TWIN BETRAYAL

Emily Tyler

This novel is entirely a work of fiction. The characters, places and incidents portrayed in it are the work of the author's imagination. Any resemblance to actual persons, living or dead, events and locations is purely coincidental.

ACKNOWLEDGEMENTS

Mary Gudzenovs. Formatting and digital preparation.
Georgina Hatchard. Editing
SelfPubBookCovers.com
rear cover created with Adobe Photoshop AI

Chapter 1

Rosin rolled over and opened her eyes. The dread that had accompanied her for moon-sweeps heavy in her gut. The tightness in her chest that never left her cramped. She sighed. Each moon-slide brought her closer to her unwanted destiny.

A surge of frustration and angst seared through her. She climbed out of bed and dragged off her moon-wash gown. She inspected her body, happy enough with her petite frame, small waist, generous breasts and shapely legs. She sighed again. She hoped the male she was to make a Bond of Le Chéile with found it satisfactory. Too bad if he didn't it would be too late by the time he saw her unclothed. Discarding her observations she washed with the cold water in the jug then pulled on her gown and an over robe against the chill sun-show. She dragged her long blond tresses into a high ponytail.

She fetched her bow from the cupboard and ran her hand over the elegant curves before snatching up her quiver and slinging it over her shoulder. After a quick glance out the door to see who had already left their beds she hurried down the corridor and slipped outside.

Her father had set up a small area for her to practice her archery well away from the gardens. The sky was tinted a delicate blue and lavender with bright splashes of pink along the horizon. It was going to be another beautiful budding moon-slide. The ground was glistening with dew and her slippers were wet by the time she reached the gate.

She fastened it behind her to ensure no one came in when she was shooting and to keep her from being interrupted. She was not in the mood to talk to anyone right now as her bonding loomed only moon-slides away. She didn't want to be Princess Apparent much less Queen in the future.

She knew her twin sister, Ciara would eagerly take on the role. She was always saying she could do better than her mother. Ciara always urged Rosin to do something to challenge her parents, but Rosin was in awe and a little afraid of her mother and loved and admired her father. She didn't have the courage to question their actions.

Rosin chose her first arrow and nocked it in the bow string. She lifted her arm, rolled her elbow and relaxed her shoulder as she sighted the target. With a gentle easing of her finger she released the arrow. It flew straight and true thunking into the bullseye. Rosin exhaled and chose her next arrow. As each hit the target a calmness washed over her. She continued to fire arrows at the target until her quiver was empty.

"Maeve, my dear bhean chéile, you must stop this greed. The people are restless. Some of the nobles are angry about Aram and his cows."

"Oh phewy, Fintain. I am the queen. I get to make the rules and take whatever I want for the realm. Keswin is prosperous and it must provide for us. Since the tithes to the High Queen our personal coffers have never been strong and they are dwindling. They must be filled again."

"But, Maeve, Keswin won't be prosperous if you keep this up. And King Baudin is upset with you for failing to assist in fending off the Chatten's last raid."

"But Fintain, it is not my responsibility to defend Wilsea.

That result falls on War Chief Bevan and if he failed to prepare his defense Keswin cannot take the burden. Fighting is expensive. Maintaining Warriors is a burden on the coffers."

"Maeve, please..."

"Enough, Fintain. Besides we have to prepare for Rosin's Bonding of Le Chéile. She must have the best."

"I don't think Rosin cares very much for having a fuss."

Rosin threw down her bow and opened the gate. She stepped out. "No, I don't need or want a fuss, Your Majesty. Mother, especially if Keswin is in trouble." She dropped a small curtesy.

"Really, Rosin, were you eavesdropping.

Her mother's scalding tone cut through her.

"No, Mother, I was merely practicing my archery."

Her Mother looked at her father and shook her head. "Well, you will have the best, Rosin. We must show your betrothed how things are done in Keswin."

"I don't want it done, Mother. Can't Ciara take my place."

"No, Rosin, she cannot. You are first born. You will be queen of Keswin in due course. Now I do not want to hear any more about it. For your information, Daughter, Keswin is not in trouble. So don't you be worrying yourself. And do stop playing with that nasty weapon. It is so unladylike and not befitting a Princess of Keswin. I'm sure your betrothed will not approve."

Rosin turned away. "Maybe he'll just have too." Her words were barely a mutter.

"What did you say, Rosin?"

"Nothing, Mother."

As her mother and father strolled back across the gardens toward the castle, Rosin picked up her quiver and began to pull the arrows out of the target. Her mood plummeted as she shoved them in their holder. There would be no reason to 'show how it was done in Keswin' if her betrothed was Garrett. Her hope struggled to survive under overwhelming odds. She loved him with a fiery passion, but Garrett had been sent away after Ciara had seen them kissing and immediately ran to inform her mother.

Rosin wandered out into the gardens in a brokenhearted fog and plonked herself down on one of the benches in the shade of an oak tree. Tears filled her eyes but as they ran down her cheeks she swiped them away.

"Sulking, are we? You have always known you couldn't have Garrett."

"Go away, Ciara."

Ciara sat delicately on the bench beside her. "You sit here and sook while Keswin is falling apart."

Rosin glared at her. "Keswin is not falling apart. Mother assures me it is not."

"It is so. You heard Father this morning. He was telling Mother to stop but she didn't listen."

Rosin frowned. "You heard them too?"

Ciara nodded. "Don't you see it, Sister. Don't you see the misery of the people. Don't you hear them talking, whining. Plotting even. Look at Aram. He hung himself only this last moon sweep. Don't you wonder why? Mother took his precious herd away from him that's why."

Rosin stared at her sister. She shook her head. "Ciara, I do see the people are miserable but our parents are the rulers of Keswin. It is not my place to question their rule. If they are doing something so wrong, why hasn't the High Queen come from Annaticcia and rebuked them."

"Perhaps she doesn't know."

Rosin shrugged. "What are we supposed to do about it. We are their daughters but to question them is still treason."

"Well, if someone doesn't stop Mother's grasping, we'll have anarchy. Do you think the nobles and commoners alike will spare you. Do you think because you pant after Garrett you will be safe?"

"I love Garrett."

"All you can think of is Garrett. Get down off your pedestal and listen to the people. You are going to be queen, and you are going to inherit the mess."

Rosin shrugged. "There is nothing I can do."

"If I was going to be queen, I would say something."

"Well, you be queen then. I don't want to be queen. I never have."

"Mother won't let me. You're her favorite. You always have been."

"Ciara, Mother loves you just the same as me, but you are second born."

"I would make a better queen than you ever will. You don't care about Keswin or the people."

Rosin grimaced. "Yes, Ciara, you probably would make a better queen. I do care about the people but there is nothing I can do about it."

"You always say that. You just don't care. All you want is to be bedded by Garrett."

"Leave me alone, Ciara. It will be soon enough when I am Queen for me to change things."

"Keswin might not survive that long." Ciara stood.

Rosin glanced up at her twin sister. "Don't say things like that, Ciara. The nobles aren't going to do anything against their Queen and the common bloods don't know how."

"Don't be so sure, Sister." Ciara turned and stalked away.

Rosin sank back into her chair. She knew her sister was right about the unrest in Keswin, but she didn't know what do about it or how. Besides she had enough to worry about being bonded to some unknown male and then having to be intimate with him. All she wanted was to be loved by Garrett. If only he was here. She sat hunched on the chair as the shadows grew longer.

~ ~ ~

Breca scuttled across the manicured lawn toward her.

Rosin flinched away from the disturbance. *Oh, go away girl, I want to weep alone.*

"Princess. My lady, the exiled ones have returned." The kitchen maid's words tumbled out in a high piping voice.

Rosin glanced up. She shook her head, unable to comprehend what she'd heard, even as the words seared her brain.

Breca hitched her skirts up as she tried to curtsey and walk at the same time. "Sorry to disturb you, Princess, but I thought you would wish to know. He's returned."

Oh, precious Maidens they have relented. Mother has brought him back. We shall be together. Rosin leapt from the garden bench and danced the few steps to her maid. Breaking protocol, she swept the servant into her embrace.

Breca squealed as Rosin swung her around.

"Dear Breca, such news. Such glorious, wonderful news."

Rosin plonked her maid back on the ground and hugged herself.

The petite young servant brushed her apron straight. "You will see them, Princess, from the tower."

"Yes, Breca, I shall go now. Thank you for telling me."

Breca curtsied again.

Rosin didn't notice as she lifted her skirts and ran across the lawn, past the rose beds and through the arch. She took the shortest way, darting down the middle of the kitchen garden. Her breath came in small panting huffs as she hurried past the herb bed.

The two gardeners weeding the vegetable patch stopped working and watched her pass.

She glimpsed curiosity in their expressions but didn't care. Garrett had come back.

Dust puffed from the little used stairs to the tower as she leapt up them two at a time. Her heart pattered a rapid staccato as she reached the top. *Garrett, my love, soon we shall be together.*

The heavy door to the tower roof resisted her efforts to push it open.

"Open. Moon dust and maidens, open. I must see him." Rosin slammed her shoulder against the ancient wood. Pain radiated down her arm. Ignoring it, she heaved against the solid resistance once more.

The door eased open.

With barely enough room, Rosin slipped through the opening. She danced across the roof to the parapet. Gripping the stone barrier, she leaned out to peer towards the approaching battalions. You could see all the way across Keswin to Shaylin Forest and the misty lavender of the mountains in the distance.

She shaded her eyes and scanned the slow-moving line of trotting horses and riders. Straining to pick out the one face she wanted to see. She wiped her eyes, frustrated at her inability to discern his features from the hundred or so other young men.

They were crossing the fast-flowing river now at its shallowest stretch.

She clutched the cold stone parapet, almost gouging marks with her fingernails. Unable to stand still, she jiggled from one foot to the other, her gaze glued to the horses and riders.

Finally, she identified Garrett's face amongst the crowd.

His blue and gold uniform appeared dusty and shabby. His hat sat askew, with his dark locks tied back in an untidy ponytail.

"There. There you are my love." Her throat clenched and sobs cramped in her chest. *So long, my love. It's been so long.*

The peal of taunting laughter snapped her back to reality.

Ciara grabbed Rosin's shoulder and spun her around. Her twin sister's dark brown eyes glittered with amber and topaz lights as she laughed, her head thrown back, her long auburn tresses fluttering down her back. "You're a disgrace, Sister. Hanging over the parapet panting after your common mongrel."

"He's not. Mother has brought him back for me."

Ciara snickered. "Oh, Maidens. You think he's back to become your betrothed. Oh, sister dear, how demented and foolish are you? Mother would never let you breed half-blood brats."

"But he's back, Ciara. This moon-slide of all days. Why is he back now, if not to make our Bond of Le Chéile?"

"Never, Rosin. This moon-wash, you will be betrothed to some aging widower or some pimply youth you had no say in choosing. Just step back for a moment and consider your choices, and know Garrett is not one of them."

Rosin glared at her twin, then turned back to watch the riders approach. Hope seeped away. She clutched at it, desperate to negate to truth of her sister's words. Shudders of revulsion rolled through her.

"You naïve fool. You're never going to feel his kisses, his touches, his member inside you. All you're going to have is short, loveless ruts with some man you despise. Life will be long and arduous for you, Sister."

Nausea burned at the back of Rosin's throat. She stamped her feet, driven by the rage burning in her soul and bile rising in her throat.

Ciara's pealing laughter battered Rosin's ears as she rested her head on the parapet and waited for her stomach to stop clenching and jerking. When she finally lifted her head, Ciara was gone.

Rosin peered again at the approaching horsemen resplendent in the blue and gold uniforms of Keswin's Warriors. Resolve solidified in her chest. *This moon-wash, my love, we shall be together. If only once, I will know your loving. Just once, to see me through the desolate years ahead.*

Rosin straightened her gown and took one more lingering look across the valley that sheltered Keswin Castle from the rest of the lands of Annaticcia before turning away and hurrying to her room to prepare. She knew he would come to her as he had come before.

~ ~ ~

Rosin jumped as the first pebble rattled lightly against the window. The signal she had been waiting for. She whimpered with the desperate need that consumed her and rushed out the doors, down the steps, and across the courtyard.

Garrett stood there, tall, gloriously dark and handsome. His brown eyes shone in the moonlight when he smiled. His neatly trimmed moustache shadowed his upper lip. He had bathed and changed into a new uniform. His black hair was slicked back into a ponytail.

She launched herself into his embrace.

He pulled her hard against his chest.

The scent of him wrapped around her. She breathed it in hungrily, greedily, immediately intoxicated by the emotions twirling through her.

How could she ever bear the reality of being with another in the moon-sweeps to come? She crushed the thought. Right now, nothing existed or mattered but Garrett.

With the tip of his finger, he traced a fiery line across her jaw and down the delicate curve of her throat.

The heat of his touch was a sharp contrast to the cool shivers of anticipation that brushed across her bare skin.

Rosin raised her face to the moons floating in the impenetrable satin darkness of the buddling moon-wash. She sighed at the exquisite waves of pleasure pulsing through her. Slowly she sank into the ache of need that spiraled through her body.

Her breath caught in her throat as the warmth from his hand that cupped her breast spread across her skin. He caressed her through the diaphanous under-gown that barely concealed her nakedness.

With a whisper of touch, he stroked across her nipple.

The small nubs hardened, reaching out for attention.

Rosin moaned. The innocence of her untouched body seeping away as the need lying deep within her passionate heart awoke into an all-consuming hunger.

"My love, my love." Garrett bent to place whisper-soft kisses on the curve of her partially exposed breasts. "So long have I wanted to touch you thus. I so feared you would be bonded before my return." The husky growl, deepened by his own desire, pushed his warm breath over her skin, teasing nerve endings into a dance of yearning.

Rosin leaned against the battle-honed hardness of his body.

Garrett's need pressed against her abdomen.

A hot flush poured over her body before a minute shimmer of fear dampened her desire just enough for her to pull away ever so slightly.

A tortured groan of protest wrenched from Garrett as his muscles contracted around her to tighten his hold. His mouth captured hers in a melting, all-consuming kiss.

Her heartbeats quickened into a frantic tattoo as the softness of her lips were consumed by the hard liquid fire of his.

He teased her mouth open and slipped the wet bulk of his tongue into her mouth.

Reveling in the taste of him, she sought a deeper connection.

His scent—a mixture of freshly washed skin, spicy cologne, horses, hay, and smoke wafted over her. An intoxicating blend that obliterated the fearful voice inside her head. The screeching of her conscience. Her body was not hers to give — not to Garrett — not to anyone, but the consort her parents had chosen for her.

Garrett released her mouth and stared down at her. The intensity in his light brown eyes signaled his sexual need. "Come, my love, I have made preparations." He took her hand and tugged gently.

She stepped toward him, trembling with the enormity of her actions. Arguments rushed through her: fulfil her love, betray her prospective betrothed, betray her realm, her mother... but her need to satisfy her love enfolded her. Nothing mattered but Garrett.

"Princess Rosin, where are ye?" Morgana's voice pierced the haze of desire clutching her.

Rosin gasped. Why now, Nanny? She pulled away from Garrett. "Go, Garrett, before you're seen. Go."

He clutched at her. "But Rosin, my love..."

"It's Morgana. Nanny. Go, you cannot get caught. Mother will have you executed."

"I shall return, my love, for this moon-wash I intend to love you. After dinner, yes?"

Rosin eyed the rooms behind her. Morgana loomed up, dark and shadowed, at the open doors.

"Yes, after the betrothal dinner. Now go before she sees you.

She might be old, but her vision is as sharp as a falcon's."

Garrett vanished into the shadows of the courtyard.

Her desire drained away, leaving the cold reality of her position as Princess Apparent of the realm of Keswin. Rosin turned and walked quickly toward the open window. "I'm here, Morgana, just taking a breath of fresh air."

"Ah, I understand, my dearest child."

Rosin threw herself into Morgana's embrace, as she had many times before. Any reason; a sisterly argument, a skinned knee or a lost pet, provided enough reason to receive one of Nanny's hugs.

"This is a hard time for you, child, but I am sure it will work out. Your parents will have chosen fairly and wisely."

"To the highest bidder, Morgana. That is all they care about, the highest bidder."

"Oh child, surely it's not that bad."

"Why can't I form a Bond of Le Chéile with Garrett? Why do I have to be queen? Ciara would welcome it all."

"Now, now. One must not cry over what cannot be changed. This moon-wash, you must go to meet your destiny with your chin held high and a smile on your lips. It is the least a good queen can do."

"But I don't want to."

"You have no choice, Rosin."

~ ~ ~

Rosin couldn't face anyone. She moped in her room ignoring her mother's maid when she delivered her new gown. The shimmering satin in purple and lavenders failed to impress her or change how she felt.

Early in the afternoon Morgana and Alanis arrived with Liam lugging the wooden tub and hot water.

She bathed and allowed the two women to pull and prod her tugging her beautiful curls into an elaborate chignon and adding a tiara especially made for this moon-wash as a gift from her parents. She allowed them to lace her into her grown. She glanced in the mirror and acknowledged she looked stunning and regal. She pouted, fighting tears.

"Morgana, I can't do this. I can't."

"Shhh, child. Now finish getting ready. They will call for you soon." Morgana took her hand and clipped a gold chain around her wrist. "I have brought this for you, for luck."

Rosin stared in awe at the piece, cold against her skin and heavy with small charms, each intricately carved out of semi-precious gems.

"My céile fir gave it to me on our betrothal. It brought me love, lust, and fertility. May it bring the same to you, child."

"Oh, Morgana, I cannot take such a precious gift."

"Shhh, child. I want you to have it."

"Thank you. I will treasure it always."

The door opened and Alanis, her lady-in-waiting, returned from her inquiry about the readiness of Rosin's parents. She curtsied low her long blue skirt billowing around her feet. "They await you, Princess."

Rosin saw judgement in the deep blue of Alanis' eyes as she hurriedly wiped her eyes and smoothed her gown. Alanis loved Garret too. Rosin refused to meet her accusing look and hugged Morgana once more, before she began the long walk to the small dining room her parents used for intimate parties with carefully chosen nobles.

~ ~ ~

Her father smiled as she came up beside him. "I know this is hard for you but I'm sure you will be pleased, Rosin."

She shook her head and looked directly into his eyes. "How can I be pleased, Father, when it isn't Garrett."

He shook his head. "It could never be Garrett. He is not even a Maidens' man." His moustache twitched as his mouth was drawn into a thin straight line. "You always knew this, Rosin."

She clutched his hand as the door swung open to reveal her destiny. Her lungs clenched and her heart contracted with a painful spasm. *Oh Garrett, my love, I cannot do this without the sweet ecstasy you and I shall share. Just once.* The sour taste of bile burned at the back of her throat. Her eyes filled with tears. She fluttered her eyelids, but the moisture remained on her lids like tiny diamonds. With an unwavering gaze, she studied her betrothed through a shimmering curtain. So be it if he sees my tears.

"Eled, Duke of Dyanwen, second son of Brigit, the Queen of Dyanwen and direct descendent of the third maiden, The Maid of War, Peace, and the Afterlife, Gavinia."

He was the same age as she but appeared older because he was tall and well-built. Dressed in dark breeches with a checked cloak that swung smartly from the large gold brooch, securing it to his right shoulder. Eled cut an impressive figure. His long curly blond hair was neatly tamed and confined in a dark green ribbon. At his side hung a ceremonial broadsword with an intricately carved gold and silver hilt. A gingery moustache covered his top lip and framed his mouth in gentle curves to his jawbone.

He strode confidently down the length of the room, his gaze focused on Rosin.

She stared back at him, her chin held high despite her eyes swimming with tears.

All eyes were on him, but he ignored the audience along with the muttering and whispers that had erupted subtly on his entrance.

Her mind acknowledged his masculine appeal in a split second before her heart hardened against him.

Eled bowed low to the three of them. "Queen Maeve, Lord Fintain, I greet you in friendship and loyalty. I thank you for bestowing on me the honor of presenting myself to your beautiful daughter."

The Queen and her father nodded acknowledgement of his greeting.

Eled then turned to Rosin. "Princess Rosin, I am honored to wait on you, having anticipated this moment for some time. I must admit, though, that those who spoke of your beauty did not do you justice. I hope you will consider my tender to be your consort. I bring skills and qualifications useful to the realm and worthy of your acceptance."

He bowed again, more deeply than before. This time to Rosin herself.

Her mother and father turned toward her. "Princess Rosin, do you accept Eled, Duke of Dyanwen's tender for your hand in a Bond of Le Chéile and to partner you in the rule of Keswin when you ascend the throne?"

Together, their voices were warm and deep. Formal words to seal a deal.

Rosin stared straight into her mother's eyes with an unblinking, tear-filled gaze. *I refuse to hide how I feel.* She hoped her steady stare radiated all the resentment and unhappiness that consumed her.

Maeve stared back with a glare that sizzled with fire and warning.

Rosin tightened her mouth just a fraction in response but did not soften her expression or drop her eyes. She did not need to be told again that to break such an agreement would bring the wrath of all Dyanwen and the High Queen of Annaticcia on their kingdom.

"Yes, I, Princess Rosin, take Eled, Duke of Dyanwen, as my betrothed."

She almost choked on the word betrothed but managed to push the word out without any telltale hesitation.

All those present applauded and murmured accolades for a good fertile match.

Eled helped Rosin to her seat, then slipped quietly in beside her.

Rosin sat stiffly, unable to make conversation with this stranger foisted on her. A chill rippled through her, a warning of what she risked following her heart.

Eled tried to make light chit chat.

Rosin struggled to find suitable responses and couldn't bring herself to ask even the simplest question, knowing she was forever trapped in this farce.

He turned to his meal; the silence heavy between them.

Rosin picked at her food, dragging it around her plate.

Loud conversation and laughter from the other guests flowed over and around her.

Dear Maidens, loosen my tongue before the others notice my silence. She took a deep breath. "You have travelled far, Eled. I trust the arduous journey has not tired you."

His smile widened. "One quickly forgets the hardship of the journey, Rosin, to find you at its end."

Heat burned up her cheeks. She glanced toward her parents. "Our parents are pleased with their arrangements. It will be good for both Keswin and Dyanwen."

"Yes, both realms will benefit. I can only hope that the

arrangements will also be good to us."

She looked up at her betrothed, not caring that he saw her pain.

He smiled slightly, his eyes dark, thoughtful pools of green as he enclosed her hand in both of his. "Rosin, I know this is hard for you, for both of us, but I will be a kind consort to you. A céile fir and consort."

Rosin nodded. "I don't doubt that Eled." *Such assurance won't win me over. For I love another and there is no room in my heart for you.*

He squeezed her hand lightly and repeated, "It is not our choice to be together, and I understand how hard it will be. Rosin, I've heard you love another."

Her breath caught and fear plunged her into an icy swirl. She nibbled at her bottom lip then flicked her tongue across her lips. With a huge effort, she snapped her mouth shut with a clack of teeth. All the time, she held his gaze with wide-open eyes. His expression held no malice, only sympathy and understanding.

He tightened his grip and ignored the sweat that had sprung up on her palms.

She tensed for the tirade or accusations to declare her unworthy.

"Do not fret, Rosin, for I love another also."

Still staring deep into his eyes, Rosin coughed and cleared her constricted throat. "Then...then..." Her voice cracked into a scratchy silence; her throat was too constricted to let words pass.

He squeezed her hand again and lightly ran his finger across her lips.

"Then why am I here?" He smiled a soft, sad smile. "I am here, Rosin, because, like you, I'm bound by duty. Duty to my parents, my realm, and the betterment of the lives of my people. My country desperately needs access to the trade Keswin can provide. My people struggle on a daily basis to be secure and fed. Especially now with Depcisians raids evermore vicious and frequent. Keswin is strong, but Dyanwen is smaller, more vulnerable. Our union will secure much for the betterment of Dyanwen."

Guilt scurried over her. She'd never considered her potential partner in the Bond of Le Chéile might just be sacrificing as much as she.

He reached up and brushed the tears from her cheeks. "Don't cry, my beautiful princess. We will do this together and if we still pine for our current loves after our first child is born, we will make arrangements, you and I."

All her angry thoughts, resentment, and bitterness died under the caress of his words. She could only nod to express how she felt. A warm ball of emotion built inside her and thawed the icy wall of resistance and resentment, blanketing her heart.

This stranger, soon to be her céile fir and consort, had offered her a light at the end of her long, dark tunnel of unrequited love. Between them, they would make this work.

Grief cut deep at her denial of Garrett, but she knew in that instance Eled deserved her honesty and her purity.

"Smile, my Princess. Together we will make this kingdom and my mother's strong and invincible realms. All our people will be well fed, secure, and prosperous. And we, we will live good lives. Together." His smile widened. "And over time, we might even get to like each other."

Something stirred inside her. She could do this. Her only worry — how to tell Garrett she would not be his this moon-wash. My poor love, I am cruel, but I must do what is right. Eled deserves my total commitment to this bonding, for he has also given up much for duty.

~ ~ ~

Rosin jumped as the first stone clicked against the shutters. Panic burned through her. A second sharp tap pierced the silence. She sat immobile in the darkened room. Her heart pattered in her chest as she breathed softly. Another tap, louder this time. *Someone will hear, Garrett. Stop, my love, I am not coming. I cannot.*

Frustration flashed through her. Surely, with all at stake for him, he would retreat to the barracks when she didn't appear. Uncertainty held her frozen. Too terrified to be close to him now, she had changed her mind. She waited.

The warm, comfortable feeling brought on by her exchange with Eled had stayed with her long after she had come up from dinner. For the first time in moon-cycles, she felt calm and steady. At the last moment, she had been given an opportunity to do the right thing without feeling cheated.

Garrett had been quite possessive of her virginity, often saying he waited patiently for her 'gift.' Garrett would not accept her decision easily.

Her change of heart, so raw and fresh, hadn't the resolve for her to see him, and touch him, then still turn away. Her love for him remained knife sharp. Misery clutched her.

Her clenched fingers ached as she sat unmoving, staring straight ahead. Her body tensed with the expectation of the next tap on the window. It came louder this time. She flinched, all her nerve endings sparking. A doleful moan escaped. If she didn't stop him, someone would hear and all would be lost, including Garrett's life.

After a moment's hesitation, she grabbed her wrap and walked to the doors. Her mouth crackled with the dryness of fear, and the pit of her stomach sagged at the risk they took. She cursed his unwise doggedness.

Very little light came from the two moons nestling on the

horizon, each one laying half hidden behind the other casting mysterious fractured shadows. The four moons waited for the turn of the season to rise again one by one until all six would float high in the sky, signaling the new seasons in.

Her eyes adjusted to the darkness, but the courtyard appeared empty and serene. Rosin paused on the first step, letting futile hope rush through her that he had given up. Would her resolve stand the ultimate test?

A slight movement alerted her.

A darker blotch of shadow eased away from the others.

Her heart jumped and her fingers twitched with the desire to touch him. All the emotions she'd tried to minimize or even deny broke loose and rushed over her like warm bath water creeping up cold, bare skin.

She gazed up at the moons, now pale on the horizon, and prayed to the Maidens.

He moved again. His shadow melted away from the archway and the hanging creeper.

With two steps, he crossed the courtyard. He immediately embraced her. "By the power of the Maidens, I need you. I must have you, my love..."

A myriad of emotions spiraled, swamping her hastily erected guard. Anticipation swept her away on a tide of passion for the man who held her in a tight embrace. She snatched at her sanity, chilling the burn of desire, but when she tried to push away, he tightened his hold.

"Stop! Garrett, this is wrong." Her voice cracked with the strength of her conflicting emotions.

"Nay, my beautiful one. Nay. This moon-wash, you will be mine. We have waited too long to be together."

The steely edge to his voice frightened her.

He applied pressure to her back in an attempt to ease her towards the darker corner of the courtyard. He held her in an ironclad and demanding grip.

Alarm seeped through her. She needed to be free of his touch long enough to tell him her decision. If he continued to hold and caress her, she would not be able to deny him.

She pushed her hands against the inflexible wall of his chest and leaned back so he couldn't kiss her. She must tell him.

His hold tightened.

"Please, Garrett, release me."

He loosened his hold.

Cool air rushed over her heated skin.

"My love do not be afraid. We will be together at last. This is your last chance to give me your gift before another man possesses you. Please, my darling, let me make you mine."

She didn't like the sudden demand in his words. "Garrett, this is wrong. I have a duty. I have made a promise."

He shook his head as he pulled her back against him.

Even as she resisted, he leaned down to capture her mouth again. She tried to turn her head to the side, petrified his kiss would annihilate her resolve.

His mouth claimed hers, hot and demanding.

Rosin's resolution dissolved as he explored her mouth.

His strong arms enfolded her, pressing her tightly against his chest.

Her heart pattered behind her breast. Liquid fire flowed through her. She clung to him, letting the passion claim her.

Sharp nails clawed her shoulders. A yank so savage and sudden it almost wrenched her off her feet. Her lips were torn from Garrett's. She yelped.

A hand covered her mouth.

Garrett's arms were ripped from her waist as a shadowy figure dragged him backwards and held him captive.

Rosin took several steps back to stay standing upright and jerked her head to the side to escape the suffocating hand over her mouth.

Perfume, so familiar, filled her nostrils. She recognized the hands that held her. "Mother?"

"Daughter?"

The single word, no more than a sharp hiss, sliced through her. A rush of icy horror swept down her body, dousing the fire consuming her core and sobering her intoxicated state like the lash of a whip on her bare skin. They had been caught and now they had to pay the price.

Her mother pulled her hard back against her body and held her there with a vicious tenacity that drew a gasp of pain.

A soft slither of metal split the silence.

Rosin looked up.

Garrett stood motionless, a dagger resting across his throat.

Her father looped a rope around Garrett's neck and tightened it until Garrett struggled to breathe freely.

The four of them stood, frozen. Their huddle was no more than a darker shadow in the corner. A breathless silence settled around them.

Rosin bit her lip as the burn of tears stung her eyes and blurred her vision. She fluttered her eyelids to drive them away, but the seriousness of her situation filled her with trepidation.

The anger that raged in her mother radiated like the heat of a fire.

Rosin cringed away from the fury; her gaze glued on Garrett.

Garrett stood tall; the strong ling of his square jaw clenched tight and held high. He did not flinch from the dagger as it grazed his skin, nor did he look away from his Queen's stare. His mouth moved as if to speak, but no sound came forth.

Rosin tried to swallow, her throat constricted and dry. Tiny trembles ran through her body. Her knees went weak and rubbery. She sagged.

With no warning, her mother flung a cloak over her shoulders. With a savage tug, a voluminous hood dragged over her hair and far enough down to almost cover her face.

Her mother held her up. "Walk, Rosin. You must not be seen, or all will be lost. My reign, Keswin, your life and Garrett's."

Her mother pushed her across the courtyard and out the gate by the castle. Darkness enveloped them. Still, her mother pushed her forward.

Rosin stumbled on the rocky path. She whimpered.

"Quiet, Rosin." Her mother pushed her forward.

The gate to the underground cavern loomed up.

Rosin twisted and railed against her imprisonment. "Garrett. Where have you taken him? What have you done to him?"

"Walk, Rosin. Do not fret your beloved. He is not dead yet."

Rosin wriggled against her mother's hold.

"Be still, Daughter. I do not wish to bind you. We still have a chance to retrieve this situation."

The dank air in the tunnel to the cavern closed around her. Panic surged through her as she stumbled down the roughly carved stone steps. She tried to pull away.

"If you wish your beloved to see this moon-wash out alive, do not resist me."

The spitting and gurgling of the fast-flowing river echoed around the cavern.

Her mother jerked to a halt and spun her around to face her. "Now we are well away from prying eyes we have much to deal with."

"How dare you treat me this way?"

"How dare you go to your beloved after committing to the Bond of Chéile with the Duke of Dyanwen. How could you be so irresponsible and disobedient? You have put the whole kingdom at risk..."

Footsteps silenced her tirade.

Garrett appeared guided by her father. He brought Garrett to a rough halt just a few feet from them.

"Garrett, my love. Are you alright?"

He grimaced. "For now, Rosin."

Her mother turned to face Garrett. "You, Garrett, have committed treason, punishable by death. Lusting after my daughter. Seducing her from her committed duty. Putting the realm in danger."

Garret stood immobile, his face ashen.

A thin line of blood showed under the blade of the dagger her father held.

A scream gurgled in Rosin's throat. She swallowed hard. "Mother, do not do this. I only came to tell Garrett my decision to be true to Eled. I never intended to let him kiss me. Please do not punish him. It's my fault!"

"This is bigger than you, Rosin. It's time you faced up to your responsibilities. You have put the whole kingdom at risk by your reckless behavior."

Cold fingers of terror clutched at her. Panic rattled through her. Her heart thudded, paused, then thudded again. Sweat beaded on her forehead. Her stomach seared with savage stabs of fear. "You cannot do this, Mother. You cannot."

"Silence, Daughter. I have decided. He did not heed the warnings. He must pay for his traitorous deeds."

"No." Her single word wailed into a screech.

Her mother's hand slapped over her mouth and silenced her scream.

She pulled her mother's hand from her mouth. "You cannot do this monstrous thing. He never touched me intimately. I'm still a virgin. Mother, I love him."

Her mother grabbed her upper arms and shook her. "You had better be telling the truth, Rosin, because it will matter. Garrett does not matter, but you do. You will be bonded to Eled tomorrow and serve Keswin. Fintain finish it."

"Noooo. Please."

Her father hesitated.

Rosin gulped. "I cannot be bonded to Eled or anyone else if I'm dead. Then it will Ciara's turn. For I shall kill myself and join my love in the Afterlife. Do you hear me? If you murder Garrett, I will hang myself in a place where all will see. I will bring shame on you both, and Keswin."

Her mother's ferocious expression crumpled. Fear etched her face.

"Maeve, if he has not touched her, then no harm has been done. Perhaps a little mercy for our daughter. It is not her fault Ciara cannot."

Her mother frowned.

"Maeve, you of all people should understand. Don't do this thing. Don't break her heart. Allow her this one thing."

Maeve shook her head, then wiped tears from her eyes.

The unreality of it all pierced through Rosin. Laughter swamped her. Peal after peal rattled around the cavern. Her head swam and her lungs froze. The air wouldn't come in. Again, wild, maniacal laughter swept over her.

Her mother's steely grip remained a manacle on one arm.

Her hysterical laughter rent the dank air of the cavern.

A stinging slap smacked onto the side of her face.

She jerked her breath in, cutting off the laughter and bringing her back into her body with a savage jolt.

Beyond the limits of coping, she coughed and spluttered on the last hysterical peal of sound, then fell silent. Huge tears poured down her face and her legs crumpled. "Please, Mother, have mercy. Please." Rosin sagged to the ground.

This time her mother leaned down with her, letting her collapse on the flagstones. She released her grip and stood tall. "Release him, Fintain. Let it be."

Released from the noose and the dagger, Garrett stood, head bowed.

"For her, Garrett, you retain your life this day. Go from this place and never show your face in Keswin again." Maeve pointed to the boat bobbing up and down next to the stone pier. "You are not pardoned, but you live because she loves you and I love her. Now you get in that boat and sail down the river to Ilara. Commander Trian will be waiting for you to report to him. You will remain in his service until I tell you otherwise. Is this clear?"

Garrett bowed low. He glanced at Rosin. Fear and resentment shadowed his expression above the sneer twisting his mouth. He didn't resist Fintain's heavy hand as he climbed down the rough-hewn steps and jumped into the rocking boat.

Despair embraced Rosin as she watched him set the oars and untie the line. Salty tears dried to a crackling coat on her clammy skin. Goose bumps sprang up, sparking a tidal wave of shivers over her body. Her teeth clattered together.

Silence drifted down again to embrace her as the boat disappeared out of the cavern opening and into the flow of the river.

"Come, Rosin."

Rosin nodded. Every bone felt like liquid. Her muscles ached and groaned. Her limbs dragged as her mother hauled her to her feet.

Halfway up, Rosin's knees collapsed, and she sagged almost back to the stones.

Her father strode to her and scooped her into his arms.

Rosin sobbed quietly against her father's shoulder.

Her mother draped her shawl over her.

Crushed and exhausted, she huddled inside the encircling cloth, letting the warmth seep into her shoulders as she clutched it together in clawed fists at her breasts.

Her mother strode forward.

Her father followed a few steps behind.

A sudden flash of fear jagged through her. "Why aren't we going to my rooms? Do you plan to make me a prisoner in the dungeon?"

"No, Rosin, you will, however, be prisoner in my suite. I will not risk you harming yourself before the bonding. You have Garret's life. If it is to remain so you will obey my bidding."

"That is not a choice, Mother. That is blackmail."

Hurt flashed across her mother's face. "Daughter, you misjudge me so painfully."

Her father carried Rosin into the luxuriously appointed suite of rooms, placed her onto the bed and pulled the quilt around her.

She lay shivering under its weight, watching her parents.

Her mother shut the heavy oak door behind them and turned the key.

"I think it would be wise to tell her the truth, Maeve. She needs to know. To understand why she must be queen and not Ciara."

Her mother looked away from her céile fir's steady gaze, her mouth drawn down at the corners, her eyes filled with tears. "It wasn't supposed to be like this. It is my shame, and I don't wish to share."

"Maeve, you must, for her sake and the good of Keswin's future."

"But, Fintain, not everyone will be as forgiving as you."

"No, but you owe your daughter the truth. Perhaps in time she will forgive you and no longer mourn the love you have taken from her."

Rosin huddled deeper under the quilt, petrified of what would come next.

Her mother paced the room, her hands clenching and unclenching at her sides.

Rosin watched her pace, then glanced at her father.

He stood silently by the end of the bed.

Her mother stopped pacing and approached the end of the bed. "Rosin, I have fought so hard to keep you from making my mistakes. It has not been easy. I understand how you feel about Garrett."

Rosin lurched up, hot tears filling her eyes. "How can you know, Mother? You have Father, have always had Father."

Her mother looked down, shaking her head. "No, Rosin." She glanced at her céile fir. "My parents chose Fintain for me like we chose Eled for you. I did not want to be bonded to him."

"But you love, Father."

Her mother looked first at her Rosin's father, then at Rosin. "I do now. On the day of my bonding, I was angry and bitter at being forced to join with a stranger when I loved another."

"As a young and rash barely adult male, I did not understand to depth of your mother's despair and fear. I didn't act with gentleness or kindness toward your mother as I should have. Once your mother suspected she carried my child she turned from me to the man she loved."

Rosin looked from one to the other. Their confessions

thrummed in her ears.

"Rosin, I was pregnant with you, but somehow I got pregnant a second time by my lover."

"Your lover?" Her voice cracked and died.

Her mother stared straight ahead, her face flushed a deep red. The High Queen Isolde sent her physician to tend me when I became ill. He told me I carried two babies. This made me happy until the birth. Only then did I realize what I had done. Ciara is not Fintain's issue. Ciara is Muireach's."

"Muireach's. Mother, how could you?"

"We do not decide who we shall love, Rosin, as you well know. If we had not come this moon-wash, you would be in the same situation, or maybe even worse."

Rosin slumped back into the bed. Tears filled her eyes. "Mother, I'm sorry for being disobedient and willful, but this moon-wash I only meant to tell Garrett that despite my love for him I had decided to honor my bonding with Eled."

Her mother smiled faintly. "Maybe, Daughter, you meant it, but Garrett would have been persuasive."

"I know, Mother. But what of Ciara?"

"She has no right to the crown, even as the firstborn. Your father and I paid a heavy tithe to the High Queen to cover it all up. She only allowed us to live because she loved your father so deeply, as her nephew and Moon Life son. We were sworn to secrecy."

"The High Queen knows?"

Her parents nodded in unison.

"And Ciara?"

"No. We do not want to destroy her. With you ascending to Princess Apparent and bonding with Eled, there is no need to spoil her life."

"Only mine."

"Rosin, I know you don't want to be queen when I'm gone, but there is no other choice. Please forgive me and your father. We did try to choose well for you. Keswin needs you."

Rosin sat back on the bed again and pulled the quilt back over her. An icy cold shivering had pervaded her body. Her throat clenched tight against the sobs rising in her chest.

Her father moved to stand beside his bhean chéile. He placed his arm around her waist. "Do not judge your mother too harshly, Rosin. Try to find forgiveness in your heart. It took me a while, as it will you, but it can be found if you want too."

She looked at them. Guilt slithered through her. "I cannot judge you, Mother, as I nearly made the same mistake and also risked Garrett's life. I will be bonded to Eled, and we will have a child to inherit Keswin's crown. The Bonding of Chéile will be a new day, a new era for Keswin and all of us."

Chapter 2

"Rosin, Lady of Keswin, Princess Apparent." The Chief Steward of Keswin announcement resonated around the ballroom, silencing the hum of conversation.

Every person, including the servants, turned to see the heir apparent to Keswin's throne enter the hall for her Bond of Cheile.

Rosin stood in the open doorway, clad in a pale lemon woolen gown cinched at the waist with a delicate chain belt. Her only other adornments, a garland of pink rosebuds, nestled in her riotous golden curls and Morgana's bracelet.

Her hands trembled. Sweat beaded on her skin before trickling down between her breasts. She wished herself anywhere but here.

The raw truth of how unhappy the people of Keswin had become showed starkly on their staring faces as they watched her. Cold dread threaded through her. Did those gathered this moon-wash hate her as much as they hated her parents? For them, the ceremony this moon-wash only perpetuated their servitude.

She despaired for the future and wished her father's brother, King Cadmar, had come to the ceremony. Only he could, at her request, have broached the subject with her parents.

The thought of citizens bearing resentment intimidated her to the point where she would have happily turned around and run. She saw no loss in forgoing her elevation to the Princess Apparent.

Only duty to the throne and loyalty to her parents held her steady on the landing and committed to this arranged union with the Duke of Dyanwen. Despite the fact she had often railed against it, she'd finally accepted that her whole life led to this moment. Not that this joining and accompanying title of Princess Apparent would allow her to exert pressure on her parents and bring about a change in the realm. For that, she had to wait for them to die.

For her mother, the Queen, the whole future of the throne hinged on Rosin forming a union with the suitor chosen for her and producing a child.

Rosin glanced around. So many nobles to witness the bonding — all Keswin's upper classes, several minor aristocrats from neighboring Wilsea, and, of course, Eled's entourage from Dyanwen.

It had been a disappointment when King Cadmar and Queen Meghan, her Moon Life Protectors, couldn't attend and that Isolde, High Queen of Annaticcia, had succumbed to a bout of the chest rattle, rendering her unable to travel to Keswin.

Taking the applause that spluttered fitfully around the room as her cue, Rosin descended the stairs with delicate poise. On the last step, she extended her hand to her father. Fintain had retained his handsome looks despite his age — blond hair, elaborate moustache, and wide green eyes that often sparkled with mischief in the privacy of the family. His green velvet jacket trimmed with gems fitted his slightly thickened frame with perfect elegance.

Rosin tucked her hand in his gloved one and curtsied slightly.

"Rise, Rosin, my firstborn." His husky purr was warm and welcoming, affectionate even. He squeezed her fingers in a silent gesture of reassurance, then led the way across the floor to her mother.

Her mother had also retained the stunning beauty of her youth — blue eyes, clear skin, and a petite but voluptuous figure. Gems and precious metals flickered and sparkled on her red gown, and around her throat rested an intricately fashioned gold torc.

Maeve had ruled Keswin for over twenty successions, taking control in her eighteenth succession immediately after her father's untimely death during a violent raid by the Depcisians. Every inch the queen of Keswin, she submitted to no one but the High Queen of Annaticcia.

Queen Maeve acknowledged her daughter with a smile and an inclined head.

Rosin lowered herself into a deep, graceful curtsy in response. As Rosin rose, she looked deep into her mother's heavily made-up eyes, starkly aware of the lingering shame and the sympathy reflected in the unblinking royal stare. Last moon-wash had changed everything.

Still drained from her emotional parting from Garrett, she still hovered in disbelief and shock at her parent's subsequent revelations. Fatigue held her in a suffocating grip. Despite bordering on tears, Rosin held her upright stance as she moved to stand behind her mother while her father returned to the entrance to escort her twin sister into the hall.

Ciara stood tall and assured of her dark beauty. So different from Rosin's petite frame and fair complexion. Now Rosin knew why.

Ciara's gaze emitted contempt as she stared at those gathered. She had chosen to wear red for this important event, a deliberate swipe at the Queen's authority.

Rosin shuddered under the blast of hatred that surged at her from her sister's direct stare. Flooded with the familiar distress at Ciara's hostility, anxiety rose like bile that threatened to choke her. Often, whispers had circulated that they were not really twins at all. Not that anybody would openly challenge the Queen. Trepidation shivered through Rosin, now she knew they were true.

Ciara had never made any effort to hide her desire to take Rosin's place as Princess Apparent. Her twin's resentment at her second-born status and relegation to nothing but a pawn to secure more riches for the realm had haunted Rosin for as long as she could remember.

Except for her sister's ill-concealed wrath, Rosin would have felt sorry for Ciara and, without a backward glance, changed places with her. Rosin had no burning desire to be queen. Especially now she'd acknowledged the unrest in the realm her sister had long harped about. It had always been easier to just ignore the whispers she heard and the things she saw that seemed unfair.

She loved and trusted her parents and didn't want to have a conflict with them. Unlike Ciara, who always pestered them about everything from extravagance to punishments for breaking Maiden law and increasing taxes.

Even her bonding this moon-wash, and the trade concessions won for Queen Brigit of Dyanwen as part of her dowry, would not solve the problem of Keswin's dwindling coffers. All she could envisage ahead was disaster.

With the formal greetings finally completed, Queen Maeve took her céile fir's hand and led the way around the ring of nobles, greeting each one with a nod of the head.

All responded politely, with bows and curtsies, but Rosin could see the dissatisfaction glinting in their eyes where their smiles failed to reach.

Maeve paused briefly to chat to Lord Wysan, representing King Baudin of Wilsea. Rosin suspected her mother offered soothing words to smooth over hard feelings because Wilsea had not only failed to secure the bonding with Keswin, but Maeve had not sent assistance against Chatten invaders.

Rosin felt eternally grateful for that failure. She had no desire to be bonded with King Baudin's oafish nephew, Tempel.

Rosin and Ciara walked side by side behind their parents, together, but apart. The degree of separation and hostility is almost a tangible object between them.

Despite her concerns for the future, Rosin determined she would walk toward her destiny in the manner befitting a future queen. But a quick survey of the fawning nobles and the seething anger behind their smiles unsettled her. Uncertainty shivered over her skin, then settled in her stomach as a lump of icy angst.

Rosin straightened her spine. She stared steadily ahead at the dais, Eled, and her future. Her parents had at least chosen well and with her happiness in mind. Only her love for Garrett stood between her and a happy future with the young Duke of Dyanwen.

She raised her gaze to meet Eled's as she approached the steps. Her betrothed's expression softened, green eyes wide and sincere, his mouth turned up in a reassuring and encouraging smile.

Hundreds of roses from her mother's garden trimmed her bonding dais. The blooms exuded a delicate perfume that lingered like an unseen mist in the room. Their beauty a stark display of her parents' excesses and luxuries.

Rosin dared another quick glance around the ballroom. A familiar face caught her attention. Her heart beat quickened. She fixated on the spot, thinking she saw Garrett at the back of the crowd. But whoever she saw, they were gone by the time she managed to focus. It couldn't have been Garrett, for he was in exile in Ilara. She sighed, glad to be mistaken.

His father Muireach, and his stunning second partner, Eileen, stood at the rear of the dais. They made an imposing couple: he, tall and dark; she, short, voluptuous, and white blond.

Rosin didn't like Muireach. His dark, brooding features and accusing manner of speaking made her uneasy, and she abhorred his ritual sacrifices. Only now did she understand why her mother kept him around as the chief priest.

As Moon Laurate, Muireach would conduct the ceremony. Rosin choked down a giggle, a tiny hiccup of hysteria. So poetic. The father of the man she loved would bond her to another.

Garrett's stepmother had encouraged Rosin and Garrett to spend time together, but Muireach had only said time would tell when asked if they would ever be together.

Rosin wondered why he had not discouraged them, or even gone to her father and prevented their association. No, it had taken Ciara's interference for that to happen.

Lost deep in thought, she hadn't heard her father deliver the bonding toast, but jolted back to reality as Muireach climbed the stairs to the platform. She sighed heavily. She had to participate now.

A vague shuffling sound distracted her from Muireach's approach. Rosin glanced over her shoulder. Ciara had backed away from her side and now stood by the edge of the dais. Rosin wondered briefly why. Any interference in the proceedings would be pointless. With Muireach already in canting the union blessing of Rianon, Rosin dismissed her concerns. Nobody could stop the inevitable.

Eled stood silently beside her, his breathing as shallow as hers.

Rosin studied him from under downcast lashes. He seemed as nervous as she. Sympathy for him wafted over her. It must be just as hard for him to be forced to leave his own realm, and parted from his own lady love as it was for her. To be matched up with an unknown princess and burdened with the expectation they would breed a new generation as soon as possible.

A tingle of amusement touched her thoughts. She doubted he'd retained his virginity like she had, because nobles like him had access to kitchen maids. She'd heard that many of the males from the upper classes got their own mistresses to tutor their sons in bedroom etiquette. *At least one of us will know what to do.*

Muireach indicated they should join hands for the completion of the blessing.

"I have come for your daughter, Ma'am! Your daughter and your throne!"

The harsh bellow reverberated like thunder through the crowded hall, accompanied by the ominous rattle of weapons.

Rosin spun round, needles of terror stinging her body.

Lord Devon, Interloper and Keswin's less than accommodating neighbor, strode toward the bonding dais.

The gathered guests fell back from his swaggering progress.

A deadly silence enveloped the hall.

Rosin glanced from her mother's ashen face to her father's snarling frown. *What the Maidens' revenge is he doing here?*

Her pulse raced; the blood pounded in her ears. She gasped in short, tight breaths. Held motionless by his aggressive approach, Rosin clutched her hands at her sides in a white knuckled grip.

This man had not been welcomed in Keswin since the day he tendered for Maeve's hand so many years ago. This moon-wash, if he thought he could carry Rosin off and make her his, he'd better think again. Even if the nobles hated her parents, surely nobody in this room would let that happen to her.

Despite his age, Devon cut an imposing figure with tight-fitting leather pants, clinging white shirt and long, dark hair drawn tightly back from his high forehead into a neat ponytail.

Bodyguards flanked him—rough, muscular soldiers, with broad chests encased in silver mail. Beefy hands clutched the hilts of swords in readiness for battle.

Devon strode unchallenged to the bottom of the steps. A

triumphant smirk distorted his face.

Rosin chewed on her bottom lip and fought to still the tremors rippling through her body. She clutched her gown, twisting it into tortured lumps. Sweat broke out on her skin even as she shivered.

"I have come, Ma'am, to collect your daughter. She is mine and will join Keswin to Ersklyn forever in a bond so strong it can never be broken." Devon's challenge cut through the silence.

Rosin's breath caught with a painful stab in her chest. Fear trickled along her skin. Why didn't someone step forward and cut him down? She glanced around and knew the betrayal in their faces. Her gut roiled, and her heart clenched in her chest.

Queen Maeve took two steps forward, her céile fir cleaved to her back, his hands on her waist.

"Go from this place, Lord Devon. No daughter of mine will ever be yours."

"Oh, yes, she will, Your Majesty," Devon sneered.

"Never! Muireach, continue the ceremony." Maeve gave a haughty wave of her heavily bejeweled hand toward Muireach.

Devon whipped out a dagger and pointed it at Muireach, indicating clearly that the Moon Laurate should refrain from obeying the queen's orders.

Muireach didn't need the direction, for he'd made no attempt to continue already slipping the bonding dagger back under his belt.

Rosin frowned. Dread thudded in a cold lump at the bottom of her gut. The hair on her skin twitched. A sense of impending doom blanketed her.

"Only over my dead body will you take Rosin from this castle." Maeve stood tall and haughty as she made her declaration.

"Well-spoken, Queen Maeve, only it is not Rosin I seek, but Ciara. Once tasted, her beautiful delights are forever in the blood, like a sweet addiction."

Rosin's breath caught in her throat. Nausea washed over her at the thought of Ciara making love with this Interloper, old enough to be her father, and a sworn enemy of Keswin. Rosin had never suspected her twin had a lover in neighboring Ersklyn, and it never occurred to her that she would lower herself to take Lord Devon himself to her bed.

All around, stillness reigned. No one rushed forward to subdue the intruders. The tension was palpable in the air as everyone waited for the next move.

Maeve's face turned ashen as she snapped her head around to stare at her dark-haired daughter.

Ciara sidled toward the steps. A smug smile contorted her crimson painted mouth. Nobody could miss the hatred and contempt in her blue-gray eyes.

"Ciara, what is this?"

Ciara's smile widened. "This, Mother, is claiming what you wouldn't give me, even though it's my right—the crown and the realm. I have known for some time the truth about my birth. The crown is rightfully mine, and with you and her"—she pointed a long, red varnished fingernail at Rosin— "out of the way, I will claim the throne of Keswin for myself and my offspring." Ciara reached down and stroked her stomach.

Rosin's heart clenched mid-beat as Ciara's words sliced through the heavy air. Every inch of her skin crawled at the thought of Devon's child, an Interloper, claiming the throne of Keswin and ruling the sixth realm of the Maiden Goddess, Rianon.

She gazed out over the crowd gathered below her, all too aware of the ill-hidden unrest among the people and the hostility against her parents' dictatorship. Their type of self-centered behavior did not engender loyalty from those they ruled.

Even if every noble remained loyal, they were soon enormously outnumbered as more of Devon's men poured in the doors.

Queen Maeve, her beautiful unlined face distorted with anger, stared at Ciara. "Are you so desperate for power that you would take by force what is not yours by right?"

"Not mine, by right?" Ciara screeched. "Do you deny, here in front of your subjects, I am firstborn, Mother? You wouldn't dare. Why did you demand it be changed on the records? I don't understand why you've chosen her over me." Ciara guffawed. "It is no longer important, for with Devon's assistance, your crown will revert to the rightful heir—me!"

A quiver of shock sparked through Rosin. So, Ciara did know she had been born first, but obviously she did not know the whole truth.

Rosin flinched as Eled pushed past her to stand beside her father, his sword already drawn.

Ciara walked delicately down the steps, then took Devon's hand as he reached for her. His single possessive tug brought Ciara into his embrace.

In her peripheral vision, Rosin saw her mother shudder, then straighten her spine before she spoke.

"So, Ciara, you have made your choice. I respect that, but in respecting your decision, I must also resolve to protect the realm by denouncing you as a legitimate child of the royal union. From this moment forward, you shall have no recognition of being born from my womb and no status as a Princess of Keswin. Your offspring will have no recognition either."

Ciara's face paled as she looked up at her Lord Devon.

His lips had drawn back in a terrifying grimace. "I think you make a grave mistake, Your Majesty." He raked the room with a contemptuous gaze. "You, Queen of Keswin, have just signed the death warrants of all your people. At least those who remain loyal, and there are not many. For with you gone, and no witnesses to your cruel ruling, Ciara will become queen of Keswin. There will be naught to stop her."

Ciara smiled again, an ugly, toothy smile that bordered on a snarl. Her expression revealed more than any words could say.

Rosin's heart skipped a beat as she quickly scanned the room. As she counted those who might be loyal, she noticed several slight movements in the crowd. A number of the women farther from the dais were backing slowly away through the crush of bodies. They knew what Devon intended. They wanted out of harm's way. Rosin watched them go, overcome with a sense of helplessness.

Eled's breath tickled the side of her face as he ever so gently placed a kiss on her cheek. "Never fear, Princess, we will rout them. Just make sure you find a hidey-hole for yourself and your mother. Keep your pretty head down until it's over."

She glanced up, ever so slightly comforted by his confidence, then reached out to touch his hand. "Eled, when this is over, we will be bonded. Together, we will crush this sickening rebellion and restore Keswin's greatness. In fact, not only crush it, but wipe Lord Devon's realm out from under him. First though, I must try to stop the slaughter."

Eled nodded, but his face puckered into a frown as she squeezed past him to stand beside her mother. Rosin took hold of her mother's trembling hand. She squeezed the icy flesh tightly.

Maeve glowered at her. "Daughter?" Her tone a mixture of puzzlement and censure.

Rosin ignored her mother's inquiry as she turned and directed her condemnation at her sister. She had to stop this massacre. "Ciara, we are sisters, twins, born from the same womb at the same time. I understand your ambition. I've always known you

41

wanted more than the second born daughter can have... but these ambitions are not worth killing those who love you. I'm happy to share my right to the Crown."

Her mother clenched her hand in a vice-like grip, but Rosin ignored her clear message.

"Join me, Ciara. You've complained often enough of the unrest that plagues our realm. Join me in righting those wrongs. Stay here, find a suitable consort, and we'll rule together."

Laughter smothered Rosin's pleas, this time a multi-tonal peal, his and hers together.

"Why should I bargain such a high price with you, sister, when I can just take it? Why should I give up the man I love, like you've had to do—have chosen to do? Why, when the throne is rightfully mine? It's not yours to give away or share. Do you understand? The throne is not yours because I am firstborn." Ciara glared at Rosin.

"A good try, Princess Rosin, but Ciara wants her crown now. I want Ciara, and I want the throne. Besides, Keswin needs us before it implodes with resentment and hostility." Devon's lips twisted in a snarl.

"My parents could abdicate for the good of the realm," Rosin said softly, acutely aware of her mother's nails cutting into the soft flesh of her palm as her firm grip tightened.

Devon guffawed. "For the good of the realm? Your parents have never done anything for the good of the realm or its people. Why would they start now?"

"Perhaps because they would have no choice." Rosin's voice came out no more than a croak.

She couldn't meet her mother's gaze, shamed to criticize her parents' rule even if she spoke the truth. At no time had she been blind to her parents' excesses, just chosen to ignore them, taking the path of least resistance. Such ignorance and self-indulgence had brought her here this moon-slide.

Devon cackled loudly. "You're so right, Princess. They have no choice. I'm not giving them a choice. This moon-wash, they will abdicate in spectacular fashion, as you will."

An audible mutter spread throughout the waiting crowd.

Rosin glanced over her shoulder to ascertain where Muireach's loyalties lay. He'd disappeared from his position behind them, and her fear grew exponentially. She flicked her gaze back to Devon and her sister.

Muireach now stood still and silent behind Devon. His sword was already drawn to do battle, but not to cut his queen's enemy down.

A tiny whimper escaped from her throat. Muireach's defection changed the balance of power in the room, for many had unquestioned allegiance to Muireach. Nothing could save them.

A new terror suddenly consumed her. What of his son, Garrett? He would be torn between her and his father. Would he betray her and become a traitor? Her heart painfully rent in two at the thought. Surely, he would not willingly support her demise this moon-wash. Even as her mind rejected the inevitable outcome, she sent a quiet plea to the Maidens that her death would be swift.

Devon smiled as if he recognized the comprehension of her fate in Rosin's expression.

She flinched at the cruelty of it.

With a quick flick of his arm, he guided Ciara over to his chief bodyguard. "Time to leave, my little, black-hearted dove. I do not want you damaged."

Ciara pouted but did not protest. The expression distorting her sister's face as she strode away left Rosin shaken. No compassion, no regret, just excited anticipation. The cruelty reflected there burned into Rosin's brain.

As Devon lunged forward, Rosin tightened her grip on her mother's hand and roughly drew her aside.

Her father stepped past, plunged off the dais, and leapt straight at Devon, his sword aloft.

Rosin reached the side of the dais in two strides. Her mother dragged heavily on her arm as Rosin towed her forward. In a clumsy rush, Rosin slipped feet first off the delicately decorated dais, crushing the roses and ivy that trailed along the edge. Her full, woolen skirt caught around her legs, and she struggled to get free.

"Oh, Maidens. Such shame to be brought to this. I have failed. Failed to command the loyalty of my people. Failed as Queen." Maeve wailed as she resisted Rosin's forceful tugs.

"Come, Mother, we must flee."

"No, Rosin, I must protect you. You must hide! With you is the future of the throne. I will not fail again in my duty as a mother." Maeve pulled free and pushed Rosin so hard she collapsed to the floor and slipped under the dais. "Stay silent and still, Daughter. I will protect you."

"Mother!" Rosin cried out in protest as she reluctantly tucked her head in under the drapes. The dais offered no real protection and her mother even less. They should have run, but all escape routes were already blocked.

The battle clattered loud around her, the air rent with the screams of the wounded and the dying. Hope flowed over her as above the racket she heard her father roar the battle cry of his people and knew he still fought for their survival.

The curtain ruffled and billowed. A booted foot stomped so close to her face she flinched back hastily, swallowing a strangled scream.

The ceremonial stage shuddered under heavy footfalls. The

screeching clash of steel on steel rang painfully in her ears. She listened to every sound, trying to track the progress of the battle. She couldn't bring herself to block out the noise of struggle—to muffle the sounds that assured her those she loved still fought to save themselves and the realm.

Devon's voice seared over her. "Ah, the beautiful Queen Maeve. Such a shame it has to end like this. If only your parents hadn't refused my tender for your hand all those years ago. Just see where their principles have brought you."

"Devon, you have Ciara. Go! You will never have the throne to Keswin."

The loudness of his laugh battered Rosin. "I already have, my lady. Observe the carnage. Their loyalty has left them drowning in their own blood. The tide has already turned in my direction. With you and your golden- haired daughter dead, it will be over. As the only survivor of this terrible massacre, Ciara will claim the crown. I will have Keswin, finally. And no blame will come my way, dear queen. No one will suspect me, because I will be the rescuer of the only survivor. Many will curse those wretched, warlike Depcisians for this moon-wash's work."

"You'll never get away with this treachery, Devon."

He chuckled. "Your black-haired child is a clever little princess. Such things are what attracted me." His laughter hacked out again, harsh and loud. "And the promise of the crown made it a totally irresistible package."

"The crown can never be Ciara's. You need to know—"Maeve's words died on a soul shattering scream.

Rosin finally covered her ears. She knew what it meant. With a thud, her mother hit the floor. One arm flopped under the curtain. Rosin reached out and tucked her hand into the palm.

Her mother's fingers closed a little and squeezed in response.

She still breathed, but from the red pool slowly spreading across the floor, Rosin knew it was only a matter of time to her last breath.

Just before she emerged from the drapes to cradle her dying mother, a barbaric roar, inches from her head, scared Rosin into stillness.

A sword slashed the curtain just enough for her to see Eled fighting Devon. The clash of steel rang out above the moans and cries that crowded the surrounding air. Eled, although taller and younger, struggled to get the upper hand because Devon had experience on his side.

Rosin watched, unaware she held her breath, and flinched with each contact.

Eled carried his left arm a little, making him slow to respond to Devon's slashes.

She dragged her gaze away for a moment and scanned the room. So many dead. Such terrible injuries. Acid rose in her throat at the number of heads separated from bodies. Such cruel vindictive injuries inflicted after death. By Maidens' Law, beheading was kept for a traitor's death; in the belief it would make entry into the Afterlife difficult. These men did not deserve such desecration.

Rosin retched. She covered her mouth to muffle the sound, even as it registered that neither man fighting out there would hear her vomit.

She fortified herself with a deep breath, for the time had come. Not many still fought amongst the carnage that obliterated the beauty of the hall. The sounds of battle amplified. She turned to where her betrothed fought Devon.

Her father, carrying terrible injuries to his leg and head, staggered beside Eled, slashing as best he could with his sword.

The knowledge her father's flailing slashes offered no more than interference for Devon clawed at Rosin.

In a flash of red, Garrett's cousin, Finlay, jumped into view.

Her sharply indrawn breath of relief that rescue had come caught in her throat as Finlay proceeded to attack her father with vicious thrusts.

Eled retreated several steps under the renewed ferociousness of Devon's assault. As they battled, the men moved around the side of the dais, away from her hiding place.

Rosin ripped the curtain apart and crept forward.

Her mother's eyes were scrunched closed against the pain. One hand clutched at the bodice of her gown where blood oozed through her fingers into a large pool at the waistband of her skirt. A huge gash had opened her abdomen, deep and wide. Her intestines bubbled out a little more with every breath. Her mother moaned. Red spittle oozed from the side of her mouth.

Rosin's stomach heaved, and she turned away just in time to throw up the remaining contents of her stomach on her mother's bloodstained skirts.

Her mother tightened her hold on Rosin's hand. "Go to Tarlic to my cousin Meghan, your Moon Life Mother and her céile fir, King Cadmar. They can be trusted and will help you. Devon must never get the crown. Go to the High Queen Isolde. She knows the truth of your birth."

In the background, the sounds of battle faded. The slaughter was completed.

"Oh, Mother, it's too late for me to escape. Nearly everyone is dead except the women who escaped earlier. They haven't brought help, so they are traitors like their lords."

"You must go, Rosin." Her mother coughed. More blood spilled out of her mouth.

Rosin used the corner of her bonding gown to wipe it away.

"You must stay alive to bear a child and claim your throne. You are the last of my line, Rosin. Promise me, Daughter."

Rosin couldn't find words to refuse her mother's plea, but struggled to forge a promise she couldn't keep. Not that it would matter, for she did not expect to make it out of the hall alive.

"I promise, Mother."

Her mother coughed, choking on her own blood.

Rosin knew she would die, but wanted to ease her distress, so with trembling hands she lifted her mother into a half-sitting position, and ripping the torn curtain free, she rolled it up, then stuffed it under her shoulders and head.

Maeve gave her a weak smile. "Thank you, Rosin. That hurts a little less, but there is naught to be done for me. Go now, leave the castle, hide, and trust no one. You must save the crown. I'm sorry I've failed you as a mother and a queen. I've also failed the Maidens. All I can do now is beg their kindness, and yours, in death."

A thud close by reverberated through the floor. Rosin looked up in time to see her father land heavily. His deep green eyes were wide open, but unseeing. The deep gash in his throat poured bright red blood onto his white shirt, freshening up the darker stains already there.

Finlay brutishly kicked his inert body in the chest before he lifted his sword to inflict the last indignity.

"No!"

Finlay hesitated, then glanced in her direction. He sneered. Ignoring her silent plea for mercy, he turned with nonchalant slowness back to the corpse and swiped his sword across Fintain's exposed throat.

Rosin swallowed convulsively, trying to stop her stomach from heaving itself onto her lap.

At her mother's keening cries, she leaned down and enveloped her in a gentle hug. "They can't hurt him anymore, Mother, and you'll be together soon."

Maeve's sobs gurgled and groaned as she slowly drowned in her own blood. "Save the throne, Rosin."

Rosin sat back from her mother as she felt a presence. The bulk of a large boot planted squarely just a few inches away pinned the hem of her gown to the bloodied floor. She peeked up at him.

Finlay already had his sword swung back to take a vicious swing.

Her time to die had come. Rosin bowed her head, squeezed her eyes shut, then covered her face with her hands. She didn't want to see it coming. She had no desire to know the moment death would strike her.

She heard and felt the thud, screaming as a warm spray of blood splattered her face and cleavage. Something heavy landed on her lap. She parted her fingers and peeped out between them. Her mother regarded her from sightless eyes, her mouth still open in speech as if begging Rosin to escape and save the crown. With wild flaps of her hands, Rosin swiped her mother's head from her lap. She screamed again and again.

His nearness filtered through her horror and the sensation of immediate danger demolished her next scream into a painful hiccup that died in her diaphragm. She focused her gaze and stared blindly at Finlay's knees. Steadfastly, she refused to watch the steely blade descend on her head.

Finlay laughed. "Don't worry, Princess, I'm not going to kill you just yet. Although before I've finished with you, you will probably wish I had."

His hand curled into a cruel vise on her upper arm. Long fingers dug into soft flesh as he hauled her up on shaking legs that could barely hold her upright.

Feverish shudders wracked her body as the room spun in and

out of focus. Blood pounded through her head and echoed in her ears.

Bodies covered the floor. So many headless corpses. Blood and gore splattered the walls and drapes. The floor glistened with pools of red. All the beautifully scented roses that had decorated her bonding dais were crushed into oblivion and the thick, sickly tang of blood obliterated their sweet perfume.

Finlay glimpsed neither right nor left, oblivious to the carnage that surrounded him. His beefy hand encircled Rosin's arm as he dragged her toward the door.

Rosin scrutinized the scene, contemplating the dead, burning the horror into her mind. Every dead noble, every dead lady and servant. This she would never forget, and if she lived long enough, she would avenge the slaughter.

She stumbled over a headless corpse close to the door, and even under the blood and gore that caked it she recognized her betrothed. Overwhelmed by the horror around her she felt nothing more than a passing twinge of sadness for the handsome stranger who would have been her bonded partner and lover by now if the demon's spawn hadn't called.

Outside in the cool, clean moon-wash air, horses milled and whinnied while Devon waved his arms vigorously to emphasize his barked orders.

Even in her shocked semi-thinking state, Rosin could tell immediately that he planned to leave in a hurry.

Finlay tightened his hand around her arm, then shoved her forward with his shoulder. But not toward Devon. Rosin revived slightly as a sliver of hope flashed. Perhaps Finlay intended to let her go and save her from certain death at Devon's hands.

"Finlay?"

The deep chuckle that shuddered through his body gave the

answer to her question as she stumbled under forceful guidance to a patiently waiting steed.

Finlay finally turned and leered down at her. "Never you mind, Princess, we're going to have us some fun, but right now 'tis not the time."

Rosin wriggled against his grip.

"Behave yourself, Princess. I don't want any trouble on the trail from the likes of you." Finlay sniggered, then snorted through his nose, like he'd said something amusing. He lifted his fist. "And if you're nice and quiet, Devon doesn't need to know you ain't dead yet."

"And you aren't entitled to take what's mine, cousin," Garrett growled from behind them.

Finlay spun round. "Ah, Garrett, now you crawl out of your hole in the ground. Now all the dirty work is done."

"Hold your mouth, Finlay. We all had our part to play."

"Well, you didn't play yours, did you? If you'd been man enough to take her then this—Finlay waved his hand toward the castle—would not have been necessary."

"You can't blame me if she wanted to be the virgin bride," Garrett snarled. "But I still intend to have my reward."

Rosin didn't bother to interpret the exchange between the man she loved and his cousin, because nothing else mattered except that Garrett had come to save her.

"Too late, cousin."

"Maidens' curse on you, Finlay. I'll have what's mine."

"You can wait your turn."

The breeze from Garrett's fist passed her face. Finlay dodged left to avoid the blow.

Immediately Rosin yanked against Finlay's tight grip pulling him into the path of the next punch.

Garrett's knuckles crunched savagely into Finlay's face. He crumpled even as Garrett followed through with a right hook.

Finaly's grip fell away.

Rosin pulled free.

Before Rosin could gather her thoughts, Garrett grabbed her arm and dragged her around the corner of the building.

"Oh, Garrett, I knew you would save me. My love, I thank you."

"Don't thank me, Rosin, for I've no intention of rescuing you from your destiny, but I do intend to have you first. I couldn't bear the waste of your maidenhead on some other, when I had to work so hard to get it."

"What? Garrett? You mean to rape me? Is that all that mattered, all these years we've been friends. You said you loved me." Rosin wriggled to free herself.

He threw his head back and laughed as he pushed her into a dark corner. Using his superior weight, he pinned her against the wall with his chest. "I never loved you, Rosin. Why should I? You, with all your privileges. You're just the spoiled little brat of those grasping tyrants you called parents. Don't you understand yet? This is not about you. It's about overthrowing the regime and bettering Keswin. And this." He pressed her against the wall then shoved her skirt up to her hips. With the other hand he undid his breeches and released his already-erect member. "This is for Alanis. Her virginity for yours. I think that's a fair exchange."

"I don't understand, Garrett." Rosin wriggled away from his thrusting hardness.

Garrett tugged at her clothing. "Your parents forced the woman I love to bed visiting nobles, amongst other atrocities."

Rosin squirmed more vigorously. Comprehending with heart breaking certainty that Garrett intended to rape her. She struggled but could barely move as he leaned against her, fumbling to loosen her undergarments.

"No, Garrett, please don't do this. I didn't know my parents had forced Alanis to provide sexual favors for visitors."

"Huh. Even if you had, would you have done anything about it? That's the question, Princess."

Shame rushed through her with burning heat. She knew she would've ignored it like the rest of the excesses perpetrated by her parents. She had never considered challenging their rule.

Forced military or domestic service for sons and daughters of poor families. Income from private enterprise being seized, excessive rents, and savage punishments for violations of Maiden law. She figured it all had nothing to do with her. She loved her parents. That love and a strong sense of duty to the throne prevented her from questioning their behavior or making any protest against their arrangements for her future. She wondered in that moment if her failure to act made her as bad as them or maybe even worse.

His cold hand pushed between her legs groping past her outer lips to find the warm moist flesh in between. Rosin grabbed a handful of his hair, yanked his head forward, then sank her teeth into his shoulder.

"You moon leech!" He yelped and smacked her on the side of the head. His quick punishment barely interrupted his probing of her body with his other hand.

"Should've let me take you when I would have been kind, Princess. Now..." He fell silent and crumpled at her feet.

Finlay stood there, a sneer on his face. "No, you don't, cousin, you had your chance."

Finlay grabbed Rosin's arm and dragged her back to his horse. Everyone but Devon and Ciara were mounted and ready to go.

Chapter 3

The lovers stood face-to-face, spitting angry words at each other.

Even as Rosin craned to see, their heated discussion ended abruptly.

Devon spun on his heel and faced the gathered men. "I need evidence. I need her body. I need to know the Princess Apparent is dead. Anyone want to confirm they killed her?" A frown furrowed his brow as he focused a suspicious stare on his best warriors.

An ugly silence ensured.

"It's pretty messy in there, my lord."

Devon glared around at the man who spoke. "I don't give a Maiden's virginity! Go find the body, now! While the Princess Apparent is alive, Ciara cannot claim the throne, and all this is for naught." He repeated his question. "Can anyone confirm that Princess Rosin is dead?"

"Moonlight and Maidens." Finlay screwed his face up as his mouth turned down into a sneer. "Just wanted to have me a little fun."

The blur of his fist hurtled toward her. She couldn't duck or pull aside. The force of his knuckles jerked her head violently to the left. Her teeth rattled. Hot blood spurted from her nose. Her vision blurred as her eyeballs jolted in their sockets. Searing pain speared down her neck.

Finlay grabbed her around the waist and hefted her over his shoulder.

Fuzzy blackness hovered at the edge of her awareness. She tried to kick, but her legs only wobbled. The scream of protest at the abuse and imprisonment strangled in her throat. Fatigue seeped through her and she hung limply over his shoulder. *If I'm going to die, so be it.* Death could erase the horror etched into her mind and she welcomed it.

Her head bounced and bumped against Finlay's back in time with his stride as he carted her toward Devon.

"Lord Devon, I've just come from the hall. I have the Princess Apparent, alive. I wasn't sure what you wanted done with her. Both parents and her betrothed are dead."

Rosin opened her eyes a fraction as the bouncing stopped and saw Devon's boots, no longer shiny but coated in dirt, stuck there by the blood splattered from his victims.

"Ahh, Finlay, isn't it? Muireach's nephew." Devon's voice sounded deceivingly pleasant.

Finlay smiled. "Yes, my lord, I am Muireach's nephew."

"His nephew and a bloody liar." Devon's words sliced the air, sharp with accusation and threat.

"My lord?" Finlay challenged the accusation.

Finlay's words rumbled through his chest—quiet and innocently questioning, but no one could mistake the nervousness that crackled underneath.

"You thought to have a little fun of your own, did you?" Devon stared directly at Finlay his teeth bared in a snarl.

Finlay shuffled his feet slightly. "No, my lord, of..."

The blow struck Finlay with devastating force.

Rosin clung for a moment to the swaying shoulder even as it descended. Her aching body found a soft landing still clutched in the muscular arms of Finlay's corpse. Without sparing him a glance, Rosin rolled off the body. She pushed herself into a sitting position on the ground.

Someone immediately grabbed her roughly under her arms and hauled her upright.

Her knees refused to obey the messages from her mind, making it impossible to stay standing. Past caring, she made no effort to help herself.

To stop her complete collapse, her captor held her in a slumped, semi-upright position.

She lifted her head slightly and peered through the sticky strands of blood-splattered hair.

Devon stood in front of her, casually wiping his sword on the edge of his cloak.

Ciara strolled up, relaxed and casual, her red gown replaced with a shorter riding skirt over trousers.

"So, Sister, you've managed to stay alive."

Rosin stared back at her twin in silence.

"You know you were not meant to survive." Ciara slapped her hands on her hips, her face highlighted by gloating scorn.

Rosin licked her dry, cracked lips with a parched tongue. She tasted blood. Her mouth stung in two places where Finlay had hit her, and she could hardly breathe through her nose. Blood still trickled from it.

"With you gone, Keswin's throne is mine. I'll never understand why Mother hated me so much she would deny me my birthright." Sharp with disdain, Ciara's voice cut through the air.

Rosin shook her head. "Ciara, you can have the crown if you so wish, but it will be an empty decoration. Mother never denied you anything."

"I know the truth. I am the firstborn, not you. You never had any right to the crown." Ciara stepped forward, drawing her dagger as she came. She waved it under Rosin's bloodied nose. "Do you hear that, sister dear? Your firstborn status is a lie."

Ciara backed away a fraction, then glanced at the guard holding Rosin. "Kill her, and I want her head to decorate a pike on the gate to this castle. When it's picked white and clean, I shall return and claim this place as mine. Kill her now!" Her voice rose to a high-pitched screech edged with madness.

Devon nodded to him, then turned away. Rosin's captor adjusted his grip and drew his dagger. The sound of metal-on-metal cut through Rosin's lethargy.

She snatched in a deep breath. "Devon, you've been lied to. If you kill me, you will never hold the throne of Keswin." Rosin swallowed against the scratchiness in her throat. "Ciara can never claim the crown, even with me dead." Her words faded.

Devon stopped walking, spun around, and strode toward her. His eyes glittered with fury under tightly drawn brows.

Shivers whipped over her. Terror at his response clenched her gut. She thought her heart would jump out of her chest.

"Devon don't listen to her. She's trying to buy time and make you afraid to kill her. Kill her and let's go. I need to leave this place."

Ciara's whine scratched down the frayed edges of Rosin's nerves.

Devon immediately held up his hand to stay any further protests from Ciara. He loomed over Rosin, a jeweled dagger in his hand. With the blade, he parted Rosin's hair, then bent down and peered into her battered face. "Tell me, little Princess, what makes you say Ciara can't claim the throne? As I see it, nothing stands in her way as firstborn."

Rosin stared into his dark eyes. She contorted her mouth but could not find enough saliva to spit in his face, so she smiled instead, a sweet, demure smile. "Maybe Muireach would like to tell you the full truth, not just the part about Ciara being the firstborn."

Rosin peeped up under her lids but couldn't see Muireach in the crowd.

"Muireach has gone ahead to prepare a suitable camp, so you had better do it, Princess. Now."

Ciara slipped into Rosin's limited view. A deep frown furrowed her twin's forehead.

"Dear Ciara, just in time to hear the awful truth." Unable to hold onto the smiling façade, Rosin twisted her mouth into a grimace. "Then again, it might be better to wait for your... for Muireach to join us."

Devon grabbed Rosin's hair and yanked her head up, forcing her to look directly into his eyes. They glittered with impatience and anger. "Out with it, Princess, before you die!"

A little flash of triumph sparked. She'd gotten to him. Refusing to cry out against the pain, she fixed her gaze directly on Devon, deliberately ignoring her sister. Ciara did not have the power of life or death over her. Devon did.

"Ciara is the firstborn, but they falsified the records because Ciara is not the legal issue of Lord Fintain, son of Adwen, consort of Queen Maeve, Queen of Keswin." She deliberately used the full titles of her parents. "She is only my half-sister, born together in the womb of the queen, but not conceived by the same father. In exchange for her life, she became second born." Rosin struggled to enunciate each word through her cut lip.

Devon stared at her, long and hard. Not a soul stirred amongst the crowd.

Ciara simply shrugged at Devon's glance of inquiry.

He turned back to Rosin, his breath hot in her face, smelling of tobacco, stale spices, and malt syrup.

She would have retched, but her stomach could no longer react.

"Can you prove this claim?"

Rosin swept her gaze over her sister, then back to Devon. "I don't have to, because the High Queen, Isolde, ultimate ruler of the six lands of the Maidens, knows the truth. If you proceed with your claim, Ciara will be executed, and you hunted down. The High Queen will enforce the right of ascendancy. But consider this, as a snippet of evidence. All Maidens' royal descendants are blond-haired and green or blue-eyed in the image of the Maidens. They are born blond, they Bond with blonds, and they have blond issue. No full-blooded descendent of the Maidens is dark-haired."

Ciara came toward her in a stumbling rush. "Liar."

Her spittle flecked Rosin's face, but it barely made an impression on the gore already caking it.

With the juicy facts of the royal scandal revealed, Rosin sagged. The last vestiges of strength sucked out of her at the reality of saying it out loud.

Her captor hauled her upright.

Sharp pains tore through every muscle. A tiny, pathetic sound squeezed out between her lips. She breathed in deeply and forced the words out. "Ask Muireach, Ciara, or should I say, ask your father. He became mother's lover, barely eighteen moon-slides after her bonding. Father forgave her for the indiscretion. It's just unfortunate mother conceived us both at the same time. Muireach wanted you to have legitimacy and a privileged life, so he traded that for you being recorded as the second-born. Besides, as a bonded man with a partner who also had just given birth, he had little choice. But even back then, he saw you as a good stepping-stone to the power he craved."

"No! You lie. Kill her!" Ciara lunged at Rosin.

Devon stepped in her way. "No. We'll do nothing until Muireach can confirm or deny your sister's accusation. If it's true, then it changes everything." Devon's voice was calm, measured, and quiet.

"What do you mean, Devon?"

"Don't fret, my little black dove. I love you still, and will make you my wife, but business is business, and I didn't do this — he waved his gloved hand at the castle — to satisfy your desires. I have my own plans. My child will inherit the throne of Keswin."

Tears sprang into her eyes. She sniffed in a vain attempt to stop them falling as she pouted. "But my lord..."

Devon put his hand over her mouth. "Do not fear, my little dove." He turned back to the guard holding Rosin. He raised his fist, then brought it down.

Devon spun on his heel and strode away, a twisted smirk that radiated evil plastered on his face.

A quick flash of searing pain brought blackness rushing in.

~ ~ ~

Her skull bounced and cracked against an undulating but solid surface. She whimpered. Her head throbbed with the jerky movement. The smells that accosted her senses — horse, male sweat, tobacco, leather, and a sickly metallic aroma riled her stomach.

Hooves clattered and lowered voices punctuated by the clank of metal wafted around her.

With extreme caution, she opened one eye the tiniest slit. Her hair dangled down, but through it she could see the ground passing below her. To ease the immediate dizziness, she opened the other eye. A man's booted foot hung down by her shackled hands suspended against the horse's shoulder. Her bound feet fell loosely into empty space.

Roughly bundled across a horse's wither in front of a rider, Rosin struggled with the hard knobs of the pommels poking into her ribs and abdomen. She couldn't identify the rider, but by turning her head the smallest degree to the right, she could see a sword swaying at his side.

A quick assessment of her battered body revealed a swollen face, tight-skinned and caked in blood. In the center, her nose throbbed with a deeper pain than the rest. Though this pain soon became totally eclipsed by the thumping headache trying to burst out of her brain where it centered on her left temple.

All her limbs seemed to be intact, but her stomach ached. It didn't surprise her, considering the number of times she'd vomited this moon-wash and the current battering from the pommel. Satisfied her injuries were not life-threatening, she let her face fall back down onto the horse's prickly coat and kept her eyes closed to ease the motion sickness. She didn't want to draw attention to the fact she'd regained consciousness either, terribly afraid of receiving another vicious blow to her head.

Her revelation about Ciara's lineage had obviously caught both Devon and Ciara by surprise. Ciara seemed both shocked and in denial. Rosin guessed Muireach would deny it.

A terrible suspicion lurked in her mind about Devon's new plans. It sent spikes of terror racing through her. Part of her wished she had kept quiet, but her revelations had provided a delay to her expected demise at the castle from a slit throat. Although death probably remained her ultimate destiny, for now she survived, a bit battered, but whole enough to make a run for it if the chance presented itself.

There would be no rescue with everyone dead or turned traitor. She could no longer trust anyone. Assuming they were headed to Devon's castle in Ersklyn, she had at least two moon-slides steady ride to escape before they reached their destination.

Unsure how long she'd been unconscious, a quick assessment

of her bodily needs suggested it had been only hours since they had left the carnage behind. She grimaced as the very thought motivated the need for action. Maidens' fall! She would just have to hold it as best she could. The constant rocking motion and the accompanying jabs from the pommel did not help. She wished fervently to be still.

"Camp ahead. Camp ahead." Gruff shouts echoed down the ranks. The momentum of the horse increased, jolting and slamming her up and down.

Her head shook and her feet flapped erratically against the undulating muscles of her mount's shoulder. A strong hand pressed into the small of her back to hold her in place as the reins slapped against her shoulders and backside. A quick glance from under her lids showed the booted foot kicking hard into the horse's flanks, forcing it to change from a trot to a canter. Rosin silently appreciated the transition to a smoother gait.

Petrified of slipping from her precarious resting place, she desperately wanted to hold on but couldn't with her hands strapped so tightly together. She shut her eyes and hung limp, praying for them to halt.

She ventured another peek out of one eye. She saw the glow of fires and the movement of shadows across the flames—people and horses, she guessed.

With her bladder about to burst, she clenched herself internally as the gelding collected its stride under the force of a heavy rein, tipping her back onto the rider's lap. Instinctively, she cringed away.

"Stay still, girlie, or you'll land in the dust." He tightened his grip, then heaved her farther onto his lap with his hand tucked around her waist.

Rosin stiffened against him, and despite trying to stay silent, she could not stop a high-pitched squeak squeezing out between her lips as he pinched her nipple between a finger and thumb, then rolled it this way and that.

He guffawed loudly. "Too good for an old soldier like me, huh?"

She didn't bother resisting his manhandling again or attempt to answer his question. Without warning, she slid, feet first, to the ground. The ruined remains of her gown rucked up around her hips. She tried to tug it back down.

The man sniggered. "Pretty legs, girlie. Pity we don't have more time and a wee little privacy. I could make good use of those legs and what lies between 'em. Ever had a real man, girlie?"

Without warning, her legs crumpled beneath her. She slid into an ungainly heap. With her hands fettered, she couldn't stop herself from toppling over, face first into the dirt. Sharp nuggets of gravel bit into the soft flesh of her cheeks, and coarse grains of dirt filled her mouth and eyes.

She blinked furiously to clear her vision. Cursing her raging thirst and the dirt clinging to her teeth and tongue, she spluttered and coughed.

Above her, the man chuckled. Silently, she wished evil on him as she lay unable to summon the strength or desire to move. Inside her stillness, her thoughts raced onto the dilemma of escape.

If they camped here this moon-wash, she might have a chance. She needed a plan and a miracle from the Maidens to achieve an escape from a camp full of enemies. Her thoughts jumped from idea to idea while her body remained immobile.

Her captor dismounted and came to stand by her. He made no attempt to harm or help her.

Rosin waited, content to lie unmoving. Her whole body hurt to varying degrees, throbbing and stinging from unseen injuries. She mentally gathered her strength, knowing the cruelty of this moon-wash wasn't finished yet.

The first set of footsteps, loud and measured, crunched meaningfully against the pebbles underfoot and seconds later they were followed by another footfall, lighter and faster. She made no attempt to acknowledge the owner of the boots that marked the dirt beside her.

A foot pushed at her. Unable to offer any resistance, she rolled onto her back. The ungainly movement twisted her legs, wrenched her hips, and flung her bound hands to the side. The fresh torment to her body elicited a shriek from her dried-out mouth. She clenched her teeth and cut the sound off short. Trapped in the awkward pose, she opened her eyes enough to see Devon standing over her. Ciara stood by his side. Her sister clutched his arm, trying to urge him away.

With a keen desperation, Rosin wanted to shut out the nightmare reality that surrounded her, but instead, she fixed her gaze on Devon's face. He would decide if she lived or died.

He folded his arms across his muscular chest and leaned back a little to stare down at her. A thoughtful, sardonic expression masked his internal thoughts. He didn't speak.

Rosin glared unflinchingly into his eyes. The ugly tension in the air pressed with brutality against her soul.

The surrounding horses moved restlessly. The men all stood silently in a circle around the three adversaries.

When the hooves clattered too close to Rosin's arms, Devon flicked his fingers at the handler.

The man moved aside, taking his mount with him.

Devon turned from her and directed a long scowl at someone obscured by the shadows.

"He's coming, my lord."

Devon didn't reply, just turned his gaze back to Rosin.

The cold lump that had settled inside her pushed goose bumps up on every inch of bare skin. Tiny shudders crept through her body until finally her teeth chattered. Her throat itched and burned, and every time she swallowed, sharp pinpricks seared down its length. Her tongue felt too big, and her mouth tasted of a sour foulness. Desperate for a drink, but determined not to ask, she concealed any sign of the physical agony and mental distress tormenting her.

Overwhelmed by angst, she withdrew from reality, curling deep inside herself. Everything retreated, shrunken and distant. In her mind, she could see herself, but she had no awareness of her body lying there on the ground.

It seemed an eternity before she heard noises. Then, as if from a long distance, Muireach's voice pierced the thick tension surrounding them.

"What's this nonsense? What has the Princess Apparent been saying? Why is she still alive?" Muireach strode forward, his expression filled with scathing.

So, they haven't told him. Rosin smiled inside. Going to be a nice surprise. Let's see how he gets out of this one.

"Devon?" The single word dripped with question, irritation, and demand. No fear.

"Ah, Muireach." Devon greeted him with a languid drawl as he waved his hand over Rosin. "The Princess Apparent has something to say."

Muireach snorted. "Since when are we interested in listening to the likes of her? She should be too dead to speak."

"Oh, I'm interested in hearing this, Muireach, and I think you might also be interested." Devon stepped forward to prod Rosin with his boot. "Speak up, Princess. Now is your only chance."

The thud in her ribs brought Rosin back to reality with an unpleasant rush. She desperately wanted to eyeball Muireach when she voiced her accusations, but she had no leverage to lift herself into a sitting position.

Devon grimaced. "Ahh, the Princess wishes to watch your reaction, Muireach." He twitched his fingers. Rough hands grabbed her under the arms before dragging her to her feet.

Rosin made no effort to actually stand until she could keep her feet steady under her. Even then, she swayed as the big, grasping paws slipped away. Her hands, still bound, hung in front of her. Her tangled blood-flecked hair covered her face, obscuring her vision. She flicked her head, and the matted curtain swayed enough so she could look Muireach in the eyes. She wanted to see his pain when she scuttled his dream. "Why don't you...?" She coughed, then spat out grit and dirt.

Again, Devon gestured toward the men waiting around him. Moments later, the hard lip of a flagon bumped against her mouth and the cool silk of fresh water trickled down her throat. She gulped thirstily; afraid she wouldn't get enough before they took it from her. Devon merely stood silently, watching her drink her fill.

The liquid revived her. She squared her shoulders and glared directly at Muireach. "Why don't you tell us all the truth, Muireach? Tell everyone that all this death is to no avail? Tell us all why Ciara has no legitimate right to the throne of Keswin."

Muireach scowled, his lip curled into a snarl that wrinkled his overly large nose and squinted his eyes under heavy, dark brows. "Depcisians' spawn, there's nothing to tell. Your parents wanted to dupe Ciara out of her rightful inheritance. I have put it to rights. You lie! A wretched attempt to extend your miserable life."

"You don't wish to enlighten us, Muireach?" Devon's voice a deceptively soft murmur as he regarded first one then the other.

"No, my lord, there's nothing to tell." Muireach's dagger was already in his hand as he lunged toward Rosin.

She twisted sideways in a clumsy movement. The blade caught in her tattered skirts.

Muireach would have buried it in her back, but for Devon's intervention.

Devon wrenched Muireach back by the collar of his coat.

The man standing behind her tugged her roughly to the side.

Her legs crumpled, and she hit the ground with a thud. With a slight twist, she managed to brace herself enough to remain sitting.

Devon swung the bigger man off his feet. Muireach landed with a thump.

Before he could rise, Devon smacked him in the face with a clenched fist.

Muireach shook his head to clear the fuzziness from the right hook. With an angry swipe, he raked his long hair back off his face, then spat out blood before he pushed himself to his feet. He glared at Devon in silence.

Rosin watched both men.

Devon turned back to her. "Speak, Princess. Seeing as Muireach seeks to silence you, I am now most interested in hearing the whole story."

Rosin hesitated, then attempted to stand. Rough hands under her armpits lifted her. She wiped her face with the rag that bound her hands, then pushed back her hair so she could glare squarely at Devon.

"Ciara is Muireach's issue. My mother took him to her bed after the first moon-slides of her bonding to my father, Fintain. Unfortunately, she conceived the two of us, me from Lord Fintain's leavings,"—Rosin pointed at her sister— "and she from Muireach's. At our birth, my mother nearly died when the physician had to cut her womb open as he had for the High Queen. With me already in the birth passage, upside down, the physician took Ciara first, the larger, dark-haired baby, then he extracted me from the birth canal, the smaller, blond, curly-headed babe. All those present knew the meaning of the dark hair, as no descendant of the Maidens ever has black hair. So, they struck a deal, Muireach and my parents. If he recorded Ciara as second born, she would be accepted as the legitimate issue of the Queen and her consort. The illegitimate child would be given the privileged life of a princess, but she could never make a claim on the crown. If this deal had not been accepted, then there would only be one live birth recorded and that would be mine."

Devon's face took on a ruddy hue, and his eyes sparked with fury. He turned to Muireach. Muireach's face had already paled to a chalky white, his complexion a perfect match to his daughter's ivory skin.

Ciara's eyes locked on Muireach. Her mouth slowly opened, then shut. Her beautiful dark eyes were wide open, as she stared unblinking at her father.

"Muireach?"

Muireach's mouth moved as he struggled to form words. He cleared his throat in a grating cough and stared back at Devon as if the man had suddenly transformed into a blood viper.

"My lord, the Princess lies. Why would I, a happily bonded man with children of my own, become Maeve's lover?

"Tell me then, Muireach, how the queen managed to bear a grey-eyed, dark-haired child?"

Muireach glared at Rosin as he moistened his lips. "The Queen may well have had a lover, but not me. No matter whom the father, if there are none to tell the story, then who will care?"

"Liar!" Rosin spat the word out. He would not deny the truth. She glared her hatred at him. Why should he be alive when her parents were dead? Why should his daughter be allowed to claim a throne not legally hers? A daughter willing to kill her mother without regret?

Rosin didn't really covet the crown, but she would not give it up easily after her sister's horrendous attempt to snatch it for herself. With a sudden certainty, she knew she didn't want to die. She wanted to live and get revenge for her parents. No matter what it cost her personally, she would keep Keswin's throne out of Ciara and Devon's clutches.

Devon pinioned her with his stare. "It's more in your interest to lie, Princess. Your life is the wager."

Rosin snorted at Devon's comment. "I know I'm going to die. Nothing I can say will change your plans for me, so I have no chance of winning that wager, but Muireach,"—she glared at him—"wants Keswin's crown for his daughter. He wants the power that will come with being the father of the queen. A young queen, an inexperienced queen. He would have a chance to shape the realm his way, in a way he couldn't with my parents alive. No matter their shortcomings or lack of vision for the realm, by birth, they had the right to rule."

"Shortcomings, Princess? That's somewhat generous." Devon snorted.

Rosin held up her hands. "Their failings do not matter anymore, for they are dead, but the inheritance of the throne is of the utmost importance. Ciara's parentage denies her that right. For what Muireach does not know is Isolde, the High Queen of Annaticcia, who rules us all, knows the full truth. She had a special interest in my mother's pregnancy because of Fintain. As one of her late sister's twin sons and Isolde's first Moon Life Child, she felt great affection for him. Besides, it's not often twins are conceived. But the difference between us spoke for itself and in the end, she had to be told the truth. My parents had to negotiate an agreement with her and pay a tithe."

"Tithe," Muireach bellowed. "You lie."

Rosin shook her head. "She even threatened to kill Ciara and foster me if they didn't comply. Overcome with shame, they never told a soul, not even you, Muireach. They just acquiesced to the High Queen's demands."

She paused, took a deep breath, then eyeballed Devon. "In his ignorance, Muireach thought he could eventually trade Ciara's life for a chance at the crown. He just needed to be patient. Then Ciara's willful nature brought a powerful ally in you, Devon. Now, Muireach is within a breath of achieving his dream, and consider what he's done to get this far."

Devon glared at his lover's father. Fury shadowed his face.

A stab of fear grazed her heart, but she had to finish this regardless of the outcome.

She had to strike while both men remained uncertain of the full truth. "Do you think, Devon, he will hesitate to dispose of you if you get in his way? Then he'll have it all. The only thing is, if Ciara takes my crown, you will all be fighting the High Queen, for she'll enforce her edict that Ciara can never bear the crown."

Muireach lurched for her again. One of Devon's men grabbed him and twisted his arms behind his back to bring him up with a jerk.

Devon spun to face Muireach. He had Ciara imprisoned with his brawny arm around her neck.

"Devon..." Ciara whimpered; her eyes wide open with fear as she craned her neck to peer at her lover.

Devon stood stiffly while he restrained her from behind. He held a short, tapered dagger pressed against her throat.

Ciara reached up to clutch at her lover's arm. "Please, Devon, you're hurting me."

"Shh, my little black dove. Your father and I are talking."

In the flickering light, Rosin saw tears glisten on her sister's cheeks.

"Once before, Muireach, you traded your own ambitions against your daughter's life. Now you need to wager it again. This time, it's the truth, or her life."

"Devon, what is this? We're friends. Behold what we have achieved this moon-wash. Ciara is your lover, already carrying your child, the future generation of Keswin royalty. The Princess lies to save her life. Of course, the High Queen does not know. She would never have tolerated such a transgression. Keswin would have been forfeit."

"Can you be sure, Muireach? I have no desire to take on the High Queen." Devon tightened his grip on Ciara, pressing the knife harder against her skin.

Even in the shadowy light, Rosin could see tiny trickles of blood running down Ciara's long, white neck and into the valley of her cleavage.

Ciara whimpered again, pressing herself back against her lover in an effort to escape the stinging touch of the dagger.

"Don't hurt her, Devon. She loves you."

"No matter, Muireach. Answer the question." Devon made no effort to release his lover.

Muireach scowled, first at Devon, then at Rosin. "If the High Queen knew, the realm would be forfeit. The High Queen does not tolerate mistakes."

Rosin squinted at Muireach. "For her favorite nephew and Moon Life Child, she did. She had a terrible fondness for my father." A rush of victory warmed her as Muireach appeared cornered.

"Moon Life Child? Fintain?" Muireach spluttered, his tone full of ridicule and disbelief.

Rosin nodded. "You didn't know, did you? It's not something one boasted about. The High Queen has many Moon Life children, but they must be discreet if she favors them."

Rosin didn't doubt Devon would kill Ciara if Muireach did not satisfy his demands. He had a goal in mind and if he had to climb over a mountain of corpses to get there, he would, without the slightest flicker of regret.

The silence lengthened.

The two men continued to glare at each other.

Ciara sniveled.

Rosin watched with a vague sense of detached amusement.

Muireach's expression contorted. Devon had him trapped.

Whatever Muireach's response, though, her future did not appear either long or pleasant.

"Muireach!" Devon roared the single word as a savage demand for an answer.

Muireach sagged, and the mask of contempt and incredulity slipped from his face. Fear showed through raw primeval fear of the man he faced. "The Princess speaks the truth. I fathered Ciara, and yes, I traded her firstborn status for legitimacy and a royal title. And yes, I hoped to seize the crown through my daughter. I had no idea the High Queen knew, or I would never have started this. No one should ever have known the truth. I killed the physician before he got back to King Cadmar's castle in Tarlic and with Maeve, Fintain, and Rosin dead, the secret would have gone to the grave with them. Ciara would have been accepted without question as the legitimate claimant to Keswin's throne. Nobody would have demurred."

Ciara whimpered; a flood of tears shimmered on her cheeks.

"You're an idiot, Muireach." Devon nodded to the man that held Muireach.

A grunt escaped Muireach, his eyes opened wide with surprise. His captor released him, and he sagged to the ground with a groan and an audible gasp. Blood seeped from under his body, staining the dirt a muddy red.

A wave of sickness crashed over Rosin at the suddenness of Muireach's death, but she watched his corpse being dragged away by two lackeys with dispassionate disinterest.

Devon had already released Ciara by the time Rosin looked back at them. He held her against his chest as she wept tears of humiliation. Ciara showed no grief for the father she never knew.

Devon stroked her hair. "Don't cry, little one. I still love you, but now I have some business to sort before we can start our lives together."

Ciara choked back her tears, her expression cold and hard. "What business, my lord?" Her tone sharp and challenging. "We hold Keswin by right of defeat. It does not matter that I'm not the rightful heir. Kill Rosin, then all is done."

"No, Ciara, my love, I must hold Keswin by right of inheritance. I will not have my claim constantly challenged by any Maiden noble. Keswin must be irrefutably mine."

"Devon, can you not be satisfied? You hold Keswin. You have more than doubled your lands. We can fight off all comers making a claim."

"Except the High Queen. No, my love, I cannot be satisfied. I must have it all." He pushed Ciara from his embrace and held her at arm's length with a firm grip on her shoulders. "I must sire a legitimate heir. It is the only way I can secure Keswin's throne."

"But..."

"You will have to be patient, my love, and understand that what I do is for us. To secure our future."

Chapter 4

A terrible numbness gripped Rosin as the sliver of suspicion blossomed into a terrible reality. Unable to move, she just sat there, letting the revulsion of this new development crawl across her skin. She knew with every beat of her heart that it must never come to pass that a child fathered by Lord Devon could claim the throne of Keswin.

The sound of the slap cracked through the silence.

Rosin flinched.

Devon stepped back out of Ciara's reach.

Ciara stared at him with eyes full of venom. "You bastard. You're mad. Obsessed with the throne of Keswin. It's nothing. Do you hear me, Devon? The throne is nothing if it can't be mine."

Devon shook his head. "I'm sorry, but this is how it must be, little black dove. Any children we have can only inherit Ersklyn. They can never inherit Keswin because of your mother's whoring ways. I must father a child with your sister to secure the throne and keep the High Queen of Annaticcia at bay."

Rosin felt removed from the drama being played out in front of her, as though it had nothing to do with her.

"You shame me mercilessly. You condemn our child to be born out of union to seize a throne you already hold. I do not want a throne that will never be mine at this price. Do you hear? I do not want it." Ciara screeched and pummeled Devon's chest with her fists. "No! No! No! You cannot mean to do this atrocious thing."

Devon easily caught her flailing hands in his. "It must be legitimate, Ciara. Such a child will make us the greatest power in the land." His face glowed with an obsessive hunger for power. "Then we can have Wilsea, Dyanwen, and Tarlic. Just think, my love, I could eventually hold all six of the Maidens' thrones."

"You intend to marry her..."

"Yes, my little dove, I must marry her."

Ciara's tormented scream of anguish rent the air. Many of those close to the couple flinched as the decibels penetrated their eardrums.

Devon shook her. "Stop keening. I'll still marry you, Ciara. Just a little later than planned. When Rosin dies in childbirth, I will be a grieving widower, free to marry you." Devon made a determined effort to soothe and explain.

Rosin heard the undercurrent of resolve and impatience in his words.

"You don't love me, Devon. I have just been a means to get the throne. It should be mine. You used me." With maniacal jerks, she tore herself from his grasp, and stomped away.

The full consequences of her situation were quite clear to Rosin. She might still be alive, but she would regret it in the moon-slides to come. It would have been better if she'd died beside her parents in the carnage of the ballroom.

A union with Devon paled into insignificance against his intent to have a child with her. She cast her gaze around the campsite. Surrounded by enemies and with her legs bound together, she couldn't flee unaided.

As she waited for the next horror, she squirmed uncomfortably, her bladder ready to burst. This could be her chance.

The man who'd earlier held her in an upright position now stood silently by her side.

She leaned toward him. "I need to relieve myself."

He ignored her.

She glowered at Devon. He had turned to watch his lover march off into the shadows of the camp.

Rosin's need pressed urgently on her body. "Devon!"

Her voice sounded shrill and scratchy, but loud enough to catch his attention. He glanced over his shoulder.

"I need to relieve myself."

Devon raised his eyebrows, as though her request struck him as totally unusual. He frowned, then jerked his head toward one of the women in the crowd. Immediately, she stepped forward.

"See to it." He pointed at Rosin.

The woman nodded, but before her head bobbed, Rosin saw adoration in her eyes. Obviously noble, but not from Keswin, and way too old to be one of Devon's lovers. Rosin pondered why he seemed to trust her without question.

"You, Slade." Devon pointed at the man standing by Rosin. "Go with them. See, she doesn't escape and keep your grasping hands off the goods. Understood?"

The man grimaced and nodded before he knelt at Rosin's feet to undo the bindings.

The woman took Rosin's arm in a pinching grip and dragged her forward. "Let's get on with it."

The numbness in Rosin's legs made it hard to keep her balance, and her flimsy slippers provided no protection against the rough, rock-strewn ground. She stumbled, tugging against the woman's directing arm.

The action immediately brought a savage shove in the small of her back and a tighter grip on her shoulder. "Don't try it, Princess."

Rosin bit her lip as she forced her legs to carry her in the direction the woman pushed her. By now desperate to relieve herself, she gave up trying to assess her chances of making a run for it.

As they left the firelight, a quiet blackness swallowed them. It seemed as if only the three of them existed, moving warily through a gloomy vacuum of darkness. As her guide pushed her through some bushy shrubs, stones rattled in ever decreasing clicks.

Rosin smiled. The stones had obviously tumbled down some distance. Over a cliff maybe. She knew of several places along the road to Ersklyn where the track ran along cliff edges that loomed above the smaller of the two rivers, winding their way across the valley that cradled Keswin Castle. Not much of a landmark to get her bearings from if she managed to break free, but better than nothing at all.

"Here will do. Get on with it." The woman released the binding around Rosin's wrists, but kept a tight grip on her hair. "You, Slade, keep your distance or you'll answer to Devon."

With the remaining tatters of her gown hitched, Rosin squatted in the shadows, deliberately taking her time so she could study her surroundings. At first, she hadn't been able to see anything, but after a few minutes in the darkness, her vision had slowly adjusted to the faint glow of the moons.

She could make out the bushes behind her, and off to the left she could see the denser shadow of Slade. The light from the moons glinted a little on his sword.

The woman's grip tightened. "Hurry it up, Princess. Lord Devon awaits you."

As Rosin stood, she pretended to stumble. The grip on her hair jerked her up leaving just enough slack for Rosin to lash out at her minder's shin. The kick didn't make much of an impression.

"You little harlot!" The woman gave Rosin's hair a vicious tug.

Rosin went with the yank and landed against her minder's large breasts. The woman's mouth opened in a cry of surprise.

As the woman sought to remove her, Rosin clawed her face.

Rosin caught her bottom lip and dug her nails into the soft, wet flesh. She dragged down hard on the sensitive tissue.

With a guttural cry, the woman lost her balance.

Slade charged toward them through the bushes, slipping and sliding over the rough ground.

As the woman fell backward, Rosin shoved her hard. The momentum ripped the woman's grip loose from Rosin's hair. Rosin scuttled toward the empty darkness to her right. At first, she seemed to be scrabbling hard, but making no progress, then her feet gained traction. She lunged forward. With sobbing gasps, she snatched air into her lungs.

Close behind, the thud of heavier footsteps crunched in unison with the heavy breathing of Slade.

Suddenly, a wide emptiness loomed in front of her. Barely slowing, she spun to the right and ran, following the cliff edge, jumping small bushes and pushing through the bigger ones. Branches scratched at her face and clutched her hair.

The crunch of his footfalls sounded loud behind her.

She expected to feel his rough hands on her shoulders at any moment.

As she lurched forward, the ground dropped away. She tumbled down a steep incline, landing awkwardly on her backside. Small pebbles and dirt showered her head as she reached out to grasp at passing vegetation to stop her descent.

Slade's large hand grasped her wrist in a bone-crushing grip. He hauled her out of the ditch.

Rosin whimpered in pain; her skin torn open by a million sharp stones. She smacked out with her free hand, trying to land a blow on the man's face.

He laughed at her feeble attempts. With minimal effort, he captured her other hand unceremoniously, dragging her back up over the shallow precipice.

She flailed her legs toward his groin and bucked her body and screeched her frustration.

He guffawed as he held her effortlessly in an ironclad grip.

Another hand tugged at her hair and Rosin yelped as thick chunks loosened from her scalp. Next, the woman grabbed her tattered bodice with her other hand — breasts, corset, and all — and dragged Rosin across the ground.

"Stop, damn you! I'll walk. Just let me stand up."

"Gonna behave yourself?"

"Yes. Just let me walk, for Maidens' sake."

Slade hauled her upright.

She made no effort to pull away as he bound her hands with the thong from his hair.

With his belt, he formed a noose, then whipped it around her neck.

Rosin gagged as it restricted her breathing.

He shoved against the small of her back. "Walk, Princess. Right back to Lord Devon. He has plans for you, girlie."

Her mind raced. Her temper boiled with rage that these two Interlopers had thwarted her escape. Even as they forced her back to the camp, Rosin watched for her next opportunity. She could not let Devon succeed in his plan to impregnate her.

The flickering light glowing around the camp grew brighter. Only a few people remained standing around the fire. These were the ones who would dictate her destiny — Devon, the priest standing by his side, and two well-dressed men that flanked them both. The priest held the Interloper's marriage book and had a Maiden bonding dagger strapped to his waist.

Devon frowned at Rosin's bodyguards. "About time, Mother. I had begun to think you'd lost my little bride-to-be."

Fury flashed through her. On a Maiden's grave, she should have given her maidenhead to Garrett years ago. It surely would have been better than having it taken by this monster. An icy frost of fear crept through her, a heavy paralysis that stole her will to resist and weakened her resolve to fight.

Even as she glanced around for some way to escape her predicament, she considered it better to kill herself before Devon succeeded in fathering a child with her. Better her throne revert back to the High Queen than go to Devon's spawn.

The priest stepped forward and indicated that Devon should move up beside his bride. Rosin wrinkled her nose as she caught his scent: sweat, blood, and horse.

Devon shook his head at the priest's instruction, then turned to his mother. "Mother, will you do the honors?"

Her female captor nodded.

Rosin looked from one to the other. Honors? Just what honors does a bridegroom's mother do?

Devon nodded at the man who held her. He tightened his grip on her upper arms so much it restricted the circulation.

Devon's mother flicked out the snowy white rug the priest handed her.

Slade grunted as he swung Rosin's whole body upwards.

She didn't even have a chance to wriggle before he thumped her down on the rug. Sharp stones pressed like needles into the strained muscles of her back.

Comprehension flooded her mind. Resistance sparked through her lethargy, and she contorted her body, twisting and writhing to free herself.

With minimal effort, Devon's two male companions captured her flailing legs and pinned them to the ground. Slade, kneeling by her head, pressed one huge knee into her shoulder and held a dagger at her throat. His body odor stank so strongly it just about suffocated her.

"You bastards! Unhand me! No! You will have to answer to the High Queen for this outrage." Rosin screeched and thrashed against her restraints.

Devon laughed, throwing his head back in a great burst of amusement. As he straightened, Rosin could see tears of madness streaming from his eyes.

"Viper's bite, murderer!" Rosin screamed as she squirmed against the restraining hands.

Devon sobered quickly. "Go ahead, Mother. I have to be sure. I know Muireach's son Garrett sniffed around her. I won't tolerate a repeat of Queen Maeve's little debacle. This child must be mine. No questions, no doubt. I can't have the High Queen question its legitimacy after its mother is dead."

The two men forced Rosin's legs apart and bent her knees.

Rosin wriggled and flailed against their efforts, but with three huge men holding her down, she had no chance. She screamed— wild, angry screeches—and snapped her head from side to side. Tears flooded her eyes as she glared at her captors, powerless to stay her humiliation.

"My dagger, Lady Edith."

Devon's mother smiled demurely as she took the dagger. "Thank you, my lord."

The older woman leaned over and snatched a handful of Rosin's silken drawers. With the other hand, she pierced the material with the point of the dagger, then sliced them open to the waistband.

Rosin cringed away from both the blade and the exposure.

With a vicious wrench, Lady Edith ripped the material from Rosin's body, then crouched on the ground, her skirts billowing around her. She shuffled forward a bit before she sank to her knees.

Rosin cringed inwardly, trying to circumvent the anticipated invasion of her most private parts.

Edith's cold, bony hands touched Rosin, parting her lips. Something pushed at her entrance, gentle but businesslike.

Rosin squeezed her eyes shut and clenched her muscles tighter in an attempt to stop the inevitable intrusion. Cold flesh and sharp nails pushed inside her, not far, just enough to confirm her virginity.

With her task completed, Devon's mother removed her hands from Rosin's body and regarded Devon with a leering smile. "She's never been touched, Son."

"And if I had, what then?"

Devon glanced at Rosin and smirked. He turned back to his mother. "Good. I don't have to wait for her moontime."

His mother moved aside with a clumsy shuffle and took the older man's place, holding Rosin's leg in a tight grip.

Rosin shuddered as she realized the man kneeling between her legs also intended to violate her. She glared up at him.

He just smiled, showing a mouth full of yellow teeth. He touched the outer edges of her private parts, running his finger through the golden curls that shielded them before easing her lips apart. Then, unlike Devon's mother, he used his fingers to explore her exposed flesh, up and down the moist skin, then over the little hooded protrusion that could give her enormous pleasure in the right circumstances. Then his cold digit circled her opening.

"Moorewood, get on with it. She's not some whore put there for you to finger, confirm her virginity." Devon stepped forward.

Lord Moorewood chuckled. "Can't blame me, been on the road a long time, my lord."

"Don't push your luck or you'll go the way of Muireach."

Moorewood pushed his fingers against her entrance. Then he withdrew. "She's ripe for the picking, my lord. A prize plum."

"Good. Get her up, Moorewood. You—he pointed at Slade, still kneeling on Rosin's shoulder—you're relieved of guard duty. Call a couple of men and prepare that tent by the cliff edge for the imprisonment of Princess Rosin."

With her legs released, Rosin snapped them together, then shrank into herself, eyes and cheeks burning, bottom lip trembling.

Without ceremony, Moorewood hauled her up and carried her to Devon.

"Go ahead." Devon waved his hand toward the priest.

The priest opened his book as Rosin watched in numb silence. He droned the short words for the Interlopers' marriage ritual.

Rosin did not respond to his questions.

They ignored her non-participation as they proceeded through each step. The priest closed the book, then withdrew the dagger from his belt.

Devon put his hand out, the underside of his wrist exposed.

Rosin kept her hands tangled in her tattered skirt.

Devon reached down and wrenched one arm up next to his own.

The priest smiled grimly as he slashed their flesh.

It stung, and Rosin flinched, but she couldn't free her hand from Devon's unrelenting grip.

Then the priest bound their arms together, the two cuts pushed hard against each other, their blood mingling in a gooey ruby puddle that smeared both their lower arms, then trickled onto their palms. As he held their arms, the priest chanted the Maidens' blessing over their bound wrists before he stepped back and plucked a rolled parchment from his cassock.

A quick tug released their arms from the binding, and Devon took the parchment from the priest. One of the nobles turned around and Devon positioned the parchment on his back so each could place their mark against the priest's and Devon's.

Rosin stood frozen to the spot, staring straight ahead when Devon held out the nib. I will not sign the parchment. She would not give her consent to the union.

Devon didn't even pause, just signed in her place with a very bad forgery of her signature.

The priest rolled and tied a ribbon around the parchment.

Rosin stared at the ground and refused to lift her head until something fluttered in her tangled hair again and again. She turned her face up to the sky. Large drops of rain splattered on her mud-stained skin.

"Damn!" Devon swore as he grabbed Rosin's arm and dragged her toward the prepared tent, snatching up the white blanket as he passed.

When Rosin resisted, he pushed her in front of him, cruelly twisting her hair into a tight knot.

"Move, my little wife. We have business to conduct and I don't intend to get wet doing it."

Devon's men followed closely as he shoved her through the flap in the canvas.

She stumbled to the ground.

Devon released her, but the two nobles pounced on her before she could gather her thoughts and limbs enough to move away.

Rosin bucked and flailed against their restraining hands, uselessly burning up her remaining reserves of energy.

Before she realized his intent, Moorewood had her hands shackled to a stake buried in the ground. He yanked the binding tight and grinned when she flinched as the thong bit into her skin.

Devon watched as his men secured her in a spread-eagle position on the white rug.

Above her, the rain rattled on the saggy canvas and the cold damp air flowed in through the opening to slip over her bare skin. What remained of her clothes hung in tatters.

Devon leaned over her; his face so close she could feel the heat radiating from his skin as he brought up his dagger to slide it threateningly over her throat.

She shrank away as he slipped it into her cleavage, then with a vicious tug, split her bodice in two. The light undergarment sprang apart, releasing her breasts. Rosin lay paralyzed, swallowing convulsively against the sour taste in her mouth. The world spun. Nothing could be done to prevent him from raping and possibly impregnating her.

Sobs strangled in a painful constriction of her throat as she tried to squeeze her legs together in a vain attempt to deny him access. Rosin didn't bother to scream because no one would come to help her. She lay there struggling to breathe against the sobs crowding her throat. Her face burned with the humiliation of being so totally exposed and vulnerable.

"Goodnight, gentlemen." Devon inclined his head in dismissal of his henchmen. "This task I can manage on my own. You have the belt, Moorewood?"

Moorewood leered in her direction. "Yes, my lord, it's just outside the door."

Both men disappeared through the opening. The only sounds were the steady drumming of the rain on the canvas and Devon's uneven breathing. Occasionally, a cold drop landed on her bare skin, momentarily interrupting the tension that held her frozen.

Devon stood between her spread-eagled legs.

She lifted her head slightly and glared at him.

He smirked at her little display of hostility, then deliberately ogled her exposed womanhood.

He smiled. "So here we are, my little princess, my bride."

"I'm not your bride or bonded partner, nor do we have a legitimate union, Lord Devon, despite your trumped-up ceremony. I never agreed to form a bond with you."

He laughed. "No matter, Princess, it is legal, in both your realm and mine, and I plan to consummate it."

A whimper escaped from between Rosin's firmly clenched teeth. She compressed her mouth tighter, determined not to give him the satisfaction of hearing her scream.

He watched her in silence as he fumbled with the laces that joined the front of his breeches. When he pulled the material apart, a strip of snowy white undergarment could be seen. Rosin watched him, determined to raze him with her contempt. He pushed his breeches down, then slipped his hand to his crotch and scooped his already stiffened manhood out into the cool air.

She looked back up into Devon's face, knowing he watched her for a reaction. Perhaps he'd expected her to scream at the sight of his member, but it wasn't the first she'd seen. She met his gaze and curled her lip a little. "I thought your One God would have given you a grown-up sized manhood to go with your ego. That's not much bigger than a desert rat." She gave a little snicker and screwed up her nose.

"Harlot." He stepped closer. "You're going to pay for that, Princess."

Her muscles clenched tightly and protectively around her virgin womanhood. She struggled to breathe in short, sharp gasps as she stared with determination directly into his face.

He climbed on top of her, the weight of his body pressing hers into the rocks underneath the blanket. His hands mauled her breasts, squashing them against her chest wall before he savagely pinched the nipples between finger and thumb. His mouth smacked against hers. His foul breath filled her nostrils as he ground her lips back against her teeth, rasping the tender skin. His tongue plunged into her mouth, twisting and plundering its moist interior even as she tried to clench her lips together.

With a violent downward thrust, he entered her. A searing pain ripped through her nether regions. A high-pitched scream tore out of her mouth. No matter how much she bucked and writhed, she could not escape his penetration or loosen her bonds. He pounded against her body again and again, inflicting slicing pain that burned into her tender flesh. She cringed away from the pain, shrinking inside herself and praying it would be over soon.

Just as she opened her mouth to scream her agony again, his face contorted into a hideous grimace. A deep grunt burst from his mouth. His eyes glazed over. Sweat trickled down his face, and he collapsed his full weight on her. He didn't move for several minutes.

Rosin struggled to breathe under the burden. She lay still, not wanting to do anything to instigate more pain.

Finally, he pushed away from her. He knelt between her legs, a sneer contorting his expression.

She cringed against the pain of his brutal attack. She hated him with red-hot fury.

Devon stood, his member covered in blood and glistening with his fluids. Without pausing, he ripped off the tail of his shirt and wiped his appendage clean.

He held up the cloth, a red smear staining the snowy white.

An evil smirk transformed his face. "You might think me small, Princess, but size enough to deflower you and make you hurt a little. And see, I have the evidence I need to prove your virginity. Untouched by any male before me, and you shall remain so until you bear me a child, one who will inherit Keswin's throne."

He tugged the blanket from underneath her.

Her bare backside scraped on the hard, cold ground, adding to the injuries already afflicting her battered body.

Nonchalantly, he leaned forward and wiped the corner of the rug between her legs. The rough material scratched like a cactus plant on the tender flesh so recently brutalized.

Rosin flinched, a tiny cry dying on her lips.

Devon laughed. A rough barking sound, sharp and cruel.

He turned away to duck his head out through the opening in the canvas. "Hand me the belt."

Rosin heard a metallic rattle from behind the canvas.

Devon filled the enclosed space again. He held some shabby-looking garments, and another rug in one hand and a metal object in the other.

She bit down hard on a scream. Dear Maidens no. Please spare me such cruelty.

The gold chastity belt exquisitely carved with symbols had a large multi-pinned lock-on the left side. Devon knelt by her side to slip it under her lower body.

Rosin didn't fight against his man handling as he adjusted it around her waist, then snapped the device closed. She bit her bottom lip in a desperate attempt to hold back the tears of pain, grief, and anger that threatened to flood her eyes. That vipers pit would not see her cry.

He hung the key around his neck, withdrew his dagger, and proceeded to saw through the bonds holding her feet.

Rosin didn't move.

He slashed the cord on one of her wrists. The other hand remained tightly strapped to the stake. He threw the garments on the ground, then chucked the blanket over her.

"Mother!"

His mother immediately popped her head through the opening of the tent.

"Help her get cleaned up. I can't stand the smell of blood and vomit when I'm taking my pleasure. Get her dressed, so she doesn't tempt the peasants and see she gets something to eat. I can't have the mother of my child dying of starvation. Besides, she needs to keep her strength up. I'll be back after I've eaten, so don't bother with undergarments." He laughed again, and still chortling to himself, pushed through the opening in the canvas.

Lady Edith stared down at Rosin with distaste, her thin-lipped mouth drawn into a distinct snarl. "Well, stand up. If you think I'm going to play lady's maid for you, then think again."

Relief flooded through Rosin. She had no desire to have her rapist's mother touch her.

Moments later, the canvas flicked back and two lackeys brought in a large wooden bucket. A young woman followed with a plate of meat and bread, a rough cloth, and some soap.

Rosin climbed to her feet but could not stand straight with the leather thong trapping her hand. Every move sent razor-sharp pains through her nether regions. She tottered to the makeshift bath, and pushing her self-consciousness aside, grabbed the cloth and soap to cleanse the blood and Devon's leavings from her thighs with her free hand. The belt made it hard to reach the parts she really wanted to wash — to scrub and scrub — and remove any trace of the violation. Even with the physical evidence removed, she would never feel completely clean again.

She glared at Devon's mother. The older woman stared her down in silence. The desire to slap or spit in her face almost overwhelmed Rosin but knowing it would do no good and might bring more abuse, she refrained from acting on her desire. Instead, she bit her bottom lip in concentration and proceeded to drag the bucket closer. The other woman made no attempt to stop her.

With the bucket up against the stake, Rosin could just manage to step into the bucket and squat. Despite the water being tepid, she sighed with relief as it cooled the burning heat that seared her tender flesh. Even as she rinsed herself, again and again, she could not rid her body of his touch, his leavings, or the taste of his mouth in hers.

"Stop fussing, Princess. I don't have all moon-wash."

In a silent challenge to Devon's mother, Rosin dared to linger in her squatting position for a moment longer, but the water had rapidly cooled to an unpleasant chill.

Seconds later, Devon's mother moved forward with her hand already raised to enforce her instructions with a slap.

Beyond bearing further abuse, Rosin stood, paused, then stepped out of the water. The sharp stones underfoot had become wet in places. Rain leaked through as it thrummed in a steady rhythm on the aging canvas. The flimsy covering sagged in places from the weight of the pooling water.

Rosin held out her hand for the larger cloth.

The girl shoved it at her.

The expression of loathing on Edith's face would have soured fresh milk, but Rosin ignored her. She deliberately made no attempt to hide behind the makeshift towel, for modesty no longer mattered. Despite struggling with one hand, she managed to get reasonably dry, then with a tortuous effort retrieved the garments Devon had dumped on the ground. They had wet patches, but it didn't matter because the garments would cover her nakedness.

The metal chastity belt chafed her waist and in the tender areas between her legs. The lock clanked each time she moved. Before she donned the skirt, she tore strips from her makeshift towel and slipped them inside the belt to pad the unforgiving surface and offer a small amount of relief from the scraping. She tied a thinner strip around the lock to silence it.

Devon had provided a roughly woven peasant skirt that had long ties to secure the waist, and a separate top that closed with wooden toggles down the front. The clothes had once belonged to a much bigger woman, but Rosin wrapped the long strip of material around her waist several times before tying it into a bow. She shivered.

Her remaining strength had slipped away with the bath water, leaving only a bone-melting fatigue that made the simplest of tasks an effort. Using her shackled hand to secure one end of the garment, Rosin tugged the material with her free hand until the side seam ripped apart along the sleeve, leaving one side of the garment gaping open. Now she could put her right arm in the sleeve, wrap the bodice around her chest, and drape the left side over her shoulder. The torn material covered her shackled arm. Rosin thanked the Maidens for the larger size because it concealed her bust with room to spare and hung down past the waist to give her additional warmth.

With no other shoes offered, she pushed her battered slippers back on. They provided no protection from the ground but kept her feet partially dry and the chill at bay. She stepped carefully across the dirt floor of the tent to avoid the worst of the tiny rivulets that formed puddles in places.

Rosin tried to gather her thoughts, but fatigue from the trauma of the moon-wash made her sway where she stood. Determined not to buckle in front of the enemy, she held out her free hand.

The younger woman shoved the plate into it, spun on her heel, and preceded Devon's mother out of the tent. The flap slapped shut behind them.

From the voices outside and the clank of metal, Rosin guessed a guard stood in the darkness and falling rain. Strangely enough, she didn't feel an ounce of sympathy for him.

Alone at last, Rosin turned her face up to the raindrops coming through the canvas and filled her mouth with icy cold fresh water. She rinsed her mouth, then spat. The action didn't eliminate the contamination from her rapist's slavering, but the liquid tasted cool and sweet.

Not sure she had the stomach to eat, she ripped the bread into chunks and paired it with strips of meat she broke off the larger piece. She bit into the first piece, surprised it tasted so good, and astounded that she had any appetite at all.

As she ate, she listened for returning footsteps. A lump of fear had settled in her stomach, fed by the dread of Devon's return and the knowledge of what he would do. Exhaustion held her in a stranglehold. She desperately wanted to lie down and sleep, to forget for a while all that had happened and silence the constant nagging dread of what would be.

She devoured everything on the plate. As she placed the empty plate by her feet, she noticed the dirt had begun to turn to mud. No matter her desperate tiredness, she could not lie down on the ground.

She studied the bathing tub and immediately decided it would make a somewhat rudimentary seat if she could turn the container over and tip the slops out. With her petite frame, she would have adequate room to sit and if she leaned up against the tent pole for support it would be relatively comfortable.

She groaned as she dragged the makeshift bath closer to the tent wall by the rope handles and cursed her tethered hand. She paused to catch her breath, listening for the guard to respond to her actions. The only sound was the drumming of the rain.

Rosin squatted down and gripped the side of the bucket with her free hand. With a grunt and a push, she tipped its bulk until the water slopped over the side.

She dragged the empty tub against the tent pole and heaved it over. The bottom looked plenty big enough for her to sit on with her legs crossed. Her improvised bed would be quite comfortable.

Once seated, she dragged the blanket around her shoulders and clutched it to her breasts, using the leftover bits to tuck under her knees as cushioning.

The moment she rested her head against the pole, the last vestiges of energy trickled away. Exhaustion filled the vacuum it left. She shuddered with cold, and a debilitating weakness caused by the shock and horror of the past few hours.

She snuggled into the coarseness of the blanket, then wrapped her free arm around her body. The drumming of the rain turned to horses' hooves, beating in a strong, steady rhythm on the sand. A gentle breeze touched her face and the sun warmed her skin as total blackness descended and she drifted into a better place.

~ ~ ~

A scratching sound penetrated her sleep. The sound of the canvas flap being stealthily lifted. Rosin stayed still, her eyes shut, acutely aware of the cold penetrating every inch of her body and a desperate need to stretch and ease the aches in her joints.

The canvas slithered back into place. Shuffled footsteps approached, the sound of water splashing with each step. Rosin cringed into herself as if she could move out of his reach. The smells assailed her senses: rain, smoke, and a lingering scent, so tantalizingly familiar. *Who is with me? Not Devon, then who? Worse perhaps.*

The intruder stood so close, their clothes brushed her arm, and she could hear the wheeze of breath over the sound of the rain that still drummed on the canvas.

Other noises in the distance registered, screams, then the crash of wood and metal. A battle, perhaps? A surge of hope rushed through her that help had finally come.

The ground trembled beneath her seat as horses galloped past. She opened her eyes to darkness, but quickly focused on a deeper black shadow hovering silently beside her. Her bonds were being loosened by smooth, long-fingered hands.

"Who are you?"

"Shh, Princess!"

She clutched at her rescuer's clothes with her free hand. The scent and the rings on her fingers alerted recognition. "Alanis. Oh, thanks to Rianon, you've come to rescue me."

"I'm releasing you, Princess, that is all. At least you will have a chance of survival. It salves my conscience to know I have let you lose."

"Alanis, what are you doing here?"

Her lady-in-waiting jerked away from her clutching hands. "I am with Devon, and Garrett, but believe me, Princess, we never meant the coup to be like this. They planned a peaceful takeover, but through it all, I have made my choice. I know as an innocent party to all this you had no choice, but without Devon Keswin is dead. Your parents were so repressive, and grasping, it had to happen eventually."

"But I would've made it better, Alanis"

"Maybe, Princess. Given time, but many of us could not wait. Muireach ordered Garrett to take your virginity as part of the plot, nothing more. He never loved you. Ciara and Devon have promised a new regime where we will all prosper. May the Maidens' care be with you, Princess."

Then the woman Rosin had once thought of as her confidante slipped away into the darkness, leaving her free of her bonds.

Chapter 5

The rumble outside echoed in her chest. The ground trembled beneath her. The tent wobbled and distorted. The collapsing tent wrapped Rosin in a heavy, wet layer.

She pushed at it. Then tugged and twisted, but her efforts to untangle herself from the heavy canvas were futile. The ground beneath her buckled and liquefied. Thick, clinging mud bubbled and flowed between dislodged rocks. She slid downward, riding on a slow-moving wave of sticky muck.

The tent wrapped tightly around her body as the slimy dirt oozed into every crevice of the encompassing material. She couldn't get her breath as the canvas molded to her face. Petrified of suffocating, she gasped in tiny breaths, and pushed frantically to free herself. The heavy material continued to press on her face as she gasped for air. Her head span and her heart pounded as she stared death in the face.

The soggy canvas flexed away. Rosin gasped in air as she kicked and writhed in the enfolding weight.

The canvas flapped and dragged away. Rosin slipped from its grip. She sank into thick freezing liquid. Terrified of drowning in the gluggy mire, she pumped her legs up and down. The mud dragged her down. She kicked and tried to lift herself, but only sank deeper.

She stilled her panicked thoughts, grappling to find a solution. *I need leverage.* Without considering its potential, she grabbed the edge of the bucket to haul herself up. It overturned, cracking the top of her head. Her eyes watered from the blow as the wooden bucket settled over her shoulders, providing a makeshift shelter.

Immersed in total darkness and up to her hips in clinging, enveloping sludge, she breathed deeply, slowly trying to calm her thundering heart.

Water splashed against the upturned bottom of her refuge. All around, unseen objects ground and scraped on the outside of the bucket.

Not sure exactly what had happened or how much danger she could be in, Rosin hooked her fingers around the rope handles and held on, grateful for the shelter. She silently prayed for the protection of her spiritual guide, the Sorceress Rianon.

A stabbing pain in her leg brought a scream to her lips. It echoed sharply in the enclosed space, so she cut it off abruptly. Saturated, she shivered with the cold that had settled into her bones. Her feet dragged and twisted at awkward angles, causing excruciating tearing pains in her ankles and knees as she slid down the slope. She endured the torture in silence.

After what seemed like an eternity, her downward movement stopped. She planted her feet firmly on solid ground. The mud continued to slide down the slope, tugging at her as it passed. She stood firm, her feet planted wide apart to secure her stance.

Rosin lifted the bucket high enough so she could breathe fresh air. Rain splashed in the mud like sprinkling diamonds. Thick, murky water flowed all around her. Overhead, heavy cloud had obscured the glow from the four moons.

Voices, angry shouts, and screams of humans and horses floated from a distance. Heavy rain drummed on the bottom of the upturned bucket. She huddled underneath, grateful for the protection it gave her from the icy deluge and the prying eyes of

Devon's men.

She suspected the heavy rain had triggered the collapse of the cliff. The camp had been swept over the precipice and down into the valley in a torrent of mud and rocks. She had no idea where she had ended up and didn't care. This mishap might be her only chance to escape and she intended to use this unexpected opportunity wisely.

With the bucket over her head, she waited, inert with uncertainty, for a long while. Finally unable to stand her own indecision any longer, she cautiously raised the edge of the bucket again, a little higher this time, and peeped out from under it. Rain blanketed everything.

The noise and clatter from the camp seemed distant and muffled by the downpour. The ruckus suggested the camp, and the survivors were in disarray. The perfect time to make a dash for freedom under the blinding curtain of rain and darkness.

Totally obsessed with possessing her, Devon would definitely come to find her. He would not give up his prize easily, or as before, demand to see her body as proof his bid for Keswin's throne had failed.

Her gut roiled at the thought.

With a grunt, she managed to tip the bucket over. Using any leverage she could, Rosin wriggled and twisted against the insidious, clinging sludge, trying to release her lower limbs. The oversized skirt tangled around her legs and dragged at her waist. Determined to get free, she undid the ties and pushed the cloth away from her body. Icy water poured in the narrow gaps, chilling her all the way to her toes. The water diluted the mud and eased its hold on her. Her lungs cramped with the intense cold. She huffed air in and out in small, sharp gasps.

She continued treading up and down, and finally, with a slurp and a glopping sound, she pulled free. Her bones ached in the frigid temperature and her body trembled with uncontrollable bouts of shivering.

Above her, voices shouted.

"Find her. Find her." Lord Devon's bellow echoed down the slope.

Fresh prickles of terror sparked over her skin. Rosin struggled to think clearly. Despair, grief and hopelessness flooded her with inertia while fear surged and confused her. With the strength of pure will power she forced it aside to focus on action and her ultimate survival. Her grieving could come later.

She gathered her strength, pulled her knees under her, and crawled across the mud. *He must never find me. Never impregnate me. I will die by my own hand before he takes me again.*

Her hair hung in great, lanky knots that dripped mud down her face and into her cleavage. She wiped the mud from her eyes, but her vision remained blurred. The combination of mud, rain and darkness obscured everything beyond the mudslide in an eerie grey light.

The clank of metal, voices shouting, and rocks tumbling from above warned her they were close. She scrambled faster across the precariously slippery surface of the mud.

For the first time that moon-wash, Rosin appreciated her semi-nakedness as she crawled. Every muscle ached. She paused at the shadowy bulk blocking her path. Her heart jerked in her chest. In the same instant, she recognized it as the carcass of an unfortunate horse killed by the landslide. She huddled down on the far side of its bulky corpse for a moment as she attempted to get her bearings.

To her left, she could just make out the edge of the mudslide and some large rocks. Behind her, more mud and rocks flowed down the slope. Directly in front of her, but at a distance were torches wavering and flickering in the hands of those investigating the damage. The left slope offered the best chance of escape from Devon and the slide.

She crawled, dragging aching limbs in clumsy uncoordinated movements through sticky mud. The mud clung relentlessly to her flesh, turning her legs into awkward logs she struggled to direct. Her elbows and shoulders burned with each movement; her flesh denuded of its substance. She struggled to support her upper body.

Rocks and other sharp objects stabbed into her knees and palms. Rosin bit her lip to prevent cries of pain escaping. She tasted blood in her mouth.

The metal joints of the chastity belt pinched and scraped each time she heaved her legs forward. Her knees wobbled, barely holding her up. With the rocks still only shadows of sanctuary, her elbows collapsed under the strain. She fell flat on her stomach.

Fatigue swamped her. She so desperately wanted to just lie there. Pure self-pity rippled through her, but as sounds of the search drew close, she picked herself up and placed one knee in front of the other, again and again. With agonizing slowness, she inched over the wide expanse of mud.

The clouds partially cleared and the glow from the moons bathed the area in a soft, silvery light. Her hunched form was now highlighted on the shimmering surface. Petrified of being seen, she flattened herself into the mud and lay still, barely daring to breathe.

The acrid smell of the searchers' torches stung her nostrils. The scrabbling footfalls down the slippery cliff pierced the quiet of the moon-wash. They were searching for her.

"Ain't never gonna find her in this bog." Slade stomped around in the mud growling his distaste.

"Bloody, Lord Devon. Don't see him coming down to help find his little floozy."

"She isn't some floozy, boy. She's the high and mighty Princess Apparent. Through her, he can more than double his kingdom. Well, her babe anyway. Some of us may get parcels of land, Edgar, even you."

Edgar snorted. "Greedy bastard. I'm wet and cold, and don't care a damn about his ambitions. All I want is me warm bed and me cuddly little wife."

Slade and his companion, Edgar boy, continued to mutter as they stumbled, slid, and bumbled down the slope. They made enough noise to scare the dead.

A crack and a roar drowned out the sounds of the searchers. A new shower of rocks tumbled down. Shouts of warning and distress echoed over the mudslide.

The falling chunks of stone hit her exposed skin and bit deeply, but she strangled her yelp of surprise and pain. Thanks be to Rianon, a distraction. Rosin scrambled to her knees, and she dragged herself as fast as she could toward some low shrubbery and the tumble of boulders.

With a final desperate lunge, she reached the potential hidey-hole she'd spied from the mudslide. The latest rock fall had piled up against one of the monoliths and the sparse shrubbery that grew beside it. There remained just enough space between the boulder and the plants for Rosin to secrete herself.

She glanced back toward Slade and Edgar. Assured they were fully occupied wading through the mud and complaining about their lot, she slid her bare feet and naked legs into the hole. Anything could be in there, but anything, even a taslot spider bite, would be preferable to capture by Devon.

At least if she died of a spider bite, he couldn't sire a child with her. *What will happen to Keswin if I die?* Rosin didn't know, but with no true heir, it would probably revert to the High Queen. She stifled a sob at the demise of her beloved Keswin.

She squeezed her partially naked body under the shallow overhang, flinching as the rough surface of the boulder removed skin from one hip, and the smaller rocks underneath scraped some more from the other. The branches flicked back and slashed her face with sharp, spiny leaves.

Instinctively she lifted her arm to protect her face from the vicious little stabs and it came away smeared with thick, warm blood.

Clenching her teeth together to stop her cries, she wiped her arm on her tattered blouse. Breathing through the pain, she dragged more of the prickly shrub toward her.

She hardly got settled before the mud started to slide into the indentation. Cold and sticky, it encased her legs and hips as it filled every crevice of the hole, she lay wedged in.

Rosin broke off some pieces of bush, grabbed a few rocks, and built a little levee to slow the flow near her face. The liquid dirt crept gradually up to her underarms, over her forearms, then up to her shoulders. She held her breath, praying it would be held back by her makeshift levee.

To help with her concealment, she scooped some of the black goo and wiped a fresh coat of camouflage on her hair and face.

The sludge rose in a creeping tide up to the top of her buffer, then trickled over until it touched her chin. Rosin held her breath, watching its passage closely. She breathed softly again when it finally slowed, then stilled.

The flickering lights of the searchers grew closer, their grumbling voices sharp in the quiet. Disgruntled foot soldiers were not going to search very thoroughly, she hoped. Most of them, like

Edgar, wanted to get home to a warm bed and a willing woman.

She breathed shallowly and constrained her mud-covered body to perfect stillness as she waited. Even camouflaged in deep shadow with all but her face and hair buried in glutinous black muck, she fretted about being detected. With desperate hope, she shut her eyes and raised her face to the sky. *Rianon have mercy on me. Make me invisible to seeking eyes.*

"I've found her!" A male yelled with excitement.

Rosin risked a quick peek. Slade's off-sider Edgar held Rosin's skirt over his head as he balanced precariously on the mud's slimy surface.

"Stupid oaf, if I'm not mistaken, there ain't no woman in that there outfit. Thought even you would know better, having held enough warm, willing ones in your time, Eddie boy."

"Well, if her clothes are here, she must be too." Edgar rolled the skirt into a bundle.

Slade took the skirt from his companion. "Well, his Lordship can come down and dig for himself because I figure she be dead by now, anyway."

At that moment, Devon scrambled down the slope. Rosin ducked her head so low her chin became immersed in mud.

"What've you found?" Devon snatched the muddy skirt from Slade.

"Eddie boy found her gown, milord."

"Well, start digging, man. She must be here." Devon gestured over the expanse of mud.

"Can't say as she'd be alive. No one could survive that, especially not an itty-bitty girl like the pampered princess, even without the chains."

Devon ignored the protest and roared at the two men. "Dig, man. I said dig. I will not let this opportunity slip from my grasp.

Get more men down here."

"My lord... the cliff!"

An avalanche of soil, boulders, and water hurtled down the slope with a thunderous roar that drowned out Devon's crazed ranting.

Edgar's howl ripped through the noise. Rosin stayed face down, hoping the fresh wave of debris would not bury her alive.

It seemed to take forever before the embankment stopped collapsing. The bulk of the fall had not reached Rosin, but a few pebbles bounced on her shrubbery shelter. She didn't feel the impact of the others through the mud blanket protecting her.

When the slide ceased, an eerie silence hung over the devastated area. Rosin remained unmoving, scared she would be discovered at any moment.

As she quivered in her hidey-hole, distant voices and the rattle of horses' harnesses punctuated the silence. She stayed perfectly still. So cold now she no longer shivered or could not really feel her legs or arms.

Somebody moved nearby.

She held her breath in response to a slight rattle of gravel and the scrape of boots on granite chunks.

"Get me out of here, Edgar, Slade, I'm hurting."

Devon's cry scraped over her nerves.

Slade's shout for assistance joined Devon's cry for help.

Shouts rang out from a distance, punctuated by thuds and periodic cracks and thumps as the unstable cliff continued to move under the heavy boots of rescuers. Hollering filled the air, coming closer. It was echoed by a clamor from farther away. The ruckus got louder as the searchers approached.

She kept her head down, trying to determine the situation from the racket. It seemed to take forever, but after much yelling and scrambling, the noises faded. She risked a peep and could just discern dark, moving shadows of people climbing the slippery slope carrying prone black shapes. Rosin assumed these were the injured.

At last, nothing moved in her vicinity. Not a sound disturbed the silence. Even the usual moon-wash sounds were absent. The distant rattle of humanity had faded completely.

In that moment, the silence that ensued so profound Rosin wondered if she'd died.

Cautiously, she twisted her head to the side, scanning the area with one slime-filled eye. A thick blanket of cloud had rolled in and blocked the remnants of light from the sinking moons, leaving the whole valley in deep darkness. Nothing moved. No flaming torches flickered on the cliff top.

A thrumming sound like the hum from a hive of angry bees filled the silence. It got louder. She poked her head up.

The noise grew louder, more defined. Rosin groaned softly. Another icy-cold downpour swamped her. Already so cold her joints had seized with a burning pain and her muscles cramped. She whimpered.

Yet despite the inevitable icy drenching, the rain made good cover and would wash away any traces of her escape by morning. Slowly, she stretched her numbed limbs. She wriggled her toes. Well, at least her brain told her toes to move. Then she shifted her feet. The mud resisted her movements as it sucked at her.

Eventually, she freed one hand, then moved the rocks from her levee one at a time, placing each quietly to the side. Even with the splash and thrum of the rain, she remained anxious about being heard. She wiped the mud from her eyes but couldn't see farther than a couple of inches through a solid gray wall of raindrops.

Hampered by fear and pain, Rosin eased out of her slimy

cocoon. Slowly, she pushed herself into a kneeling position near a huge chunk of rock. She surveyed the area without exposing herself too much.

She wore only the metal chastity belt and her tattered shirt. She'd lost her slippers in the mud. Her hair stuck out in a semi-solid frame of stiffened spikes. Without clothes and shelter, she had little chance of surviving.

Chaotic thoughts tumbled through her mind as she studied the landscape. The betrayal, the dead, her rape and her future. With determination, she pushed them away. First things first. Her escape.

Suddenly, the rain stopped. The silence left behind, shocked with its depth as it pressed onto her ears, but at least she could see again her eyes now well adjusted to the darkness. With the muted glow of the last moon still peeping above the horizon, she could see right across the mudslide and up to the top of the cliff. Nothing moved, and no light showed above. She suspected — hoped — that Devon had moved out during the rain and headed for his castle.

She stood up, using the rock for support.

A low moan broke the silence. Rosin dropped back to the ground, lying flat on the rocks, their sharp edges pressing into her freezing flesh.

The moan came again, a dull drawn-out dirge that ended with a low gurgle.

Someone lay dying on this muddy bank. She trembled with indecision. Did she leap up and run, naked, from the slide in the hope she could find clothes later or did she risk everything to get the clothes she needed from the injured enemy?

One of Devon's men would be dressed in a tunic, breeches, and a warm cloak. Just what she needed. She hesitated. Could the injured man still be capable of overwhelming her by size and skill?

Did she take the risk of being caught?

Wracked with terrible bouts of shivering, Rosin weighed up the risks and benefits. Devon could return at any time and recapture her. Then all would be lost. If she did nothing and slowly perished from exposure and cold, it would be just as bad. I have to get his clothes. I don't want to die naked. I cannot let fear ruin my chance to wreck revenge on them all.

An appalling thought lashed at her: what if they were a Keswinian? Someone she knew, Garrett even. A wave of sickness nipped at her, but she pushed it away. Loyalty had died this moon-wash and so would he, whoever he was.

She climbed to her knees, muffling a scream of agony as her bruised flesh pressed into the rocks. At first, her legs refused to obey, so she reached up and, with gritty force, dragged herself into a semi-standing position.

Forcefully expelling a warm breath into the icy air, she pushed herself upright. She swayed. Her knees threatened to buckle. Determined to remain standing, she tightened her grip on the rock. If she went down now, she might not be able to get back up, and she had no intention of dying at the bottom of a mudslide this moon-wash.

The commitment to her mother and the promise to herself left no room for hesitation. No room for weakness. She would see the throne with its rightful owner.

Rosin shuddered as the vision of her mother's head in her hands filled her mind. Grief took a stranglehold. She choked on the sobs clawing their way up her throat. With a vigorous shake of her head, she banished the vision. No time for grief right now.

Rocks sporadically tumbled down the fractured cliff face. She flinched, unable to determine if they were just a few remnants of the last slide or a warning of things to come. Rivulets of water ran freely over the surface of the mud, diluting it into a treacherous, sucking mire.

A little farther down the hill, the flow backed up and Rosin peered intently through the gloom to see the cause. The carcass of a warhorse lay partially submerged in a small lake of water. The saddlebags still hung behind the saddle. Clothes. Food. Weapons. Her heart leapt at the unexpected treasure offered. Gifts to help her fight for survival.

Rosin hobbled closer; each step torturous. At the horse, she dragged the bags free, and tugged them open. Her heart sank. No clothes, just travelling food, a bottle of vinegar, a mug, and various eating utensils. Not much. Nevertheless, she heaved the bags over her shoulder.

A moan drifted across the mud.

Rosin squinted through the darkness.

The dark mound of one of Devon's men lay jammed up against a small, rocky outcrop. He lay helpless on the broad of his back. The mud had built up beside him. Soon, it would bubble over him.

With cautious steps, she moved closer.

He groaned.

She froze. Help of the Maidens'. Her breath caught in her throat and her heartbeat in a palpable tattoo behind her breast.

Devon's men had left this man here to die a long, agonizing death. But then, he deserved no less for siding with ambitious, murdering thieves.

She spied a skull-sized rock sliding slowly past her and picked it up in both hands, coldly assessing it as a possible weapon.

Horrified at the thought of killing a man with it, she went to drop it. As it slid in her fingers, reality bit deep: she no longer had the luxury of being squeamish.

With carefully placed steps, she moved closer to the injured man. She held the rock in a grip so tight she expected her handprint to dent the surface. She stepped closer.

Slade. Rage hardened her heart while recognition strangled her conscience and obliterated her compassion.

He made no movement or sound.

She shuffled closer, wary at first, but when he didn't move, she put the rock down. With her hands free, she immediately set about removing his clothes.

She tugged off one of his boots. With no response to her groping, she wondered if he had just died. She removed the other boot, struggling with the unwieldy weight of his strapping leg. As his boot slipped free, his foot dropped with a splat. She breathed hard and fast with exertion.

After a quick glance at the man's face to assess his condition, Rosin knelt down to attack the front of his breeches. Her freezing fingers struggled to manipulate the wet laces and belt buckle. Cursing and swearing under her breath, she persisted until they loosened. She wrenched the opening apart then yanked and tugged on the tough pliable material. Wedged under him and stuck to his body with the thick pasty muck the breeches wouldn't budge. She crouched by his side and pushed hard until she succeeded in partially rolling him over.

He groaned.

Rosin flinched and clenched her muscles in preparation to flee.

He made no movement and didn't resist her manhandling.

She continued to manipulate his pants at the waist. Finally, she managed to roll them down over his backside. She dragged them past his thighs and let him fall on his back with a plop. His undergarments came off with the trousers, exposing his manhood tucked like a wrinkled sausage against his hairy balls.

It didn't matter that the breeches were filthy, wet, and way too big for her. She dragged them on. As she pulled up the pants, Slade's slingshot, metal pellets, and a small used flint fell from the pockets. She retrieved them before she laced up the front, folded the excess material over, and drew the belt in tightly at the waist. The material felt strange against her skin as she bent down to push her muddy feet into the oversized boots. The heavy leather footwear slipped and slopped as she walked, but she didn't care. For now, her cut, bruised, and aching feet had a modicum of protection from the rough ground.

Rosin also wanted his cloak and shirt. She moved to stand by his shoulders. She leaned down and grabbed the material.

With a jerky movement, he grabbed her ankle in a clawed clasp, groaning with the effort. His eyes opened. He looked straight at her. "So, girlie, you survived, but now I have you."

She glared down at him but made no effort to escape his grip. "You're a dead man, Slade, and capturing me is not going to save you."

He frowned, coughed, and spat out blood, but didn't let go of her leg.

Adjusting her stance, Rosin swung her free foot and kicked him in the chest.

His grip tightened.

She slammed her boot into him again, this time floundering to keep her balance.

Her captor coughed again, spitting up globs of blood. It sprayed over his shirt and vest, then trickled down his chin. He moaned.

He would die, but not soon enough for Rosin. No matter how much murder might conflict with her conscience, she needed to hurry his demise. She scanned the mud for the chunk of granite she'd discarded earlier. In one smooth movement, she snatched it up and raised it above her head.

Fear shadowed his eyes. He knew she had no mercy.

For a moment, she wavered, feeling sick at killing a helpless man where he sprawled, injured and covered in mud.

Even as he faced death, he still ruthlessly clung to her leg. Slade made no attempt to defend himself, though. "Make it quick, girlie, for even a man like me deserves the mercy of..." A sickening gurgle in his throat and chest silenced his plea.

Rosin stood over him. Stared down into his eyes. Hatred burned so fiercely it filled her with a heat that banished the cold from her battered body. "To hell with what you deserve." With a vehemence that surprised her, she brought the rock down on his face. The hollow thud and sickening crunch that followed sent her stomach into a spinning whirlpool.

She had no time to react as the vomit rose in her throat and spewed out. She wiped her mouth before she inspected her victim.

Slade was no longer recognizable, his face crushed into a pulp, bits of skull sticking up like rocks in a mudslide. His eyes had popped out of their sockets and were now nestled in the hollow where his nose had once been, floating in her vomit as they stared blindly up at her.

She swallowed convulsively and held back another heave. It took all her willpower to control her stomach as it churned painfully, desperately wanting to expel its remaining contents. She stared at the dead man and summoned cold indifference. My survival comes first. Slade, you are collateral damage.

She quickly found that physically, the killing had been the easy part. She twisted and agitated the sword wedged tightly under his arm and entangled in his cloak. The sharp edges of the blade sliced through the dead man's flesh until it hit bone. Only then could she wrench it free.

One of the new rivulets formed in the last deluge of rain had washed some of the mud from around his body, so despite being hampered by the stiffness of her fingers, she easily scraped the remaining sludge away from his arms. Leaning on his chest, she worked fast. She ripped open the toggles that held his shirt closed. As the shirt fell open, she found he also had an undervest. With an enormous effort, she yanked one arm out of the shirt sleeve, then the other. Barely pausing to catch her breath, she rolled the body again, and dragged both the undervest and the cloak out from under him.

To her surprise, she found a small leather satchel attached to his torso by a thick leather thong. She pursed her lips. She just didn't have the strength to move him again, so she grabbed the sword and sliced the strap on either side of the pouch before she scooped it up. She transferred the slingshot from her pocket into the pouch with the unknown contents.

The mud oozed fractionally slower than the thin layer of water that flowed over its surface, making it difficult to keep secure footing. The silence faded with the familiar thrumming noise of rain approaching.

A flash of fear buzzed through her. More rain made it imperative she get onto solid ground, away from the rock fall, before the cliff disintegrated further under the new deluge.

With her newly acquired belongings clutched to her breast, Rosin waded through the thinning mud. Her progress was slow as she placed each foot blindly. She secured each step before she took another, scared she'd fall and not be able to get up. Her heart sat like a chilled lump behind her breast. Her mind seemed unable to comprehend or process the moon-wash's events and the dire circumstances affecting her.

She needed to get away—as far away as possible—before Devon's men came back to hunt for her. If Devon couldn't find her alive, he wouldn't accept her death unless he'd seen her corpse. Only then would he accept he'd lost all chance to make his grotesque dream come true.

Rosin acknowledged without protest she would never be safe while Lord Devon remained alive.

With the saddlebags hanging over her shoulder, Rosin paused at the edge of the muddy river to pull on the rest of her new clothes, not caring they were wet, muddy, and swamped her fragile body. They didn't provide much warmth either, but she only cared about feeling less vulnerable. To ease her walking, she stuffed Slade's undershirt in one boot and his undergarment in the other. The padding made the oversized boots moderately comfortable. At least her journey would no longer be an ungainly hop from one foot to the other in a painful dance across the valley floor in the dark.

Determined to put as much ground between her and Devon as possible, she stumbled through the darkness. With every step she listened for any sounds of pursuit, petrified Devon would return to recapture her. She guessed Devon had received some injury in the second rock fall, but that did not guarantee he would not send men back after sun-show to search for her or her body.

Rosin hunched over as she walked, seeking a modicum of relief from the freezing rain that slashed at her. She cursed it, but also thanked the Maidens because it would wash away any evidence of her passing.

She hated being wet, cold, and dirty, but those physical discomforts paled against the sense of being totally alone in the world. The fact that no one in the world knew where or how she was weighed heavily on her soul.

She trudged through the darkness, putting one aching leg in front of the other. The fast-fading moonlight glowed faintly through the scudding clouds that danced along the darker shadow of the horizon. There was just enough illumination to prevent Rosin from tripping on rough ground. With the last moon-sweep of the awakening season, the rain of the misting would become more constant, the air colder and the light hours each moon-slide shorter. The rivers would swell with the constant rain, flooding low lying areas along their banks and making them treacherous to navigate. She would have to time her crossings with the tidal washes. Rosin fretted she wouldn't find a haven before the freeze.

Sometime in the pre-sunshow darkness, she entered a wide stand of trees. She trudged under the wide, straight branches that entwined with their neighbors to form a canopy that thinned the rain to a sprinkle. Unfortunately, the canopy also cut out the muted moonlight, and she struggled to find a safe path. The thick carpet of pine needles muffled her unsteady footsteps and muted the patter of the rain. Out of that quietness, the spit and gurgle of rapidly flowing water caught her attention. Optimistic, she'd found the smaller of the two rivers that flowed past Keswin Castle. She moved cautiously toward the sound. Unable to discern other sounds above the cascading water, she peered closely at each shadow, splash of moonlight, and tree trunk for movement.

All remained still. Not even a breeze whispered through the branches. She stood on the bank staring at the deep, fast- flowing water. Jagged boulders jutted out of the watercourse, tearing the flow into multiple tumbling surges that frothed and sprayed. The bed of the stream was littered with rocks and boulders. In places, the stream bed was pitted with deep crevices.

A guttural moan squeezed out as she sank to her knees. How do I cross this? Why? Haven't I suffered enough without this? Have mercy, Rianon. She wrung her hands and bit hard on her bottom lip. The only solution mocked her. She glanced downstream.

Sighed, stood, then turned upstream.

She cursed the wasted time and deviation from the direction she needed to go. The rise in the ground didn't seem much, but her legs ached as she trudged through the sodden undergrowth. Rosin peered over her shoulder more and more often. Anxiety burned through her. This detour would not put any distance between her and Devon.

A terrible screech rent the air.

Rosin jumped and ducked for cover under some shrubs. Her heart thundered in her chest.

The screech changed pitch to a shriek punctuated by sharp cracking and tearing sounds. A long, drawn-out groan vibrated through the air.

Rosin's throat tightened. She struggled to drag air into her lungs as she peered around, trying to ascertain the cause.

An ear-splitting crack punctuated the groan, followed by a thud and the sound of branches being tortured.

She peered around the bush and several paces from her hiding place lay the wreckage of a huge alpine tree, its branches still jerking and bouncing from its brutal demise.

Its massive, straight, branchless trunk rested across the stream, just above the surging water. The enormous ball of mud that surrounded the base of the tree already dissolved to expose a gnarled tangle of roots. On the far side of the stream, the wide branches had virtually annihilated the encroaching trees on the bank.

Rosin leapt up and broke into an ungainly jog. "Oh, Rianon, my protector, thanks be to you." She scaled the tangle of exposed wood and inspected her windfall.

She inhaled deeply through her nose, then exhaled forcefully out of her mouth. I can do this.

With precise movements, she removed her boots and tucked them in her saddlebags. The rough bark dug into her soles as she curled her toes to get a secure grip. With her arms out to balance herself, she walked steadily. The saddlebags weighed on one side, but not enough to over-balance her.

Rosin placed her feet with precise action on the rough surface. After each couple of steps, she would glance up to her destination. Below, the water surged and splashed, frothing, as it forced itself around the boulders rising out of the stream bed.

Almost there.

The bark underfoot loosened as she transferred her weight. A lump broke away and hurtled into the torrent. Her foot jerked sideways, leaving her precariously balanced. She let the saddlebags slip to the trunk as she tried to regain her balance. Her muscles protested. She toppled forward and hit the trunk with a thwack. Her breath expelled under the force.

Her body skewed sideways. Her lower body slipped over the curve of the trunk and dropped into nothingness. Her fingers clawed at the bark as she buried her face against the tree, muttering for Rianon's help as she levered her lower body upward. The tough material of her stolen breeches protected her from the rough bark. The chastity belt hampered her flexibility. The pitted bark tore into the skin of her hands.

She scrabbled at the bark, jamming her fingers into the crevices of the surface. Rosin could barely heave her leg to hip height and failed to gain a purchase with her toes.

Sobs threatened to choke her as she slipped back. She clung with desperation to the pitted bark. The spray from the tumbling water misted her skin. She breathed deeply, then heaved her leg upwards again. Her bare foot barely reached the top of the trunk. As it slipped back, the rough surface of the bark stripped several layers of skin off her ankle.

Sobs of frustration cramped her ribs. She glanced down at the raging torrent. To fall was to die.

Above her, the rounded bulk of the trunk loomed. She glanced to the other bank and weighed up her chances of being able to move her body sideways one hand grip at a time. Her shoulder joints already screamed in agony. She tightened her grip with one hand and let go with the other and grabbed for the bark a few inches to her left. With that grip solid, she let go and moved the second hand beside the first. She gasped in air and hung for a moment, then repeated the action. Blood seeped from her palms and dribbled down her wrists. She snatched for the next hand hold. Her hand slipped. She tipped and swung sideways; her shoulder wrenched. Panic surged through her as she grabbed at the bark and dug her fingers into the crevices. Tears flooded her eyes. I'm never going to make it. It's too far.

She glared up at the trunk. A small protrusion caught her attention. A snapped branch. Not particularly sturdy, but short and pointy. She lifted herself and grappled for it but couldn't reach it. Dangling by one hand, Rosin dragged the belt from her waist. And using her teeth, she managed to turn it into a noose. Her trousers slipped to her hips.

She rested for a moment. Her whole arm seared with pain. Eyeing the branch, she swung the belt up. It dropped back, slapping her in the face. Her fingers slipped. She clutched the timber harder, and her descent jerked to a stop.

Again, she flung the belt up over the trunk. With a click and a jolt, the belt landed on the stubby branch. She pulled on it. The leather groaned as it tightened, but the belt remained secured on the branch.

She gasped in a deep breath and tightened her hold on the

leather. Once secure, she let go of the trunk with her other hand and snatched hold of the belt. She hung suspended on the leather. It creaked and stretched but held.

She hauled herself upwards hand over hand. With her knees tucked up as high as she could, one more tug allowed her to dig her toes into the fissures in the bark. The extra leverage gave her the lift she needed. Despite the exhaustion that gripped her, she managed to drag herself atop the trunk.

Clutching the bulk of the trunk, she lay flat on her stomach breathing deeply, sobs fluttering in her chest. She choked them down and gathering her residual strength, she pushed upright. For a moment she swayed but raised her arms and steadied. With renewed caution, she grabbed the saddle bags and her belt before she continued her precarious crossing to the dubious safety of the far side.

Without pausing, she scrambled through the branches and out onto the bank. She glowered at the stream as she pulled her trousers back up to her waist and secured them with the belt. Her toes were numb lumps as she pulled her boots back on. The leather immediately rubbed the damaged flesh. Shouldering her saddle bags, she turned her back on the stream and hobbled across the meadow. The ground kept rising in a long, steady slope. She didn't know how long she'd trudged, but barely dragging her feet through the grass, she started to climb yet another hillock.

By the time she reached the crest, the rain eased off again. She could see rocky outcrops studding the meadow below. Off to the left, the forest loomed, dark and brooding, still shrouded in the gray curtain of misty rain.

She turned into the shadowy bulk of trees, unwilling to go out into the open meadow so close to sun-show. On the other side of the meadow, she hoped to find the Fiery Moon River that flowed across the middle of Keswin.

Every plodding footstep pushed her beyond endurance. Pain speared through her back and shoulders with every step she took. Fatigue sucked at her. Fear prickled across her skin. The tiny crescent of the sixth moon sank behind the horizon where the sky had already begun to lighten. She had to find somewhere to hide.

In the darkness, under the trees, Rosin struggled to see. Moments later, she stumbled over the gnarled roots of a gigantic tree. She crumpled into the wet pine needles and lay there breathing hoarsely, her face buried in her arms.

Dragging her knees up, she tried to rise. Her legs sagged, and she dropped back to the ground. I can't do this. I can't.

She lifted her head and glanced around. She had fallen into a hollow carved between two twisted roots sticking out of the ground. With further effort beyond her, and not caring about the risk of a deadly poisonous blood viper being in residence, she snuggled down into the sizeable hollow filled with dried leaf litter and twigs. She wrapped the cloak around herself and sprinkled leaf litter on top of it. To complete her concealment, she tucked her hair under the cloak and brushed dirt on her face and hands. To be sure no one would see her, she squeezed right back into the hollow, then laid her head down and closed her eyes.

Even as she drifted into exhausted sleep, she flinched and jumped at the slightest sounds, quickly dragged into wakefulness by the dread of being found.

Sometime during the long moon-slide she woke, her throat dry and rasping. A terrible craving for a mouthful of water from the stream she could still hear in the distance tortured her. She cursed her failure to fill the flask belonging to Slade.

A faint vibration of the ground dragged her from an uneasy sleep. Horses galloping close by. She cringed deeper into her hollow and held herself motionless. They didn't stop, and she breathed a sigh of relief. Tense and trembling, she didn't sleep again as she waited for the fading and darkness to cover the countryside.

~ ~ ~

For five lunar passings she walked, cold, tired, and terrified of being recaptured by Devon. The chastity belt had rubbed her raw around the waist and groin. She'd used the dagger to pick the lock but ended up with a puncture wound on her hip. She didn't bother to try again, preferring to keep moving. She only stopped to grab a few bites to eat out of the saddlebag and relieve herself. She drank sips of rainwater as she needed it.

Soaked to the skin after constantly being rained on, sloshing through mud, and wading across a couple of bogs, Rosin so desperately wanted to stop and rest, but fear pushed her on. Each step and each moon-slide brought her closer to King Cadmar's castle and safety. Her determination strengthened against her weariness.

Chapter 6

When she hid on the sixth moon-slide, she tried to calculate how much farther to the Fiery Moon River.

The last five nights she'd had plenty of light from the five moons higher in the sky, with the sixth one floating a little more above the horizon each moon-wash of the moon-sweep. The synchronization of all six moons high in the sky heralded a powerful time for those descended from the Maiden Rianon: increased fertility, successful crop planting, and unexplained healing of illness in those who made sacrifices to the Goddess. The combined force of the six moons caused a pull strong enough to part the river waters and drag them toward the sea. In this moment, it would be possible for her to cross the dry riverbed safely.

On that moon-wash, she also expected her moontime to start, as all women descended from the sixth maiden, Rianon, did on the moon-wash of the tidal wash. She prayed hers started on time, for only then could she be assured she had not conceived a child by that monster.

As the shadows lengthened, she mentally prepared herself to face another moon-wash of travelling and the problematic river crossing. The moons floated into a crescent across the sky, lighting the moon-wash with a soft glow as she made a quick survey of her surroundings before setting off. Apprehension shadowed her, for despite the shallow waters that would remain in the riverbed at moon-peak, the crossing could still be a difficult venture alone.

As she headed toward the river, the ground flattened out and the vegetation became sparser. She made good time despite the awkwardness of the oversized boots.

Having eaten the food from the saddlebags, she discarded all the useless items in a hastily dug hole. She stuffed the flask for water, a small bottle of vinegar to use for cleaning wounds, a dagger, a snare, slingshot, and the bag of metal balls she'd removed from Slade's pockets back into the trouser pockets.

With one eye on the ground so she didn't stumble, she kept a close watch on the moons, knowing she had to reach the river before full moon-rise. In that moment, the tides would pull back, leaving the riverbed free of water. She only had a small window of time to cross the muddy riverbed before a wall of water would rush back, following the moons as they descended to the horizon

From what little knowledge Rosin had of the Fiery Moon River, she knew this watercourse ran wide, deep, and slow moving. She had been warned on the trip she did with her parents of the treacherous dangers for the unwary in its debris-riddled bed: quicksand, spinning eddies that could drag a human under and the speed with which the waters returned.

Just before moon-peak, she reached the sandy bank of the river. Afraid of possible watching eyes, she crawled under a thorny bush to wait for the tidal wash.

It didn't take long before the moons slid into a crescent high above the horizon, the sixth one gliding silently up to join her sisters in a glorious display of lunar beauty.

Rosin gazed up at the iridescent orbs that represented her Maidens: the silver white of Arawen; the spangled multi-colored Blodwen the clear blue of Morgwen; the subtle lavender depth of Gavinia and the hot yellow of Carwen. The last one held her spirit and soul and glowed with a deeper burnt orange. Her own moon,

Rianon, sixth Maiden, Sorceress and Spiritual Guide to all. A sense of awe always overcame Rosin when all six moons rose high in the sky, wonderment at their beauty and their mystery, but this moon-wash she watched with a different concentration, yet no less amazement.

At the instant of synchronization, she leaped up and ran down the sloping, sandy bank. The waters moved, slowly at first, then faster, gurgling and spitting as they raced down the curving bend of the river toward the sea, invisible and unreachable so many miles away.

The last remnants of the tide had barely been swept away before she hurried across the littered mudflats. Winding her way around boulders, rotting tree trunks, tufts of reeds, and other unidentifiable objects. The muddy riverbed clutched and sucked at her ill-fitting boots as she increased her pace.

Her breath came in burning gasps. A sharp pain stabbed in her abdomen. She clutched at her side in a vain attempt to ease the pain as she scanned the ground for the telltale signs of quicksand and concealed ditches. Barely three-quarters of the way across, Rosin heard the splashing and hissing sounds of water. The tidal wash was returning faster than she had anticipated.

The over large boots slipped and skewed on her feet, slowing her down and she wished she'd removed them before starting. Too late to rectify that problem, she lengthened her stride and increased her pace, gasping and whimpering as the cutting pain in her side ramped up.

The water swished around her feet. Only a few more steps. The returning tide touched her knees, tugging at and wrapping around her limbs. It clutched at her. Pulled at her. Slowed her pace.

Then, with one more stride, she took a flying leap and landed with a thump in the reed beds that grew on the edge of the river.

Without pausing, she crawled up the slope, away from the swirling wavelets that lapped at her feet.

She collapsed in the middle of a thick stand of rushes. Gradually, her breath slowed to normal, and she stopped trembling from the terror of being drowned, just like the original Maidens of Annaticcia legend. How in their human form they were drawn deep into the lake, their lungs filled with icy fluid that had extinguished life.

With the moons sinking, the darkness deepened. Soon the sky in the east would lighten again. She needed to find somewhere to sleep. Dragging her tortured limbs, she walked slowly through the scattered trees along the edge of the river. The sky had already changed to the soft hues of pale pink and gray when she came to the edge of a meadow.

The leaves thick and green, hiding the rich colors of the ripening fruit, plump and juicy as part of the harvest season. Following immediately would be the glowing and the withering, when those leaves would turn gold, red, and brown and rustle in the morning breeze, whispering age-old secrets to any who would listen.

These signs made Rosin uneasy and anxious. She must make it to Tarlic and King Cadmar's protection before the freeze began. The next tidal wash in seventy-two moon-slides — the tidal wash heralding the withering. It would be her last chance to cross the Sacred River. If she missed this deadline, she would die in sight of safety from the vicious blizzards of the frost and freeze.

Stumbling on in a daze of exhaustion, she watched the growing lightness of the sky.

She stepped forward. Her foot pressed into nothingness. Too slow to save herself, she tumbled over and over, down a rock-strewn slope, stopping with a bone-jarring crack against a monolith. All around her, thick vegetation pressed in, obliterating the light and muffling sounds. A thick bed of leaf fall cushioned her exhausted body. She shook her head to clear the spinning dizziness, dragged her hair from her face, and studied her landing.

She sat at the bottom of a stony crevice that ran partway along a narrow gully that ended abruptly in the middle of the meadow. Both ends of the gully were blocked by rocks, with her end completely overshadowed by two stone-studded hillocks.

The lay of the land made it virtually invisible from the meadow and probably impenetrable by a man on a horse. The sound of running water tinkled nearby.

Rosin crawled deeper into the tumble of massive boulders. Still in a crouch, she inched her way between the rocks until she came to a narrow passage low under an overhang.

Wary of unknown occupants, she crawled slowly through the passage. She sighed with relief when she emerged in a cozy little cave with dry sand on the ground and enough roof height to allow Rosin to stand upright.

With the entrance so well concealed by scraggy bushes and a small spindly tree, it made a perfect hidey-hole.

Anxious to get dry before she developed the dreaded chest rattle and died all alone in the wilderness, she retrieved the flint from the small pouch she had taken from Slade. Although still afraid of being caught by Devon, she decided to risk lighting a fire to get dry and warm for the first time in six moon-slides. She had not seen or heard another human since she fled the mudslide and the dead Slade. She figured it would be worth the danger.

Before she started, Rosin sought out the stream to refill her water flask. Even in the gloom of the dense foliage when she knelt by the brook, she kept watch over her shoulder. A glitter of silver caught her attention, and she snatched up the sword and jerked back into the undergrowth. The sword wavered in her trembling hands as she lingered in the shadows. Just as her heart calmed, and she stepped out of the undergrowth, a huge trout flipped out of the stream, then flopped into a shallow pool with a splash. Rosin flinched at the unexpected movement, but immediately saw a meal flapping in front of her. She leaped forward and stabbed the hapless fish in the side. The water turned pink as she swung the blade to lift the fish onto the grassy bank. She mumbled a quick prayer of thanks to the Maidens before hurriedly washing her face and hands. With one more glance around, she gathered up her prize, the sword, and the flask, and scurried back to her cave.

She used the dagger to scratch the scales off. With clumsy slices, she opened up the fish's gut, and with tentative movements removed the innards in a clumsy replica of what Morgana, the castle cook and her nanny, had done. Waves of revulsion pulsed through her at the messy job. *It's not neat like yours, Morgana, but it's the best I can do.*

Laying the fish aside, she set about constructing a smokeless fire by digging two pits, one for the fire and one to generate airflow, as her cousin Keegan had shown her last time, they had mucked about by the river on a visit to Tarlic Castle.

She struggled to dig with bare hands. The abrasive sand reopened the slices and cuts on her hands and her blood stained the sand red. As she measured the depth, one pit collapsed. She dragged her arm out. Tears of frustration threatened, but she sniffed them back and re-dug the second pit off to the other side. The sand held its shape. This time, both pits were stable.

She went outside and gathered dry grass and bits of wood small enough to fit in her hearth. Three strikes of Slade's flint lit the grass. It smoked and crackled. She blew gently on it. When the fire burnt hot and smokeless, she put the fish whole on a large flat rock that just balanced halfway over the fire pit. While it cooked, she stripped off her wet shirt, under vest, and sopping wet, tattered blouse. She hung the cloak over a rock near the fire, then she poked a couple of sticks into the sand and hung the other garments on them. It didn't take long for them to steam and even though she remained naked from the waist up while the clothes dried; she felt warm for the first time in a moon-sweep.

She dug around in the saddlebags for the battered metal mug, filled it with fresh water and added a few drops of vinegar. As the fish started to roast, juices dropped into the fire, making it spit and sizzle. She added more wood before she set the mug on one side to heat.

When the water steamed, she drank some to warm her from the inside, then used the rest to wash the irritated skin under the chastity belt in an effort to ease the inflammation caused by the constant friction against her body.

Feeling better than she had in a long time, she sat forward and basked in the heat of the fire. After a short time, even her soggy breeches started to dry. Using her dagger, she turned the fish. The smell of the cooking flesh made her mouth water. Unable to wait for the whole thing to be done, she picked bits of white meat from the cooked side. The flesh melted in her mouth, the taste exquisite, and the warm mouthfuls comforting to her very empty stomach.

With her stomach full, she struggled to keep her eyes open as fatigue dragged at her. Not prepared to sleep mostly naked, she dragged on the partially dry vest and shirt. With extreme reluctance, she banked the fire before lying down on the sand.

She stirred restlessly for quite a while, her thoughts a tumult of agonized memories. Tears squeezed out between her lids as she sniffed and fought back the sobs that threatened. She breathed deeply in an effort to calm her thudding heart until fatigue seeped in and stilled the tormenting thoughts. She didn't hear the rain start again.

~ ~ ~

As consciousness returned, Rosin lay still and silent for a long time, letting the bleak awareness of her situation wash over her. She'd never felt more alone than at this moment. All she knew had been ripped from her and she didn't know what lay ahead. The instinct to survive would be her strength.

A disguise, no matter how minute, might provide a second or two advantage in a confrontation. With just a twinge of regret, she picked up the dagger, tugged her hair over her shoulder, and sliced through it with the sharp blade. She continued hacking and slicing until she had chopped every muddy strand off close to her head. Then she started on her nails. Those that remained long she trimmed roughly with the dagger blade, right back to the tips of her fingers.

Rosin tore a strip from the front of the cloak, the cleanest bit she could find. Then she stripped off the vest and shirt, and even though she found it awkward, she wound the material around her back and across her breasts, tugged it tight, then wound it again. When she'd finished, her bust had been reduced to distorted bumps. Pleased with the result, she slid the vest and shirt back on, satisfied that at a glance, or at a distance, she wouldn't appear obviously female.

Fatigue clawed at her again, so she stretched out on the sand with the cloak over her. This time, she slipped easily into a disturbed slumber.

When she opened her eyes much later, the light glowed soft and gloomy. Birds cooed and tweeted in the nearby foliage as if they were settling down for the moon-wash.

Rosin cast off the cloak and crawled to the opening. With infinite caution, she made her way toward the stream, pausing every few minutes to listen. All seemed quiet.

She knelt by the edge of the fast-running stream, dipped her hands in, washed them clean, then scooped up some icy water and drank deeply. With the worst of her thirst quenched, she splashed more water on her face, but she wanted desperately to be clean.

With hurried movements, she stripped off everything except the locked chastity belt. Taking up the dagger, she poked and prodded at the lock again, twisting it this way and that. She tugged at the contraption, but it would not budge. She threw the dagger aside.

The lock rattled as she stood. She glared at it then waded into the water. She gasped as the icy water chilled her skin, but ducked under, anyway. Using her hands, she scrubbed her hair, face and body vigorously. She really wanted some soap, but it wasn't an item men like Slade carried in their saddlebags. Besides, she suspected, no amount of soaking, rubbing, or rinsing would cleanse her body of Devon's violation.

Afraid to stay too long and acutely aware of how vulnerable she felt naked, Rosin climbed out of the water. Using the cloak, she rubbed herself dry before she hurriedly got dressed in the dirty clothes. On her knees again, she washed Slade's under vest and drawers. The blood and mud dissolved and flowed away in the water. Despite the lack of clean garments to put on, she felt so much better as she weaved her way back to her hidey-hole.

Her heart suddenly jumped into an uneven rhythm. Panic flashed through her. *I'm lost. This is not the way to the cave.*

Tamping the alarm down, she moved slowly forward until she came to the edge of the wide meadow. Nothing moved on the open grassy area except a couple of birds. She relaxed enough to get her bearings, then cautiously made her way through the vegetation. Not far from her hiding spot, she saw some spots of color ahead.

Round balls of red hanging all over one of the taller trees. Apples.

They were a bit withered due to the lateness in the season, but she didn't mind at all. Using the undergarments as a container, she stripped the tree of its crop. Pleased with her find, she heaved the makeshift bag over her shoulder, then headed downward until she found the opening to her cave.

Once inside, she relit the fire and hung the washed garments in front of it to dry overnight.

The air cooled rapidly when the sun dropped below the horizon, leaving it very dark outside. Only one moon, Arawen, would ride in the sky for the next twelve moon-slides. Rosin roasted four apples for supper and ate them, hot and sweet. With her stomach full and warm, she banked the fire, then snuggled down in the cloak.

Sleep did not come easily now the edge of her exhaustion had been dispelled. She mulled over the ugly happenings of the last few moon-slides.

She cursed Ciara for her deadly ambition, murderous jealousy, and conspiring with one such as Devon. Despite everything her sister had done, Rosin reluctantly accepted that Ciara's protest about the wrongs in Keswin were within her rights, but the outcome of her protest seared Rosin's soul.

Perhaps if she had also rebelled, things might have come out differently. Rosin burned with shame at the way she'd accepted or ignored the suffering of Keswin's citizens happening right in front of her eyes.

Wrongs done, even to her own lady-in-waiting. She thought of Garrett and Alanis and their betrayal. The desire she once had for him had died, but it still hurt to know he'd never cared for her. That his declaration of love had just been part of a plot. But that plot had gone awry, ending in a massacre from which there could be no redemption for all who had participated.

Seething anger at her parents for their failure to be competent rulers burned deep, as did her mother's confession, lying at the root of everything.

Generally, life would be short and hard for the lower classes, coaxing a living from the land with a limited growing period, fighting off the raiding Depcisians, and traveling long distances to trade with neighboring realms. Only now did Rosin fully comprehend how much harder her parents had made it by always demanding more tithes and higher rents.

Under such tyranny, all people would eventually rebel. Yet despite her disappointment in her parents' ability to rule, she still loved them, and despite trying to block out the gruesome vision of their passing, grief overwhelmed her.

Self-pity wrapped itself around her, tears welled up and escaped to trickle down her cheeks. Her twin's savage betrayal, without warning, had ripped her comfortable existence to shreds, taken her loved ones, her support systems, her home, her innocence and left her desperately alone.

Her pampered life had not prepared her to survive such a catastrophe. She didn't trust herself to make the right decisions and doubted she had the inner fortitude to face the inevitable hardships in front of her. Curling into a fetal position, she covered her face with her hands and sobbed.

Her chest ached and her throat rasped as she finally stifled her sobs to hiccupped sniffles. She scrutinized the barren cave and refused to accept this would be the end. Mentally, she acknowledged how far she'd already come, what she had done, and the fortitude it had taken to achieve. Determination warmed her. She could do this, one step at a time. She would stay free, find her way to help, and re-claim her throne.

Her mother had made her promise to go to Tarlic, to her Moon

Life Protectors, King Cadmar and Queen Meghan. She carried the hope they could be trusted with her safety. She immediately rejected her only other option: to give up. To lay down and die.

When Cadmar's riding accident had prevented them from attending her bonding, she had been disappointed and even though she felt grateful they had not been at the slaughter, she wondered if things would have turned out differently with them and their contingent in attendance. Had their absence been deliberate? Rosin pushed the disloyal thought away. The only other option she had would be the High Queen of Annaticcia, Queen Isolde. A daunting prospect and a lot further away.

In the past, with good mounts and plenty of support, her family had traveled to Tarlic in about two, sometimes three, moon-sweeps, depending on the weather. But on foot through harsh country, alone, it would take longer and she couldn't afford to reveal herself to anyone before she crossed into the safety of her Protector's realm.

She hoped a few moon-sweeps of arduous travel would bring her to her destination. On a makeshift map in the sand, she marked Keswin, Devon's realm of Ersklyn, and the approximate location of the mudslide. With landmarks in place, she reviewed the journey to her Protector by drawing in things she remembered, like the Oasis of Birds where her family had stopped, rested, and swum for two days before going on to Tarlic.

She remembered from her childhood they always headed toward the horizon of the sinking moons for ten moon-slides before they arrived at Cottam Village. After a couple of days' rest, they had climbed the pass through the mountains.

From the summit of the pass, they could see the flood plains, the river, and magnificent Tarlic Castle as it stood on a plateau rising out of the flood plains, it's enormous rammed earth mounds topped with wooden walls and great, carved gates. A treacherous journey under the best conditions. The thought of doing it alone filled her with anxiety.

The delicate princess had been annihilated by the cruelty of the last few moon-slides. She could no longer afford tears, tantrums, or her sense of entitlement. To survive this horror and reclaim her throne, she had to fight her fears, use her strengths, and find ways to overcome her weaknesses.

Tomorrow, at moon-rise, she would continue her journey.

Chapter 7

Rosin woke just before sun-show energized and optimistic. She slipped out of the cave and inspected the meadow from the shadows of the vegetation. Only a few small birds flittered through the long grass. She scanned the sky for signs of dust, but nothing marred the clear and cloudless sky. She climbed the hill to scout for unwanted company.

As she neared the crest, she dropped to her hands and knees and crawled through the grass until she could scan the valley below.

The tiniest creak of leather on leather crashed into her ears.

Her breath whipped away. Horses. Her throat constricted and her heartbeat slammed in her chest. She froze, then gulped air and tensed, ready to flee.

A weight slammed onto her back, shoving her to the ground. The air in her chest grunted out with the force.

"Oh, no you don't, my pretty. You is just what we been searching for."

Rosin writhed under the weight.

It pressed harder onto her back.

She collapsed completely.

"What you reckon, Felix? Perhaps we could have ourselves some fun before the others get back. Devon would never know."

"Nah, Caleb, not worth the grief, besides I hear she's under lock and key."

Her captor grabbed her hair, shifted the weight off her back, and hauled her upright. "Is that so, girlie?"

Rosin nodded. Relief sliced through her. She could not be raped by these two.

"Get the horses, Felix. We'll go down and meet the others."

Rosin cringed away, flailing and twisting, ignoring the savage burn on her scalp. "Free me. You commit treason. Unhand me."

Caleb chuckled.

She kicked back.

He grunted, clutched his genitals with one hand, then stepped backward, dragging her with him.

Rosin threw her weight onto him, and they fell in a tangled heap.

His grip loosened.

Rosin twisted round, snatched his dagger from his belt, and stabbed wildly in his direction. The blade slowed as it sank into his abdomen.

"Arrg. Whore. Felix, she's gutted me."

Rosin rolled away. She saw Felix in the corner of her vision, leading the horses closer.

He hurried.

She didn't wait to see but scrambled to her feet and ran headlong down the hill, her feet moving so fast they barely disturbed the grass.

"Get her, Felix." Caleb rolled around on the ground, spreading his blood over the grass.

Her legs burned with the effort. Her lungs dragged in great gasps of air. Her boots slopped around her feet, and sharp pains radiated through her hips as each foot thudded into the ground.

Hoof beats thundered behind her, getting closer, louder.

The rattle of the harness, the squeak of leather and the laboring grunt of the horse bearing down on her whipped her onwards.

Another sound caught her attention. Five of Devon's men trotted sedately toward the meadow.

She had nowhere to go. No escape.

Sobs jerked in her chest, strangling her gasping breaths. She veered to the left, then forced her legs to stride out farther on the uneven ground. A slicing pain ripped through her abdomen. Her steps faltered fractionally as she risked a glance behind.

They came. All seven of them riding abreast at a slow trot.

She pushed forward. I cannot get caught. I cannot.

On they came, wheeling around her now.

She turned to avoid the nearest.

Relentlessly, they drove her toward the meadow.

Her legs shook. She stumbled. With wide, thudding strides, she regained her balance, but she had slowed. The agony of air dragged into struggling lungs and the grueling jab of the pain in her side crushed her stamina and dragged at her momentum.

She stumbled again, her feet flying out from under her. Her body lurched forward, and she fell into nothingness. A bone-jarring thud shuddered through her as she connected with the ground. Shocked into inertia, she rolled over and lay still, waiting for them to come and get her.

As the hooves closed in, stirring the dust and clattering on rocks, she pushed to her feet, then stood bent over, panting.

The horses stirred restlessly. The men waited for her to run.

She glared up at them.

They leered down at her, ribald comments staining the air.

Her heart clenched in a painful grab. This is it. Tears welled and spilled down her cheeks.

The thunder of galloping horses echoed above the men's jeering.

The earth reverberated under her feet. She glanced to the crest.
Four horses galloped toward them.

"The Queen's Warriors! Prepare for battle."

"The Princess?"

"Forget the bloody Princess. Ain't no good to you when you're dead."

The seven horses wheeled away from her.

She didn't wait to see the battle begin, but turned and ran toward the cave.

The clash of metal, shouts of pain and anger, and squealing horses pursued her down the slope.

Halfway across the meadow, she heard the sounds of pursuit. She glanced over her shoulder.

On the slope, the skirmish continued with the flashing of metal, milling horses, and the clunk of shields.

Off to the side, coming her way, a horse and rider. She didn't pause long enough to identify her pursuer but turned and ran. Her lungs pumped air out in painful scrapes, her knees burned each time her foot hit the ground.

Rosin threw herself into the shadows of the vegetation.

The horse squealed as the rider reined in.

She heard the thud as he landed on the ground. Forcing her limbs into motion, she crawled deeper into the bushes, ignoring the stab and slice of debris on her knees and hands.

She paused and listened.

He came thrashing and blundering through the vegetation.

Whimpers pushed their way up her throat, but she clenched her jaw shut against them as she scrambled deeper into the gully toward the stream.

With a thud and a tight grip on her hair, he had her restrained and lifted off the ground.

"I have you now, girlie. All mine."

Caleb. She could smell blood over his body odor. He had to be struggling with the injury she inflicted.

"No." She kicked out with her feet, swiping at his face and hands with her nails.

"Oof." He grunted as her fist caught him in the chest.

Her hand came away with blood on it.

She hit him again.

He dropped her.

Barely able to stand, she staggered toward the meadow, shoving the bushes aside with thrashing arms.

The injured Caleb staggered right behind her.

She burst into the open.

He snatched at her clothing. Dragging on her. His grip slipped.

Rosin leapt forward.

"God damn it, girlie." Caleb gasped through laboring lungs.

With a fresh surge of energy, Rosin darted forward, then dashed away. She risked a glance toward the battle. Four men remained standing. Three still fighting and one struggling to mount one of the restive horses.

"Oh Maidens, spare me, I beg you." She spun around to retrace her steps, swinging wide of the lumbering Caleb. Blood soaked the whole front of his shirt. She figured Caleb would soon succumb to his injury. Once in the gully where a horse could not follow, she would be safe, but her energy flagged, and she slowed.

The thunder of hooves grew louder. She gave a fleeting glance at the horse bearing down on her. A Queen's Warrior.

"Princess Rosin, hold up. I'm here to save you."

With faltering steps, she came to a halt. She glanced toward Caleb.

He staggered toward them. He had drawn his slingshot.

The horse swung sideways as it reached her.

"Up, Princess. Give me your hand."

She looked up. The Warrior was young and handsome, with twinkling green eyes. Blood splattered his tunic and breeches.

Rosin reached toward him and heaved herself upward.

His grip tightened on her wrist, and he tugged her forcefully.

With a scramble, she managed to drag herself behind the saddle. As the horse jumped forward, she wrapped her arms around his waist.

He flinched at her grip and she could feel the wetness of blood under her linked hands.

"Halt, you spawn of the devil. Halt, I say, in the name of Lord Devon." Caleb's words came out disjoint by great gasps of air, before they trailed off into a groan. He swung the slingshot.

With a faint whistle, then a plop beside them on the ground, the first went wide.

She glanced over her shoulder just in time to see Caleb release another metal projectile. His aim flew true. The metal ball slapped into the horse's rump. It shied, then bucked.

"Hold on, Princess."

The third ominous whistle ended in a crack. The horse screamed as it stumbled.

She still clung to her rescuer after they hit the ground.

He grunted, then lay still.

The horse squealed and thrashed around.

Rosin ducked away from the lashing hooves, but not quickly enough. A flash of agony and a soft thud right by her ear made the world spin. Sickness wallowed in her gut, and darkness hovered on the edge of her vision.

~ ~ ~

The sharp ring of metal on metal cut through the throbbing in her head. She reached up and touched the sore spot. "Ouch." Her hand came away covered in blood.

She focused her gaze toward the sound.

An arm's length away, Caleb and another of Devon's men viciously attacked her rescuer. All three men staggered, almost on their knees at times. Blood soaked their clothing. Her rescuer slashed with a sword and cut the unknown soldier down then turned thrusting his weapon toward Caleb. Caleb dodged out of the way and turned to rain a barrage of blows from his axe on the Queen's warrior and slash at him with a sword in his other hand.

Her rescuer faded under the fusillade.

Rosin pushed onto her hands and knees, then lurched away in an ungainly crawl. She hadn't gotten far when a terrible screech rent the air behind her. Then silence. She cowered for a moment, then resumed her crawl, faster now.

She heard him coming. His limp was audible in his stride. Guttural grunts punctuated the rattling gasp of breath. Despite his struggle, he advanced on her.

Almost at the vegetation, she veered and increased her pace toward Caleb' horse, waiting patiently. If I can get to it. If only I can get to it, I'll be safe. Groaning with the effort, she pushed her body harder. Her head still spun, and her vision filled with black spots interspersed by a red mist.

She could smell him, feel him behind her. In a desperate effort to elude capture, Rosin dropped and rolled.

He grabbed her ankle.

"Let go, you moon leech." She screeched, lashing out with her free foot. She connected.

He grunted. "Whore."

"Oof." The air spurted out of her lungs as his weight crashed onto her, forcing her face into the dirt.

"Got ya. Now you and me are gonna have a little fun, girlie."

"Get off, you oaf. Do you know who you're manhandling? You'll pay."

Caleb guffawed. "Oh, I know, Princess. Now up with ya." He eased off her but snared her hands behind her back as he did so.

She tugged against his hold.

He shook her.

The world spun with dizzying oscillations and the black spots danced. Her stomach clenched and heaved, and she vomited on the grass.

"Move, girlie." Caleb pushed her roughly.

Forced by his pushes and shoves, Rosin moved inexorably toward the patiently waiting horse. As she dug her heels into the ground, a sharp thrust in the back propelled her to the ground. By the time she had lifted her face out of the dirt, Caleb had bound her hands and feet together behind her back. This awkward position stretched her ribs so much she could barely breathe, and her spine arched in a painful backward curve. Her legs already ached. Twisting her neck to the side, she watched her captor.

His movements were jerky and constricted as if he suffered terrible pain. With one hand, he dragged his bedroll from the saddle and spread it on the ground. Barely upright, he retrieved another bag from the horse. He plonked down on the blanket. "You know what, girlie, all I need is a bit of patching, then I'll show you what a real man can do for a woman. Just you wait and see."

"If you let me loose, I could help you."

"Ahh. Think I'm stupid. A brainless peasant. I'd let you lose, and you'd be gone. Besides, mended myself often enough to do this little job." He eased his shirt off. Blood poured down his arm and his pants were soaked in blood.

Rosin closed her eyes. She had no desire to watch him stitch himself up. His grunts and curses battered at her ears, and she wished he'd just get on with it.

The sun beat down on her. Her mouth became dry and prickly as sweat beaded on her skin. The rope cut into her wrists and ankles. Her back muscles pulsed with cramps. She wriggled to ease the pain.

Behind her, all remained still and quiet. She twisted her neck and peered at her captor.

He lay scrunched up on his side.

"Hey, you, oaf, are you dead yet?"

"Shut up, Princess."

Damn, he still lives. "I'm thirsty."

"Tough."

"I need to relieve myself."

"Too bad."

"Damn you..."

He rolled over. With a series of grunts, he climbed to his knees then pushed himself to his feet. He ambled toward her.

She assessed his condition. Can I take him? He's weak. Lots of blood loss. Must watch for a chance.

His momentum faltered. His expression contorted as his beefy hands clutched his abdomen. His knees buckled. With an ungainly crash, he hit the dirt.

Rosin waited for him to get up.

He didn't move.

"Hey you, Caleb."

No response.

Rosin lowered her head to the ground to ease the crick in her neck. She closed her eyes against the brightness of the sun and wiped her tongue around her mouth to relieve the dryness.

"I need a drink." She writhed against her bonds. The ropes cut deeper. Bone ground against bone in her knees and shoulders. "Damn you, get up, you moon leech peasant. You can't leave me like this."

Birds twittered, and the wind whispered through the grass.

She twisted her wrists back and forth, tugging and pulling.

The sun burned down. Sweat beaded on her skin and she fluttered her eyelids to wipe the grains of dirt from her eyes.

Stinging pinpricks scattered up her bare skin. She flinched. The tickle of crawling feet made her jump and cringe. Ants. It could be worse. It could be a taslot spider or a blood viper. She shuddered. Dead bodies attracted both.

Her bladder hurt now. She whimpered. Ignoring the grabbing tightness, she twisted her neck to see the recumbent man. "Please, Caleb, have mercy. I need to relieve myself." Nothing. "Caleb, for Maidens' sake."

For the first time, she wondered how long she could last out here in the harshness of the weather. The weight of her predicament was intolerable. The sun floated high in the sky. Insects buzzed in the grass, and birds hopped almost up to them. I cannot die here. I cannot. She squirmed on her belly. Her back muscles cramped. "Oww." She howled, paused, then thrashed about some more.

Stones stabbed at her belly where her movement had torn her shirt open. Dirt stuck to her sweat coated skin. The sun's rays burned down on her head and back. She lifted her shoulders and heaved. Her upper body moved fractionally toward Caleb. She rested, then with a deep breath, she dragged her lower body over. Her crushed lungs burned as she forced air into them. Again and again, she lifted her upper body as she maneuvered closer to Caleb.

He showed no sign of life in response to her grunts and whimpers.

As she moved again, she lost control of her bladder. The heat of embarrassment washed over her and tears poured in hot salty trails down her cheeks. She sniffed the tears back.

Despite the indignity, she quickly found she moved easier with her bladder empty. After three more ungainly lurches, her head smacked into Caleb' legs. She rested. Flies buzzed around her and the bloodied abdomen of Caleb.

The heated rays burned relentlessly down. Nausea squeezed her stomach. She swallowed several times. The thought of wallowing in her own vomit revolted her.

With an ungainly lunge, she maneuvered herself next to the body. His small hunting knife poked out above his belt. She stretched her arms out as far as they could go, then wriggled her fingers. The tips just brushed his belt. She extended herself some more, but still, she couldn't grasp the handle. Sobs crowded in her chest, choking her. Whimpers bubbled out as she twisted and turned. The hardness of the handle teased her fingers. Please maidens, please. I don't want to die.

"Maidens' curse, come here, you moon-dusted knife." She flipped back and forth in an effort to inch closer. Her fingers brushed the handle. Yes. Nearly got it. Come here, little knife, I need you.

The next movement landed her up against Caleb' side. Her fingers curled around the handle of the knife. She wrenched on it. It didn't move. Tightening her fingers, she tugged again. With excruciating slowness, it slid from the belt. Yes. Yes. Yes.

But her triumph quickly faded. Getting the weapon into a position to saw through the rope would prove another challenging hurdle. Terrified of dropping the blade, Rosin manipulated it in her fingers.

"Ouch." The blade sliced her hand. "Moon leeches and lunar

dust."

With a deep exhale, she sagged into the dirt with the knife clutched tightly in her bloodied hand. All around the grass whispered, and the insects clicked. The sun's rays burned down on her, drying out her skin and toasting it in the heat.

She struggled to swallow, her mouth so dry and prickly. A growing fear she would die out here in the heat and the dirt beside her dead and bloodied captor tormented her.

No. I will not die. I will not. With renewed enthusiasm, she manipulated the knife some more. The blade snagged on the ropes. She sawed the blade over the binding strands. Struggling to breathe, she rested, then began again.

Joy danced through her when the first stands gave way. She licked her lips with a parched tongue, then continued the jagging movements of the blade. The tense pressure on her legs eased as another strand popped apart.

A movement in the grass caught her attention. She jerked her head around, but it had gone. The hairs on her arms tickled as they rose. Uneven trembles raced through her body. It took all her concentration to shut the dread out and continue sawing. Each rope frayed with excruciating slowness until it finally tore apart.

She sensed a movement beside her. She cringed but kept sawing. A flicker of red, then a whisper-soft touch against her side wrapped her momentarily in a gripping paralysis. The grass wavered. Rosin resumed sawing, her momentum swift and erratic.

The distinct squelching sound of blood being sucked by a viper drowned out the sounds of her sawing. With slicing arcs, Rosin attacked the rope with renewed ferocity. The last strands sprang apart, freeing her feet.

With her hands still bound behind her back, she dropped the knife and rolled away from the body, over and over again and again, ignoring the creaking of her bones and the clenching of muscles. Dizzy and sick, she finally lay still several feet from the corpse and the feeding blood viper.

Grunting with the effort, Rosin rocked her body from side to side. She flopped over, bent her body at the waist, and pushed up into a sitting position. She sat gasping in air and summoning her fading strength. With a grunt and a cry of effort, she lifted her body from the ground, scrambling to get her feet under her. Even as she swayed, she quickly untangled her hands from the loosened bindings.

Caleb's horse grazed just across the meadow. She moved toward it. The horse threw up his head and trotted away.

"Damn animal, stand still." As the animal settled to grazing again, she moved closer with slow, steady steps. "Whoa, boy. Steady there."

The horse snorted. The carrion birds up the slope fluttered and squawked. The horse snorted again, flicked its tail and cantered out of sight.

Rosin sighed. Hopelessness enveloped her. Every bone in her body ached, blisters swelled on her feet and the chastity belt had rubbed her skin raw and bleeding.

Keeping an eye out for the blood viper, she limped back across the meadow and snatched up Caleb' travel kit. With one last glance across the death littering the meadow, she hobbled toward the cave. She pushed through the vegetation and dragged herself into her sanctuary.

The cave seemed suddenly very precious, but the urge to leave this place and the carnage behind overwhelmed her. She took a quick dip in the stream before she dressed in Caleb's spare trousers. Feeling revived, she returned to the cave to wait for darkness and the safety to flee.

~ ~ ~

At last, the fading came, and the shadows lengthened. Wolves howled in the distance.

Rosin shuddered. They would feed well this moon-wash, but she would be long gone, and unless she became injured or got caught in the snow of the freeze, they wouldn't trouble her.

As it got dark, she crept down to the stream, washed her face, then filled her water bottle. She had already stuffed the undergarments back into her boots, so she simply slipped Caleb' travel kit over her shoulder and set off.

The only way out led past the battlefield of corpses, but after all that had happened, she no longer feared the dead. Careful not to lose her bearings in the dark, she climbed the small slope and ducked under the leaves.

A hand latched onto her booted ankle. She started, then let out a small squeak as she peered down.

"Water, please, water."

Instinctively, she flinched away from the grotesque apparition that confronted her. Her feet slipped from under her, and she tumbled backward down the slope, landing with a thud. Free of his grip, she scrambled up and dusted herself off. She drew the sword, then cautiously moved closer to determine if the injured man be friend or foe.

Her would-be rescuer stared up at her. He made no attempt to grab her again, but his eyes remained open. One, at least, the deepest of green and filled with reflections of the agony his mangled body held him in. The socket of the closed eye appeared to be filled with congealed blood.

"Water, please." His voice cracked, then he spat out the blood that flowed from his gashed lip.

Dumbfounded he still lived after Caleb's beating — for that matter that Caleb had not ensured he was dead — and that he had managed to get himself this far. Rosin just stared at him. She suspected he'd heard the stream, and desperate to relieve his thirst, had dragged himself from the meadow.

Agony contorted every line of his body. His pain etched on his face. "Please..." He held out his hand. Two fingers were missing and the gash right across the palm still oozed blood.

This man had helped her. He had called her Princess. Her plans to leave this moon-wash caved in as she knelt by his side. She slid one hand under his head, then with infinite care, placed the lip of the water bottle against his damaged mouth, tipping it just enough to trickle water into the opening.

He let it dribble down his throat, then coughed before he swallowed.

As she tended him, she struggled not to flinch away from his terribly wounded face, with a long wide gash from his neck up over his jaw and nose before crossing his forehead and disappearing into a vicious dent in his helmet. Wet with blood, his ripped tunic clung to his chest with flesh and gore peeping through the shredded material. Caleb had intended to kill him.

She felt the weight of his head in her hand as he fell back, his eyes closed.

Again, the wolves howled. They sounded nearer now.

She contemplated the wounded man. Now what do I do? Leave him or tend him? For her own benefit, she should just leave him and get moving, because Devon's men could return at any moment. However, despite the horror of the last few moon-slides, she realized she had an obligation to help this warrior as he had tried to help her. His determination to survive touched a place deep in her soul. Convinced he would die soon of his horrendous wounds, warm compassion burned inside for this beaten stranger who had killed her enemies.

Instinct told her to reduce her sympathy to the bare basics and secure her own survival, but she couldn't bring herself to be so callous. She couldn't leave him here, and she didn't want to stay exposed.

He appeared unconscious, his breathing shallow, his face a grotesque mask, porcelain white in patches, and the rest of it covered with congealed blood and lumps of sticky, wet globs.

The lightest touch on his shoulder and his eye flew open.

His hand came up to protect himself.

She stayed his arm. "It's all right, I'm here. I will not hurt you."

He sighed and let his arm fall back by his side. He regarded her out of his one good eye. "Who are you? I thought you were the Maiden of the Fallen come to take me across the bridge to the Afterlife."

He didn't recognize her, and although it disconcerted her, she figured the trauma to his head had caused memory loss. Reluctant to remind him of her identity, Rosin just shook her head. "We need to get you out of sight. If Devon's men return, they will kill you and take me prisoner."

He frowned. "Devon's men?"

Uneasiness gripped her. "Yes, those soldiers you killed came from Lord Devon's personal guard."

He frowned again. "I don't remember..."

Her uneasiness grew into an uncomfortable lump in her stomach. "Never mind. Are you up to moving to shelter?"

He immediately tried to push himself into a sitting position. He bellowed with pain but cut it off with a grunt as he collapsed to the ground.

Rosin went behind him and tucked her arms under his armpits.

"Push with your feet if you can. It's all downhill."

She half carried, half dragged him. He had no strength and drifted into unconsciousness.

Rosin knew he must be in horrendous pain and considered it a blessing for him to sink into the blackness. It made her task easier as she tugged and dragged his tall, muscular body down the slope and through the boulders. Her breath came in painful, dragging gasps, her legs and back throbbed from the effort required to shift a dying male twice her weight and considerably taller than she.

His wounds had bled heavily, and he hadn't regained consciousness by the time she had him at the crevice. Panting with the effort, she took a long gulp of water from her bottle, stretched tall to ease the twinges in her muscles. Exhaustion threatened, but she managed to haul him through the opening.

He lay on his side, just inside the opening. His skin felt cold and clammy. The blood seeping from the wound to his torso stained the sand crimson and his breathing remained very shallow. She straightened his legs and eased him onto his back. Using the dagger, she cut away his tunic spontaneously, crying out at the severity of the wound that left his chest flayed open.

Through some miracle, the weapon had not broken his ribs or pierced his intestines. She doubted he would survive but, in an effort to comfort herself, she poured some of the vinegar into the wound to help fight infection, then tugged the flap together and bound it tightly with strips torn from the clean under vest.

As she undid his helmet and eased it off, she could see the damage to his face would make him virtually unrecognizable to those who had known him. His reddish-blond locks were stained and matted with blood, and his scalp wound immediately started to bleed profusely.

Keen to stop more blood loss, she quickly disinfected the

exposed flesh then eased the edges of the wound together to cover the white of his skull. Struggling to hold the flesh in place, she applied more strips of torn undervest to bind it together.

The slash had opened his forehead, cleaving his face open along the side of his eye and across his nose, which now sagged as a loose flap, then down across his mouth, skimming his jaw all the way to the bone. The gash ended at the side of his neck and shoulder.

She cleaned the wounds out, then bathed his eye, pleased to see the eye itself wasn't damaged. A good thing, if he survived. Tomorrow, if he still lived, she would find some herbs to help with the pain he would suffer. Having done all she could to help him, she turned him again onto his side to stop the blood still seeping from his mouth and running back down his throat.

With him comfortable, she wrapped herself in the cloak and lay down to rest. Sleep eluded her. She should be well on her way toward the river by now and cursed herself for being so gullible and soft. Instead, she remained in the cave, waiting for a total stranger to die so she could continue her journey. Her mind shied away from the selfish thought. She had no wish for the warrior to die of his wounds, but feared he would succumb in a nightmare of suffering.

It occurred to her that she could have hastened his death with a slice of her dagger, but by rescuing him, she had placed his life in the hands of the Maidens. She would do what she could to ease his pain, whatever the outcome. Without the fire, dark and cold filled the cavern. Rosin sat huddled in the cloak staring into the darkness, unable to stop the voices in her brain from debating her decision.

In the distance, the wolves howled.

The man's labored breathing sounded harsh in the quiet of the cave. His presence unexpectedly comforting and she tensed every time his painful wheezing stalled, fearing death had come with the last breath.

Loneliness wrapped cold fingers around her as she lay huddled under the cloak. Her body ached for the touch of another human, for gentle fingers caressing her skin, or the tight squeeze of a hug. Tears welled in her eyes as sobs pressed against her ribs. Finally, unable to bear it any longer, she threw off the cloak and climbed to her feet. Dragging the cloak behind her, she crossed the cave and stood watching him struggle to breathe. With the slightest hesitation, she dropped to her knees and stretched out against the stranger's back. She tugged the cloak over them both.

He didn't stir.

The only sign he lived showed in the shallow rise and fall of his breathing against her breasts. She rested there for quite a while until finally the warmth seeping into her body let her sleep.

~ ~ ~

He lay still, indescribable pain throbbing through his body centering on his chest and head. He opened his eyes but found he could only see out of one as the other was swollen shut. Above he could see rock. Firelight flickered across the craggy surface. A moan escaped. He reached vainly for the water bottle, his single good eye squinting with concentration.

He sensed her presence before her hands touched him. She lifted his head and touched the edge of a flask against his mouth. The water was cool and fresh. He tried to swallow a little but even that hurt. He groaned as she rested his head back down. He focused on her. A petite woman with short hacked blond hair, blue eyes in a heart shaped face. She was nibbling her bottom lip as she studied him.

"You are badly hurt. I will go shortly and get some herbs to help with the pain."

He tried to smile but immediately his lip split open and bled. When he shook his head in refusal of more water, she laid his head down again.

"Thank you." He grimaced and his lip cracked open and bled slightly.

She smiled. "I'm going out to get some herbs for pain, but I will come back."

He reached out and squeezed her hand.

He cast his mind back but came up against a blank space. He couldn't remember what had happened or how he came to be injured and in the cave with this woman. He closed his eyes and sank back into the blackness that came with the pain.

~ ~ ~

Before she left cover, she surveyed the field of corpses, but the injured horse belonging to her rescuer seemed to be the only living thing out there. The poor creature must have sensed water, then managed to hobble to the edge of the meadow. It surprised Rosin that the wolves had not attacked it, but then again, why would they trouble when easier pickings were scattered over the meadow.

The injured animal still wore the saddle, although the bridle had broken loose. Behind the saddle a pair of bulging saddlebags hung.

She walked slowly toward the horse, determined to retrieve those items. Consumed with pain, the injured horse pranced away.

Frustrated and more than a little desperate, she decided to resort to more brutal tactics and retrieved the slingshot from the cave.

The man remained unconscious, but now he moaned and stirred restlessly, and when she pressed her hand on his forehead, it felt hot and sweaty.

Unable to help him, she returned to her position by the bushes. The horse had moved closer and now stood unsteadily at the top of the slope. She only needed to hit the horse in one of its good legs to bring it down, then she could administer a merciful death with the sword.

She popped a metal ball in the sling, then swung it as fast as she could. With a clumsy flick, she released it. It missed the target by a wide margin.

The horse stood still, watching her as she sent another missile toward it. The projectile whistled slightly, before it landed well left of the animal. The horse snorted.

She used metal ball after metal ball until, with only two balls left in her bag, her aim flew straight and true. The lump of metal hit with a thwack just below the horse's knee.

The horse squealed, reared up, then crashed to the ground, its front legs crumpled underneath its body. It snorted in panic and pain.

Rosin hated causing additional pain to a blameless animal, so she moved in quickly, keen to deliver mercy and retrieve the bags.

The horse snorted at her approach, but she walked quietly and spoke gently. As soon as she stroked its forehead, the horse calmed. She wrenched the saddlebags free before turning back to the horse's head.

For a moment, she rested her hand between the horse's eyes and prayed. "Dear Maidens, please accept this noble animal as a suitable sacrifice to my survival and the survival of the unknown warrior lying in the cave. I thank the horse and ask that it be brought to a better existence in the Afterlife."

After a couple of moments of reverent silence, she brought the sword across the neck in a deep slicing action. Blood burst out of the wound. Within seconds, the horse's eyes glazed over and it collapsed on its side.

Without pausing to contemplate her actions, she hid the saddlebags in the vegetation, then headed up the slope where she had seen some native wortilzion weed the moon-slide she arrived.

She hurriedly picked the herb in great chunks, making a quick scan of the surrounding country as she did so. The surroundings appeared deserted, so she quickly walked back down the slope.

On the way, she found a small bush of danilciet. She uprooted the whole plant, knowing she could make a potion to bring on her moontime, since it hadn't come on its own as expected on the moon-wash of the tidal wash.

The sound of the warrior's moaning reached her as she entered the overhang.

He thrashed about. The wound on his torso had bled enough to seep through the dressing. Sweat layered his face and chest, and his forehead felt hot.

His eyes flickered open for a second, but when she put the flask to his mouth, he just flailed around and knocked the flask from her hand.

She tore another strip off the cloak, then went down to the stream where she refilled the bottle and soaked the rag in the icy water. When she got back, he had calmed, so she placed the wet rag on his forehead.

His severely heated flesh made the water sizzle on contact and dry up in seconds. Again and again, she wet his exposed skin, trying to cool the fever that raged through his body. She trickled a few drops of liquid on his dry lips, but he didn't swallow any.

Moments later, he shivered, his skin cold and clammy.

She covered him with the cloak, then lay down beside him, rubbing his back and shoulders to increase his warmth as she hugged him close. The moon-wash dragged into a marathon effort of cooling, then warming as the fever of infection consumed him.

In the early sun-show, she gave up on any attempt to sleep and went through the saddlebags. She found clothes and various food items in one side and in the other she found more food, a horseshoe and nails, a bag of gold coins, another bottle of vinegar, and to her delight, several farrier tools.

She immediately stripped her breeches off and set to work on the belt. She captured the sides of the lock in the heavy nail extractors, then twisted it round and round. It stayed solid. She threw the tool down and snatched up the hoof trimmers. With several forceful clunks, she attacked the lock. It remained intact. Exasperated, she tossed the tool away.

"Damn it, why won't you open?" She gazed up at the roof of the cave and made a desperate plea. "Please help me, Rianon? If you wish me to live and claim the throne of Keswin in your name, please help me get free."

She re-inspected the device, then decided on a different approach. She used the nail pullers again and, twisting herself sideways at the waist, she attacked the hinges of the lock, squeezing them between the clenching blades of the tool. Using both hands, she pressed the handles. The joints squeaked and tightened, then all of a sudden buckled under the pressure, but they did not break. "Oh, moondust just break." She chucked the tool away from her and stared balefully at the lock.

~ ~ ~

Infection ravaged the warrior's body. His wounds had become red and bloated with thick, foul-smelling pus oozing from the blackened edges.

She paced the cave, muttering to herself and pleading with Rianon for help in tending him. In between, she would kneel beside him, shaking her head and hugging herself in a vain attempt to face ending his life and agony.

He drifted in and out of consciousness, his face haggard and gray, his skin paper dry and burning with fever.

Her nose wrinkled at the stench coming from his wounds as gunk seeped out from under the bandages. She turned away as her stomach twisted. He might not have died from his immediate wounds, but he would almost certainly die from the infection that had come after them.

For a long time, she watched him thrash and moan, overcome with frustration as he became weaker. She had nothing to kill the infection and no training in the healing arts to help him survive. Despite being unable to help him, she couldn't bring herself to end his suffering through death.

She wished she had listened more closely to her father and ignored her mother's joking dismissal of his healing talents.

With the moons of Arawen and Blodwen now lighting the sky in the second moon-sweep of the harvest, the delay to her journey also weighed heavily on her mind.

She had to make the deadline or die. If she didn't reach the Sacred River in time to cross with the next tidal wash on the last day of the withering, she would either drown trying to swim the treacherous waters or freeze to death in the blizzards of the freeze to follow. Restless and no longer able to just stand by watching the warrior suffer, she hurried from the cave and out to the edge of the battlefield. It lay deserted under a gloomy blanket of cloud. Rosin went cautiously among the dead, revolted by what she saw.

Most of the corpses had horrendous wounds, but even with the extensive damage, she could see where blood vipers had sucked out the congealing blood. They were long gone now, preferring fresher dining.

In an effort to cut the smell of decaying flesh, she wrapped a strip of material around her face as she carefully walked amongst the putrefying bodies.

She found a number of kit bags, a shield, several daggers, bedrolls, eating utensils, and on the last body she found a bow. Just like hers. Joy burst through her. She had a reliable weapon to hunt or kill. She scratched around in the long grass and found the quiver. It had five arrows. Precious few but enough. She covered her hand with material to protect it from infections as she took what could be retrieved without disturbing the dead too much. She shouldered her finds and went to turn away. A movement on a corpse's face caught her attention.

She examined the corpse more closely. Maggots, hundreds of them. Big fat ones, tiny little ones, just hatched, and flies lightly landing on the flesh to lay more eggs in the rich feeding ground.

As she stared down at the corpse, a vague snippet of memory — a story she'd overheard from her Protector one moon-wash popped into her head. He had often gleefully related his experiences on the battlefield. King Cadmar, well known for his healing knowledge had saved many lives. His methods often used experimental techniques and invented herbal concoctions.

This particular, rather disgusting method of curing infection remained one of his most bizarre. She hesitated, unsure if she should proceed, knowing full well that Father Cadmar enjoyed embellishing a good story. She hoped fervently the healing method she now contemplated using did not turn out to be one of his exaggerations, for if true, maybe it would provide the Warrior's only chance of survival.

She retrieved a metal mug from one of her piles, then returned to the body. Without getting too close, she knelt and studied the maggots. On one side, hundreds of squirming little ones had just started to get busy on the dead flesh.

She put her hand out, hesitated, then drew it back. Oh, dear Maidens, how should I do this? She shuddered. Her stomach somersaulted and hot bile rushed up her throat. She went to her pile and scratched around amongst the salvaged items. At the bottom of the second kit bag, she found a battered spoon and dragged it out. This would suffice to do the job.

Back by the corpse, she leaned in, and using the spoon, scooped as many of the baby maggots as she could get without taking any decaying flesh. Most of the others were leaving the body already fully developed. Seeking tiny ones, she moved from corpse to corpse, collecting hundreds and hundreds of seething little white bodies.

Taken from their source of food, they wriggled frantically, tunneling under each other, seeking sustenance. Afraid they would escape from the mug, and revolted by the idea of them crawling on her, she covered them with a piece of cloth then hurried back to the cave.

As quickly as she could, she prepared some additional strips of material for her task.

He didn't move. His breathing slow and shallow. Except for his occasional moans, he could be mistaken for a cadaver.

She unwrapped the dressings, then used the spoon to remove as much of the evil-smelling material in and around the wounds as she could. The wounds had horrible yellow and black flesh around the edges. His flesh was putrefying from the germs, which were breeding furiously, creating an indescribable stench.

Her stomach rebelled, but she held the sickness down by force of will as she considered the wounds, then the maggots. Revolted by what she planned to do, she steeled herself and tightened her grip to steady her hand before spooning the maggots over the putrefying flesh on his chest, face, head, neck, and shoulder. She even released a few on his hand to heal the stumps of his amputated fingers.

With morbid fascination, she watched them wobble over the infected flesh. Immediately some of them began to wander, so she quickly covered the wounds with strips of material. With longer strips she firmly tied the cloth down to stop the maggots from falling out of the wounds, or venturing into parts of his body she didn't want them in but not too tight to stop them having air and light.

Once she'd covered all the wounds and the little parasites, Rosin went to the stream and washed her hands several times before she hurried back to the battlefield and retrieved her treasures.

Chapter 8

Gently, she touched his forehead. His skin had cooled slightly. His thrashing had eased during the last moon-slide. She eyed the bandages. Her stomach clenched and bile climbed her throat. How long should I leave the maggots? What if they eat the healthy flesh?

Three more moon-slides had passed.

With ruthless efficiency, she trickled the painkilling liquid down his throat, then wiped the leaves inside his mouth. At least he wouldn't suffer any pain.

She climbed to her feet and turned.

The red diamond shaped head extended a foot from the ground, the fangs exposed and dripping venom.

Rosin froze, her breath balling in her chest.

The blood viper swayed; beady, black eyes fixed on her.

Blood beat inside her head. Her throat constricted. Pure terror clamped her gut. Without pausing, Rosin threw the container of painkiller.

The viper reared up and hissed as the fluid splattered.

Rosin sidled to the side, scanning the cave. Where in the cursed Maidens did I leave the sword? As she stepped back to retrieve it the viper propelled itself at her. She kicked at it. The fangs sank into her trousers just below the knee.

"Owww." The fangs scraped her skin. She screamed. The intensity of the bite searing right up her leg.

With her leg dragging, she leaned over and snatched up the

sword. Holding the hilt in both hands, she swiped.

The viper dropped to the ground.

She swung again. Missed.

The viper headed for the man.

His blood. The viper wanted his blood. Moon leech, no. She leapt forward. Her leg collapsed under her, burning and throbbing.

"Owww." She hit the ground.

The viper had almost reached him.

Stretching forward, she managed to poke it with the sword.

It turned to her and hissed.

This time she managed to reach close enough to slice the side of the viper's abdomen open.

Despite the injury, it sprang at her.

She kicked out as she shuffled backward.

The viper slithered toward her.

Before she could pull her leg away, it sank its fangs through her trousers. Pain seared along her skin. I'm going to die. Oh Maidens, I'm a dead woman.

With a well-placed clout, she dislodged the viper.

It slithered away with its insides trailing in the sand.

She pushed up and hopped after it. With a massive thwack, she brought the sword down. The blade severed the head.

The tail end quivered then lay still while the head with the fangs still bared landed with a splat right by the warrior's boots.

Rosin sank to the ground, whimpers and moans slipping past clenched teeth. Her whole leg pulsated, the skin hot and tight. With trembling hands, she peeled her trousers off and inspected her leg. The two sites were burning infernos, already turning red. She fought down sobs. On closer inspection, she could see they were not actual puncture wounds, but scratches. Is there hope? Perhaps I have not been injected with venom. What to do?

Rosin choked back her fear. Her hand shook as she picked up the sword. For a moment she sat frozen, the sword blade hovering over the scratches. The blade wobbled. She tightened her grip, then brought the blade down across her skin, slicing the chunk of flesh bearing the first scratch mark from her body. Before she could lose her will, she sliced the second site.

Blood spilled out and ran down her leg onto the sandy floor. She let it bleed as she hunched over, hugging herself to ease the shuddering of her body. If some venom had filtered through her system, thinning her blood, it would soon leak out of her very pores.

She dragged her shirt over her head and ripped it into five pieces. With the two smaller pieces, she padded her sword wounds then bound them around very tightly with the other pieces. Her leg throbbed and had already swollen to twice its normal size.

The world span. A misty red fog obscured her vision and her head felt like it would explode. She crawled toward the man and collapsed by his side. Sobs choked in her throat because she didn't even have the energy to cry. I'm sorry, Mother. I'm sorry I didn't save the throne.

Blackness hovered at the edge of her mind; fatigue gripped her body. She let her head rest on the ground and allowed the blackness to come.

~ ~ ~

Coldness clutched her. She curled in on herself, whimpering against her discomfort. She sought the blackness, but it wouldn't come. One leg pulsated with a dull grinding pain. The world spun as she lifted her head from the ground. Oh, Maidens' curse. The blood viper bit me. I'm not dead?

With shaky arms, she pushed herself into a sitting position. She had no idea how long she'd been unconscious. Her leg remained hugely swollen, and the flesh showed blood above and below the bandages. Not fresh but dry, crusty layers on her skin. It hurt like a lunar storm. Fatigue gripped her body with a heavy pressure and her head throbbed. Maidens, I need a drink. She glanced around.

The viper's head with the gaping mouth had become partially buried in the sand by her warrior's restless feet.

A shudder ripped through her. She should be dead. Giving the viper head a wide berth, she crawled around the warrior. She snatched up the water bottle and guzzled much of the remaining contents. Her wounded warrior writhed and moaned.

She dragged herself to his side.

His one good eye opened, and he focused on her. "Luna dust, you're bleeding."

"I'm all right, it's not my blood." She shook her head, too bewildered by her survival to explain.

He nodded, then with his one good hand, he clawed at the dressing on his face. "Please, help me. Take it off. Moonlight and Maidens, it's unbearable... "His voice cracked; his agony reflected in his eye.

She hesitated to acquiesce, not sure if the maggots had completed their job. He seemed less feverish, so maybe it might be time. Nerves fluttered through her. How could she explain it to him?

She stayed his hand. "I will remove the dressings, but you must trust me." She stared down at him, meeting his serious gaze with a warning one of her own. "You must lie still until I say you can move."

He nodded.

"Here, take some more painkiller. You will need it."

Except for the occasional low moan, he watched her preparations in silence. His tortured gaze followed her as she lit the fire, heated water, then tore more clean rags. Finally, she laid out her materials by his side.

He smiled encouragement.

"The problem is, even if the infection's gone, your wounds will still be open. I'll need to close them, although I'm not sure how."

He gave a wisp of a smile. "Most warriors carry needle and thread for mending wounds or clothes. Perhaps you should try some of the dead."

A flash of guilt seared as Rosin dug through the items she had taken from the battlefield. It didn't take long before she found what she sought, but what he proposed horrified her as much as the maggots had. The needle seemed huge and the thread thick. The thought of piercing his flesh to sew it together made her shudder.

"Give me some more of your brew and just get it stitched."

Her hands shook as she held the makeshift surgical tools out to him. "You can't be serious."

"Think about it. In the meantime, get these moon leech dressings off. They're agony." He squirmed and moaned.

Suddenly concerned he would attempt to remove them himself; she hurriedly finished her preparations.

Finally ready, she knelt by his chest. "I would suggest you shut your eyes. This won't be pleasant."

A ghost of a smile touched the good side of his mouth. "I'm sure I've seen worse, my lady."

"So, you remember me now?"

He frowned. "I know nothing of you, my lady, other than what your dulcet tones, soft hands, and delicate features tell me. You are no wretch from the streets and far too beautiful to be mistaken for a boy, no matter all you're trying."

"My disguise is a dismal failure?"

He nodded. "So now will you stitch my wounds?"

"Please close your eyes."

He closed his eyes and clenched his fists. His body tensed, then stilled, as if in anticipation of more pain.

Grateful he didn't bother to argue, she released the bindings and delicately lifted the bulk of the dressings.

Even though she had prepared herself for an onslaught of stench and the sight of the maggots, when actually confronted with the broiling mash of fat gray creatures, she could not stop a cry of anguish escaping. They spilled out of his wounds and rolled, crawled, and tumbled in all directions. Revolted at the thought of them getting on her, she reflexively shuffled back.

~ ~ ~

At her cry, he opened his eyes. "Is it that bad, my lady?" He lifted his head a little to examine his chest. Nausea rushed through him. His blood receded and the world span. He swallowed hard, against the bile that rose in his throat. "For Maidens' sake! Get them off me!" He brought up a hand to swipe them off.

The woman grabbed his wrist and held it well away from his wounds. "Don't touch. Your hands are dirty."

"Dirty!" He screwed his face up with distaste and pain. "What the moon's fall do you call that?" He looked again at his chest cringing inward on himself as if it would remove him from the seething mass.

"I said to trust me."

He scowled up at her his revulsion pulling his expression tight. He gasped and sagged back down giving up the fight. He closed his eyes unable to face the sight. The pain raged through him accompanied by the crawling sensation as the maggots crawled over his flesh. Vomit rose in his throat. He swallowed hard.

~ ~ ~

Working as fast as she could, she gathered the maggots into several mugs and, putting them aside, she flooded the wound with the boiled water and vinegar.

He yelled and groaned, then his eyes rolled back in his head as he broke out in a sweat. With him unconscious, it would be far easier to do what she had to do.

Fear made her body leaden. She hovered over him, reluctant to start. She inhaled and exhaled deeply, then leaned forward so she could see better. Her hand shook as she made the first stitch.

The flesh appeared amazingly healthy with very little bleeding or other seepage.

She plied the needle and thread, stitching slowly and steadily, joining the flesh as neatly and as closely as she could. She cursed the fact she wasn't a seamstress and that his scars would be extensive and permanent, but again, at least he would live.

Using the dagger as a razor, she shaved his head around the edge of the damage. As a precaution, she rinsed the wound again with the boiled water before she started to sew. Working with a steady rhythm, she stitched each wound, bringing the clean sides together as best she could. They wouldn't meet completely, leaving a wide, jagged scar that would scar him permanently.

Her whole body trembled with concentrated effort by the time she finished and applied clean bandages. He remained unconscious, and for his own comfort, Rosin hoped he would stay that way for a while.

She snatched up a clean, but ragged pair of pants from her

stash of stolen items, some clean cloth for bandages, then hobbled to the stream. It took a bit of scrubbing, but she cleansed her skin of blood where it had leaked out of her cuts and grazes. The cold water soothed her swollen leg. The gaping cuts had scabbed over, but she doused them with vinegar, then re-dressed them.

She touched her stomach. *Am I still carrying the babe? Surely it would have been lost in the aftermath of the viper poison.*

With just a little light bleeding marking her underdrawers, she knew she had not lost the babe. She struggled to walk back to the cave. Every muscle ached. She stared up at the moons, two fully risen, the third just peeping over the horizon. Time passed quickly. A sense of urgency discomforted her. *What if I miss the tidal wash? What then? Do I just curl up and die in the snow? No, I've come too far. I can do it. I can reach the river in time.*

Exhausted by her excursion and beset by vexing thoughts, she didn't even bother scratching around to find food. He lay unmoving, so she just dropped down to lie beside him and pulled a couple of cloaks over them. She snuggled into his side and it didn't take long for the chill in her bones to ease and the darkness to descend.

~ ~ ~

Her first awareness came as a sense of being watched. She opened her eyes, just tiny slits, afraid of what she would see.

His rumble of laughter vibrated through his chest and hers. "Peek-a-boo, my lady."

She started fully awake and scuttled away before peering up into the quizzical gaze of one deep, green eye. The injured eye continued to be just a slit in the bruised and swollen socket.

He smiled. "Suddenly you're afraid of me? I thought you might give me some more of your magic potion. These wounds are hurting like a moon leech."

She handed him the mixture, feeling disappointed her ministrations had not eased his pain.

He drank deeply, screwing his face up.

"Is the pain any less?"

"A lot, thank you, my lady. It hurt like a Maidens' fury last moon-slide. I wanted to die, but this morning it's just bearable. I think sleep would be the best thing." He lowered his head and shut his eyes. "Wake me for dinner. My ribs are dancing with my backbone."

A jet of laughter burst out of her. He surely had to be on the mend if he could make witty little asides. Pleasure wafted through her, but the light relief didn't last long. The chastity belt had rubbed her raw, and her moontime had still not come despite the viper poison. Three moon-sweeps past her date. Relentless queasiness and fatigue plagued her. Her greatest fear had been realized. She must resort to using her store of danilciet. The sooner, the better. She hesitated, fearing the harm it could cause. Whispers through the castle had never revealed how much she should take, or what strength she should mix. Only the risk of illness or death had been broadcast openly.

She mixed the potion as strong as she dared, knowing it would be better to die than carry that monster's child.

She gagged as she drank the potion, the taste so rancid and bitter it made the wortilzion seem like a sweet cordial. It had to work, and soon. She wanted the thing growing inside her gone.

Dry retching and gagging, she picked up the sword and tottered toward the pond. With two mouths to feed now, she planned to catch one or two of the plentiful fish. The task of disemboweling the fish tested her gut. After several pauses, she had completed the unsavory task. With the bodies spiked on the sword, she limped back to the cave.

The warrior remained unconscious.

She put the fish down, then crept up to her lookout by the battlefield. Pain throbbed through her injured leg even as she used the sword to ease her weight from the limb. Nothing moved, so she made her way up the slope and scanned the vista all around — no dust, no clouds, and no smoke — just the clear pale blue sky starting to turn grey and lavender with the sinking of the sun. Satisfied there'd be no immediate threat to her haven, she returned to the cave.

The warrior still slept.

She returned outside and gathered pieces of very dry bark from the nearby trees, then broke up varying size twigs and wood. With nimble fingers, she set the fire in the bigger of her fire pits. When the blaze caught, she placed her flat rock over the bigger hole then set the fish side by side to cook to tender sweetness. In anticipation of the tasty meal, she breathed in. A wave of nausea washed over her.

Rosin leapt up and raced outside just in time to throw up. After she vomited several times, the sick feeling eased. She rinsed and wiped her mouth, then went back inside.

The Warrior lay on his side wide awake. One green eye focused on her as she entered. He would have heard her vomiting outside.

She deliberately avoided meeting his questioning gaze, unwilling to explain her situation.

"Are you all right, my lady?"

Rosin nodded. "I'm fine. What about you?"

He grinned. "Still in pain, my lady, but definitely improving."

"Then perhaps you are well enough for formal introductions."

~ ~ ~

169

"Of course, my lady, my angel and savior. I am... I am..." He scowled. His mouth moved in hurried little movements. He stared at the woman before him as if she would give him the answer he sought. Confusion rushed through him as his mind reached a blank space.

"You don't know who you are?"

He saw unease in her expression. He frowned. "I can't remember. I have no idea who I am, why I'm here, who you are. Help me, my lady?"

The woman pursed her lips. "I know you are from the High Queen's Commissioned Warriors. You tried to rescue me from Lord Devon's men."

"Lord Devon?" He shook his head even as he searched his mind. "The Queen's Commissioned Warriors... I don't remember."

She touched his shoulder lightly, a sympathetic smile touching her mouth.

He floundered in his mind but there was nothing. He reached out again and again into emptiness. "Tell me what you do know, my lady, please? Maybe I'll remember something."

She knelt beside him.

He rested on his back. His posture tensed against the severe pain throbbing through him from his newly stitched wounds. The slightest movement brought on waves of agony.

She took his uninjured hand in hers. "I'm sure your memory will come back when your horrendous bash to the head heals. Not only did it crush your helmet, it pared the metal open then sliced through your scalp. Trauma to the head has been known to cause memories to dissolve, but mostly, they come back in time."

He continued to frown. "Maidens' curses. I know I got a crack on the head and it still hurts like the bite of a moon leech to remind me, but I wouldn't have thought it would erase my whole life. And you, my lady, why did you need rescuing? What is this Devon to you?"

Again, the woman shook her head. "Devon is my enemy. He wants my... ouch!" She doubled over, clutching her abdomen making small cries and whimpers.

"My lady?"

With her face flushed even hotter than it had at admitting her robbery of the dead, she brushed her distress aside in the hope of dampening his interest and concern. "Just women's problems, nothing important."

She picked up the mug of painkilling potion and downed the contents.

Embarrassment flowed and heat rushed through his body, but he didn't take his gaze off her face as he waited for her to finish her story.

"I am the Princess Apparent of Keswin. Devon came and massacred everyone on the moon-wash I was to make my Bond of Le Chéile to a man chosen by my parents." Her voice cracked and faded as she told him what had happened. Tears filled her eyes and she fell silent.

He did not move or prompt her. He just waited patiently as she brought herself back from the brink of emotional collapse.

"Devon decided he needed to conceive a child with me. He... he raped me." Hot burning tears welled in her eyes, then spilled over onto her cheeks. "I escaped. I killed a man, then I ran until I found this place. I am walking to Tarlic Castle, but then you needed saving..."

He reached out and took her trembling hands in his. Horror and rage seared through him. *What sort of viper's curse did such things.* "I might not have been originally trying to kill this lord, but if I ever come across him, I will kill him, regardless of who I am. What are your plans now, my lady, or should I say, Princess?"

"Rosin will do, sir. I am going to my Moon Life Protector, King Cadmar of Tarlic. I am going to find a suitable consort, then I'm going to reclaim my kingdom and kill Lord Devon. I am going to bear a legitimate heir to the Throne of Keswin, and rule my realm more wisely than my parents did. I will make changes for a better Keswin."

Her voice rose as she spoke as she outlined her plans with determination and resolution.

Sympathy raced through him for this petite young woman who had already been through so much was outlining plans that would put her though more. He had little to offer but his sword arm and protection. "Do you wish for some company and help on your journey, Rosin? I don't know who I am, but when I'm healed— thanks to you—I would be honored to guard you, fight for you, and lead the battle to get your throne back."

She sat back and stared at him, hoping to read his intentions. "And what do you want in exchange, sir?"

He shook his head. "Rosin, my Lady of Keswin, I'm offering you my fealty and my sword arm as payment for my life. I owe you that and will honor my debt."

"That is a big offer you make to one such as me."

He nodded. "But you have given me my life. What I offer is little in exchange."

~ ~ ~

Rosin still felt uneasy and suspicious, but he seemed to be vowing in good faith, and she had, after all, saved his life. She stood and gave a small acknowledging curtsey before she picked up the sword. "My lord"—she touched him on one shoulder — "I dub thee the First Knight of Keswin"—then followed with a touch on the other shoulder and accept your fealty in the manner it is offered. As of this day, I charge you with the duty of protecting my life until I return to reclaim my throne. At my ascension to the throne, you shall be duly rewarded and free to follow your own choice of trails that lead to a rich entitlement in the Afterlife."

He bowed his head in solemn acceptance of her charge and her bestowal of a title.

A sudden bubble of laughter rose in her chest. A smile curled her mouth upward. "The only problem I have, First Knight of Keswin, is what to call you."

He smiled in response to her obvious amusement. "What is your preference, my lady?"

Rosin felt a weight of responsibility, because it might be a name he would live with for the rest of his life. He might, sadly, never remember his former self. A spark of excitement filled her when a moniker came to her. It had meaning, and she liked the name as it rolled off her tongue.

"Can I suggest Arlan? Its meaning is 'to make an oath of trust', and it is also the name of the first son of the sixth Maiden Goddess, Rianon. It reflects our shared oath and also that you are the First Knight of Keswin." Rosin stopped speaking, suddenly uncertain how he would feel about her suggestion. She didn't want him to feel obligated to take on the name she suggested because he had to wear it and be known by it.

He smiled. "I accept your name of choice, my lady. I will bear it with pride and be known in Keswin only by this name. If, at a later date, I remember my real name, then I will adopt one as a first and the other as a second, depending on my preference at the time."

Rosin really smiled for the first time in quite a while.

She liked her companion, and it comforted her to no longer be alone.

The smell of burning tickled her nose. "Oh no, dinner!" She turned to rescue the fish. Grateful on inspection that only the fins had charred. The flesh, still sealed in the leathery skin, remained white and succulent. She placed the metal plate between them, and without another word, they broke the fish apart and devoured the sweet, juicy flesh. By the time they settled back, full and sated, they had left little but skin and bones.

Arlan lay back with a groan.

Rosin noticed a little trickle of blood seeping from under his bandages. "I will need to change those dressings and clean your wounds with some boiled water and vinegar. I'm afraid the infection will return."

Arlan gave her a mock scowl of capitulation and lay back with his eyes closed. "Do what you must, Lady Rosin, but no maggots, please. I now have a charge to fulfill, which I can't do if I'm dead."

With infinite care, Rosin removed the dressings, then bathed the wounds with boiled water and vinegar mixture. Despite the blood, all his wounds showed signs of healing. The scars would be pretty ugly and remain with Arlan for the rest of his life.

"I'm sorry. I'm not much of a seamstress, Arlan," she said as she covered his wounds with new dressings.

He placed his big hand over hers where they rested in her lap. "Do not fret, Rosin. You have given me my life and for that, I am eternally grateful. A warrior does not have to be pretty."

His words failed to soothe her, although she smiled and pretended they did. Once plenty of pretty young maidens would have fluttered their eyelashes at him as he passed, but she doubted that would happen, with the scars now distorting his features.

During her treatment of him, she hadn't found any bonding scars on his wrists, so at least he didn't have a bhean chéile or children pining over his absence and who would be shocked at his disfigurement. Of course, he might find a woman who would love him for him, or he might make a union for practical reasons. Only time would tell. But she hoped he didn't come to regret having his life saved by a princess without a throne.

"Do not worry about me, Princess, it is you we need to concentrate on. You have a kingdom to reclaim. I have studied your map and would like to suggest a few things."

Rosin pushed her concerns about Arlan's future aside and focused on his observations. "I would welcome your help."

"Firstly, I will need a while to heal. Then when I'm up to it, I suggest we walk by moon-wash until we find the first village and see if we can buy a horse or two. I'm in no state to fight this Devon and his men, but I would suspect once we are on your Protector's land, we should be safe to travel nonstop. A disguise would be useful, I think."

Rosin nodded in agreement. "Do you think the dead up there will mind if we use the money from their pockets? I feel sort of uncomfortable being a thief."

A warm rumble of laughter rolled out of him. "I don't think they have a use for it, Rosin... owww, owww." His hand went to his ribs, and he gasped for breath. "It hurts. I must not laugh."

As she laughed at him, the sharp cramping began again and took the edge off her enjoyment at Arlan's predicament. She needed to get the chastity belt off, and soon. The constant chafing left her skin weeping and inflamed. The thought of having to resort to maggots for her own body repulsed her.

"You've gone pale, Princess, are you all right? Oh, sorry, I forgot."

A hot blush now rushed up her face. "I'll be back." With a vague smile, she left the cave.

Once outside, she doubled over with the full tearing force of the cramps. When they eased, she staggered into the privacy of the thick vegetation then huddled against a sturdy trunk, letting the pain rip through her. She stayed for a long time, but finally the cramps eased. On inspection, she confirmed the baby remained snug in her womb.

~ ~ ~

Arlan moved restlessly beside her. She stayed still, her eyes closed.

"My lady?"

"Mm-mm?"

"I need some help. I need to get up and go outside."

"What?" Vague and fuzzy with tiredness, she didn't register the urgency in his tone or the meaning of his request.

"Princess, please, I...I have a call of nature that is getting urgent. Can you please help me?"

She stiffened, then flicked her eyes open and studied the cave roof while her thoughts bounced around her brain.

She scrambled to her feet. "Sorry, Arlan. Of course, I will help you. Do you think you're up to it?"

He nodded. "Once I get on my feet."

She leaned down, put one hand around his waist, the other holding his good arm as he awkwardly climbed to his feet.

He stood for a moment, swaying slightly. After a moment, he gathered his strength and adjusted to the pain the movement caused. He leaned heavily on her shoulders.

She tightened her hold around his waist, supporting him.

He shuffled with each painful step across the cave and outside. The sweat poured down his face, which had turned a sickly gray by the time they reached a small private area.

Rosin eased him onto a large boulder in a half sitting position. "I will leave you, Arlan, if you think you can manage. I won't go far, so just call me when you're ready to return to the cave."

He nodded, his eyes closed, and his teeth clenched against the pain.

She moved away through the foliage to give him some modicum of privacy, and to complete her own business.

Arlan reached down and struggled with the laces at the front of his breeches. Pain seared through his hand where his fingers had been amputated. He couldn't get the laces undone.

"My lady, could you help me please."

She appeared.

Embarrassment flushed through him. "I'm sorry but I can't get the laces undone."

She blushed.

"Sorry, my lady."

She smiled up at him. Then leant down and loosened the laces.

"Thank you, my lady, I can manage from here but I might need you to re-lace them."

She stepped back and disappeared. He sensed her just behind the bush. He managed to uncover himself and do what he needed. He struggled to re adjust his clothes but finally he was covered.

"My lady, I'm ready for your aid, please?"

She knelt before him and re-laced his breeches. Arlan inhaled deeply as an ache of desire rushed through him at the light touch of her hands against him.

She completed the task and stood. "Let's get you back to the cave and lying down before you collapse." She tucked herself under his arm, his weight immediately heavy on her shoulders.

"Sorry, Princess, to be a burden, but I feel weak as a kitten. My legs are shaking, and the blood is pounding in my head as the world spins around it."

They had to stop and rest several times, his chest heaving as he struggled with the exertion. "Oh, fallen Maidens, Rosin. I can't believe I'm this weak."

"Arlan, do not expect too much so soon. Only two moon-sweeps ago you were dying, your body consumed by a massive infection. You lost so much blood from your wounds. I have no idea how you survived in the first place. You did not eat and barely drank for almost a moon-sweep so don't be so hard on yourself."

"But I'm holding you here, stopping you from reaching safety."

"Don't worry, Arlan, just concentrate on getting well. I have some time to spare before I need to reach the Sacred River for the tidal wash. I have no doubt sharing my journey with you will be safer, quicker, and far more pleasant than on my own. Now, are you ready to continue?"

He nodded, accepted her support, and together they slowly negotiated the entrance. He sighed deeply when he finally climbed back onto his makeshift bed.

When he settled, she immediately gave him some painkiller, then insisted on checking his wounds. He lifted his head and looked at his chest. Moondust and Maidens it was a mess but seemed to be healing with just a little seepage from between a couple of the stitches. If his face was the same he'd be lucky if anyone recognized him.

He might mend and fight again but even as he thought that he cast his mind back into the looming blank space in his mind. He flinched back from the nothingness and tried to calm the fear that swirled through him. He had to go on with what he had for he might never know who he really was.

~ ~ ~

To make doubly sure no infection would restart in the wounds,

Rosin swabbed them with vinegar and re-covered them with fresh dressings.

Under the influence of the potion and exhaustion from his small excursion, Arlan quickly fell asleep. His face had swiftly regained its color.

For a long while, Rosin watched him sleep, still able to admire the handsomeness of his strong square features around the puckering lines of his wounds.

With her companion comfortable, she gathered some clean clothes from the retrieved saddlebags, her water bottle, and her bow and quiver, then headed for the stream. She wanted to soak her aching leg and finally take a real bath using the rough soap she found in one of the saddlebags. After a quick check of the surrounds, she undressed. She had brought one of the small, pointed tools from the saddlebags to have another go at the chastity belt.

Sitting naked on the grassy bank, she bent over the lock and poked it with the sharp end of the tool, but no matter how she jiggled and made it rattle and click, it did not open. The futile effort left her hot, sweaty, and extremely frustrated with her failure.

Finally admitting defeat, she dropped the tool and waded into the icy water. After a quick duck under the surface, she soaped her ragged hair then scrubbed thoroughly before rinsing it clean. She bathed her whole body, careful to get in under the chastity belt. It irked her that she still didn't feel cleansed of Devon despite having had three complete washes. She doubted she ever would be completely rid of his violation.

Desperation clenched. She had to rid herself of this thing inside her. The mixture of danilciet had failed to loosen its hold. If her moontime did start soon, she would have to find a healing woman to help her.

Rumors had often circulated the castle of a strong potion that could be purchased in the time of need from a healing woman or a white witch. There were risks, of course. She'd heard of women dying after taking it or having a damaged baby. No matter the risk, she would take whatever a witch could offer her to get rid of it, even if it put her future fertility or her life at risk. A strangled sob bubbled up in her chest. She would not even contemplate her other option. She could never bring herself to commit infanticide, nor could she ask anyone else to do it for her or trust them to complete such a heinous act.

But if she carried Devon's child, it could not be allowed to live.

By the time she'd washed her old clothes, a relentless chill had settled in her bones. She climbed out of the pool, dried with a cloak, then got dressed in some overlarge but clean clothes. Her next task was to find food.

The other moon-wash, some ducks had flown into land, and she suspected she would find them hunting worms in a swampy area nearby. Sure enough, she heard the ducks before she saw them. Hundreds floated on the widespread wetlands and swamp area at the bottom of the valley. They rested on their long migration to the coastal areas for the freeze and made easy targets for her experienced bow arm.

Crouching in the bushes, she crept close, nocked an arrow then stood and released the arrow in one smooth move.

With a terrified squawk, the ducks rose as one in a black cloud of feathers and beaks. One remained floating near the edge of the water.

She hurried into the shallows and retrieved it.

Arlan still slept, so she headed up across the battlefield to the hill. Nothing moved within her view. On the way back down the hill, she snatched up some more painkilling herb. Back in the cave, she hung up her washed clothes, lit the fire, then prepared the duck.

Arlan woke soon after, probably lured back to consciousness by the aroma of the roasting bird.

"You are a lady of many talents, Princess—doctoring, hunting, rescuing the wounded—and also of great beauty. Whoever you finally choose as your consort will be a lucky man."

Embarrassment heated her face at his words of praise. She scowled a little. "Many of the men from whom I will choose do not value such talents, Arlan. What they value is a throne, the people ruled by it, its riches, and the value of its treaties. The most important, of course, is the ability of the princess to produce a legitimate heir. As you know I am not currently able to offer these."

"Then he would be a fool."

She chuckled. "Nobility does not provide immunity from foolishness, idiocy, or any of the other less complimentary human traits."

"No, I suppose not. Anyway, my lady, could you help me sit, perhaps with a couple of saddlebags behind me for support?"

She brought the bags, then helped him sit. Awareness rushed through her of her hands touching his bare skin and the way it made her nerves dance and tingle.

He leaned forward and breathed in deeply. "Mm, you smell nice this moon-wash."

"I went down to the stream and bathed with some of the soap from one of the saddlebags. It is so nice to be clean and fresh. It's been so long since my last real wash..." Her words flagged as she realized the vision she had painted for Arlan.

"Don't blush, Princess. It would've been a beautiful sight, I'm sure, but not for the eyes of a battered warrior like me."

The heat coloring her face and neck increased. She gazed into his eyes, humming with awareness in response to the lights sparkling in his. The recognition of each other as man and woman.

An immediate need to squash that spark urged her to speak. "Arlan, I... I'm not free... do not have the luxury of... the freedom to follow my heart's desire..."

He placed his large hand over hers. "I know, Princess. I understand, and you will never be in any danger from me. I have the ultimate respect for our situation."

"I just didn't want to give you a false impression, Arlan, and always need to be on my guard."

"Say no more, my lady. Now, how long is that duck going to be?"

"A while."

"Then perhaps you could help me outside to sit for a while in the last of the sunlight."

~ ~ ~

She helped him to stagger outside. The sun felt good on his skin. He lifted his face to the sun with his eyes closed letting the rays warm him.

An easy companionship was developing between him and his savior. He was attracted to her. Her litheness, her energy, her determination, the lilt to her voice and the tilt of her mouth when she smiled. This was woman he could easily bed and perhaps even fall in love with. She was very capable and didn't turn away from the hardship of the challenges she faced. He admired her.

He looked at his arms and knew he was not bonded. But he was acutely aware of her position, a princess, and one that needed to find a suitable consort to reclaim her throne. Arlan doubted he was consort material. His calloused hands told him he had been a fighting man for a long while. Sadness washed lightly over him. She had been fair and made it clear that she was not available even for a short interlude or a long term future. Besides, Princesses did not fall in love with common-blood warriors. Mostly they bonded for the good of the realm.

He sighed. His future loomed up grey and distorted. He knew nothing more than he needed to heal and get Rosin to where she needed to be. He would do that and walk away leaving the possibilities that whispered in his mind behind.

Chapter 9

Each moon-slide, Arlan went outside and sat in the sunshine, then walked back and forth a little farther each time. At last, he could manage most things without assistance, and his wounds were healing nicely.

"Perhaps you could bathe, Arlan."

"Are you saying I'm on the nose, my lady?"

"No, Arlan, of course not… I didn't mean …"

Her words fluttered into the silence of embarrassment.

He started to laugh, a rich, deep chuckle, then grabbed his chest as if to suppress his mirth against the pain it caused. "Oh, Princess, no offense taken. Yes, I would love to bathe."

She gathered up a change of clothes and a cloak for him to dry with, then they made their way to the water.

Arlan walked slowly, leaning just a little on her shoulders for support. At the bank of the stream, he sat on a boulder and fiddled with his tunic.

Rosin immediately saw his struggle to remove it and stepped forward.

Together, they dragged it over his head.

He turned to her so she could remove the bandages.

She undid the knots, then unbound the dressings on his chest, but as she lifted them away from his body, her fingers grazed his skin. She flinched in response to the whisper-soft touch of the springy hairs as they brushed the tips of her fingers.

With Arlan's quick, indrawn breath, the awareness between them exploded into a tangible entity.

Rosin held herself in check not to act on the chemistry that called to a primitive need within her.

With concentrated interest, she studied his wounds. "You're healing well, Arlan. Now lean down and I will take the others off."

He didn't answer, just eased forward so she could reach his face and head.

She unwound the strips of material. With his head near her breasts, the warmth of sexual awareness buzzed through her.

The sizzle of desire flowed between them, sparking and tingling in the air. Guilt filled her when her body responded to his nearness, but she had no power to stop it.

Arlan's breathing became ragged. Both fists clenched on his thighs as he stared at the ground between his feet.

Rosin almost stepped back from him, knowing the fault was hers, but instead she inhaled deeply and continued removing the dressings.

As she lifted the material from his head and face, she realized how much his hair had grown, much of it still matted with blood. Being unable to shave, he had also grown quite a bushy beard and moustache. His mouth twisted by the scar and his nose no longer straight took his handsomeness away, but both eyes were clear and a crackling green when he looked up to meet her contemplation of his features.

"Is it so bad, my lady?"

Unbidden, tears sprang into her eyes. "Oh, Arlan, I have not repaired the damage very well. I am not much of a seamstress."

He reached out, clasped her upper arms, and gave her the tiniest shake. "Do not fret, my lady, for I am alive."

"But, Arlan, I have not been able to restore even a fraction of your handsome features..."

"Do you find me repulsive, my lady?"

She reached out and rested a hand on either side of his jaw. "No, Arlan. No matter how badly you are scarred, I would never be repulsed, but then, I am used to the damage, too. Your injuries will perhaps be difficult for strangers to become accustomed to."

"As long as you are not repulsed, my lady, I care not for what others think." He rose, unlaced his breeches, and let them and his undergarments drop to the ground. He stood totally naked, not at all self-conscious, even with Rosin's blatant observation of his magnificent body.

"Can you please help me into the water, my lady?"

At over six foot three, with broad shoulders, well-defined chest muscles and a flat abdomen, he dwarfed Rosin, lucky to stand five-five in bare feet. A light sprinkling of reddish-blond hairs grew on his chest and trailed down his torso into the springy bush around his manhood. She could not tear her eyes away from every inch of him. Well endowed, he had a long, thick shaft snipped as all Maidens' males were at birth. His long muscular legs ended in large, well-shaped feet.

A warm, liquid sensation pooled in her womanhood, and she wanted Arlan to hold her close and make love to her. Only he couldn't, with the physical barrier of the belt and her commitment to the throne. Part of her cried inside. It took considerable effort to lift her gaze up to meet his.

He smiled just a little, his expression full of sexual awareness. "The pool, Princess?"

"Ahh, yes." Throwing off her trancelike state of mind, she moved forward.

Arlan waded in a few steps before he lowered himself into the water, his magnificent body disappearing. She held out the soap, but he shook his head.

"Can you wash my hair, please? I'm worried I might damage the stitching because I can't see it, and my shoulder is not working all that well."

The desire to touch him, no matter the excuse, tugged at her so strongly she didn't consider refusing his request. In a flash, she kicked her boots off, rolled up her breeches, and paddled into the shallow water at the edge of the pool.

Arlan ducked under the water, then came up blowing bubbles. He turned and slid backward, so he ended up sitting on her feet.

She bit back a squeak of surprise at the feel of his naked buttocks against her flesh and stood very still as she leaned over and soaped his hair. With infinite care, she massaged his scalp, gently easing out the tangles, the matted knots, and the dried blood from the golden blond strands.

By the time she finished, her breath came in ragged gasps.

~ ~ ~

Arlan fared no better, his bare chest rising and falling in time with his uneven breathing. As he ducked under the deeper water to rinse his hair, she had no doubt of his physical response to her touch.

"Come and join me, my lady. The water is wonderful, cold and refreshing."

She shook her head. Not because she feared crossing the line with a man she found so attractive in body and spirit, but due to her shame at being locked in the chastity belt.

"Then if you do not want to join me, perhaps you would go back to the cave and get me the razor and mirror from the black saddlebags. I need a shave."

"You be careful while I'm gone. No straining those wounds."

"No, my lady."

She turned and hurried through the vegetation, puzzled by Arlan's desire to be clean-shaven. Most males from the six thrones of Annaticcia had moustaches. Moustaches of great size and elaborate shape, like her father and Cadmar. The lower classes also had beards but kept both moustache and beard short. Only the nobles who had the time to take such pride in the hair on their faces wore longer styles.

She hurried back to the pool, worried about leaving Arlan alone, knowing he still had dizzy spells from time to time. At the pond, she found him floating on the far side, not moving. His face turned up to the sun.

"Arlan?"

He rolled over slowly in the water, made to stand, but immediately yelped and sank under the water.

With her gaze fixated on the spot where he had disappeared, she fought down the panic that engulfed her. Her insides quivered. She danced on the spot, counting the seconds since he went under. Arlan, where are you? Surface please. She fluttered her hands as she scanned the water. Surely, he would surface in a moment. She waited for what seemed like a whole moon-sweep, but unable to wait a moment longer, she threw the razor down and barged into the water fully clothed.

At the spot where Arlan had disappeared, her ankles were grabbed, then whipped out from under her. Dragged below the surface with barely time to catch a breath, she came face to face with Arlan in the slightly cloudy water, tiny bubbles floating up from his crookedly smiling mouth.

With no time to react, she shot to the surface, where she managed to snatch a breath before Arlan grabbed her around the waist and tried to drag her back under. With a mock scream of terror, she wriggled away. Her ill-fitting trousers slipped and dragged over her hips. Arlan tugged again.

"No, don't," she cried. But too late to stop them sliding off and she could only kick free of them and her undergarments as they tangled around her legs.

~ ~ ~

Seconds later, Arlan popped up in front of her, her garments clutched in his fist. Anger surged through him so hot it almost boiled the water streaming off his skin.

He wiped one hand over his face, then back through his hair. "Who put that on you? That thing? Why didn't you tell me? I could have helped you."

He saw her tears mingled with the water on her face. Tears of shame, anger, and frustration. She shook her head, unable to speak, as emotion choked up her throat.

His anger melted away, and he tugged her against his chest, his arms wrapped around her as he dropped gentle kisses on the top of her head. "Tell me, Rosin, who locked you in that instrument of oppression and servitude?"

She peeked up at him, calmed by the gentleness in his tone and the closeness of his body. "Devon. After he raped me, he put it on. He intended any child I carried to be his and only his. I've attempted to get it off."

"Moonlight leech, I will have his head for this abomination. Come, my lady, out of the water. Let's see if I can release you."

After Arlan waded side by side with her to the shore. She helped him out of the pool. After a cursory wipe with the cloak, he dressed in his clean undergarments and breeches. He wrapped the cloak around her, then kept her embraced by his side as they walked back to the cave.

She shivered against him igniting his protective instincts. They came unbidden from out of that blank spot in his brain. A desperate need to soothe her hurt. He knew he was falling for her. The woman he couldn't have. His heart clenched tightly. He wondered if he had ever loved before. He didn't remember ever feeling this way about any particular woman. He sensed he knew woman though. A softness balled inside him and a determination that he treat them right. He didn't know where it came from but he accepted the knowledge as part of who he was.

While he lit the fire, Rosin quickly pulled on a dry under vest and tunic. He stoked the flame up into a roaring blaze, then patted the cloak he'd spread next to it. "Sit, Rosin. Warm your bones while I deal with this entrapment. The dull ache of his wounds made his movements cautious and slow, but he seemed to be getting around easier than before, and none of his wounds had bled since his time in the water.

He dug around in the saddlebags, finding a selection of instruments.

Some looked downright dangerous, and Rosin cringed a little.

He smiled. "Do not be afraid, Rosin, I know how to use these so I will not hurt you in my attempts."

The scent of her newly washed skin tantalized him as he leaned over to inspect the belt. Although she was somewhat exposed with no undergarments and her legs bare, he wasn't immediately sexually responsive as any sexual awareness on his part had been suppressed by the task at hand and his fury at her imprisonment.

He experimented with each tool. Some targeting the actual lock, then others against the hinges, but even after heating the heavy nail extractors, he could not break the lock. Frustration soared through him, as his desire to free her was thwarted. He couldn't force harder in case they slipped and she was injured. "I'm sorry, Princess. I cannot get it open. It pains me grievously that I cannot release you, but any rougher attack could hurt you seriously." He leaned forward and kissed her cheek.

"Do not fret, Arlan. I'm sure we will find some way soon."

~ ~ ~

She found Arlan seated outside in the sunshine when she returned from the stream. He had her small collection of weapons and shields spread out beside him.

"Are you preparing to do battle, my First Knight?"

He shook his head. "No, my lady. I'm in no state to do battle. I'm just preparing the best of the weapons."

"Arlan, will you teach me to use a sword?" She looked down at the ground, then back up to him, fully expecting an instant and disdainful rebuff.

He frowned at first, then his expression became thoughtful. "Hmm, I don't see any reason why you shouldn't learn." He held up a shorter, slightly narrower blade that he'd already cleaned. "This sword would be about your size and weight."

"My father allowed me to have a bow as a child because he thought it a quaint novelty for a princess to use a weapon. I became quite good at it, but my mother forbade me from using it when I got a little older. Arlan, I wish to learn how to defend myself from those who have an inclination to harm me."

"Yes, Princess, I think it would be wise to develop such skill. With me in such a weakened state, I would not be much use against even one experienced warrior, let alone two or three. If you're trained, we will have more chance of survival if attacked."

Arlan wiped the cloth slowly down the blade he held.

Alarm sizzled through her. "You think we might be attacked?"

Arlan shrugged. "I don't know, my lady, but I must do my best to protect you, even if it means teaching you to protect yourself."

"You are wise, my Arlan. Do you think I could be any good?"

He chuckled. "I hope, my lady, you will never need the skills. It does not matter if you're never good enough to be a Queen's champion. If you can at least parry and thrust, it might mean the difference between life and death." He pushed himself off the rock. "Here, take this sword."

Keen to use a sword for more than stabbing fish, Rosin took the weapon and held it straight out in front of her body.

Arlan chuckled.

She let the blade drop in front of her, the point resting on the ground. "Don't laugh, Arlan. As a pampered princess, no one taught me such things."

He came around behind her and put his hands on her hips.

"Now, my lady, you stand thus."

His words brushed like butterflies' wings against her ears, his breath warm on her neck as his arms came around her body to lie along hers. His body so close she could feel the warmth radiating from him.

He interlaced his fingers with hers as they rested on the hilt.

"And you swing the weapon so. Feel the weight, feel the curve of the blade through the air." They worked on this for a while then Arlan took one of her hands from the hilt. "Now, take the sword in one hand." He picked up a light shield and handed it to her. "Here, hold the shield in the other, across the front, to protect your body. Move fluidly, left and right, sweeping the sword like this. Always keep the shield up, for it can be used to stop the path of the enemy's weapon if it slips past your blade. Keep moving, swing that sword.

Good."

She followed his instructions. Her breathing had become uneven and ragged, but not from the exertion.

His body melded to hers as they moved in unison around the clearing. Then his hands slipped away, and she moved on her own.

"Keep going, Rosin. You are doing very well, but I need to rest."

The weight of the weapon and how it balanced in her hand started to feel familiar as she continued the pattern they had begun. Occasionally, she glanced over to where Arlan sat propped against the boulder.

Each time, he smiled, and a blast of warmth reached out to her.

Not only did she want to please him, and earn his respect, she also wanted to master the new skill for her own satisfaction.

She smiled inwardly. If she got good enough, she might eventually have the pleasure of killing Lord Devon herself.

After a few more rounds of the clearing, she panted, and perspiration ran down her face and between her breasts.

"Enough, Rosin, it's time to rest... or take a swim, perhaps."

She put the weapon down and sagged to the grass, acutely aware of the ache in her arms and legs from the unfamiliar exertion.

"Come, my lady..." He held out his hand. "Up you get."

She took his hand but didn't allow him to take any of her weight as she jumped to her feet.

This time Arlan did not seek her support, even though his gait remained slow.

At the stream, he kicked off his boots and lifted his tunic over his head before he paused to watch her. "Shy, my lady?"

Heat instantly rushed up her face, increasing her self-consciousness tenfold.

"Shall I come over there and help you?"

"Arlan, no. I can manage."

He chuckled as he proceeded to undo his breeches. His naked magnificence drew her gaze like a magnet. His manhood thickened under her lustful scrutiny.

Suddenly shy, she dropped her gaze as she fumbled with her clothes. She heard a splash. Eager to cool her heated flesh, she quickly stripped down to the maligned chastity belt and climbed into the water.

Arlan swam up to her. "Come, my lady, swim with me." She kicked off from the bottom and scudded through the water. Arlan followed her as she swam with clumsy strokes across the pool. The icy water cooled her heated skin, but did not ease her acute awareness of Arlan.

As she neared the other side, Arlan skimmed in front of her, then stood in her path. Unable to stop her forward momentum, she crashed into him.

His hands immediately steadied her, then pulled her close. She shivered, scared of how close they were and how much she wanted to be right there. With a soft sigh, she surrendered to her desire to touch him and slid her hands over his chest and up to his shoulders. She reveled in the smooth silkiness of his wet skin under her fingers and the fiery touch of her nipples against his taut muscle.

He stared deep into her eyes, as if analyzing the shadows flickering across the depths. He leaned forward.

She tensed when his face loomed close to hers, torn between desperately wanting him to kiss her and being trapped by duty. Acting on their desire would only increase the depth of the chemistry between them, and the pain that would follow.

Even with her unavailability, he made no effort to hide or deny his attraction.

She feared hurting him. Consumed by her own inner turmoil,

the whisper-soft kiss he dropped on her nose surprised her.

He released her, then flipped away in the water, reaching the other bank in a few easy strokes. Obviously aroused, he ignored his state as he climbed out of the pool and quickly dressed.

"Come, Princess, time to check the snares, eat, make plans, then get some rest. There is a storm is coming."

Warring thoughts bounced through Rosin's mind. She felt cheated because he hadn't kissed her, but ever so grateful he had not, especially given their obvious attraction. With a sedate paddle, she crossed the pool and climbed out.

She dried herself with the cloak before she got dressed, very conscious of Arlan watching her. A frown marred his face, and she suspected he still harbored anger about the chastity belt.

Heavy drops of rain already splattered the leaves and ground by the time they reached the shelter of the cave.

Arlan brought in all the weapons.

Rosin set about lighting the fire. The temperature had dropped considerably outside, but as the fire warmed the cave, Arlan took a couple of swigs of her painkilling potion and lay down on the makeshift bed.

He patted the cloak beside him. "Come, Princess, join me for a nap, I think I've overexerted myself."

Not bothering to debate the rights and wrongs, she lay down beside him, offering no resistance when he embraced her and covered them both with a cloak. He eased himself right against her back, then wrapped one arm over her and cupped her breast with his hand.

Rosin made no protest at his closeness even when he stroked her breast through her clothes and nuzzled the back of her neck, nibbling and kissing with tiny gentle movements.

The rain sounded loud, pelting down outside, but the cave

embraced them in a warm, semi-dark haven of safety tinged with desire. Rosin snuggled close to Arlan.

~ ~ ~

Arlan cuddled close. His body immediately reacted to her closeness. His member hardened and his balls ached. He pressed against her buttocks knowing full well she would feel his need. She made no attempt to move away. Arlan sighed and enjoyed the pleasant ache in his groin letting her scent waft over him. He closed his eyes and dreamed of making love to her.

Sometime later, his arm tightened its hold as he turned to her. "I know what you said, Princess, and I respect that, but you know this feels so right.

"Yes. Arlan, it does feel right, but it cannot be in the future, and the closer we get, the harder it's going to be when the time comes for us to part, and I am bonded to another man."

He hugged her close. The knowledge of what would be cut him deeply, but he had known this from the start. He couldn't help the feelings that had risen unbidden in his heart or the reaction his body had to her closeness and the inbuilt desire to protect her. "I understand, Rosin, but even you cannot deny what there is between us."

She stretched up and softly kissed his cheek. "I'm not denying anything, Arlan, just reiterating the reality of our situation."

"Then I will love you forever and hold you in my arms for as long as I'm allowed, but let you go when it has to be. I do respect your dedication to the throne of Keswin and understand the way it must be. Now, my lady, we must make some plans for moving on as I have improved a great deal in the last few moon-slides. You need to get to Tarlic Castle so we have a deadline to meet the tidal wash at the Sacred River?"

"Yes. We have about twenty more moon-slides before the glowing season tidal wash. I figure it will take four moon-slides to get to Cottam village, then an additional two moon-slides to cross the mountains through the pass. If we make good time, then one more moon-slide to the river itself. That leaves a few moon-slides in case we strike trouble or need to rest. I do not want you to overdo it and have a setback."

"I don't want a setback either. So, I think we should have this moon-wash and tomorrow moon-wash here, then leave the next moon-wash, as soon as it gets dark. I think we should only travel at moon-wash until we cross into Tarlic."

"Are you ready to travel, Arlan?"

"I'm much better, but we will rest when I need to. We'll also need to be cautious about being seen, as I'm in no fit state to fight. It will be better if we can procure a couple of horses."

"Maybe in Cottam Village, it's just inside Tarlic's border."

He needed to move to do something physical to dampen his desire to make love to her. Another defensive skill would be useful.

"Right. Now, in the meantime, my lady, enough of this lying around like the Princess you used to be. I have more lessons for you."

"But it's pouring outside."

"Up you get, Ma'am. I'm going to teach you how to throw a dagger. To kill."

"Really?" Excitement flared. "I've always admired knife-throwing skills in the warriors of Keswin, but I wasn't allowed to learn. "Is it hard to learn?"

"Well, get ye up and you'll find out." He instinctively lightly smacked her thigh, just below the belt.

She rolled away from him, then climbed to her feet. "Now who's lying down on the job, and after you've taken such liberties with my person?"

"And very nice it felt to smack, too." With a light laugh, he climbed to his feet. "You're not offended, Rosin?"

She grinned and shook her head.

"Then come, Princess, to work."

He retrieved his own daggers from his black saddle bags and drew a line in the sand. She watched him as he set up a couple of shabby saddle bags as the target. "Okay let us begin."

From the moment the lesson started, he set exacting standards. Time after time, Rosin threw the dagger, adjusted her grip, smoothed the path of her arm, then set her eyes square at the target, but she didn't seem to get any better. The more she concentrated, the less she achieved. "Its so frustrating Arlan and my arm aches."

"Take a moment, get a drink then we'll try again."

She returned to stand beside him and took the proffered dagger.

"Again, my lady. Think it through, slowly, one step at a time." Arlan walked it through with her.

This time, the dagger flicked free of her fingers and flew straight and true. Thwack. It became embedded dead center in the target.

"Yes! You did it, my love." He grabbed her, pulled her into a bear hug, and planted a hard, smacking kiss on her mouth. "You did it."

She gazed up, stunned by the flood of sensations that ripped through her. The dagger success, the hug, the kiss. The force of her emotions silenced her voice.

His eyes shone as his face moved closer. This time he took firm control of her mouth, thoroughly exploring the willing softness she offered.

The taste of her intoxicated his senses.

Willingly, she answered with the response his mouth demanded.

He closed the gap between their bodies with the slightest of movements. His hands cradled her face, and he drank deeply of her love.

The world receded, leaving only them and the emotions generated by their mutual attraction. Nothing else mattered but the feel of their hearts beating in unison, the warmth of their melded bodies, the heat of their passion, and their desire to be joined.

Arlan released her mouth, then lifted his head. "My love, my love." Desire and sadness deepened the huskiness of his voice and he cursed the emotions burning through him.

Tears welled in her eyes. "Oh, Arlan, I'm hurting you so... I never meant to."

Tenderness rushed over him. He didn't want her feeling guilty. It was mutual. "Shh, my love, let us just enjoy what we have for as long as we can. We'll deal with what comes after when we have to."

She rested her head against his chest and wrapped her arms around him. "I wish it could be different."

"You never led me to believe otherwise, my lady. My eyes are wide open and..." He chuckled as he put her from him. "My stomach is mighty empty. Shall we roast that hare you shot with your arrow earlier, then go to bed early?"

~ ~ ~

For the next two moon-slides, Arlan became her taskmaster. He demanded she work on both her dagger throwing and her sword wielding. He even became her opponent, meeting her thrusts, then showing her how to dodge them in return, to parry and deliver lunges of her own. He paid particular attention to her footwork and demanded she hold her opponent's gaze. He made a competent opponent for her, but he would not be much of a match for the full onslaught of a warrior.

Finally, she started to feel comfortable with both weapons, pleased with the thought she would be able to at least fight off an attack to some extent.

She showed Arlan her skills with the bow hitting her target every time.

"You are very skilled with that weapon. Not many use archery but it definitely has its uses and advantages. Can you show me the rudiments? I'm not sure how I'll go with my shoulder weak like it is but archery would be a useful skill so I could attack from a distance.

Rosin retrieved her arrows from the tree trunk she was using for a target.

Arlan watched with interest as she explained how to nock the arrow in the bowstring and how to aim for the target. She let the arrow loose then handed him the bow.

He carefully nocked the arrow then lifted his arm. Rosin went around and pushed his elbow a little higher and squarer to the bow. She reached out and adjusted his fingers on either side of the arrow and got him to demonstrate how to let the arrow loose before she allowed him to pull back on the string.

He grinned at she instructed him but followed her instructions to the letter. "Make sure you keep your stance wide, your elbow rotated thus. She adjusted his elbow position. And once you find a comfortable position always try to keep it the same with each shot."

He sighted the target and let the arrow loose. It hit the trunk to the right side.

"Not bad for a first shot. Try again. Just make sure you line up the arrow from back to front. Stay relaxed and hold you form until the arrow hits the target."

Arlan took another arrow from the quiver and nocked the arrow. He took his time aiming carefully.

Rosin watched him as he concentrated. His arm was steady as he slowly and smoothly released the arrow. It flew but missed the tree trunk completely.

"Viper's pit. This is harder than I expected."

Rosin grinned. "It's not just for pampered princesses."

He smiled back down at her. "Definitely not."

She helped him correct his stance. As she touched his leg, he became still. She looked up at him.

He grinned. "You make it hard for a man, my beautiful princess."

Rosin removed her hands and straightened. "Sorry."

His grin widened. "Don't be. I enjoy you touching me."

She blushed and guilt rushed over her at the thought she was teasing him when she was not willing.

"Don't be embarrassed, Rosin, we are both aware of what is between us even if we can't act on it. I will never take advantage of that."

She smiled and stepped around the other side and helped him move his elbow into the correct place. "Now remember keep your draw and the release smooth and slow. Hold your stance right through."

He drew back and released. The arrow hit the tree trunk dead center.

"Yes. That's great, Arlan."

He smiled, dropped the bow and cupped her face in his hands. He leant in and kissed her softly on the lips. "Thank you for teaching me. All I need is some practice. I might get to enjoy using the bow but will probably always prefer my sword and a dagger or two. I seem to be most familiar with them and I suspect that is what I have been trained to use."

"It must be hard for you, Arlan. Not remembering anything of your past."

He nodded. "It's very frustrating. I lie awake in the moon-wash trying to remember but nothing comes. Maybe I'll never remember."

She kissed him lightly on the mouth. "Maybe we can find out something about your past when we reach Tarlic Castle. If you want to?"

He shrugged. "Maybe."

~ ~ ~

On their last afternoon, she climbed the hill to check out the valley. All appeared still. On the way back to the cave, she gathered some more painkilling herbs, although both of them seemed to have improved beyond the need of a pain-numbing potion.

When she arrived back at the cave, Arlan had already made two bundles. He'd fashioned loops from strips of cloth so the packs could be carried over their shoulders. Two leather pouches bulged with unknown contents and four metal canteens she had stolen from the dead sat by the bags, ready to be filled with fresh water from the stream.

He had lit the fire and put a couple of fish on to cook. "I thought we should cook some food to take with us. We'll leave as soon as it's dark and go as far as I can before we find somewhere to bed down. I expect to get stronger each moon-slide. As long as I don't overdo it, the walking should be good for me, to build up my strength and stamina."

Chapter 10

As they entered the open meadow Arlan took her hand and they walked side by side through the long grass that rustled in the wind. The shadows from the moons were disjointed and fractured making navigating the ground precarious. He felt strong although his head and chest still hurt when he moved suddenly or too much.

He was glad to be on the move for too much time alone with Rosin with nothing much to occupy him allowed him to focus on how he felt about her. Vipers spit it was going to be gut wrenching when she took another man to her bed. He wondered what he would do when that happened. Would he be able to stay in proximity and maintain that distance? He wasn't sure he could.

By the time the moons topped their crescent and slid down the other side, his energy was flagging. His steps slowed.

"Arlan, are you getting weary?"

"Yes, Rosin, besides its getting too dark to walk safely. We need to find somewhere to hole up for the moon-slide. Keep and eye out for some boulders or vegetation."

They walked down into a gully. It had a stone strewn bottom that led to some boulders.

"I think this will do. Come, let's get settled before its completely dark." He helped her weave through the boulders until they found an almost enclosed space surrounded by thick vegetation.

Arlan dropped his pack and helped Rosin with hers. He pulled out a blanket and lay it on the ground. "Get settled as comfortably as you can. We will be here for quite a while."

She grinned up at him. "I'll be comfortable as long as I'm laying with you, Arlan."

He smiled but underneath a pent up need to love this woman undulated through him. He squashed it down. That was never an option.

He went and relieved himself frustrated that his member was semi hard from just being near her. *Viper's curse how am I going to get through this and over this.* He relaced his breeches loosely knowing full well what was going to happen when he lay beside her.

She smiled up at him as he lowered himself to the ground.

He groaned as pain shot through his shoulder and chest.

"Arlan, are you hurting?"

"A bit. Do you have some of your potion? Just enough to take the edge off the pain so I can sleep but not enough to knock me out. I need to be alert to some extent in case we're disturbed.

She handed over the bottle. "Just take one mouthful."

He did and handed the bottle back and lay down behind her. He shuffled closer and pulled two blankets over them. He rested his head on his arm laying still and letting his body's needs wash over him and subside.

Rosin's breathing eased, and he knew she slept. His whole body ached, but the edge was gone. He closed his eyes, but sleep eluded him. He delved deep into his mind seeking those intangible memories. He rubbed his hands down his breeches feeling the callouses. He knew he was probably descended from the Maiden Arawen if he was part of the High Queen Isolde's Commissioned Warriors. The callouses told him he was probably a long term warrior which meant he probably wasn't an officer or a royal as they tended to move upwards quickly. He stilled. He had read the names on Rosin's map drawn in the sand. *Moondust and Maidens, I'm literate.*

He clenched his arm more firmly around Rosin's waist then tucked his hand under her breast. He sighed trying to relax. He delved again. Surely, he had something there: his childhood, a romance, a bad battle, his parents, his age. Anything. The blankness of his mind mocked him. He sighed again.

"Arlan, are you in pain again?"

He squeezed her tighter. "Not physical pain, Rosin, mental. Sorry I disturbed you."

She snuggled down. Arlan lay still with his eyes closed and finally he slipped into a light sleep.

The moment she moved he woke. "Rosin?"

"I need to relieve myself, Arlan."

He chuckled. "Me too. It's just light better go now."

She scrambled to her feet and held out her hand. Arlan ached all over and allowed her to help him stand. He swayed slightly.

Rosin grabbed his arm her expression full of concern. "Are you in pain?"

Arlan shook his head. "I'm just tired." He didn't want her worrying about him. Frustration at his lack of strength and stamina irked him. He glanced around but nothing other than some birds and the grass moved. "Go, Rosin just behind the rocks. I'll keep watch." He rested his hand on the nearest boulder as he indicated she should go.

She slowly walked away from him but glanced over her shoulder before she disappeared behind the boulder.

He glanced out over the grassland and peered up into the sky looking for signs of company. He inhaled and exhaled deeply trying to relax his body.

A rustle of grass and she was beside him.

"Go, Arlan. I'll keep watch."

He smiled down at her before he slid his finger over her cheek. He turned away.

On his return they sat together and Arlan opened up his pack. He handed Rosin some cold fish. He took a piece for himself. It was nice enough cold and silenced his grumbling gut.

The warmth from where her thigh touched his flowed through him. He reached down and pulled out a water carrier. He handed it to her.

Her fingers touched his sending a buzz through his arm.

She glanced up at him then brought her other hand up to cover his. "I'm sorry, Arlan."

He shook his head. "Do not be sorry, Rosin. Now snuggle down and sleep."

With another small dose of potion he drifted into a deep sleep and didn't wake until Rosin kissed him lightly on the cheek. "The light is fading, Arlan."

He groaned and pushed himself into a sitting position. "Time to get moving." He felt better the pain at a dull ache.

She stood and held out her hands.

He took them letting her ease him up. He picked up his bag and hung it on his shoulders.

Rosin did the same and then added her bow over the top allowing easy access.

He took her hand, and they set out.

The ground was flat and boggy in places. He guided them around what they could but the one that lay in front of them now was huge. He couldn't see how far it spread in the dark.

He looked down at her. "Looks like we are going to get wet feet."

She grinned up at him. "More than our feet I think."

"Perhaps we should follow it awhile for a more suitable place to cross."

Rosin shook her head. "I seem to remember going through a wide bog when we came to visit Tarlic. On horseback it wasn't a problem. I think this area drains into some marsh land on the other side. Father said the bog runs right along until it spills into the twin rivers that run passed Keswin Castle."

Arlan sighed. They had no change of clothes, and he didn't fancy traipsing around the country covered in smelly bog mud or laying all through the moon-slide in wet clothes.

He leaned close to Rosin and grinned. "I suggest we strip and place our clothes on our shoulders then wade through the bog. We will have to take our chances of finding some fresh water on the other side to wash it off.

Rosin giggled as she glanced around. "Well, it's dark and we are all alone. At least we will have clean clothes on the other side."

"Are you sure?"

She giggled harder. "Its not like we haven't seen each other before, Arlan."

"True, my beautiful Princess." He wasn't averse to seeing her 'almost naked' again although anger flared when he saw the chastity belt. He stripped his clothes off and stuffed them in his pack. This he put it on his head. "Follow right behind me, Rosin. Make sure you have your balance before you take each step and point your toes as you step as it makes it easier to pull your foot back out."

He stepped through the grass bunched on the edge and immediately sank up to his waist. He clenched his manhood and pulled in his stomach as the cold water hit his skin. "It's cold, Rosin."

She stepped forward and squealed as she sank up to her breasts.

He took two steps and paused glancing over his shoulder as he watched her take three steps to reach him. Once he was sure she was balanced, he stepped off again. The weight of the mud dragged on his legs. The constant ache in his shoulder turned into a sharp throbbing pain from his arm being held upright. He struggled to keep his arm up. He turned and watched her take three dragging steps. "You managing, Rosin?"

"Yes, Arlan. What about you?"

"I'm okay."

He waded another two steps.

Rosin came up behind him. "It's getting deeper, Arlan."

"And thicker." He waded again. His foot stuck. He tugged, but it refused to release. "Viper's spit I'm stuck."

Rosin came up behind him. "What can I do to help?"

Arlan turned and handed her his pack. "Hold this for me." He groaned and let his arm drop. He leaned forward and tugged. He leaned further forward and tugged again. He fell forward and landed splat in the mud the dark water closing over his head. He scrabbled to surface by pushing up and gasping for air. The mud sucked at his body. "Viper's curse I can't get out or up." He groaned as pain radiated through his body banishing the numbness of the cold.

"Stay still, Arlan."

He glanced at her. She carefully laid the packs on a mound of short green vegetation and stepped closer to him. She grabbed him around the waist and hauled. He pushed with his hands. She lost her hold. He fell forward. She grabbed him again and pulled. This time they both flopped into the mud. They lay side by side in the mire. Rosin giggled as she took his hand. He entwined his fingers with hers and squeezed.

"Nice as this is, my beautiful Princess, we need to get out of here before we freeze to death."

She pushed up until she was on her knees. Arlan did the same. They clutched each other and pushed upright. Their hands slipping and sliding off muddy skin.

They were both panting.

Rosin couldn't quite suppress her giggles.

Arlan leaned forward and slid his hands around her and pulled her to him. She pressed against his chest and wrapped her arms around him. They stood there together as he kissed the top of her head. "Maidens curses, Rosin. You're a special woman."

She looked up at him mud smearing her face and covering her breasts.

"Lunar dust I so want to touch you, mud and all." He reached up and slid his hand down over her breast wiping the mud off and revealing her erect nipples to his touch. He ran his thumb over the nipple. Rosin moaned softly. He slipped his arms around her waist and lifted her. Her body came free, and she eased her feet out of the mud.

She grabbed his hands, and he leaned forward and wriggled until he felt the mud give. He hauled himself up again and finally he stood in front of her.

She giggled. "Oh, Arlan what have we come to, the two of us. A dispossessed princess and an unknown warrior stark naked in a bog covered in stinky mud in the middle of nowhere?" Her voice cracked then tears tumbled down her cheeks.

He reached out and wiped the tears away leaving more muddy smears on her face. "We have each other, Rosin, and we will overcome this." He embraced her in a short hard hug then turned and scooped up the packs. The rain began to fall.

"Come, my princess, we need to get out of here. They wrapped arms around each other and side by side they dragged their way through the bog. The ground eventually became firmer. Then hard and grass sprouted in tighter and tighter clumps. Once more on hard ground the rain poured down washing away the layer of mud. Arlan sluiced the water off his body. The sky was beginning to lighten. Sun-show wasn't far away.

"Come, Rosin, we need to find somewhere warm and dry to sleep. They walked wet and naked hand in hand. The rain tumbled down washing the mud from their bodies. Just on sun-show they found a huge tree with the trunk hollowed out. They stepped inside. Arlan poked and scratched around in the leaf litter until he was sure the space was free of vipers and spiders. He handed his underwear over and Rosin dried herself.

He watched her wipe the feminine curves of her body, her breasts and legs. His manhood ached.

"I'm going to relieve myself, Rosin, just behind that boulder. He couldn't stay and watch her wipe herself intimately under that filthy chastity belt. Anger surged through him. He wanted to rip it off. He wanted to be the one to wipe her intimately. He spun on his heel and strode away.

He found a spot, he leaned against the trunk and breathed deeply. But he couldn't shut out the vision of her wiping herself. His manhood hardened. He shook his head. *Oh viper's I want that woman. To hold her to love her to bury myself in her.* He wrapped his hand around his shaft and stroked hard and fast. There was no gentle enjoyment of pleasuring himself. All he wanted was his release. Relief from the constant ache. He closed his eyes and let himself imagine. It didn't take long. His manhood throbbed and his release surged over him. He sagged against the trunk breathing hard. Fatigue washed over him. His knees almost buckled. He inhaled deeply then pushed away from the tree and walked slowly back to Rosin. He shivered and ran his hands over his arms the skin was covered in goose bumps. He gave his body a cursory wipe and pulled on his breeches, shirt and jacket.

Rosin had already laid a blanket on the ground in the back corner of the hollow. She sat and opened the pack. She held out her hand and drew him down to her.

He carefully lowered himself to the ground.

"You're hurting, Arlan?"

He nodded.

She handed over the bottle of potion. He took a sip.

"Have some more, Arlan, you need to sleep without pain."

He shook his head. "I need to be able to protect you, my princess."

"No one will see us in here, Arlan. If you don't rest, you will not be able to protect me. It is my turn to keep watch."

He smiled and took another deep gulp of the potion. He felt like he was shirking his duty, but the pain was almost unbearable, and he was exhausted from climbing through the bog and the usual fatigue of his sexual release tugged at him.

Rosin leaned back against the inside of the trunk and stretched her legs out. She patted her lap. "Rest, Arlan."

He didn't have the strength to argue and laid his head on her lap.

He felt her draw the other blankets over them. He sighed deeply as the potion took effect.

~ ~ ~

She sat there with Arlan's head on her lap. He slept almost immediately. She pushed his dark golden locks from his face where it had come loose from his thong. She studied his face. From this side the scar was barely visible. She stoked his cheek. He murmured in his sleep. She tucked her hands under the blanket and closed her eyes reveling in the warmth that radiated from him. Her heart ached with the knowledge that she could never have this man as her own.

She slept and woke. It was light outside. The rain still fell in a grey sparkling curtain. She was glad to be warm and dry. She slept again then started awake. It was still raining. She listened intently for what had woken her.

Sleep eluded her now. She studied Arlan. She wondered about him. She was so drawn to him. She had seen him naked and aroused but he hadn't tried to force anything between them. She had never felt afraid when he held her or been naked in front of him. His manhood was bigger than Devon and a tinge of fear clouded her mind. Would it hurt with Arlan? Would it hurt with whoever she had to take as a consort? She knew loving between a man and a woman was supposed to be pleasurable. But hers would not be loving just a means to an end; the making of an heir. She shuddered at what the future held for her. If the Maidens were with her, the man she accepted as consort would be gentle and kind. She eased her position and rested her hand on her stomach. She feared that a babe grew inside her. One that could not live. She fretted over what she needed to do and how she was going to get it done. By the time they reached Tarlic Castle it would be too late and there would be others that might prevent her doing what must be done. A sullen darkness washed over her. She sighed and eased her position again. Her bum was numb, and the rough surface of the eroded wood dug into her back.

Arlan barely stirred.

Loneliness washed over her. She had come to rely on Arlan's company and support. She sipped some water and closed her eyes. Finally drifting into a troubled sleep half her mind alert for danger.

Just on the fading Arlan stirred. He lifted his head and yawned. "Rosin are you alright?" He took her hand in his as he pushed into a sitting position. He dragged his hair back and retied the thong. He rubbed his hand over his face and grimaced. "Maidens, I need a shave."

Rosin smiled. "You're so unlike Maidens' men, Arlan. They all love their moustaches."

Arlan frowned. "I can grow one if you would like. It might cover the scar a bit."

She touched his face. "No, Arlan, I really like you clean shaven."

Arlan shrugged. "I have no idea why, but I don't like hair on my face. Anyway, enough of my appearance. It's getting late. I think we need to get some fresh food. No time to set snares. What about your bow and arrows? I'm sure you could hit a hare or two."

She pushed up and took up her bow and slipped her quiver on her shoulder. "Come on, my First Knight of Keswin, lets go get dinner."

He pushed up and took her hand.

They walked together through the trees.

On the edge of the clearing Arlan squeezed her hand and pointed. There were several hares hopping in the clearing.

She pulled out her arrow, nocked it in place and aimed carefully. The first hare squealed and fell writhing and kicking. The others scattered. She went to retrieve her kill but Arlan stayed her movement.

He leaned down. "Wait, we need more than one."

They stood side by side unmoving. Only Arlan's thumb stroked across her hand sending warm sensations swirling through her.

The hares returned. She raised her bow already loaded and killed another one. It fell in silence barely disturbing the others.

Rosin handed her bow to Arlan and held out an arrow.

He frowned and shook his head.

She mouthed yes.

He took the bow and with a serious expression nocked the arrow. She turned and adjusted his elbow slightly and checked his fingers were positioned right. Then she nodded.

Arlan relaxed and took his time picking his target. She watched him her heart somersaulting.

He released the arrow and stood still watching his arrow fly. It felled the hare.

"Yes, Arlan you did it." She latched onto his arm bouncing up and down.

He grinned, dropped the bow and swept her into his embrace crushing her against his chest. "So, I pass?"

Firey emotions soared through her. "Of course you do, Arlan."

He let her go. "Let's get these cooked so we can move on by dark."

Chapter 11

As the sky started to lighten on the third moon-slide, they climbed steadily up a steep, lightly wooded slope. Arlan stopped periodically to catch his breath and to survey the landscape for danger. They needed somewhere concealed to rest up for the moon-slide, and he had left it much later than on the previous moon-slides to start searching because they'd hoped to reach Cottam Village by sun-show.

As they reached the crest of the hill, they lay down to study the vista below. They could see a huddle of cottages in the deep shadow of the mountains. Most appeared deserted. The only sign of life slim plumes of smoke curling lazily up into the sky from some of the chimneys.

Rosin pointed into the valley. "That's Cottam. We're in Tarlic." They had made excellent progress. "I think we're far enough into Tarlic to approach the villagers and be safe from Devon."

Arlan glanced from the village to her, then back again. "So, who's going into town? Me, with my ravaged face, or you, with your identity to hide? Do you feel secure enough to go into the village as Princess Rosin?"

Rosin shook her head. "I don't want to reveal who I am, because I can't trust anyone. I'll need a disguise."

"Any suggestions?"

"Stay here." She jumped up and retraced her steps.

Less than five minutes earlier, she had smelt the scent of the cardemony bush. Women used the plant to dye cloth in dark brown, gray, and black, so she assumed it would make up a crude dye with some vinegar to color her hair and make her skin a deeper color.

As for Arlan, perhaps he should just wear a cloak low down over his face and pretend to be a Moon Laurate.

Arlan nodded when she explained what she planned to do.

Rosin held out her dagger. "Can you trim my hair shorter, and tidy it up a bit, before I color it, please?"

She sat with her back to him, her legs crossed awkwardly to accommodate the restrictions of the chastity belt. Warmth emanated from his body, and she could feel his breath on her neck as he leaned forward to slice her hair gently.

At times, he stroked her scalp, and she relaxed under his ministrations, wallowing in the glowing heat simmering quietly at her inner core. When his skin came into contact with hers, she shivered, just a little, as sexual sensations whispered over her body. The desire to lean against his chest beset her as she shut her eyes and soaked up the exquisite tenderness of his touch.

The dagger clattered as he dropped it, but he didn't move away. His hands rested on her shoulders, and he gently massaged and caressed her through her shirt.

"Mmm, that's so nice, Arlan."

His breathing changed tempo, becoming faster and uneven. His warm breath skimmed the back of her neck, quickly followed a whisper of a kiss. He slipped his arm around her waist and brought her gently against him.

She relaxed and enjoyed his embrace and the sensual nuzzling of his mouth on her neck until she could bear it no longer. She eased away with a deep sigh, tears welling up. "We need to get going, Arlan."

He moved slightly, creating a chill gap between them.

She sensed his sadness as she reached for her dye mixture. With one hand, she rubbed it sparingly into her short, spiky hair. Her pale blond became dark brown. With her male clothes and ill-fitting shoes, she could perhaps pass for a boy at first glance. She couldn't bind her breasts any tighter because they were swollen and tender. She guessed, after all her hopes for it not to be the case, she indeed carried a child.

By the time she finished, Arlan had darkened his hair to black, donned a cloak and tugged it down to cover the worst of his scarred face. He had also applied a little of the dye to his face to further disguise the scars. He had become an intimidating character, not at all like her Arlan.

No one came out to meet them as, side by side, they entered the eerily quiet village. No children played in the streets. No animals wandered freely on the verges. All the cottage doors were shut, and the curtains drawn or the shutters pulled tightly closed.

Unease shivered through her. What had happened here to change the open, carefree village with the hospitable welcome to weary travelers she had experienced before? They hurried down the narrow street until they came to a blacksmith working in his forge.

He furtively glanced over his shoulder, then without a word, turned back to his work.

Arlan tapped him on the shoulder. "Sir, we could do with your help."

The man sidled away from Arlan's touch and shook his head. "I'm busy."

"We need to buy a horse or two. Would anyone here have one for sale?"

"No. Nobody here has a horse. We're just poor farmer folk, loyal to our King." He didn't lift his gaze from his work.

"Surely someone would have an animal they can spare?"

The smithy looked Arlan square in the face. "I said, no one here has an animal. Be on your way."

The lack of hospitality, or even civility, shocked Rosin. The expectation in Maiden Creed demanded hospitality be offered as best as could be afforded. Offered, even before the purpose of the travelers' presence had been revealed. This village, despite its deserted appearance, seemed to be reasonably prosperous, and the unexpected attitude reflected badly on the inhabitants.

"Who is your king?" She knew the answer, but she wanted to provoke the man in some way.

The smithy stared, long and hard, straight into her eyes, as if trying to convey a message or a warning.

"King Cadmar of Tarlic. We're loyal subjects even if we don't see him much out here in the borderlands. If another, stronger chieftain decided to become master of the village, there would be naught we could do to stop it. Now, on your way, *laddie,* and take your dark-faced friend with you. Ain't nothing here for the likes of you." The obvious, unnecessary growled insult reflected his determination to get rid of them. The stark shadow of fear filled his eyes.

In that moment, Rosin knew Devon had visited the village. She met Arlan's look, then nodded. They could not ask for help from these innocent folks and put them at risk.

All the way through the village, past the vegetable gardens, the well, and the cow paddocks, Rosin could feel the heat of the smithy's stare.

He wanted them gone and expected his hostile reception would be enough to put them off ever returning.

At the last cottage, Rosin noticed a small, colorful talisman hanging on a tree indicating a healing woman lived in that cottage.

Rosin decided immediately she had to return, regardless of the smithy's refusal to help them or the reasons behind it.

As they walked in silence, Rosin puzzled over her need to return without Arlan. Anxiety tingled in her gut. Not just at the perceived danger in the village, but what Arlan's reaction would be to her secretive mission.

When the ground started to rise again, they stopped and rested in the dubious shelter of some scrawny, leafless mountain oaks. A cold wind whipped down from the mountains, but the sun still burned in the clear sky.

They had made good time, but the signs in the landscape filled her with dread. The first snow would fall soon, signaling the beginning of the frost, and before that she had to be at the river for the tidal wash.

Surely by now news of the brutal massacre had reached Tarlic. She must reach the castle soon, or Keswin would be shattered by Devon or taken over by the High Queen. She had come too far and given up too much to have that happen.

Arlan couldn't settle. He climbed to his feet and paced back and forth a few feet from her. "Something's just not right down there. The smithy seemed very keen to move us on. Do you think this Devon has been around?"

"Arlan, I know Devon has been in Cottam. There would be no other reason for them to treat us as they did. I would have thought even he would not be foolish enough to mess with King Cadmar, especially after the massacre."

"I'm tempted to go back to the village and check it out." Rosin rose to stand beside him. "Do you think that's wise? You're not in any condition to fight." She didn't want Arlan prowling about while she needed to get the potion.

He shrugged. "You're probably right, and I didn't see any animals around, so maybe he told us the truth. Besides, I've got a bit of a sore head this moon-wash. Perhaps some medicine and a good moon-wash's rest are in order before we tackle the mountains."

She laughed lightly. "Very wise, my First Knight. Now take this and rest."

"Your wish is my command, Princess." He swallowed the liquid, then lay down again. He patted the blanket. "Come, Princess, lie by me and we shall both keep warm. Besides, holding you in my arms for just a little can do no harm, and it gives me great pleasure. He patted the blanket again.

Tears already wet her cheeks as she lowered herself beside him.

"Do not cry, Princess, for now we have each other, and a friendship that will last forever. I will not cross that line unless you demand it, and who knows what the future will hold?" Her tears continued to flow.

Arlan held her close and murmured reassurances between stroking her face and shoulders and placing whisper-light kisses on her cheeks and neck.

She turned to him and offered her mouth, which he immediately claimed with a firm, exploring caress. His taste so sweet and addictive. He increased the pressure and demanded access to the moist interior. She responded. Both took long intoxicating drinks of the other. As they drew apart, they stared deep into each other's eyes. Sexual tension and an unnamed emotion swirled between them.

"Sleep, my Princess, for tomorrow is another moon-slide and we have an arduous journey ahead."

When the remedy took hold, he stilled, his arm lying over her waist.

Only then did Rosin roll away from him and cautiously stand

up. She paused by the line of bushes nearby in case he woke and missed her.

He did not stir.

Rosin walked softly for a short distance. Once well away, she turned and hurried down across the valley. She gave thanks to Rianon that the witch lived on the mountainside of the village, and she didn't have to risk going right into the cluster of homes. Danger lurked in the hamlet. A danger the smithy had warned her of, with his cryptic comments, and lack of the much-prized hospitality. The smithy's sullen attitude, so out of character, seemed to be driven by fear, not malice.

Her desperate need for the potion outweighed the suspected dangers in the village. The potion was now her only option other than to kill the child immediately after birth.

Rosin almost tiptoed down the side of the road. She glanced around, feeling vulnerable and exposed. Jumping at shadows and rustling bushes moved by the breeze, she fervently wished she had risked Arlan's disapproval just to have him accompany her. Even though her eyes had adjusted to the darkness, she had walked two steps past before she spied the witch's talisman on the white picket fence.

Down a short footpath, she came to the cottage where a weak light glowed from behind the drawn curtains. It appeared to be the only light in the village, and the darkness made her even more nervous and jumpy.

When the gate screeched, Rosin flinched, her heart fluttered, and her skin tingled in panic. She stood in front of the door, her knees trembling as she lightly tapped. Her breath came in jerky huffs. She could barely swallow past the dryness of her mouth. Impatient for a response, she tapped again, louder this time.

Footsteps tapped from inside the cottage. The door creaked

open, just a crack, and a youngish woman with long black plaits peeped out.

When she saw Rosin, she opened the door wider, then peered up and down the street. "Enter. I knew you would come."

Assailed with a strong urge to run, a greater fear of the dark street had her entering the home. Inside the house, everything seemed normal. A meal bubbled on the stove and the table had been set for two.

"Welcome, Princess." The woman rested a well-manicured hand on Rosin's arm.

At the use of her title, Rosin froze mid-step, her hand raised to smack the woman's hand away. She snatched her arm away and turned to flee.

The woman caught her other arm. "Do not be afraid Princess, I will help you."

Rosin stared at her.

Compassion filled the other woman's eyes, and a serene smile curved her mouth.

Rosin resisted the desire to pull free from the woman's hold. "How do you know me?"

The woman smiled. "I saw your coming, many moon-cycles ago."

"Do you know why I'm here?"

"Come, let me shut the door. Things are not good in the village. No one must know you have been here. Sit, let us talk. I have food ready."

Calmed by the woman's gesture of kindness and her serenity, Rosin walked to the table and sat as if held by a trance.

The woman talked as she dished up the food. "I am Nevanthi, a healing woman, taught by my mother and grandmother. They say my family is descended from the Water Spirit, Koloria. Because

I am so obviously of mixed blood, not everyone would make me welcome, but here, they accept me as I am. They are kind to me and pay for healing and love potions."

The smell of the hot stew made Rosin's mouth water, and she struggled not to snatch up the spoon and start shoveling.

Instead, she sat quietly, not quite relaxed, watching Nevanthi as she broke a fresh loaf into chunks.

The woman's olive complexion, high cheekbones, and almond-shaped eyes all contributed to her exotic beauty and the rich aura of expectation around her. Her eyes were like none Rosin had ever seen before — lavender with a navy border around the iris — piercing, but full of shadows and lights. They were heavily made up with purple and black powder that accented the unique color and the long, dark lashes. Her hands were fine and long fingered with shapely nails, also colored purple. Around her wrists, gold bracelets jangled each time she moved. Her long tidy plaits decorated along their length with beads swayed as she walked.

Nevanthi handed Rosin a large chunk of bread. "Eat, Princess, there is plenty and I will give you some to take to your companion when you leave."

A tranquil, comfortable silence blanketed the room. The only the sounds, the crackling fire and food being consumed with enthusiasm, disturbed the quiet.

The warmth flowed down her throat and spread through her body. The food tasted delicious, the meat tender and aromatic. Rosin scraped the bottom of the bowl, then picked up the last crumbs of bread. When she finally put her spoon down and lifted her head, she found Nevanthi watching her closely.

"There is not much time, Princess. You must go from here. You have come for the woman's potion?"

Heat flared in her face and the lump of fear and shame resting dormant in her lower torso suddenly fermented and started to rise. It disturbed Rosin to reveal her predicament, for a Princess of the Maidens had a reputation to preserve. But then again, considering the circumstances, what did it matter?

In her own mind, Rosin had expected an old hag-like woman with rotting teeth and an evil disposition to dispense such concoctions. It would have been easier to ask such a woman for her potion. Nevanthi, barely older than Rosin, seemed too beautiful, gentle, and normal to be a witch.

"Yes, Nevanthi, I have come to get a potion to make me lose the child I'm carrying. The child of Lord Devon conceived through rape." Already just a whisper. Her voice cracked and her face flushed even hotter as she voiced her shame.

"Oh, Princess, what he's done to you is inexcusable and you are right in this action. The child you carry must never take a first breath. Even so, Devon is determined to have you and the child you could bear. He hungers for the throne of Keswin and has no regard for whom he hurts in his pursuit of it. He has even sent soldiers here, so far into Tarlic."

Rosin gasped. She covered her mouth with both hands as she rose out of her seat. "I guessed as much. He dares much, this Interloper. I should go before I bring harm down to the villagers."

"Sit, Princess, you are safe with me. They left two soldiers here to wait in case you came by. This is why you must not be seen. The villagers will not help you. They have good reason, but I do not. You wish to abort the child you carry? Do you know this can kill you or stop you from having another child? It's always risky."

Every nerve end sizzled with fear. "Please, just give it to me, Nevanthi. I understand the risks. I must leave here quickly. I cannot be found by those soldiers, and this child cannot be born. I cannot let an Interloper's spawn rule my country."

"Wait here, Princess, and I will get you what you ask for. I have it made up, for it's not such an uncommon request."

"Oh."

Nevanthi nodded as she bent over the dresser in the corner of the room. "There is no shame for you to carry, Princess." She handed over the package.

There would be shame soon enough. Once she reached Tarlic Castle, everyone would know her shame.

Rosin took the neat package eagerly, but immediately felt repelled and had to fight the urge to fling it away. She extracted a gold coin from her pocket. "Is this enough payment, Nevanthi?"

The witch shook her head. "For you, Princess, payment is not required. Now, here is your food. You must go before you are found."

Nevanthi turned the lamp down before she went to the door. After she'd surveyed the street, she turned back to Rosin. "It appears all clear. Now go, hurry."

Rosin slipped through the open door as she pushed her precious package into the binding around her breasts. It lay there, cool and smooth. A trauma waiting to overtake her. Her eyes gradually adjusted to the darkness as she walked quickly up the lane, the container of food held tightly in her hand. She kept close to the mottled shadows of the bushes that lined the overgrown path, hoping no-one would see her.

The slightest sound crackled in the distance. She froze and waited with bated breath. All remained silent. She walked. Again, a whisper of sound. Someone stalked her. She hurried, as caresses of fear danced across her skin.

A heavy thud broke the silence. A large, muscular arm circled her neck. The sharp prick of a dagger stung in the middle of her back. The food slipped from her hands and spilt on the ground.

The fetid odor of foul breath and unwashed body swamped her. One of Devon's soldiers.

"Aha, the runaway bride. And where would you be off to, girlie? Not back to your long-suffering husband, of course. Bad girl. Perhaps I'll have to help you remember your wifely place. Now walk. Slowly."

He spun her around to face the village. With the insistent prick of the dagger in the small of her back, she had no choice but to step forward.

The weight of melancholy pressed against her chest as she wondered if the healing woman had betrayed her, or if dumb good luck allowed Devon's man to find her.

~ ~ ~

Arlan woke with a start. Something was different. Missing. He rolled over his heart thudding in his chest. "Rosin."

Her space in the blanket was empty. He paused. Maybe she had gone to relieve herself. He pushed into a sitting position. He could see right down into the valley by the light of the moons. He climbed to his feet. His stomach clenched. "Rosin."

He walked in a circle, but the area was deserted. He glared down at the village, guessing she had gone to see the healing woman. He suspected she was with child from the rape by Devon. He shuddered as thunderous anger surged through him. How dare a man treat a woman thus? Even though he didn't know who he was instinctively, he felt a need to be gentle, supportive and respectful to females. He cast back in his mind finding only emptiness. He snatched up his sword and with a brewing rage simmering he strode back down the hill.

Hurt wafted through him that she could not trust him

enough to ask for help. But then he debated with himself. There is considerable shame attached to her condition and what she obviously planned to do. He reminded himself they had only a short, if intense, acquaintanceship.

He entered the village looking for the talisman he had seen as they left. He had seen Rosin looking intently at it as they passed. He had expected her to ask to stop right then but when she hadn't he had stayed silent.

He spied it and opened the gate and strode up the path, knocking a hard rapid tattoo on the door.

He waited and knocked again.

The door opened. He started back at the sight of the woman who peered out at him. She was stunning in an exotic way.

"Excuse me but I am looking for a woman. Dressed in boy's clothes."

The woman frowned, glanced at his face then looked him up and down. "And who are you?"

Arlan scowled. "I am Arlan, First Knight of Keswin."

She smiled. "I am Nevanthi. The Princess has been and gone. She should have returned to you by now."

Fear rushed through him as he shook his head.

The woman opened the door wider. "Then she is in danger. Two of Devon's men are here in the village. They may have captured her."

Arlan heart clenched and his stomach somersaulted as anger exploded through him. "They will not have her. Where will I find them."

"They billeted themselves at the stables."

"We need to lure them out one by one. I am not fit enough to manage two at once."

"Wait here. I will get Shaw to help us." She hurried out the back door.

Arlan scoured the area in the light of the moons. The shadows were deep and fractured. He couldn't hear anything.

He jumped as Nevanthi touched his arm.

"Shaw says only one remains at the stables. They are a little worse for the drink but the big one has stumbled out to do a patrol."

Arlan unsheathed his sword.

Nevanthi leaned over and snatched up the bronze candle stick from the middle of the table. "Shaw is going to lure the second man out and down the street in a short while. If we go that way, I think we will find the princess."

"I do not know why she came alone."

Nevanthi touched his arm. "What she came for, Arlan, was deeply personal and not what men would approve of. The woman's potion."

"She wants to abort the child I think she is carrying. Conceived from rape by some monster called Devon. I would not disapprove, Nevanthi."

Again, the hurt washed over him that Rosin felt she could not ask for his help.

They walked steadily down the street. Nevanthi holding the metal candle holder across her chest. Arlan had his sword balanced in his hand.

He saw them. Two bulky shadows in the middle of the road. One of them was writhing and struggling. The bigger one laughed and made a ribald comment.

He heard footsteps and saw two shadowy figures walking toward them.

Viper's bite three of them. It was going to be a struggle but he would not let them take Rosin. He lurched forward Nevanthi right beside him.

~ ~ ~

Two sets of heavy footsteps hurried up the road toward them.

Her captor halted and stood breathing heavily.

Nevanthi had said the villagers would not help her, so she didn't expect to be rescued. Whatever their reasons, she couldn't really blame them. The villagers were simple, good-living people with families to protect. Devon would have threatened dire consequences for the whole village if they didn't cooperate.

Out of the darkness loomed another of Devon's men, followed by the glum faced blacksmith. A feeling of doom descended, and she gave no resistance when the one holding her tightened his grip.

"Bind her feet, Dai, stop the little lady from damaging me." A suggestive snigger rattled in her ear.

Rosin kicked out at the second man's face as he knelt to bind her ankles together. She wriggled, pushed, and shoved against the vise-like embrace her captor held her in.

"Go for it, girlie. Does a man's heart good to have a beauty like you thrashing against his balls."

Horrified at the implication, she stilled. By the time she'd gathered her thoughts enough to resume her resistance, Dai had her feet in a rough-handed grip.

He struggled with a thong to bind them.

She fought against his efforts. A flash of silver in the moonlight and a dull thud distracted her for a moment. A sideways wrench and the soldier's strangling grip loosened.

His dagger clattered to the ground.

She wrested free. Snatched her own blade out of her belt and brought it up over her head.

A little worse for the drink, Dai failed to react to his companion's crumple to the ground and still knelt, head down.

Rosin bore down with every ounce of strength she had. The knife shuddered when it hit clothes, but she pushed through the resistance, shoving the dagger easily past his ribs.

Dai grunted, then peered up, the surprise etched on his face almost comical.

Rosin hauled the dagger out of his flesh, then brought it down again, this time a little higher up his back.

The kneeling man continued to stare up, his face set in a mixture of agony and astonishment.

She lifted her foot, pressed it against his shoulder, and pushed.

He toppled over, his pain-filled gaze raked over her length as he fell backward onto the road.

She heard the rattle of metal behind her and spun round, bringing her dagger up. Confronted with Arlan, she brought her thrust to a stuttering halt in mid-air. He stood over the body of Devon's lackey, nonchalantly wiping his sword clean.

Nevanthi hovered beside him, the metal candlestick she had used for light during their meal clutched in both hands. It dripped blood.

"Arlan?"

He nodded. "Princess."

She couldn't really determine his expression in the dark pools of his eyes, but the clipped, sardonic tone to his voice meant she would be answering some questions before the moon-wash finished.

The smithy fell to his knees at her feet his closely shaved head bowed. "I am Shaw, please forgive me, Princess? Forgive us all. The soldiers had our children held hostage in the Baird's house. I did warn you off when you arrived earlier..."

Rosin smiled down at the contrite man and rested her hand on his broad brawny shoulder. "Stand, Smithy, stand. Of course, you had to put your children first, this I understand and if I," — she glanced over her shoulder at Arlan — "had not been so foolish as to return this moon-wash, all would have been untroubled."

"What can I do, Princess, to repay your generous spirit?"

Arlan shook his head. "Rise, man, nobody is asking recompense."

As the man rose, Rosin touched his hand. "There is something that you might be able to help us with."

His light blue eyes sparkled. "Anything, Princess, anything."

She took a deep breath and squashed the humiliation she felt at revealing her shame to this humble man. "I need this removed, please." She turned down the edge of her breeches and revealed the metal monstrosity that held her lower body in a cruel, chafing grip.

The blacksmith frowned rubbing his chin through the neat stubble of his beard. "The moon leech. May the Maidens send a terrible plight upon his black soul and those close to his icy heart. Come, Princess, I have many tools and I will fire up the forge if required. No matter what, I will free you from this atrocity."

She fought the instinct to hug the man and tempered her response with a dose of queenly decorum. "Thank you, Shaw. I am most appreciative of your assistance."

"Shaw, did these men have horses?"

Shaw nodded. "Yes, young man. They're stabled at the back of the inn and yours to take. Come, Princess, I do not want you in that thing a moment longer."

Shaw's bhean chéile waited in the forge. She paced up and down, wringing her hands, only stopping when she saw her céile fir's companions. "It is done, Shaw?"

He nodded. "This young man's plan has worked a treat."

Rosin turned to Arlan. He smiled but did not enlighten her.

"Gwendolyn will take you to the horses. She has already packed some supplies for your journey. I would suggest you ride hard to our king's castle, for the snows will come before long. Lord Devon's men are expected to return here before the freeze. When they left, they headed for the mountains, but I doubt they would venture any deeper into Tarlic. It wouldn't be safe for them, especially as all the realms are up in arms about his monstrous deeds. Nevanthi, please stay for the Princess's modesty while I remove this belt."

Arlan left.

Shaw rattled through his tools, then came back with a selection.

Embarrassment held Rosin's tongue still when Shaw began to work on the stubborn lock holding her trapped in the metal casing.

After half an hour of struggle, Rosin remained encased. She tamped down her desperate need to have it removed. The failure made her jumpy and irritated.

"Please, Nevanthi, may I have some water?" As Rosin drank, her parched throat soaking up the cool liquid, she swallowed the first packet of yellow powder.

Nevanthi watched her. "Remember, Princess, six hours, then another dose."

Rosin just nodded. Tired of being poked, prodded, and shunted back and forth, she struggled to remain perfectly still and outwardly calm.

"Curse this contraption to the Maiden's pit. I cannot break it. I will have to use heat, Princess. Please be patient and I will work the forge."

She squashed down the urge to scream at the delay, but she didn't want to hurt Shaw's feelings. He had tried his best. The heat from the forge radiated to her back by the time Arlan returned.

Shaw came to stand beside her. "This is a very dangerous maneuver, Princess, so please listen carefully. I need you to lie down flat on your back on the table. I will bring my anvil right next to you. When you are ready, I will place the lock square on the anvil and apply a red-hot sharp tool to the lock. With a bash from my hammer, it should give way."

Arlan frowned as he moved closer to her side. "Are you sure this won't harm the princess?"

Shaw scowled. "I have no other options, but would not some small harm be better than staying confined in that disgusting contraption?"

Arlan frowned in concern, but nodded agreement. "Well, let's proceed then."

Arlan held her so she couldn't flinch or roll.

Nevanthi steadied Rosin's feet.

Gwendolyn applied wet cloths to her body nearest where Shaw would work.

Rosin held herself motionless, hardly drawing a breath. The wretched lock hung only a minute distance from her bare skin.

The smell of heated metal assaulted her nose. The heat from the metal warmed her skin. The ring of metal and the pounding of the hammer on the flat head of the tool thudded through her head. She flinched as some hot metal drips seared her skin, but she clenched her teeth, determined not to cry out.

The belt wriggled, then loosened.

"Yes!" Shaw's jubilant yell echoed around the forge as the metal disintegrated under the joint assault of heat and force.

Arlan helped Rosin sit up.

She sagged against him, exhaling a deep breath and glancing up to the heavens, offering thanks to the Maidens for their assistance. The two pieces of the belt grated against each other. One side was still warm as Shaw took them away.

She touched his shoulder. "Dear Shaw, I can never thank you

enough for what you have done."

The blacksmith bowed his head slightly. "It has been an honor, Princess."

Tears welled in her eyes.

Gwendolyn wrapped a towel around her as she slid off the workbench. Her knees buckled beneath her.

Arlan grabbed her waist and supported her until she felt secure on her feet.

"Come, Princess, I have a bath and clean clothes ready for you and some nice undergarments." Gwendolyn held out her arm to guide Rosin from the forge. Heat rushed up her neck and face at the talk of undergarments in front of the men.

Both Arlan and Shaw kept straight faces, although they both suddenly, inexplicably, needed to clear their throats.

"Come, lad, I have the same for you and some food. Then you will be sustained and ready to leave before we release the children. I think it's best they do not see you. Then little tongues can't waggle to those who shouldn't hear."

Chapter 12

The sun peeked over the horizon as they swung up into the wide leather saddles. With a clatter of hooves and a chorus of goodbyes, they departed the village.

Rosin halted momentarily to wave once more before they broke into a gallop.

In front of them, the mountains rose majestically above the valley, each rugged peak crowned with a cap of glistening, white snow.

Between the village and the Oasis of the Birds, they only stopped to rest their mounts. Even though the sun shone, a distinctly cold breeze blew from the mountains.

Rosin knelt by the pool and sipped some cool water to wash the second dose of Nevanthi's potion down her throat. A dull ache had already developed across her back and low in her abdomen during the last couple of hours.

Arlan squatted by her side, wincing as he moved, his face haggard with tiredness.

An immediate wave of tender concern rushed over her. "Are you all right, Arlan?"

He nodded, even as he grimaced. "I'm a bit sore. Done a bit much, I think."

She looked up at him and covered his hand with hers, soaking up the warmth of his skin. "Come, you need to rest, and I want to inspect your wounds."

His eyes filled with indefinable shadows and lights. Drawn to him, as a magnet to steel, she wanted so desperately to lean forward and press her lips against his, to taste his masculine flavor, and feel his mouth explore the softness of hers.

He must have sensed her desire for he smiled, just a little, his mouth an open invitation.

They knelt inert, neither making any move to close the gap. He wouldn't and she couldn't.

Swamped with desire and taunted by indecision, Rosin broke the spell. The stark reality of what must be haunted her. Without a doubt, it would tear her to pieces. She couldn't take a lover even as she aborted the illegitimate child she carried.

"Come, Arlan, I need to check you out before we move on to a little less frequented area to bed down for the moon-wash. We will make better time tomorrow if we rest. I do not want you to have a relapse."

Disappointment at her withdrawal flickered across his face.

He hid it with a gentle smile as he stood up, drawing her with him. He made no move to bring her closer, even though his expression indicated he wanted to. With a barely perceptible hesitation, he let her go.

She recognized it would never be he who jeopardized her claim to the throne.

"You can check me out when we stop for the moon-wash, but you can explain now why you went back to the village last moon-wash on your own."

She turned away, afraid to tell him what she had done. Afraid of his anger and disappointment that she had made such a choice.

"Rosin, you owe me an explanation. You put yourself in danger. I don't understand why you had to sneak off. Why did you not talk to me?"

"I'm sorry. Arlan, I never meant to put you in danger or myself..."

"Maybe not, but why drug me then take off alone? Whatever you wanted, Rosin, you just had to ask, and I would have helped you." His remonstration was husky and gruff.

She couldn't bring herself to meet his gaze and instead stared at the ground. "I'm sorry, Arlan. I needed to see the healing woman."

"I know why you needed to see Nevanthi, but to go alone?"

She glanced up and met his gaze.

Anger, puzzlement, and hurt reflected in his eyes.

"I needed a potion to... to make me miscarry, and I didn't think you would approve. Most men don't. We are told to just keep our legs closed and we won't need it." Her words faded into silence.

"I know what the potion is for, Rosin. I suspected you were with child, but I didn't know what to do to help. I wish you had told me. Trusted me."

The tears welled up, and she covered her face with her hands. "I was afraid you would think less of me by bringing on a miscarriage. This child by Lord Devon...from the rape, can never live, Arlan." She swallowed several times to ease her constricted throat and wash away the sour dryness in her mouth as she prepared to face his disapproval.

His open countenance flickered, then became shuttered.

She couldn't read his thoughts at all. The need to explain burst out of her. "This child cannot be, Arlan. A monster's spawn. With this child, he can seize my throne."

"But the High Queen would..."

Rosin shook her head. "He conducted a bonding ceremony, then an Interloper's marriage ritual, before he raped me. It is a legitimate child. If I do not get rid of it now, or kill it at birth, the High Queen will be forced to accept this child as heir to the throne."

"But you would be queen..."

"No, Arlan. Devon planned to kill me after the birth, then with Devon in control until the child comes of age, Keswin will be destroyed. It would be nothing more than an adjunct of Ersklyn. I could not bear that. I fear Devon will never give up trying to rule Keswin."

"But the risks to you, Rosin. Is there no other way?"

"Please, Arlan, don't you see? I have no choice. It is for the throne, but also for me. I could never love this child. Every time I saw it, or held it, I would see Devon and remember that moon-wash: the deaths and the rape. An innocent child does not deserve to bear that burden." Her voice cracked and tears sprang into her eyes.

Arlan's expression changed to one of resignation and sympathy as he held out his arms.

In this moment of grief and shame, Rosin couldn't take his offered comfort, didn't deserve it. Filled with sadness, she turned away.

She'd hurt him. Firstly, going to the village alone, and now, again, by rejecting his offer of comfort. He hadn't argued with her decision, but he didn't voice his agreement either. Uncertainty rushed through her. Did he now think less of her knowing she had used the risky potion? She felt too afraid of the answer to ask. In an uncomfortable silence, they remounted and rode on.

~ ~ ~

Not long after the shadows started to lengthen, Arlan scanned the countryside for a place to bunk down for a few hours' rest.

By the time they entered a narrow canyon that ended in a deep overhang of rock with a flat sandy floor, darkness had fallen. Even the horses fitted under the ledge, with the entrance well concealed by spiny bushes.

Despite the silence that lay between them, Arlan insisted on helping her to dig out the adjoining holes to light the fire, then assisted with heating some of the food Gwendolyn had given them.

Rosin watched his every move with growing concern. He moved slowly in small, restricted motions that often ended abruptly, and although he made no sound of pain, it was obvious he felt considerable discomfort.

She ate her meal, even though she had little appetite.

Arlan ate even less before he pushed his plate away. Rosin turned to rummage inside the bag Nevanthi had given her for the strong antiseptic powder and several vials of painkilling crystals she had concocted from the local plants and herbs.

Without a word, Rosin spread out a blanket and patted it.

Arlan eased out of his shirt before he lowered himself carefully to the ground, making himself comfortable on his back.

She examined him all over.

His eyes remained open, but he did not focus on her as his muscular chest rose and fell in a steady rhythm.

She indulgently allowed her gaze to linger on the body she'd come to love. Every inch of him attracted her sensual being; the well-defined muscles and broad shoulders and the little of his smooth, creamy skin she could see. Warmth flared in her nether regions. Regardless of the scarring under the bandages, he remained an attractive man, and the smell of the soap he had used last moon-wash teased her nose as she drew closer.

It didn't matter that his battle scars marred the smoothness of his skin because it wasn't just his outside that enthralled her. His essence, his soul, and the beauty of the inner person drew her like a moth to a lamp.

She fought an unbearable urge to lie down beside him, throw

off the shackles of duty and beg him to make love to her, to place her head on his shoulder and feel his arm tuck around her. To feel loved and safe.

Instead, she breathed through the cramps in her abdomen, knelt beside him. The wounds on his face were healing nicely, the skin tender and pink. Carefully, she lifted the bandages from his chest. A small stream of blood trickled down his skin. She wiped it away. Two of her stitches had broken and the flesh around the wound seemed a little inflamed.

Guilt seared through her. If she had not gone to the village last moon-wash, he would not have put his wellbeing at risk. With infinite tenderness, she wiped the new flow of blood away, then sprinkled Nevanthi's antiseptic powder over the whole area.

Arlan stared into the distance, his eyes warm liquid pools, his mouth relaxed and his lips slightly parted. A couple of moon-slides growth of facial hair gave him a rakish appearance that made her want him even more.

She replaced the large dressing with a smaller, fresh one.

He didn't move, and as she finished, Rosin realized he'd fallen asleep.

She leaned down and pressed her lips against his skin in feather-soft kisses. She dared to rest her cheek against his chest for a moment. Hot tears of anguish welled up in her eyes. She lifted her head before the salty drops fell on his skin.

Pushing back the sadness that held her in an iron grip, she tucked a blanket over him, then lay down by his side. As she closed her eyes, she breathed in his scent and consciously tried to relax.

The ache in her back got progressively worse. The cramps twisted her lower abdomen into knots that weighed heavily deep inside. Eventually the pain got so bad she moved away from Arlan, because she wanted to spare him the sight of her suffering.

On the other side of the shelter, she lay on her side and drew her knees up to her chest as she bit down on the moans that escaped when the waves of pain washed over her. She swallowed a couple of crystals of Nevanthi's painkiller with sips of water and stayed very still.

All around, moon-wash noises crackled and clicked. The breeze rustled the leaves, and the horses snuffled and moved restlessly. Loneliness tormented her. She missed the closeness of Arlan's body. That special sense of closeness they had shared for many nights.

The pain intensified. Her whole abdomen clenched, then twisted in wave after wave. It hurt right down to the bones in her pelvis and deep inside her womanhood. She rocked side to side on her hips, but the movement didn't help. She clamped her mouth shut against the whimpers and cries rising in her throat.

Finally, she staggered to her feet. Bent over in pain, she climbed past the bushes into the open. Her feet dragged in the grass as she shuffled forward, bowed in half. She clenched her teeth against the screams tearing up her throat. Her whole body trembled as she made her way to a small hollow on the side of an outcrop she had seen just before they'd stopped.

By the time she'd reached it, agony made it difficult to stand and blood ran down her legs. She whimpered in pain and fear as she collapsed to lie scrunched into a ball. As each cramp ripped through her, she rolled back and forth, writhing and moaning each time the pain sharpened.

Nausea washed over her. Tears streamed down her face. Tears of pain, humiliation, and sorrow. She swallowed another couple crystals of the Nevanthi's painkiller then lay down, praying they would ease the torture she endured. Full of guilt and misery for what she needed to do, she hugged herself in a vain hope of comfort. It had to be done, but the killing of her child stabbed unexpectedly at her heart and soul.

The cold wrapped itself around her. The pervading dampness of the approaching frost seeped through her clothes onto her skin. Her body vibrated with shivers and her skin pimpled with goosebumps as she stared out into the darkness, wishing the moon-wash over.

The physical pain became far greater than she had ever anticipated. Blood flooded from her, clotted with membranes and unidentifiable lumps. She gagged and closed her eyes against the mess. Terror held her petrified at the amount of blood she was losing. The fear of death hovered. All the while, the guilt and emotional confusion stabbed through her.

Up until now, she had not even been aware of the child as an entity except for the failure of her moontime to start, her tender breasts, and periodic sickness. Until this moment of annihilation, she had felt no attachment or love for the thing growing inside her. Only hatred, resentment, and a desperate need to get rid of it.

With unexpected savagery, grief wrenched at her. It came unbidden, unwanted. This child, conceived through the terrible act of rape. The spawn of a monster, this child had no place in this world.

Rosin moaned and whimpered. Clutching at consciousness, her head swam and her stomach churned as the blackness crept in from the sides. As the pre-sun-show light paled the sky on the horizon, she let it come, beyond fighting to stay conscious and beyond bearing any more of this wretchedness.

"Rosin?"

His voice whispered in her mind, but she couldn't rouse herself.

"Rosin?" His touch caressed her skin.

Maybe she dreamed, but amid her desolation she reached out

and found him strong and solid.

He held her.

She clung to him and buried her face in his chest to hide her shame and humiliation.

Arlan lifted her from the cold ground and carried back to their camp. He ignored her tears and her blood as they wet his clothes.

~ ~ ~

He carried her to the overhang, her blood soaking into his breeches and shirt. Panic seared through him. *Maidens' curse so much blood. Surely, she will die.* Waves of despair washed over him. Knowing she had no choice but the terrible results and again she had been afraid to ask for his help. Frustration flooded through him but he sort of understood. They were in a sense strangers.

He laid her on the blanket. He stood and looked down at her, not knowing quite where to start. It wasn't like a wound; he couldn't stem the bleeding.

She shuddered and moaned.

He opened the saddle bags and found one stuffed full of rags. He pulled them out, knowing she had made provision for this.

He snatched up some tinder and small wood and lit a fire. He placed one of the pots Devon's man had attached to his saddle full of water. As it warmed, he stripped her breeches off and her underwear. Blood was everywhere. He discarded the clothes and grabbed a couple of cloths and the warmed water. He wiped the blood away and then washed her inner thighs and her abdomen and buttocks. He hesitated for a moment before he wiped the blood from her womanhood and washed her clean. More blood flowed. He didn't know how woman wore the rags so he tucked them between her legs and tied a strip around her waist to hold them in place. He lifted her to a fresh blanket and tugged a spare pair of breeches out of the saddle bag and pulled them on her. He was glad she was unconscious so there was no embarrassment between them. He lay down beside her and pulled a blanket over them.

He didn't sleep. He could do nothing more.

She moaned.

He held her close to him. Several times during the darkness her changed her cloths. The blood had not slowed its flow. He fretted. Would she survive? He nuzzled her neck and kissed her lightly. "Don't leave me, Rosin, my love. I am here. Come back to me."

He added more wood to the fire and pulled a jacket from the saddlebags on top. She shivered in his embrace. He held her as the sky began to lighten with sun-show.

~ ~ ~

The unrelenting ache in her pelvic region rudely brought awareness back. She squirmed and whimpered, reluctant to be dragged back from the painless oblivion of unconsciousness. Relentlessly, it clawed at her. She stirred. An awareness of warmth and the cessation of the savage gripping pains washed over her. Maybe she'd died. Drained of energy, she floated in a surreal calmness.

Strong arms held her, and the steady thud of a heartbeat matched her own.

She opened her eyes to find Arlan's hand lying loosely across her breasts. She listened with a sense of wonder to the sound of his steady breathing and slight snores.

Not wanting to disturb him, she lay very still, trying to piece together what had happened. Vague snippets of memory flashed through her mind, memories of Arlan carrying her, cleaning her, and whispering gentle words in her ear as he cradled her in his embrace.

He stirred.

Rosin pretended to be asleep because she didn't know how to face him in the cold light of sun-show. She kept her eyes closed even when he leaned over her shoulder.

"You didn't have to do it alone."

Heat rushed into her face. She opened her eyes and looked up at him. Guilt and shame loomed, ugly and bitter in her heart. "I couldn't have coped with your disapproval, along with my own remorse."

He shook his head. "I do not disapprove, my lady. In normal circumstances, it is hard to accept when a woman chooses to rid herself of a child, often for flimsy reasons. But I understand the need for what you did. To be honest, I don't know how you could bear the thought of that rapist's get inside you for as long as you did. Even without the throne in jeopardy, I believe you made the right decision. I just wish you could have trusted me enough to accept my help."

Rosin turned away from his troubled, earnest gaze. "The men in my life would never have coped with such. Childbirth and other things are considered a women's realm. I didn't want to shock you or disgust you."

"Rosin, I love you. Nothing about you would disgust me, but it did terrify me to see you in such a condition."

"I thought I would die. Nevanthi did warn me that to abort this way would be a horrendous process."

"You could have died, my love, and I couldn't bear it if you had, for without you, life would not be worth living. I love you with all my heart."

"Oh, Arlan."

"Now, you rest, my love, while I hunt up some food and appraise our situation."

Rosin watched him making preparations, fighting back a tide of embarrassment flooding through her. She wore a pair of black breeches several sizes too large, an undershirt, and a long grey tunic. Obviously Arlan had cleaned her, dressed her, and made adequate provision for her bleeding. It hadn't been a dream. "Thank you, Arlan, for taking care of me."

He smiled, a bit crooked and self-deprecating. "I will never tell, Princess, that your First Knight has seen you naked and applied some very personal ministrations."

Her face flamed. "Thank you."

All the next two moon-slides, he cared for her, made sure she had all she needed, cooked food, and kept watch for any sign of followers. Rosin began to feel better, physically. The bleeding eased.

At the fading on the second moon-slide when Arlan returned with a small fish and a vexed expression marring his face.

A sudden surge of cold enveloped her.

"Are you up to moving on? I can see campfires about a moon-slide's ride behind us. I guess they're settling in for the moon-wash. I suspect it's Devon. If he's returned to the village, he will know you are alive."

She nodded.

Arlan helped her up.

Her legs were a bit unsteady. She wobbled with light-headedness. "I'm so dreadfully thirsty, Arlan."

He instantly proffered his arm.

With his support, she managed to totter across the cave to the water bottle. She took a long drink and washed down some of Nevanthi's painkilling crystals.

"I'll get the horses and give you a minute. If you need help, call me. I'll be just outside."

A dull ache held her body in a relentless grip and she still bled heavily. She wanted to lie down and sleep, but with riders only a moon-slide behind, they had to move on. Rosin forced herself to prepare and hobbled outside.

Arlan helped her onto her horse.

They rode through the darkness, only stopping to attend her needs. As the five moons slipped below the horizon, a veil of blackness flooded over the land so deep it made moving forward a risky proposition that would only change when the grey of sun-show lightened the sky.

Rosin's body ached, and she struggled to stay conscious. Mustering all her reserves, she clutched the pommel in a white-knuckled grip and clamped her mouth shut on her whimpers. She wanted to keep her discomfort from Arlan in case he insisted they stop, but also to spare him her misery.

Finally, with it too dark to carry on, Arlan allowed them to stop for a short time. On the brink of unconsciousness, Rosin swallowed some painkiller and eased her aching body to the hard ground. Exhaustion engulfed her immediately, and she knew no more.

Arlan's hand on her shoulder forced her back into reality. As the sky lightened, they moved on. Rested, her pain had subsided to a bearable throb.

Concerned about those following them, Arlan suggested they kick the horses on and cover the ground at a steady canter.

Rosin nodded her agreement.

They didn't even pause to eat until they reached the bottom of the first steep rise into the mountains.

When they stopped, Arlan peered into the distance behind them.

The unknown riders had dropped back, their presence nothing more than a swirl of dust in the clear sky. They were too far away to identify, but it seemed to be a reasonably large contingent. One, they would have no chance of fighting off if it caught up with them.

Their only chance of freedom relied on them moving at a fast pace and keeping the distance between them. Surely Devon would not follow them over the pass and so far into Tarlic.

As they moved higher into the mountains, their pace slowed. The horses struggled with the uneven, rising ground, scattered with rocks and thick vegetation. Up ahead, the peaks jutted into the sky, their summits already blanketed in glistening, white snow.

All around them, the denser foliage grew right to the edge of the path. Huge ferns and creepers filled in the spaces between the clumps of alpine trees that rose tall and straight into the sky.

Lichen carpeted the branches and trunks of the trees and, in the dark coolness of the shadows, tiny high-country flowers peeped out of the damp richness of the fertile black soil. Low clouds hung as an eerie mist in the stillness between the trees. The cool moisture in the air flowed over their skin in a damp caress.

Rosin shivered as she gazed up at the snow on the crags above them, rugged and imposing under a gray, sullen sky. The temperature had dropped dramatically in the past hour as they steadily continued upward.

After a particularly steep section, they paused to spell the horses, who breathed hard from exertion and the thinner air. From this vantage point, they could make out the dust on the plains, where the riders moved toward them at a steady pace. The gap between them had closed considerably since their ascent began and slowed their progress.

Conflicting emotions sliced through her. She clenched and unclenched her hands on the reins. Blood pounded in her ears.

Threats of violence upon his person rested on the tip of her tongue. Damn him to the Maidens' pit. How dare he cross so far into Tarlic? She whimpered at the thought of being in his grip again.

"He will not touch you again, my love. Do not fear."

The effort it took to smile proved beyond her. His comment made it obvious he kept a close eye on her. While grateful he cared, it made it harder for her to hide her physical and emotional suffering.

The air became colder and thinner as they continued toward the summit. Her fingers and toes had turned into lumps of frozen flesh on the end of her limbs, her nose so cold it hurt and dribbled uncontrollably. The icy air chilled her throat and burned in her lungs.

The path became rockier. The cliffs loomed up on either side, signaling the start of the pass. The massive cliffs would soon have them completely enclosed in a narrow channel with only a sliver of sky between the two peaks. They could only move slowly upward in single file.

Scrawny trees clung to the walls of the pass their roots buried deep in any small crevasse that retained the tiniest bit of soil. Lichen covered the rocks in a blanket of soft green and clumps of small spiny grasses crouched together between gnarled tree roots.

Both the horses struggled with the rough terrain, but despite the physical effort required, they were skittish and jumpy. The hoof-falls echoed eerily off the rough rock walls.

On tenterhooks, Rosin strained to hear any other noises above the clatter. It was impossible. Instead of fretting, she put her head down and concentrated on staying in the saddle.

Several icy touches on her face made her glance up. Tiny soft flakes fell like miniature stars, silently drifting to the ground, landing on her skin and melting into oblivion. She shivered and tugged her sleeves down to cover her hands. A cloud of frosted air formed in front of her each time she breathed. She tugged her cloak closer, seeking any skerrick of warmth she could.

A loud clatter and a shower of small stones wrenched her out of her reverie. She jerked her head up.

Her horse shied and half reared.

Rosin clutched the pommel.

Her horse staggered backward as an additional weight attached itself to its rump.

A beefy arm curled around Rosin's waist and the sour smell of common soldier breath fanned the side of her face. She screamed, yanked on the reins, and savagely kicked her horse. It baulked, reared, and unseated her unwanted passenger.

"Uuff." The air exploded out of his lungs when he landed hard on the boulder-strewn ground.

Fighting down panic, Rosin turned her horse. With a savage thud, she kicked it hard in the ribs again even as she reined back.

Confused by her conflicting signals, the already skittish horse reared again with a squeal of frustration. It lashed the air above the prone soldier with flailing hooves.

Rosin pushed her weight forward, forcing the horse to drop down with a clatter of iron-shod hooves and an explosion of rock. A crack and squelching sound echoed when her horse trampled forward.

The animal squealed, not at all happy about the squirming human underfoot.

Relentless, Rosin yanked on the reins and kicked until the terrified animal turned. She adjusted her seat, urging the horse to rear and bring its feet down again on the already trampled soldier.

Devon's man didn't move. His eyes were closed and his face set in a grotesque mask of horror at what he'd last seen.

Her horse neighed loudly before it scrambled for safer footing on the slippery ground.

Rocks rattled and men's grunts rose above the heavy breathing of the horse.

Rosin turned. She gasped. Fear speared through her.

Arlan fought hand-to-hand with another soldier. In the narrow enclosed space, his sword flapped uselessly at his side. His breathing heavy and uneven as he grappled with his opponent.

Anger roiled in her gut. She hissed her dismay as she withdrew her short sword from its scabbard. With another sharp kick, she urged her horse forward, but it danced sideways, still unsettled by its brush with the corpse.

She lifted out of her seat. Her foot came loose from the stirrup, and unable to get her balance, she slid from the saddle.

She hit the ground with a bone-jarring thud. Excruciating pain ripped through her leg and shoulder.

The horse collapsed to its knees but immediately struggled to get up.

Rosin rolled free of its struggles. "Rotten Maiden's pit! Stupid horse." Her leg twisted at an awkward angle with a searing blast of agony shooting up past her knee. Barely able to lift herself high enough, she made a grab for the reins, but the animal threw its head up and scuttled backward.

Rosin snatched again for the reins.

The horse snorted, spun around, and trotted back down the pass, its tail flicking high in the air.

With all hope of retrieving the animal gone, Rosin turned back to the combatants.

Arlan struggled to stay upright on the sloping ground a few feet up the ravine. He had managed to draw his sword.

The second, larger man wearing Devon's colors grappled with

him.

Arlan's wounds obviously handicapped him as he battled to swing his sword in a full arc.

Rosin gritted her teeth against the agonizing pain as she dragged herself forward through the icy slush, so cold it burnt her skin as it seeped through her clothes.

If anything happened to him, she would die inside, her heart mangled to pieces. Even her own well-being and the reality of what would happen if Arlan went down came secondary to the thought of losing the man she loved.

The two men angled and twisted around each other. Muscle strained against muscle. Sword slithered against sword.

Unable to rise, Rosin dragged herself closer on her backside until she virtually sat under their feet. The splatter of slush from their scuffling sprayed up at her as they nearly stomped on her legs. Panic gripped her chest tight at the sight of lots of blood on Arlan's chest and thigh and on the shoulders and back of his opponent.

Huddled in each other's arms, neither man could swing his weapon and deal a fatal blow.

Arlan had obviously weakened. His knees buckled slightly as he struggled to find purchase on the slippery ground.

The two men stumbled around and around, each searching for an opening to finish off the other.

Arlan saw her over the man's shoulder and shook his head.

Rosin nodded back vigorously, indicating she had the sword ready to drive home.

He nodded and immediately leaned heavily into the soldier. When his opponent counteracted the unexpected shift in Arlan's weight, Arlan jerked himself free of his clutches.

The man swayed and barely kept his balance as he went to

lunge after Arlan.

In that split second of exposure and hesitation, Rosin thrust the sword directly at her enemy. The blade caught the soldier in the thigh. Not satisfied to just injure, but determined to finish him off, Rosin leaned her weight on the weapon and pushed the blade right through until it poked out the other side of his leg.

The soldier yelped with pain and surprise at the unexpected attack. He spun round to face her but lost his precarious footing and collapsed to the ground face down, his damaged leg unable to take his weight.

With a flash of silver, Arlan drove his blade into the man's back. Blood spurted out of the wound, melting the ice it landed on before freezing into a permanent red splotch. Arlan withdrew his sword before the man rolled over.

Their foe stared up at them, his eyes filled with pain. "Lord Devon intends to get the Princess. His contingent is only a moon-slide or two away." His voice gurgled and scraped.

Arlan stood over the man. "Are there more of you here in the pass?"

The man shook his head. "We're the last outpost. He wasn't keen for us to go any further into Tarlic, but he wants the Princess. He's determined, in his madness, to rule Keswin." He glanced from Arlan to Rosin. "We dinna agree with it, the raiding and the marauding around the land, and him making orders from his sick bed. He's been confined to it with a crushed leg since the mudslide that terrible moon-wash. We didn't have a choice, being in his service and all. Besides, he's quick to kill opponents to his demands. Go now and escape the mad bastard. He has no right to Keswin, especially as he don't care for the people he already has." The wounded soldier groaned. "Finish me off. Let me die a quick death."

Arlan's expression twisted into a grim mask of contempt as he drove his sword into the man's chest.

With a deep rattle in his lungs, the soldier died there in the slush.

Not interested in observing another corpse, Rosin swung around, seeking her horse, but it had vanished. "Moon dust, just what we need."

"We will manage with one, my love."

"But Arlan, I cannot walk. My leg is broken, and how badly did he hurt you?"

Arlan shrugged. "Not so bad, my love. Come, let's get you patched up before we go."

Arlan's horse stood patiently just behind him, but as he gathered up the reins, he held his arm close to his chest and blood leaked heavily enough from a gash on his shoulder to seep through his cloak.

He knelt awkwardly beside her, and with a tender grip under her chin, he lifted her face so she would look directly at him. His thumb stroked her icy skin. With obvious discomfort, he leaned forward and gently kissed her tears away. With his other hand, he brushed the snow flakes off her face.

"Don't cry, my love. We're still alive, but we must leave this place quickly, for Devon's men are not far behind, and he will know from this carnage we've crossed the pass."

Suddenly desperate for a connection with him, Rosin placed her hands on either side of his face and drew him to her.

Their lips met.

At the first touch, he took command of her mouth, a firm, demanding, and caressing touch.

Her lips parted in response, fire igniting in her belly. She breathed in his scent, reveled in touching him, and drowned in a whirlpool of sensation as her body answered the call of his and soaked up the emotions from his heart.

Without warning, tears poured down her face. She couldn't stop them or the overwhelming sense of grief at her own loss, fear for Arlan, and the pain of her broken leg. She hadn't been trained to cope with what she'd been through, and everything now washed over her in a rumbling destructive wall, demolishing all her defensive strategies. She still bled heavily, and her blood stained the slush.

Arlan allowed her the luxury of crying for a moment as he knelt beside her. He stroked her hair, then showered tiny kisses on her face and whispered gently in her ear, "Don't cry, my love, it will be all right."

As her tears eased, Arlan retrieved a couple of short spears and bits of torn cloak out of his saddlebags.

Arlan handed Rosin a piece of rag. "Bite down on this, my love. It's going to hurt like a Maiden's revenge, but it has to be done. I'll be gentle and quick." He kissed the top of her head, then proceeded to straighten her leg.

The pain grabbed hold, and she bit hard down on the rag he'd given her. She groaned against it, but didn't cry out when the bones moved and grated together. Arlan gradually pushed them back into place.

Finally, with her leg splinted, he helped her to stand.

She insisted he pause long enough for her to place a couple of pads of cloth under his tunic, then bind his shoulder to stem the blood flow before he hoisted her into the saddle. With her help, he managed to scramble up behind.

Rosin let the horse pick its own way through the boulders and slush as they climbed the steep path. She had to nudge the poor horse forward, burdened under the weight of two. Progress was slow.

At last, they crested the pass and began the torturous journey down the other side. They didn't pause to admire the magnificent view of Tarlic dressed in the vivid oranges, reds, and yellows of the withering.

A canyon of agony engulfed her. Each lurching movement jarred her leg until she could feel the bones moving and grating, end against end.

Arlan held onto her waist as he leaned against her, but only one hand held her in a firm grip. His injured limb merely rested there.

Relief filled her that she no longer had to drive their overburdened mount forward. She let it carefully choose its own secure footing on the roughness of the downward slope.

Below them, she could see Tarlic spread out in a muted brown-and-yellow checked pattern of dying pasture grasses and fallow ground. The Sacred River flowed majestically down the middle of the valley.

In the distance, high above the river, on the summit of a large plateau, Tarlic Castle stood. The castle itself appeared as a mere smudge against the gray of the sullen sky.

Tears welled up, but she smiled through them. "We're nearly there, Arlan. I can see King Cadmar's castle."

He responded with a light squeeze on her waist.

They continued the descent in silence.

Rosin summoned the little remaining reserves of courage and stamina she had to complete the torturous journey down from the mountain.

As the ground leveled, Rosin kicked the horse on even though every movement sent searing pain stabbing up her leg and back. She cried silent tears of pain.

With the fading, the sun dipped toward the horizon, and already the first of the six moons peeped above the hills. Time was short. "Arlan, are you up to a faster pace?"

"Go, Princess, a nice steady canter, until we reach the river. The six moons will rise soon enough with the close of this moon-slide. We must be ready as soon as the tidal wash happens. There will be plenty of light and once the tidal wash comes back, we should be safe from Devon. No one can cross the river without the tidal wash. We can rest until sun-show, then make the castle by high sun tomorrow."

She couldn't shake the unnerving prickle along her skin. They were being followed. Several times she glanced over her shoulder to scan the path, sure their pursuers were closer than expected. There was no sign of them. Still unconvinced of their safety, she turned the horse toward the river and with a hard kick from Arlan, the horse sprang forward, almost unsettling their precarious seat.

Birds filled the sky, not hunters or carrion eaters, but waterfowl. Ducks dropped in V-shaped formations to take a rest on the river before migrating south to avoid the harshness of the freeze.

Huge trees, their roots buried deep into the rich river loam of the flood plains, had already shed their leaves, covering the ground with a carpet of red and gold.

The horse cantered through the colorful blanket and leaves swirled up around them before they settled back on the ground.

When they neared the river, Rosin slowed the horse to a walk. Worn down by exhaustion and injury, both struggled to stay in the saddle.

With plenty of grass on the side of the trail, the horse happily loped along, snatching quick mouthfuls of feed in passing.

Icy air flowed down from the mountains. Clouds had formed on the horizon, gray and sullen. They would soon hide the moons, and Rosin didn't know whether to be pleased or worried about this development.

Every inch of her ached, her bottom numbed from hours in the saddle, her injured leg swinging back and forth, the bones gating with each movement and the remnants of her miscarriage throbbed abysmally in her abdomen.

On the edge of the river, she halted the horse but made no attempt to dismount. Not only because they wouldn't be able to get back up, but because they would also be more vulnerable to attack.

Still unable to shake the feeling of being followed, she glanced nervously over her shoulder from time to time. She feared Devon's men lurked not far behind them. Unable to see up into the mountains, now shrouded in deep shadow and misty clouds, she could only guess how close they might be.

Craving concealment, Rosin picked out a tall, bushy shrub, then backed the horse in under it. They wouldn't be easily seen by those approaching from the mountains. She fought her body's desire to sag, keeping her back as stiff as a well-forged sword.

"Not long now, my love. See, there are five moons up and the sixth is just nudging the horizon." His words were faint and forced.

She guessed his wounds were more serious than he'd admitted. Rosin watched the moons float slowly across the sky. The reins clenched in tight fists as she fought the desire to fidget in the saddle. Gnawing on her bottom lip, she stared at the moons, silently urging them to rise faster. She needed to treat Arlan, lest he bleed to death on the horse behind her.

"Are you all right, Arlan?"

"I'm hurt, my love, but we are nearly there. Once we are over the river, you will have to mend me again. Then we'll finish this together. I've managed to loosen my belt. It is long enough to go round both of us. Here, can you reach the buckle?"

She let the reins go and sought the ends of the belt. She held them out level in front of her. She slid one end through the buckle and tightened the strip of leather over her aching stomach.

"I don't want to fall off, my love, in case I cannot fight the blackness. Do not be afraid, my love, only the river to go."

"But Arlan..."

"Shh, love."

She gazed up at the moons. Move, Rianon, move. Join your sisters, weave your magic.

But nature could not be hurried. The air swirled with expectation. An unnatural silence encompassed them.

Arlan remained silent and still.

She feared he'd lost consciousness but fought against the urge to jostle him into awareness. Rosin fought to keep her hands and legs still and relaxed so the horse wouldn't fidget.

An overwhelming need to flee besieged her. She stiffened in resistance to the urge and waited.

The sixth moon had risen beside the other five, its golden orange glow lighting the countryside with a warm, translucent light and bringing a whisper of movement in the flow of the river.

She flinched. Her heart somersaulted as a loud crack shattered the heaviness of the silence. She turned and stared into the darkness behind her but saw nothing.

More rocks tumbled. Sounds of certain pursuit. The crunch and rattle of rock on rock and iron horseshoes pounding on stone, somewhere behind her.

Unable to see those who followed, she turned back to the river where the water slid gracefully down the riverbed toward the sea. It would be awhile before the water drew back far enough to fully expose the riverbed. She glanced from the moons to the river, then back again through narrowed, intensely focused eyes. Every nerve tensed, poised to leap into action. With her jaw clenched hard, she struggled to hold back. "Arlan."

He didn't respond.

She assumed he'd succumbed to unconsciousness. Her responsibility for getting herself and the man she loved to safety weighed heavily. She analyzed her situation. If she guessed correctly, her pursuers had not yet seen her hidden in the bush by the water's edge. From the echoes and sharpness of the displaced rocks, she calculated they were still coming down the mountain trail.

Even knowing the risk of being swept away, she intended to wait until the very last minute of the tidal wash before making her dash. If she timed it correctly, they would not have time to follow her before the water returned with its usual turbulent rush. The torturous waiting, silent and still as the water receded, tightened like rope around her senses. Her body itched to leap forward. She watched the moons. All the time, she heard her pursuers coming closer. Not the clatter of rocks anymore, but the thud of galloping hooves on hard ground.

She waited and observed. The slightest movement in the moons gave her the sign she needed. In the blink of an eye, it had come and gone. Rosin booted the horse hard. One hand clutched the reins, the other the pommel, and they took off at a gallop down the soft bank into the muddy bed, dodging and weaving through the debris.

Off to her right, the water swished as it reversed its flow. Fear sizzled along every nerve as she inclined her body against the horse's neck, slapped it with the reins, then kicked and kicked with her good leg.

The animal flattened out and yanked the reins roughly through her hands as it took the bit and bolted, driven, not by her urging, but by its instinctive fear of the returning water.

The gushing water swirled around the horse's legs. Above the sounds of the water, Rosin heard the whoops and cries of Devon's men as they hurtled down the soft sandy bank into the riverbed. The roar of the water returning filled her ears. Gurgling, eddying, and frothing as it raced back up the riverbed, chasing the moons.

The water rose to her horse's shoulder, so cold it hurt her skin as it swept past. The force of the motion pushed the horse off its feet. Swept forward with a sudden rush, the horse swam strong against the tide, but they continued drifting with the flow. Rosin held on with clawed hands to both the saddle and reins, praying Arlan's belt would hold.

The horse jerked, then slowed as it found its feet on the river bed. In a clumsy scrabble, the horse lunged up the other bank.

The roar of the water was so loud behind Rosin she felt the vibrations in her chest. Anxiety ripped away from her. She sagged, gasping against the sobs that threatened to choke her.

Free of the river, the horse stumbled to a halt and stood, shaking. Its head hung down as it snorted froth and snot to express its disapproval.

Ignoring the ache in her bones, she tightened her grip on the reins and squeezed the horse's sides. The water behind her slowed to a gentle swirl. She glanced over her shoulder.

A group of Devon's men and horses were milling on the far bank, the rattle of harness and swords slicing through the air.

By the fading light of the sinking moons, she saw a couple of bodies eddying in the settling water. A quick scan along the length of her bank showed no other survivors of the crossing. Nobody would try to cross now.

Rosin watched from deep in the tall reeds as her pursuers turned away from the river and galloped toward the mountains.

Relief washed through her as they faded into the darkness. With imminent danger gone, she turned the horse and set off at a brisk walk. She had to find shelter and treat Arlan.

Again, she let the horse find its own path. She clung to the saddle, struggling to stay conscious as pain ripped through her. At last, they emerged from the reed beds and into a meadow.

Arlan hadn't spoken for a long time.

The full weight of his body rested against her back. A sense of urgency gripped her. Dear Maidens, protect him, hold him close to your hearts. I love him, I need him. She fought down the sobs that bunched in her chest and tightened her grip on the reins. The horse halted.

"Arlan?"

When he didn't answer, she shook her body a little to jiggle him awake but got no response. Her throat tightened and tears filled her eyes when she couldn't discern any sign of life. Gutted by the knowledge she could do nothing at the moment, she kicked the horse on, searching for a suitable campsite.

Chapter 13

Without being too choosy, she directed the horse to the biggest group of trees and rocks she could see.

The rocks stood in a semi-circle; the opening faced toward the castle so anyone coming from across the river would not see if she lit a fire until they were right on it. Its aspect also provided some protection from the icy wind that whistled down from the mountains.

She didn't expect anyone to come, not after seeing the bodies left in the river by the tidal wash, but caution had become a natural action.

A huge boulder towering above the surrounding ground had tumbled sideways, forming an almost-enclosed space. Getting as close to the overhang as she could, she rested and pondered just how she could manage her dismount with a broken leg and Arlan, either unconscious or dead, behind her. It would be tricky and painful, but she worried most about damaging her leg more and not being able to care for Arlan. At this moment, she refused to consider how she would get back on the horse in the morning.

She deliberately switched her thoughts off. Arlan's death did not bear thinking about. All she could manage was one small step at a time.

She undid the restraining belt, then leaned back onto Arlan.

He didn't respond to her weight.

She choked back panic. Concentrating only on the task at hand. Using both hands, she lifted her injured leg up and over the pommel. Her foot dragged through the tangled mane. The horse snorted softly and shifted on the spot. Horrendous agony exploded along her broken leg and she screamed as the grinding pain shot through her. Blackness hovered at the edge of her mind.

She waited for the ache to ease before twisting her body around. Hanging onto the pommel and horse's mane, she slid down the horse's shoulder, her injured leg held up so only her good leg touched the ground.

After she landed, she clutched the stirrup leathers in a white-knuckled grip and turned her eyes up to the sky. Tears sprang up in her eyes and every inch of her body trembled from the searing throb. Fortunately, after a while, it eased to a dull roar.

Without her support, Arlan slumped forward in the saddle. His head hung so low his hair touched the horse's withers. Blood had soaked through his clothes.

She reached up and pressed her fingers on the lifeline in his neck. With her breath held, she pressed in several places until she found the tiny erratic thump-thump of the blood flowing. Alive, but death lurked not far away.

Using her sword as a crutch, she moved the horse well into the shadows of the outcrop. Her frozen fingers scrabbled at the ties on the saddle bags. "Moon leeches, open." With her fingertips burning, she finally loosened the ties and dragged a blanket from the bag. She draped it on the ground.

Her breath came in tortured gasps, jerking to a halt as pain sliced through her with each movement. She clenched her jaw, then reached up to haul the unconscious Arlan from the saddle.

He hit the ground with a bone-jarring thud, even though she had eased his fall.

A tiny groan escaped.

She firmly tethered the horse to a nearby tree, afraid it might wander off. Without it, she would die out here in the shadow of her refuge. With unsaddling beyond her, she left the horse as it was.

Finding plenty of leaf litter and dried twigs, she quickly started a fire, making no attempt to conceal it in smokeless fire pits this time. As soon as the flames burned strongly, she put water on to boil, then dug around in the saddlebags for more rags and potions. The clean rags prepared for her use would suffice to patch up Arlan.

Every movement of her leg sent stabs of agony through her. Sweat beaded her face and ran between her breasts and down her back. She cringed at the sound of the bones grating, but finally, with all her materials gathered, she managed to lower herself to the ground beside Arlan.

Fighting back sobs, she split open his blood-soaked tunic, worried about what she would find. His old wounds were still closed and healing well.

What troubled her more were the two deep gashes across his shoulder and bicep that bled profusely. She washed the blood away with hot water, then before it could overflow the wounds again, she scattered the antiseptic powder over them and pressed the edges together. This time, she didn't hesitate when she plied her needle and thread to the gaping wounds. As she inserted the last stitch, she paused a second to admire her handiwork, very happy she'd managed to align the edges and neatly sew the full length.

Satisfied they would heal; she covered them with clean dressings then quickly inspected the rest of his body. He must be bleeding heavily somewhere else to go downhill so fast. His breeches were soaked in blood from the groin all the way down the right leg. She picked up the dagger and slit both legs of his breeches up to the waist. He wore soft white undergarments. They were also drenched in blood. Two slashes with the dagger and one tug left Arlan naked.

His life-force flowed freely from a deep stab wound high up his thigh. She had to stop the bleeding, or he would die. She pressed hard with a dry pad of cloths directly on the wound. With no way of telling what damage the sword had made inside, she sat there in the dark and kept the pressure on the gash, praying it would stop bleeding.

Blood soaked through to her hand. She whimpered in frustration as she added another pad on top and pressed down hard.

A moan escaped from Arlan, but he didn't open his eyes.

The fire started to die down, so Rosin threw some more sticks onto the flames without releasing the pressure on the wound. The moons had dropped below the horizon and stars were obscured by the clouds rolling in. A deep darkness surrounded them. The crisp, icy air produced a frost plume in front of her with every breath, even with the fire taking the edge off the cold.

His blood seeped slowly through her pad of rags.

Shivers raced through her body. She added more cloth and pressed harder. She looked to the sky and beseeched Rhianon. "Stop the bleeding. Please help me or he will die."

The sullen clouds slid across the sky. Wolves howled in the distance.

Her arms ached from applying pressure to the wound. Still, blood gradually seeped through.

Arlan lay still and pale, his eyes sunken into the sockets, his mouth open slightly as he breathed in small huffs of icy air. He was dying before her eyes.

Fury surged through her at the unfairness of it all. "I will not lose you. I will not." She released the pressure on the bandages, snatched up her dagger and held it over the flames. Guessing the blade was hot enough. She withdrew it from the heat and held it over his thigh as she pulled the blood-soaked dressings from his wound. Fear and angst surged through her. She hesitated a moment, her hand shaking. She tightened her grip and steeled herself against the pain she would inflict. "Sorry, Arlan. Sorry, my love, to cause such pain." She clenched her teeth and pressed the searing blade on his wound. Her stomach clenched at the stench of burning flesh, and she cringed at the hiss. Sweat poured down her face, mixing with her tears. Bile rose in her throat, but she held the blade on his flesh.

A quick inspection assured the wound had sealed completely. With trembling hands, she tied a new pad over the area. She sat beside him, breathing deeply, ignoring the tears streaming down her cheeks, praying it would be enough to save him.

Relieved to be finished, she discarded his ripped and bloodied garments in a pile, then covered them with dirt to hide the smell from any nearby vipers. She hauled some fresh clothes from her bag and, heaving and dragging his inert body back and forth, she managed to get some ill-fitting clothes on him.

Arlan hadn't regained consciousness by the time Rosin had re-dressed him, and the beat of blood in his neck remained weak.

Sweating and panting, Rosin added some heavier logs to her fire, aware for the first time of her own blood staining her pants. She dragged them off and inspected her leg. Arlan had set it well. The wooden splints supported her leg and held it straight.

Taking the last pair of clean pants, she cleaned herself up and eased the pants over her legs. Lurching from side to side on her bottom, she managed to get them all the way up. Nausea washed over her. Her head spun and stars flickered in front of her eyes. She swallowed repeatedly to ease the need to vomit as she dug out a couple of Nevanthi's painkilling crystals. She swallowed the crystals, and dragging herself close to Arlan, she curled up by his side. She snuggled close before dragging two cloaks over them. Her feminine curves fit so closely to his masculine ones. With a sigh, she laid one arm over his chest and rested her head on his undamaged shoulder.

Before she slept, she covered every exposed inch of skin, for the cold had intensified in the last hour. The blackness surrounding them had become absolute. The smell in the air foretold of early snow.

Despite her exhaustion, she couldn't settle. Her face burned with cold. The excruciating pain in her leg almost consumed her sanity. With Arlan unconscious, she felt dreadfully vulnerable, exposed, and alone. All the time, her ears remained attuned to the movements outside their small hollow of safety. While she suspected all Devon's men who attempted to follow her across the river had perished in the tidal wash. She couldn't be certain and didn't want to be taken by surprise.

In the distance, wolves howled. The horse snuffled and stirred uneasily.

She refueled the fire several times as she struggled to combat a terrible sense of loneliness and guilt. Foolish woman. Foolish, foolish woman. I should have stopped it, never let it start. Oh, what a mess. The emotion that flowed between them placed both of them on dangerous ground. Her heart ached afresh for the fact that she would have to turn away from a man who loved her.

She mulled the past few moon-sweeps over and over in her head. Her emotions somersaulted from anger, bitterness, and resentment to grief and fear.

Deep down, though, she didn't think she could betray her people and walk away from her kingdom when it needed her the most. She'd killed her baby to save the throne and had killed men to escape and save her own life.

Now within reach of the refuge, her Protector's castle offered she could not have doubts. She must not weaken, no matter how much she loved Arlan.

Again, she turned over and threw some more chunks of wood on the fire. For a long time, she stared into flames, hoping to extract an answer from the golden glow. It had grown even colder, and she checked that the rugs completely covered Arlan before she snuggled down and closed her eyes. Several times during the long, lonely moon-wash, she examined Arlan's thigh, pleased to find no sign of more bleeding.

~ ~ ~

She heard the chirps and whistles of early birds before she realized the sky had lightened ever so slightly. The fire had burned down to embers, and the air remained icy. She peered out of their shelter. Snow covered the ground in a light sprinkling that lay thicker in the hollows and on the mountainside of the rocks and boulders.

She eased out from under the covers, lifted one of the cloaks off Arlan, and wrapped it around her. She stoked the fire and put some water on to boil before she went back and shook Arlan. "Arlan, wake up. We need to go and I cannot lift you into the saddle." She shook him hard, tears of frustration and helplessness imminent when he failed to respond. In a moment of rashness, she leaned down and kissed him.

He immediately opened his eyes and stared up at her. He groaned. "I hurt everywhere. What happened, Rosin? Are you all right? Are we across the river?"

She nodded as she handed him some warm bread and a cup of hot herbal tea. "You passed out from loss of blood. I've dressed your wounds and stopped the bleeding for now, but we cannot stay here."

He squeezed her hand. "I'm sorry, my love, I failed you."

"No, Arlan, you did not fail me. We are both alive. Before we crossed Devon's men came. They tried to follow but left it too late and died. They can't follow us here. I heard wolves howling in the moon-wash and the frost has begun and brought early snow. We need to hurry to the castle because we won't survive out here for long once the temperature starts to drop."

She held out her hands.

He took them and managed to sit up. "I feel woozy. Just give me a minute."

Hopping on one leg and the sword Rosin dealt with her personal needs behind the nearest rock. As she hobbled toward the fire with her makeshift crutch, the horse nickered.

Arlan had brought it around to stand by a couple of flat rocks. "Ready?"

She nodded then hobbled toward him.

With his good arm he helped her get onto the rocks. She managed to scramble into the saddle.

Her head spun and her mouth filled with saliva as she clutched the pommel and fought off encroaching blackness. She swallowed then shook her head to make the dizziness slowly recede.

Arlan also used the rocks.

She tugged on the waist band of his breeches to help him clamber up behind her.

He grunted with the effort but did not cry out against the pain. He then wrapped a cloak around them, tucking it into his belt. "Let's go, Princess."

He turned the horse, then nudged it forward. They set out at a brisk walk. Both scanned the terrain for evidence of company. Nothing moved except a couple of birds hopping across the snow and the reeds by the river's edge that rustled in the breeze.

Keen to get to the castle, Arlan kicked the horse, and it leapt into a steady canter. Arlan held her around the waist, the joint warmth from their bodies wrapping them in a comfortable cocoon.

They travelled over mostly cleared ground used for agriculture by Tarlic's farmers for many years. Silt from the river floods when the big thaw came created rich, dark soil. But nothing grew here at this time, allowing a renewal for the river flats' fertility.

Like all the Maidens' descendants, the farmers worked with nature, not fighting the inevitable. Unlike the Interlopers, who always wanted to grow more crops each succession and on less and less fertile ground or dammed up the river to provide water for dry pastures that should only run sheep or goats.

Rosin bubbled with joy when she could make out her Protector's standards flying from the outer gate as they cantered across the valley. Snow fell again in a light but steady sprinkle. The ground rose in a gentle slope toward the plateau the castle stood on.

They passed cottages. Small ones used in the growing seasons of the mist and awakening by the farmers of Tarlic. They were deserted now, for all the families had moved into their winter quarters in the castle. Soon, all this land would be the domain of wolves and occasional hunting parties who left the castle by the secret entrances to secure fresh meat.

A long, drawn-out shout sliced through the frosty air.

Rosin's heart jumped.

To the right, a large, straggling group rode toward them from out of the woods. A chariot followed with a driver and an obviously female passenger. Two riders broke away from the group and galloped toward them.

Her breath caught in her chest. She clutched the reins in a fierce grip. The searing burn in her gut sparked the foul taste of bile. Not now. Not this close to sanctuary?

Arlan tightened his grip as she went to kick the horse to a faster pace.

"Go, Rosin. They can't stop us now."

The lead rider yelled out a challenge. "Halt, in the name of King Cadmar. Halt, I say."

Rosin sagged. Relief flooded through her. They had arrived. Sobs bucked in her chest to be released. She forced them back, but she couldn't stop the tremors vibrating through her body. Her hands clutched the reins and drew the horse to a halt.

It breathed heavily, snorting plumes of frost from its nostrils, and foam and saliva dribbled from its mouth. It danced on the spot, nervously aware of kindred spirits galloping toward it.

Rosin patted its neck, then spoke gently to calm the fidgety mount.

Arlan leaned forward. "Seems we'll have an escort the last distance."

"Yes, we've made it, Arlan."

The two horses skidded to a halt just off to their left.

One of the riders, a blond-headed young man who stood slightly upright in his stirrups, yelled, "Identify yourself. Reveal your faces."

His orders were backed up from a short distance behind by the second rider with a slingshot armed and aimed at the horse's legs.

A bubble of joy flared, warm and comforting in Rosin's chest as she recognized her slightly older cousin Keegan.

She pulled the cloak hood from her face. "I am Rosin, Lady of Keswin, Princess Apparent to Keswin's throne. I seek safety and support from your father, King Cadmar, as his Moon Life Daughter."

Keegan's jaw sagged, contorting his mouth open. Ashen faced, he moved forward, peering at her. "Praise the Maidens, it is you.

Cousin Rosin, you live."

He reached over to hug her.

She squeezed his hand. "Can we leave the greetings till later, cousin? My companion and I are both injured and need healing and some warmth in our bones."

"Surely, cousin, come unto the gates." Keegan waved at his armed companion. "Gale, go to the castle and warn my parents. I bring the Princess Apparent of Keswin and a companion. Father's healing skills will be required and tell the cook to prepare some food."

Gale stowed his weapon, kicked his horse, and took off in a flurry of mud at a mad gallop.

"Ashlynn, come forward, it's Rosin."

The chariot rattled across the snow and swung around a few feet from their horse. "Cousin Rosin. Dearest cousin, we thought you were dead." Emotion choked her words into broken syllables.

"I nearly died several times, Ashlynn"

"Do you want to ride the rest of the way with me?" Her cousin eyed Arlan, suspicion and curiosity clear in her expression.

"Thank you, Ashlynn, but no. I have a broken leg and my passenger is injured, so we best stay aboard the horse until we arrive."

"Let's go, Fenton."

Her driver obediently whipped the horses, and the chariot took off at a fast clip toward the gates of the castle.

With the rest of the party as escort, Keegan rode close beside their horse. He kept glancing at her all the way to the gates.

Rosin withered under his scrutiny, dreading having to explain her situation.

The outside gates opened, and when they approached, trumpets heralded their arrival.

They slowed to a walk to negotiate between the inner walls and the steep slope up to the living quarters.

The first faces she recognized in the inner courtyard were her Moon Life Mother, Queen Meghan and her Moon Life Protector, King Cadmar. Dread seeped cold into her heart. How will they take it? How would she face telling them?

Cadmar's thick coat flapped open as he reached up to take her horse's bridle, revealing his splinted leg. His mouth was drawn into a tight line.

A sudden rush of emotion gripped her chest. Tears sprang into her eyes, then tumbled down her cheeks as sobs shuddered through her.

Arlan tightened his hold. "You've done it, Rosin."

"Not without you, Arlan."

"Nor me without you, my love." His voice cracked, and he fell silent.

Cadmar and Meghan were beside them. Servants helped her out of the saddle. Pain seared through her, and she cried out as they lay her on a stretcher. In that moment, she also flushed with shame as she realized her pants were soaked in blood.

The servants also helped Arlan down, but when he lifted his cowl from his face, they gasped and stepped back.

Undaunted by his appearance, her Protector stepped forward and held out his hand. "I am Rosin's Moon Life Protector, King Cadmar. Welcome to my home."

Arlan took his hand and shook it. "I am Arlan, First Knight of Keswin."

The king frowned at his use of the title.

"Sire, forgive me if I offend, but I suffered a blow to the head, and this is the name the Princess gave me because I could not—still don't—remember my own. She saved my life, as I have hers, on our journey here, and I ask only that you offer me some healing, accommodation, and hospitality worthy of a good warrior. It is not my intention to impose upon your patience or goodwill, but you should know that I have sworn fealty to Rosin, Princess Apparent of Keswin, and will fight to protect her, and if she so desires, to the death, for her to regain her throne." He bowed low in respect but fell to his knees as the blood loss from his wounds took effect.

Rosin cried out as he thudded to the flagstones.

Cadmar stayed her forward lunge. "Go, child. Meghan and Rowena will tend to you. I'll have him taken care of."

He intended to separate them quickly, before anyone asked questions or drew assumptions. She understood his protective actions but resented them at the same time.

Nevertheless, she bit down on her protest when a couple of servants came forward and bundled Arlan onto a stretcher and carted him away. There would be time enough later to set Cadmar straight.

Unable to do anything else, she slumped back, letting go of the thin thread she had clung to since the moment Devon had made his first demand.

With Meghan at her side, Rosin took the two draughts the physician offered so he could re splint her leg and ease the fever that wracked her body. She drank it all. Immediately the blackness rolled in, not the terrifying oblivion she'd often fought in recent moon-sweeps, but a soothing nothingness that she fell into without argument.

~ ~ ~

Arlan opened his eyes and stared at the ceiling above him. He went to push himself up and the world span around him and a ripping pain seared through his shoulder.

"Don't try and get up, warrior, you've lost a lot of blood and have a couple of savage gashes to your shoulder.

He flinched. He didn't recognize the male voice. He lifted his head and looked at the man sitting beside him.

"I'm Dragorn, one of King Cadmar's healers. You brought the Princess Rosin to the castle."

Arlan nodded. "Is she safe? She needed healing."

Dragorn smiled splitting his ginger beard and moustache in half showing a mouthful of yellow teeth. "The Princess, she be taken care of. Did you set her broken leg?"

Arlan grimaced. "I did."

"You did a mighty fine job of it, young man. And who mended your face and chest such as it is."

Arlan shook his head. "Princess Rosin. I all but entered the Afterlife after the battle with Devon." He shuddered involuntarily. "I was dying with infection, and she put maggots on me. Hundreds of them wriggling and crawling. They cleaned up the infection then she stitched me up."

Dragorn chuckled. "She's a bonnie little lass is Princess Rosin. King Cadmar always tells that story. I've used them before. Work a treat they do. I'm surprised Princess Rosin remembered that story it's been a while since they visited."

Arlan shuddered again. "I hope never again."

"Let's get you sitting up. You need sustenance to build up your blood and stamina."

A maid entered with a tray. Arlan stomach growled, and he realized how hungry he was.

He looked around the room as he ate. "Where am I, Dragorn?"

"You be in the officer's quarters of Tarlic Castle. King Cadmar has insisted you are looked after in style. Carrick one of his

Commanders will come by soon with a uniform and boots for you when you are able to get up. There is no rush."

"I need to get well, Dragorn, I made an oath to protect Princess Rosin with my life."

"As I said young man there is no rush. The princess is healing too. She won't be going anywhere anytime soon."

Arlan lay back exhausted.

Dragorn covered him with a blanket and gave him some potion. "Sleep, young man, so you can heal."

~ ~ ~

Arlan started awake as the door opened and footsteps crunched across the floor.

He opened his eyes. A tall, lean but muscular man stood by the bed his arms loaded with clothes.

He smiled and dumped the clothes on the chair by the bed then held out his hand in the warrior's grip.

Arlan shook his hand.

He was quite a bit older than Arlan believed he might be with short cropped blond hair and a neat moustache that framed his mouth and curved onto his wide square chin almost meeting in the middle. His blue eyes twinkled under bushy eyebrows. "I'm Carrick, one of King Cadmar's Commanders. It appears you are somewhat of a hero, Arlan, bringing the Princess to safety."

Arlan pushed up into a sitting position.

Carrick frowned. "You fought some viper's battle to get those. I figure you're lucky to be with us."

Arlan grimaced. "If it wasn't for the Princess and her maggots I would not be. Unfortunately, they are not pretty."

"You bonded, Arlan?"

Arlan held out his arms. "Doesn't appear so." He reached up and touched his head. "I lost all my memories from a blow to the head. I don't even know my real name. Arlan is what the Princess chose for me."

"Viper's curse that's pretty rough. You don't remember anything?"

Arlan shook his head even as he delved into the blankness in his mind. "The Princess tells me I was one of the High Queen Isolde's Commissioned Warriors but other than that I know nothing."

"Well don't go fretting about it. Most memories eventually return. In the meantime get back on your feet. The nobles from around are coming to meet with King Cadmar. They are planning to do something with Devon in the thaw. A joint campaign."

"Hopefully I'll be ready to fight by then. I want to kill that viper's bite for what he did to Rosin."

Carrick frowned.

Arlan bit down on his next words. "I apologize, Carrick. The Princess Rosin."

"You taken a liking to the Princess."

Arlan frowned. "Yes. She is a smart, brave, multi-talented, and beautiful woman. We helped each other through the journey but I assure you, Carrick, I was respectful at all times. Only thing is a man can't help how he feels when in the company of one such as her. She is here to find a consort and I would not have the audacity to assume I would be suitable."

Carrick smiled. "But you might be royal, Arlan, who knows."

He grimaced. "Not royal enough to be her consort or King Cadmar would have recognized me or someone would have missed me."

"You might be thankful for that, Arlan. It will be a brave man that takes the young Princess on. Devon has a hold on the country and lots of soldiers. Her consort may die before even reaching Keswin. And who knows what damage has been done to a young woman going through such terrifying experiences. I mean she was raped for viper's sake, and you can't expect her to take well to being bedded after that by some noble that's been foisted on her. She has no battalions to fight him with, and no one knows what the High Queen will decree. She might just annex Keswin then the Princess will be exiled."

The weight of Carrick's comments thudded into him making his stomach roil and his heart thump. He straightened up and looked directly at Carrick. "I would take her on if I was given a chance."

Carrick smiled. "I think you might have a touch of fondness for the Princess."

Arlan looked away as the heat rushed up his face. Then he looked Carrick squarely in the eyes. "It's more than a touch of fondness and it leaves me gutted that nought can come of it. But I assure you I kept my place throughout our time together."

Carrick patted him on the shoulder. "I would not think otherwise, Arlan. Now I suggest you rest up for a couple more days then you and I will begin training to get you back to fitness. King Cadmar has indicated you can join Tarlic's warriors under me if you don't remember who you are and chose to stay here."

Arlan held out his hand.

Carrick took it in a firm warrior's grip. "Oh, and by the way if you want to conceal the injury to your face why don't you see Magee, the king's jeweler and engraver. He might be able to make you a mask to cover your scars."

The idea appealed to him. He didn't like the way people recoiled from him the first time they saw his face. He knew if he was around people for a while they would get used to his deformity, but it jarred on him. "Can you send him to me please?"

Carrick nodded. "I suggest you rest. You are starting to look pale and breaking out in a sweat."

Arlan nodded. "I'm struggling. No stamina, aching all over. My leg throbs and my shoulder burns like a viper's bite.

"I'll send Dragorn too. I'll check on you in a couple of moon-slides."

"Thanks, Carrick."

After Magee and Dragorn left Arlan took the potion and lay down. He stared at the ceiling. He liked Commander Carrick and if he stayed, he might find a friend. He thought about Rosin. He had heard nothing. He tossed and turned as he waited for the potion to weave its magic. Dragorn had indicated her leg was healing. He wondered about the outcome of her miscarriage. Was she healed? Was she well? Did it haunt her? He wrapped his arms around his chest missing her closeness, her smile, the strength she showed when faced with adversity and their easy companionship. He wriggled a little at the familiar ache in his groin as he remembered her scent, the soft curves of her body and the swell of her breasts.

He groaned. *Losing her is going to kill me, viper's curse. To know she is being bedded by another male and perhaps not in the sensual way I would do it.* His lungs cramped at the thought of her being afraid, of being handled roughly or even insensitively. He groaned again.

Two moon-slides later Magee brought his mask. It was an elaborate bronze with intricate filigree and engraving around the edges.

Arlan took it and tried it on. It fitted snugly to the injured side of his face and was held in place by thin lengths of plaited thong. He thanked Magee for his efforts pleased with the results.

~ ~ ~

Shortly after sunshow the following moon-slide Carrick rapped on his door and entered. Arlan had washed and was dressed in a basic uniform for training. He wore his mask. He liked the air of mystery it gave him, and he felt more relaxed knowing his scars were not visible.

They entered the training arena. The weapons boy offered him several swords. Arlan chose his favorite, the broadsword. It felt heavy in his hand, the weight pulling on his shoulder.

He slipped on his helmet and picked up his shield.

Carrick led with the first thrust. Arlan responded. They sparred for a short time circling around each other.

Out of the corner of his vision Arlan saw a man watching his arms crossed over his chest.

He ignored him as Carrick continued to attack. His shoulder ached. With a lithe flick he transferred his sword to his left hand and sliced an arch through the air. Carrick baulked then lunged forward with a long thrust. Arlan instinctively flicked his sword, spun his hand on the hilt, and caught Carrick's sword mid thrust. With a sharp flick the sword was ripped from Carrick's grip and went flying across the arena to land with a clatter. Arlan heard gasps from behind him.

Carrick stood motionless, glancing from Arlan to his sword his mouth hanging open.

The sound of single slow applause broke the silence. Arlan looked toward the sound. A dark skinned man walked slowly toward them.

Carrick turned and inclined his head.

Not knowing why Arlan did the same.

"Well done. So, you were trained by Master Warrior Garven of Annaticcia. And trained well."

Arlan stared at the man. Then shook his head. "I don't know, my lord."

He waved his hand in the air. "Call me, Kynan. I am King Cadmar's Master at Arms. And young warrior, I was not asking if you were trained by Garven. I was making a statement of fact."

Arlan shook his head. "How can you make such a statement, my lord, when I do not even know my own name."

Kynan laughed. "Only warriors trained and trained well by Master Warrior Garven can successfully execute that move. Carrick, consider yourself dead."

"Yes, Master Kynan. I've never seen anything like it before just about ripped my hand off."

"Sorry, Carrick."

"Do not be sorry, Arlan. I know it was friendly sparring, but you are not even back to full fitness yet. When you are fitter you and I will spar then perhaps you might meet your equal."

Arlan gaped at the Master of Arms. "I would not assume as much, my lord."

"Oh, but I do. And when you are back to full health I want you to train three of my best in that very move. Are you willing. You will be recompensed."

Arlan inclined his head. "I am more than willing, my lord."

Kynan frowned. "I would prefer you use my name not a title I am not eligible for."

"Yes, Kynan, as you wish. So will Carrick be one of my students?"

Kynan smiled and shook his head. "No, Carrick will not be one of your students."

Carrick grimaced. "No, Arlan, your talents would be wasted on me. I am past learning such moves."

"Carrick, you are a good solid swordsman and warrior and a wise and admirable Commander, but you are right. You have many years of experience and you are a might set in your ways. That move, and others I am sure Arlan is accomplished in, need the speed, flexibility, and sharpness of a young man along with the willingness to endure the accompanying discipline and discomfort that comes with learning such a tactic."

Carrick grimaced. "So, Master Kynan, you are saying so politely that I'm past it. Too old to learn such exacting maneuvers."

"Not exactly. I was not in any way denigrating your abilities as a warrior, Carrick, or saying you are too old. That move can take one to two successions to gain the flexibility of the wrist and the ability of both hands to manage the weapon with equal strength and accuracy to master that tactic. I would expect that Arlan was learning that move at around twelve to thirteen successions and had mastered it by the time he had his first shave."

Arlan grinned. "Is that why I do them instinctively even if I don't remember learning them?"

Kynan nodded. "Now, Arlan, I want you training every day. Carrick is a good sparring partner. When I determine you are ready, we will spar."

Arlan nodded.

Kynan turned away and disappeared into the castle.

Carrick grinned at Arlan then turned away to retrieve his weapon.

Arlan watched him return. "Maidens, Carrick that was harsh."

Carrick grinned. "Kynan is always honest with warriors. He says it will keep them alive. I know my limitations. I will be thirty-eight successions in a couple of moon cycles. I came to fighting late at twenty successions. My father thought he could provide a different path. It didn't happen. But I have my Commander's compensation, and I intend to step down in a couple of successions before I become too slow and get killed. I thought I would take up a plot and breed horses."

Arlan smiled. "At least you have a plan, Carrick."

"I do and I have a plan for you. Would you like to join me on my additional training routine. I need it to keep me fast and agile and build muscles." He held up his arm. "I've always been lean. Muscles don't come naturally to me."

Sympathy and admiration washed through him for the older man. "I would, Carrick, thank you, but make it tomorrow I've had it for this moon-slide."

Fatigue washed over Arlan, but it wasn't enough to extinguish the elation rampaging through his brain. He knew another thing about himself, and it had brought him the privilege of working with the Master at Arms and finding a task he would enjoy to keep him occupied. He had also made a friend. He knew he needed activity to make him so tired he could at least fall sleep without hours of restless grieving his lost love and haunting unrequited sexual need.

He trained hard with Carrick pushing his body into a finely tuned machine. He fell into bed each moon-wash exhausted, slept heavy and woke each morning with a strong determination to do better.

On the fifth day Carrick paused at the door. "Arlan, why don't you come with me to the barrack's dining hall. I'll introduce you around to my men and some of the others.

Doubt surged through him. He reached up and touched his mask.

"Don't worry about that, Arlan. Rumors have already circulated about you, the Princess and your injuries. Most of men carry scars of their own, especially Kinnard he got slashed across the cheek a couple of successions ago. He is a good looking lad, but he has convinced himself the ladies are turned off by his face."

"Well, he's probably right, Carrick."

Carrick smiled. "Wouldn't know myself."

"You've never found love or bonded, Carrick."

His smile faded. "Never been that lucky, Arlan, and as I'm always off at battles I haven't really made an effort. I'm thinking that leaving a woman alone or with babes so much wouldn't be fair. There are plenty of service woman to satisfy my needs in the small town to the west."

Longing crushed onto Arlan's chest. He looked across at Carrick. "I thinking only one woman will ever satisfy my need these days, Carrick, and I can't have her."

Carrick placed his hand on his shoulder. "You have to get over it, my friend."

Arlan sighed. "I know."

The dining hall was crowded and noisy. As they entered it fell almost silent. Arlan looked over the sea of male faces looking at him with eyes filled with curiosity and something else. He determined it was pity, and he recoiled from it. He didn't want pity. He didn't need it.

A handsome young warrior with a scarred face jumped up and came forward. He held out his hand and Arlan took it in the warrior's clasp. "Commander Carrick, Commander Arlan come, join us. Welcome to Tarlic Barracks, Commander Arlan. Everyone is keen to meet you as we have all heard about your epic journey to save the Princess Rosin." Kinnard smiled and touched his face. "And your survival from your injuries. They're saying she used maggots."

Arlan grimaced. "She did at that."

"Viper's curse, you should be dead."

"Enough, Kinnard."

Kinnard inclined his head to his commander. Then moved around to re-claim his seat opposite Arlan.

Carrick gestured toward two older men. "Commander Teague and Commander Goraidh. King Cadmar has such a large legion he needs three Commanders. He's like Annaticcia. The High Queen Isolde has around a thousand warriors."

Arlan grinned. "So, she won't miss me then."

"She probably wouldn't miss any of them. There is no status in Annaticcia unless you have royal blood. King Cadmar is better. The compensation is good and he pays restitution to the family if you die."

"That's a good thing."

They slid into the bench seats and were served a hearty meal.

Arlan began to relax.

After they ate Carrick guided him around introducing him to his men. Always as Commander Arlan. They accepted his rank without question.

He knew he wouldn't remember them all so he concentrated on the officers and any that stood out for some reason.

Kinnard and Rogan were his young Sub Commanders. Kinnard he would remember and Rogan had a shock of thick white blond hair that hung in his eyes and he was clean shaven.

Maguire was a stocky slightly older man with a bushy red moustache. He gripped Arlan's arm tightly. "You did a good thing, young man."

"Thank you, Maguire. I was pleased to bring the Princess to safety."

"All that time alone with the little Princess, bet you'd be pleased to be chosen her consort."

The gravelly words raked over him, obviously an accusation. As he turned five warriors entered via the side door.

The huge warrior leading them slammed his fist into the man's smirking face then as he fell snatched him up by his arm and hauled him to his feet. "And who are you to be making such accusations. A measly scullion maid besmirching a princess and a hero."

The man squeaked his protest.

The warrior holding him looked directly at Arlan.

Arlan inclined his head.

Carrick growled and stepped forward. "You speak out of turn, Tain. How dare you make such a crude accusation."

Arlan clenched his fists at his side.

Carrick turned to him. "There has been talk, Arlan. The men don't know the facts and therefore speculate and gossip. It's something that's piqued their interest"

"Well, I'll give them the facts then they can keep their mouths shut." He pulled out a chair and stepped up onto it. He looked around the room. "I'm Commander Arlan and I'm only going to say this once so listen closely. The Princess Rosin has been through the viper's pit and back. Her parents, loyal nobles and her betrothed were massacred on the moon-wash of her Bonding of Le Chéile by Devon because he wants Keswin's crown. After the slaughter was over, he dragged her off and raped her. He then placed her in a cruel metal chastity belt. She escaped and walked across the country. She crossed rivers at the tidal wash unaided always hiding from her pursuers. In a rescue attempt my comrades were killed and I sustained severe injuries that wiped out my memories. The Princess saved my life and when I healed I assisted her on her journey. At Cottom village we were set upon by two of Devon's men but with some villager's help we killed them and took their horses. Unfortunately crossing the pass we were again set upon by Devon's men. I was struggling to defeat our foes with my injuries but with Princess Rosin's help we overcame them. Princess Rosin was thrown from her horse, breaking her leg and causing her to miscarry the child of that monstrosity. I was bleeding like a stuck pig but we managed to cross the river at the tidal wash and get to the castle. Despite these horrendous experiences the Princess is now trying to find a *suitable royal* consort so she can return and reclaim her crown and save her people from Devon." He surveyed the men watching him. No one was talking. "I will not tolerate anyone speaking badly of the Princess or making crude innuendoes about her journey. She is a courageous, brave, intelligent, capable and dedicated woman who has suffered much and yet still desires to save her realm at great cost to herself. If I hear the slightest wrong whisper about her that person will either front King Cadmar or me at sun-show in the training arena. Do I make myself clear."

A murmur rose around the room, all eyes on him. Arlan watched them closely.

Kinnard rose from his seat. "And with that there will be an empty place or two at the dinner table."

"Kinnard, take Tain to the lockup. He's confined until he learns some manners."

Kinnard nodded to Carrick and pointed to Maguire. "Give us a hand, Maguire."

Arlan replaced the chair and sat down. Carrick sat beside him.

"Who's the big warrior with the tattoos."

Carrick leaned close. "He's Dominus Trystan from Sanjeva. King Mostyn's half brother."

Arlan's heart clenched. "So, he could be a potential consort."

"Not likely. He's half Gaudi."

"So."

"Rexus Mostyn wouldn't have it. He despises his half brother."

Arlan glanced up, but Dominus Trystan was gone.

Kinnard returned grinning. "That stilled his tongue. He was full of apologies."

Tormey a lanky young man leapt out of his seat and grabbed Arlan's hand. "Stupid milkmaid. Always running his mouth off about others. Glad you told us your story, Commander."

Arlan guessed he was only sixteen or so successions.

"I saw you training the other day. What you did with that sword was incredible. Will you teach me?"

Arlan smiled as he released his grip on Tormey's forearm. "Maybe, Tormey. Master Kynan will be choosing who I train."

Tormey smiled faded as he dropped back in his seat.

Beside him sat a young man with short dark blond hair and a fine moustache on his top lip. His deep blue eyes almost bordered on grey. He smiled slightly and inclined his head. "I'm Kaiden, a new recruit." He didn't offer his hand.

Arlan acknowledged him with a slight smile as he pushed out of his seat. "Peaceful rest all. It's been a long day."

Later back in his room he stared at the ceiling. He ached with need for Rosin. He had heard nothing, and he fretted for her health and safety.

As he trained with Carrick the next moon-slide he could see he was being watched. They paused.

King Cadmar and Prince Keegan stood at the fence with Kynan.

Carrick gestured they should go and greet them.

Arlan looked Cadmar over. And older man with a clean shaven head and an elaborate grey moustache. He used a stick to ease his stance.

Arlan remembered Rosin saying he'd broken his leg.

He bowed deeply beside Carrick. As he straightened the King spoke.

"Arlan, I see your health is improving."

Arlan inclined his head. "Yes, Your Majesty, I am grateful for your care and the provision of my clothes and weapons and my access to training."

"Kynan tells me you were trained by the Master Warrior of Annaticcia."

Again, Arlan nodded. "He tells me I have Master Garven's special tactics."

The King smiled.

Arlan looked directly at the king. "May I, with respect, Your Majesty, inquire after Princess Rosin's health? We struggled together on our journey, and she saved my life. I would wish she is regaining her health."

King Cadmar smiled. "The Princess Rosin is recovering well. She is convalescing under the Queen's care. Nobles from Wilsea, Dyanwen will arrive on the next moon-slide, the Sanjeva Rexus Mostyn arrived last moon-slide. They will draw up a plan for a campaign in the thaw to defeat Devon. With the nobles here I hope the Princess can find a suitable consort to be by her side. Then she will return to Keswin and defeat that monster Devon and re-claim her throne."

The King's words pierced Arlan's soul. His heart clenched and a lump dropped in his gut. He knew it was going to happen but having it said out loud slammed it into reality.

He inclined his head. "I am glad the Princess will have the support of others and I wish her and her chosen consort well in their campaign."

King Cadmar smiled as he turned away.

Arlan's heart clenched. Had she asked after him? Did she care for him at all? Had he misinterpreted her attention. Coldness flooded through him.

Keegan grabbed his hand as he went to follow his father. He leaned close. "She asks after you every day, Arlan. I think you made an impression on my cousin."

The heat flared in his face. "Your cousin, the Princess made an impression on me too, Your Highness. She is a remarkable woman, brave, strong, intelligent, capable, and compassionate and caring. And if I may say so without disrespect, Your Highness, she is beautiful."

Keegan smiled. "No disrespect taken, Arlan. My cousin is a beautiful woman."

"She will make an incredible Queen, Your Highness. I hope she finds a consort who will appreciate her qualities and provide the support she will need in her battle to re-claim her crown. Please could you pass my wishes onto her for me, if I am not taking too much liberty."

"She will, Arlan, and I will pass on your wishes and I'll update her on your progress. Father is reluctant. He is concerned for her mind and her reputation."

Arlan inclined his head as Prince Keegan turned away.

His own words seared his soul. He looked at Carrick. "Let's go for a run, Carrick. A hard run."

Carrick patted his shoulder. "You poor lunar curse."

Arlan turned away from Carrick's sympathy and started around the parapet of the wall at a slow jog.

Arlan kept running until he stumbled and his knees collapsed. He dropped to the stones panting and gasping sweat pouring off him his wet clothes sticking to his skin.

"Stop, Arlan, before you hurt yourself. Having a relapse if not going to change it."

He pushed to his feet. "I know, Carrick. I'm going to wash and sleep I can't face anymore this moon-slide."

~ ~ ~

Two moon-slides later the long boats of Wilsea sailed up the river.

Carrick came to stand beside him. "The barracks will be full this moon-wash. And they will set up camp behind the castle. Wilsea brought two hundred men, Queen Brigit of Dyanwen one hundred and I think Sanjeva's Rexus Mostyn has brought a couple of hundred."

Arlan watched the ships as they were hauled to the shore and tethered. He sighed. Those ships were bringing a consort for the woman he loved. His heart sat like a cold lump of snow behind his ribs.

The next moon-slide Kynan appeared at the training arena. Carrick withdrew to the sidelines. A shiver of doubt flickered through him, but it didn't time to get a hold for Kynan lunged at him with a deadly thrust and Arlan was fighting to protect himself.

Kynan gave no quarter.

Nor did Arlan. He circled and thrust protecting himself with his shield.

Their grunts and deeply exhaled breaths and the crash of metal on metal echoed around the arena.

As the strength in his shoulder faded he flicked his sword and changed hands but his complicated twist failed to catch Kynan's weapon. He sidestepped and thrust just touching Kynan's tunic.

He spun away fast and lunged.

Arlan stepped back and swept his sword in an arc flicking Kynan's shield out of his grip but as he brought the sword down Kynan's sword point touched his throat.

Arlan lunged aside spun and brought his sword in almost touching Kynan's abdomen. He was panting and gasping his body throbbing with pain.

Kynan flinched back and lunged aside. He spun to face Arlan. "Enough."

Arlan stilled before lifting his sword in a sweep in front of his face. He inclined his head to Kynan. He drew in huge breaths of air, his legs trembled and sweat poured from his body.

Kynan lifted his sword and also inclined his head. "Well done, Arlan. A return to full fitness will once again make you a warrior to be reckoned with even for me."

Arlan bowed. "Thank you, Kynan for your praise."

Kynan smiled as he collected his shield. "I only give praise when it is deserved, Arlan. I never allow Warriors to overestimate their skills for it will get them killed."

"True, Kynan. I just hope my shoulder improves. It is my weak spot."

"We will spar every day, Arlan and I want you to continue your training with Carrick. Tomorrow, gentlemen."

~ ~ ~

At last, Ashlynn came with permission for Rosin to leave her suite. Her ambulation, aided by a pair of crutches fashioned by the castle carpenter, and a maid to help her with every task, was slow but steady. She cursed her lost vigor.

From the moment her fever had abated, and she could sit up in a chair, she'd grown restless and frustrated beyond bearing. There had been no sight of Arlan since their arrival at the castle, only messages passed on by Keegan. She fretted for him. No matter her resolve, she missed him with a primeval ache that only he could appease.

Meghan and Cadmar had visited her every moon-slide, and both assured her Arlan had made a full recovery. Cadmar had settled Arlan in the officers' quarters and had him training with the Master at Arms to regain his strength.

Arlan apparently asked after her often and sent messages of support and concern, but he had not come to visit her. She wondered whether he hadn't asked or hadn't been allowed. Rosin didn't know, and Cadmar always changed the subject by urging her to get well.

Ashlynn had been her constant companion during her convalescence, playing hauntingly sweet tunes on a small silver whistle, talking to her about happenings in the castle, and puffing her pillows. Oddly, Ashlynn had not asked once in the whole twelve moon-slides of her illness what had happened.

Rosin suspected she'd been strictly instructed by her parents not to ask questions.

Keegan had often brought her news of Arlan and his respectful messages of good wishes. Unlike his sister, Keegan hinted at his desire to know what had happened.

When Rosin just shook her head, he either had the good manners not to persist or had also been placed under a strict rule of silence.

She headed to Cadmar's parlor, determined to outline her plans for the future.

Meghan and Ashlynn helped her, fussing and clucking as she made her way slowly down the corridor.

Cadmar sat in a large chair close to the open fire where he had already been served a sumptuous morning tea. He indicated the chair opposite him.

Ashlynn helped Rosin get settled while Meghan plied her with a hot posset and some freshly baked cake.

Rosin shook her head at the offerings.

Meghan didn't insist merely sitting back and studying her intently.

Rosin knew Meghan and Ashlynn waited impatiently for

Cadmar to ask the questions uppermost in all their minds.

"You look well, my child. Is the leg still paining you?" Cadmar asked.

"I'm fine, Father Cad, but I have many things to discuss with you. Nobody has spoken to me about what happened or asked any questions about my state when I arrived? For this I am grateful, but I'm unhappy I've not been allowed to see my companion, Arlan."

"A decision I made in your best interests, child. You needed to be cosseted and cared for. Time to heal from your significant injuries."

"Father Cad, with respect, I need to say this. I have been through so much these last moon-sweeps. I am no longer the darling, doted-on daughter of a happy queen and consort. I have seen things, done things, and experienced things that many battle-hardened warriors haven't. I'm changed forever. I cannot afford to be gentle and soft and will no longer tolerate being cosseted or patronized. I no longer trust easily, and I will not bear being lied to or told half-truths to spare me."

"You are, but a child, Rosin, a full succession younger than Ashlynn." Cadmar frowned as he protested.

"No longer, my dear Father Cad, nor can I afford to be. I am the Queen of Keswin but will not call myself thus until I can reclaim my throne."

"There is no rush, child. You are safe here."

She pushed herself awkwardly forward in her chair. "Please stop being soothing. I need you to understand what I am saying. I do not want to disrespect you, Father Cad, but I must make you understand the new order."

Cadmar frowned as he leaned back in his chair. "To me, you're Maeve and Fintain's little girl, and you are ours now they is gone. It's hard for me to bear the weight of guessing at the atrocities you have seen, and the pain you have suffered just from your state when you arrived here. But it also pains me to have you speak to me thus."

"I know it is hard for you. Be assured I don't ever want you to stop loving and caring for me, but I cannot have you clip my wings with what you see as kindness. The time has gone for that."

He nodded. "Then tell me, Rosin, what happened, and what you want from me. Place before me your plans for the future. I will try to understand the changes in you and give you the respect that is your due. Meghan and I will help and support you as best we can."

"Thank you for understanding. Please, I would suggest Ashlynn leaves us, for what I have to say is not for her ears."

"Cousin, I'm older than you. I wish to hear your story."

"Dearest Ashlynn, what I have to say will give you nightmares you need not suffer. Please respect my wish that you leave us."

Rosin nearly smiled at her cousin's sulky expression and the hard lines etched on the queen's face. Meghan did not appear pleased her daughter would be excluded.

"Ashlynn and Mother Meg, I wish I could once again be blessed with the innocence Ashlynn has, but that will never be. They savagely ripped my innocence from me, and I do not want to be responsible for that loss of innocence in you, Ashlynn. I will give you an abridged version later, though, I promise."

"Leave us, Ashlynn, please."

The young woman frowned at her father but stood and left the room with reluctant obedience. She quietly but firmly closed the door behind her.

Rosin eased back in her chair. She glanced from Cadmar to Meghan, then down at her hands. "This story began much earlier than the moon-slide of my bonding. Some you may already know, but I will try to weave the background into the telling in an attempt to make some sense of this nightmare."

As her story unfolded in all its gory details, she spared them nothing. Queen Meghan's face blanched, tears welled in her eyes, and her tongue flicked out to moisten dry lips.

Cadmar's face alternated between red and gray, and he fidgeted in his seat at each new revelation.

When she spoke of her rape, Meghan covered her face with her hands and dropped to her knees by Rosin's feet. Her Moon Life Mother took Rosin's clenched fingers in her own and held them tightly as she stared up at her with tears pouring down her face. Her blue eyes filled with sparks of anger, and her carefully crimsoned lips clenched in a tight line as she bit down on words of sympathy.

By the time Rosin had finished speaking, tears poured down her beloved Father Cad's face, his tea and cake untouched on the tray.

Drained by the emotional retelling, Rosin struggled to go on, but believed she must finish making him aware of her demands and plans.

"Enough, my child. You should rest."

She shook her head. "Perhaps a sip of your prized brandy would revive me."

He snorted with suppressed amusement. "You are your father's daughter, Rosin."

He handed her the spirit and Rosin warmed it with her hands, as her father had taught her. Cadmar poured a double for himself and one for Meghan.

Rosin took a sip, welcoming the burn down her throat. "Please don't hold it against me that I aborted my child. I could not allow it to live."

"You will not be subject to judgment by anyone, my child."

Meghan looked at her céile fir. "Will she, Cadmar?"

The king shook his head. "Despite my dislike of such actions, I know you did the right thing this time."

"I want to see Arlan."

"He concerns me, child. He is unknown. He claims he does not remember, but I am, like you, untrusting. You rode in here in his arms, injured and bleeding from an obvious miscarriage. I think to see him again would perhaps set tongues wagging."

"I am a little beyond caring what others think of me. I have done nothing wrong. Arlan knows where my future lies. He knows I must find a suitable consort to be able to claim my throne."

"How do you feel about that?"

"How do I feel?" She repeated his words. "Bitter, angry, and cheated. I did my duty in agreeing to be bonded to the appropriate person, even though at the time I thought I loved Garrett. Following the horror, I have to deny my feelings for an unknown warrior to form a Bond of Le Chéile with someone—anyone—suitable, to reclaim my throne. I have even thought of abdicating."

"You cannot..." Cadmar protested.

Rosin stayed his protest with her hand. "No, I cannot. But to reclaim my throne, I must have a consort, and I will need your help with this."

He nodded.

"And I wish to find out more about Arlan—to identify him, if possible—for no one should spend their life with a pretend name. I will also need some support in the way of warriors, food, and equipment as I intend to return as soon as possible to retake Keswin, then seek out Devon and kill him."

Her Moon Life Protectors both nodded. "We will give you what you need and so will the others."

"Others?"

"I have several of the lords and chieftains gathered here to work out a strategy to hunt Devon down. Even Queen Brigit has come with her heir and the twin siblings of Eled. Most cannot spare much because the Depcisians are raiding heavily again and Devon has already attacked the smaller towns and outlying villages right through the withering season. He has claimed them for his own. We will all meet here tomorrow. I will find a consort for you and see what the others can offer in support. Do you feel ready for this, child?"

"Yes, Father, I'm impatient to get this done."

Chapter 14

Just after sun-show the next moon-slide, King Cadmar's valet, Bryne, summoned her to the parlor where Cadmar and Meghan sat by the fire, a tray arranged before them.

"Come, Daughter, sit and eat before we talk."

Rosin tried to do justice to the spread, but she had no appetite and finally gave up the attempt. She rose and paced the room. Her heart danced with fluttering beats in her chest as a gigantic lump of cold apprehension collected in her stomach.

King Cadmar indicated the chair.

Rosin flopped into it; her countenance deliberately set into a serious mask. The next hour or so would define the path her life would take. She desperately wanted to run away and hide. With a calming breath, she stilled her restlessness and fixed her gaze on her Moon Life Protector.

Cadmar's expression mirrored her own. "We need to sort your wee little mess out, child, before word reaches the High Queen about your un-stewarded kingdom."

Rosin responded with a simple nod of acknowledgment. She knew what she had to do. Make a Bond of Le Chéile and bear a legitimate child. Her heart lurched. Not like the baby she'd murdered who had been neither legitimate nor descended directly from any of the six maidens.

"I know what I must do, Father Cad."

"But you cannot do this alone, child. Already you've been

through more than any person, especially a Princess Apparent of such a tender age should go through. Your eyes and mind should never have been tainted with such horror." King Cadmar stirred uneasily in his seat.

Rosin sat up straighter and stared directly at her Moon Life Protector. "It's too late to mourn the loss of my innocence, as it is too late to mourn my purity. You talk of bonding, but who of the nobles gathered here will put their son forward to be my consort? My kingdom is in a state of mutiny. The traitors have taken down its monarchy in a savage coup, because they were not happy with the rule they lived under. I'm damaged goods, in that a man has already impregnated me. I have killed not only men of war, but my own child. My throne is at risk and who shall ever stand beside me as my consort will have to fight? He will have to lead whatever ragtag army I can bring together from farmers and laborers. All my knights are dead or have betrayed us to Lord Devon, even... even...the man I once thought loved me."

Tears sprang into her eyes, not because she still loved Garrett, but at the pain of the betrayal. He had never loved her. A convenient pawn in Muireach's grab for the throne and Lord Devon's murderous games. He had been charged with taking her maidenhead outside of a legalized bonding to bring her purity and the legitimacy of her first child into question. He would never have formed a union with her but left her dishonored and abandoned.

"You can only move forward, my beloved Daughter of Rianon. We must gather the chieftains and request who will show the strength of character to put forward their son, or even themselves. There are a number of options." Her Protector's words trailed off into an uncomfortable silence.

Rosin lifted her chin in a gesture of defiance, then drew a thin veil of anger around her vulnerable heart. For all her show of bravery, she perceived herself as a piece of merchandise or other discarded item in the market, to be sold to the highest bidder. Only in her case, the bids were not expected to be high.

"Do you wish me to do this through a secret ballot, child? It would save you much heartache and personal torment..." Cadmar's words faded, stifled into silence by his own embarrassment and anguish.

Pride and anger held her stiff and strong. She shook her head at the barest minimum. "No, Father Cad. I will face their scrutiny, their refusals. I will look them straight in the eye and hope to see some embarrassment in their own."

Up until now, Meghan had remained silent, watching the exchange between her céile fir and her Moon Life Daughter. She leaned forward in her seat, reached out, and touched Rosin's tightly clenched hands. "It will gain you nothing, Rosin."

Rosin lifted her head and stared directly into her eyes. "I will face them as I have already faced such tragedy, and no doubt will again. But I refuse to slink off into some secluded corner while they decide my future. I have no shame to hide that Devon raped and beat me and that I saw my parents and my betrothed murdered. I will not bow my head, dearest Mother Meg and my beloved Protector—for you, for them, or anyone. I have done nothing to be ashamed of."

"That you have not, Rosin, but..." Meghan shook her head, then gave Rosin's hands a light squeeze as she fell silent.

Far from comforting her, the warmth of Meg's hands over hers overwhelmed Rosin and she shrank away from the humanness of her touch, back into her emotional place of refuge—her cold place—the place where no one could reach her.

In the face of her determination, Cadmar summoned the nobles from the adjacent parlor with a barely perceptible flick of his fingers.

They had come from all the surrounding counties, duchies, and kingdoms, any place over which her Protector had even the smallest influence. They stood in an untidy knot just inside the door. Each noble shuffled to keep their space in the tightly knit group. No one wanted to come farther into the room. They all stood with eyes downcast, immediately after flicking nervous glances over her and the King of Tarlic.

Rosin accepted without question their responses—she already knew what their answers would be—so she lifted her chin and stared directly at them. She studied the various stages of baldness that afflicted the older lords and the flurry of thick curls or long, pony-tailed locks of the younger men. Men her own age, ones who should have been clamoring for her hand in partnership. Actually, had been in the not too distant past. Rosin wondered what thoughts now filled their heads and hearts.

With all that has happened, Rosin knew these young men in front of her did not have the maturity or the fortitude she needed. She studied the older nobles and wondered if any would take her. None appealed to her sensibilities, but her desires no longer mattered. In fact, they probably never had. This confrontation would determine her consort.

"So, my lords and ladies, you know why you're gathered here. Firstly, Brigit, I must express my condolences on the loss of your son. He would have made worthy consort for my Moon Life Daughter."

Rosin stared hard at her late betrothed's mother, Queen Brigit of Dyanwen. She allowed her mouth to soften just a smidge as she met the woman's tortured eyes.

"Your Majesty, your son, Eled, appeared to be an exceptional young man. I would have been proud to be his bhean chéile, to have him stand by my side and make Keswin a worthy kingdom. I am sorry for your loss, but I can say he died a hero, fighting by my father's side to protect the queen and myself from harm. He killed many before being at last overwhelmed by several of Lord Devon's soldiers. He did not go easily, Your Majesty."

The Queen gave a sad, solemn smile as she stepped forward. She reached out and took Rosin into her embrace. "Thank you for your kind words, Princess. I am appalled at the happenings of that moon-wash. I had eagerly anticipated a stronger bond with your kingdom." Brigit inclined her head ever so slightly toward King Cadmar. "Rosin's words give me some comfort, Cadmar, some small comfort. I have three other children, Bryce, my successor and Eled's twin, and Tearlach and Una, but the deeds carried out that moon-wash horrify me, so I wish to make some small contribution to Rosin's campaign for her throne."

"You wish to offer your third son to my daughter?"

Queen Brigit reddened. "Sorry, my lord. I would ask to be excused on that task. I need my sons at my side. While Tearlach is not my heir, he is very young, and the task of consort to Rosin is not without its dangers." She paused for a moment, overcome by her emotions.

Rosin nodded respectfully. "Of course, gracious Queen." Her voice barely rose above a whisper, but it sounded loud and grating in the silence that enveloped the cringing nobles.

"But Princess, I would like to offer you a small token of my esteem and condolences. When you find your consort, I will put at your command one hundred of my best men, fifty horses, including some of my best breeding stock, and twenty male servlings educated in useful trades. If you so desire, I will put ten female servlings at your disposal as cooks, seamstresses, maids, and ladies-in-waiting. Each person will be appropriately armed."

Tears sprang to Rosin's eyes, and she swept a deep curtsy at the Queen's feet. "My dear lady, your generosity shows no bounds."

Queen Brigit placed her hands on Rosin's shoulders, indicating she should rise. "Princess, all I ask in return is that you secure your kingdom and provide the neighborly support your parents have in the past."

Rosin nodded as she choked down her emotions. "It will be done, Majesty."

The Queen nodded. Rosin saw tears in her eyes and sweat on her brow and realized how this noble woman had struggled with this interview, and she empathized with her pain.

"You are thanked, Your Majesty, and dismissed. We will talk later of details." Cadmar indicated for the servant to open the door for the Queen.

At King Cadmar's dismissal, the Queen and her son Bryce turned on their heels and strode from the room.

A heavy silence descended again, and no one made any attempt to break it.

They waited for what seemed like an eternity until finally, the King cleared his throat. "Well, gentlemen, after that generosity, who will make an offer of their son or a suitable noble of good reputation to become Princess Rosin's consort. You have all been told of her dramas and the state of her kingdom. No information has been spared, so you can make an informed decision."

Rosin leaned on the chair for support. She wanted to flee the line of lords as each one stepped forward to refuse Cadmar's request.

As Rexus Mostyn waited his turn his younger brother Dominus Cerdric pulled at his arm and whispered hasty words in his ear. Rexus Mostyn shoved his half brother aside with a savage "No." And a shake of his head.

Rosin watched the exchange closely but could not interpret the exchange between the two men.

They all had excuses but other than Rexus Mostyn each of the others made an offer of help with men, horses, and weapons in a gesture of goodwill.

Rosin flopped back in the chair when the last lord and his gangly man-child son left the room. The silence became so intense, it pressed painfully on either side of Rosin's head. She closed her eyes to hold back her tears and ease the pounding in her skull.

Even when Meghan touched her shoulder in a gesture of sympathy and reassurance, she couldn't respond. Totally drained of purpose and self-esteem, her limbs rubbery and unresponsive, her chest burned with the effort it took to hold back her anguished sobs. All this shame for nothing. Even their offers of help hinged on her finding a consort.

Anger burned brightly for a moment, then faded, tempered by understanding. She had little to offer, and her kingdom would have to be fought for and resurrected. Whoever would take on the task of being her consort would have a mammoth chore ahead of them and no guarantees of a peaceful life.

As if from a distance, she heard the King ease himself into his chair. He remained silent.

Rosin sought relief in his silence, grateful for his thoughtfulness while she mulled over her failure to secure a consort. If no suitable noble could be found, how did she solve the impasse? The laws on these matters are clear. No consort, no throne.

Her hands stung with shooting pains when she finally moved them from under her thighs. The surrounding silence was so profound it filled the room with tension that made even her uncomfortable. She opened her eyes.

Cadmar still sat opposite her, smoking his pipe, staring deep into the flames of the fire, which now heated a kettle of water.

"At last, you are back with us, child. Let us share a mug of my favorite herbal tea, and then we shall talk."

Rosin hiccupped, swallowed, then spoke. "My Lord Protector, Father Cad, there is nothing to talk about because I have no options left. The law cannot be satisfied. No one wants me." Tears fell down her cheeks and onto her hands. Each droplet seared the newly awakening flesh. "I don't blame them, but I thought in honor and respect for my parents, someone would step forward. Even offering one of their older nobles, perhaps a widower. It did not have to be an heir."

Cadmar shook his head. "They fear Lord Devon. They fear what he might do to retain the throne. They fear for their sons lives and also what the High Queen Isolde will make of it all. If she steps in and annexes Keswin as part of Annaticcia, even if you try to regain your throne, you and your consort would be homeless. All your sacrifices may be in vain if Isolde declares it so."

Rosin sighed deeply. "So, what do I do now?"

"Tell me, my daughter, about your companion. This young man, Arlan?" Meghan broke her silence for the first time since the nobles entered the room.

"There is no point, Mother Meg. To speak of such only causes me considerable pain."

"Why is there no point, child?"

"Meghan, perhaps it is best not to pursue this line of questioning. It is upsetting Rosin. I'm devastated by the responses. That alone is enough upset for one moon-slide."

Meghan shot her céile fir a stern glare. "I would guess she is fond of this young man. Perhaps he is to be considered."

Cadmar frowned. "The laws are clear. She must make a union to a man of noble birth and produce an heir, or else the throne is forfeit to the High Queen."

"I cannot let that happen." More tears welled and spilled over to run down her cheeks in wide, salty rivulets. "Is there nothing I can do?"

"I do not know what we should do next, Rosin, but I will give it some thought. Perhaps you need some rest before you get overly distraught." Cadmar patted her knee in a soothing gesture.

"Come, child, dry your tears." Meghan stepped forward and clasped Rosin into a tight embrace.

As she clutched her Moon Life Mother and buried her face in the proffered shoulder, she heard Meghan speak to Cadmar.

Her tone was slightly sharp with emotion. "Cadmar dear, as you know from Shamir's studies, the laws are not as cut and dried as you and Rosin's parents believed they should be lived by. We have discussed this many times, Cadmar. The depth of the laws should be shared with all. Do you not think there would be a clause in the laws to guide us in this situation? It can't be the first time in history such a tragedy has occurred." Her question a direct challenge for her céile fir and King.

"Meghan, dearest, I do not think it is the time to be putting forward unrecognized laws out of Shamir's dusty, handwritten book. I do not think we should be giving Rosin false hopes. The High Queen will not tolerate a high-handed approach to this matter."

"Cadmar, if the laws are written, then even the High Queen must capitulate. We owe it to our daughter to leave no stone unturned in the search for a solution. She deserves that, at the very least, after what she has been through at the hands of ego-driven males."

"Meghan. It is unfair to include all of us."

"Are you going to forbid me, Cadmar, to seek the truth?" She stared intently into his eyes.

Cadmar slammed his drinking vessel to the table. His moustache twitched as he drew his eyebrows down into a frown. "Would it do me any good, my queen, if I did?"

"No, Cadmar, it would not. I did not form a bond with you to become your puppet, as you well know. I have my own brain and thoughts within it to be used to better this family's life."

"Oh, Meghan, the love of my life, and the precious stone in my boot." Cadmar groaned as he wrapped his huge arms around Rosin and the queen, squeezing them in a tight embrace. "Go, do what you must. I'll pray to the Maidens you find something, but in the meantime, I shall pursue all other avenues. There is always an option from the High Queen for a consort." His voice held no anger, just acceptance.

"Thank you, dearest, for your agreement. It is one of the many things I adore about you. You can and do keep an open mind, and are willing to face change and challenge in the seeking of a better life under the laws of the Maidens." Meghan kissed him on the cheek.

With the disagreement obviously ended, Rosin lifted her head and glanced from one to the other. "Is it safe?"

Both Cadmar and Meghan burst into raucous laughter.

"Of course, child. There is no danger here, just a lively discussion between two equals who love each other." Cadmar smiled and squeezed them again before he stepped back.

"Daughter, come, we will go and visit my Moon Laurate. He is a man of great education and wisdom. He is very wise in the word of the law, both of the Maidens and the Interlopers. But first, tell me of your companion."

Frustrated with Meghan's insistence, she quickly outlined her time with Arlan wisely, leaving out their shared kisses.

Meghan listened intently, watching her every expression. "You care for this man, Daughter?"

Rosin nodded.

"Come, we are going to see my Moon Laurate. He will have a solution."

"What do you mean, Mother Meg? Surely you can see there is no solution to my dilemma. The laws are clear."

Queen Meghan smiled. "Your mother and I, although cousins, had differing beliefs in how the laws should be interpreted. Fintain and your mother chose to live by the first level of laws only. These are very specific and have no options to help in situations out of the ordinary. But I have come from the more liberal land of Wilsea and have gently been trying to educate my dearest love in the wider knowledge contained in the laws. He is coming around, albeit slowly."

"I don't understand."

"You will, child. Meghan turned to Cadmar's valet. "Bryne, please carry Rosin down the old flagstone steps, and do be careful, because they are crumbling with age and heavy use. Soon they will be repaired." She turned to Rosin. "Once, only I descended to speak to Shamir, but now, many enter his chamber to seek his knowledge."

The roughly carved stone steps appeared to heave and drop in the flickering light from the torches.

Rosin clung onto Bryne, terrified they would fall as they followed the queen into darkness.

Staggered to learn her knowledge of the Maidens' laws was but a stunted version, she refused to let hope to find a foothold. She dared not, despite Meghan's confidence in the laws' provision for just such a thing as her dilemma.

At last, they came to a huge oak door with an old-fashioned, metal rod-type handle that clanked as Meghan lifted the rod from its cradle. The door moaned when she pushed it open. The dimly lit room had an unexpected welcoming air, warm and cozy.

Shamir sat before a large fire on a wooden bench covered in luxurious furs, leisurely smoking a pipe. The pleasant aroma, strong and pungent.

"Shamir, I have come to seek your advice for my Moon Life Daughter. You already know of her difficulties."

Shamir nodded. "Ahh, the Besieged One. Be at peace with the Maidens, child. Be seated, both of you."

"And their peace and blessing be upon you too." Rosin's words were barely a scratchy whisper from her aching throat and tightly clenched chest.

Bryne helped her perch on a small, fur-covered bench by the fire. Rosin luxuriated in the heat of the flames, as she hadn't been totally warm since she lost her child. The emptiness that dwelled inside brought a deep chill to her soul.

Meghan gracefully lowered herself onto a smaller fur covered bench to Shamir's right as Bryne backed quietly out the door.

Shamir reached for a large, leather-bound book. "These are the laws of the land as decreed by the six Maidens: Arawen, Blodwen, Morgana, Gavinia, Carwen, and Rianon. I have taken the liberty of copying them down several times in both our language and the Interlopers' for fear they will eventually be lost in our mostly oral culture." Shamir opened the book. "Even now, it means many of these laws are unused because people have simplified them. Or, they have chosen to ignore them because they cannot remember all the laws. But they are here, in all their complexities, for all contingences, especially one such as yours, child."

Shamir's words captured her interest. There were six laws, as she knew them, always verbally passed from generation to generation. She'd been drilled into them by her parents from an early age. They had not tolerated any deviations from the stark rules by her, her sister, or the nobles of the court. Even the peasants were expected to follow them as strictly as possible, regardless of their heritage.

She watched the reverent way Shamir handled the heavy book, its bulk filling his lap. Anger and frustration at her dead parents filled her mind. Why had they chosen to live by such unbendable rules?

With careful consideration, Shamir opened the book. He shuffled through several pages before he stopped to read. "Mmm, yes, this is what we need. Her Majesty, Queen Meghan, has informed me that all the eligible nobles of the first order have turned you down." His gaze focused directly on Rosin.

Rosin's face flamed with the indignity of being considered unworthy. To be rejected so publicly, for such dismal reasons, brought on intolerable shame.

"Yes, Shamir, the first order, second order, and all the rest." Her voice cracked. A vision of her becoming an old spinster and never being able to reclaim her throne loomed up. "Nobody wanted me."

"Do not feel shame, my child, for doing what you have had to do to survive and ensure you fulfill your destiny. He placed his gnarled finger on the text.

"The law states the following:

'No first born, male or female will ascend the throne without a consort.

All first born heirs to the throne will submit to a Bonding of Le Cheile to a male of their parents' choice to ensure that the Kingdom is strengthened and that inbreeding within the realms of each Maiden does not occur.'

This, child, you already know, but the rest of the text reads thus:

'In our turbulent world of violence and struggle, if something

happens to prevent that betrothal becoming a bonding that is consummated, then another consort will be chosen by the parents in consultation with the first born.

'If the first born becomes an orphan after having accepted their parents' choice, but said arrangement has failed to progress either by the suitor's refusal, the suitor is ruled unsuitable, or becomes deceased, then the first born is free to find a suitable consort of his or her own choice.

'This choice is to be made wisely, and firstly, from the first order of nobles whence the original betrothed came from.'

In your case, the descendants of the third Maiden, Gavinia, The Maid of Peace, War and the Afterlife.

'If, for whatever reason, there are no suitable nobles of the first order available or willing to take on the role of consort from the preferred Maidens' descendants, then the first born may choose a noble of the first order of any of the Maidens, bar her own and her parents, and if that cannot fulfill the need, then she may choose a noble of any order of any of the Maidens, bar her own.'"

"I'm sorry Shamir, but this does not help because no one who is eligible wanted me!"

He smiled as if he recognized the exasperation in her voice and secure in his own right not to interpret it as disrespect.

"I have not finished, child. All I ask is a little patience."

"Sorry." She hung her head.

Shamir reached out and lifted her face up so she had to meet his gaze. "I understand your anxiety, child. This next bit is for you, I believe."

She smiled, immediately embarrassed at her show of impatience. "Shamir, please continue."

"'If the circumstances behind this choice are so dire that there are no nobles of rank willing or able to assume the role of consort,

then the following checks and balances must be adhered to if the first born has the need to choose a commoner.'"

"A com—" She snapped her mouth shut, determined to stay silent until the Moon Laurate finished.

"'This commoner must be the firstborn's uninfluenced, personal choice. A person of undisputed worthy character. A clean living, contributing member of the community, who has done well through trade, compassionate works, or in defense of his or her ruling noble and/or the borders of the noble's realm.

'Should the first born choose such a commoner, such commoner will be assessed and approved by such nobles as have refused to or been unable to offer a suitable consort for the said first born.'"

Shamir watched her closely after he read each criterion. One at a time.

"'Criteria by which said commoner can be assessed for suitability:

'One—royal blood or connection of any minute amount.'"

Rosin shrugged.

"'Two—a worthy warrior of note who can demonstrate a sacrifice in defense of their ruling noble and the Kingdom they have declared their fealty to.'"

Her heart jumped and then beat unevenly as she nodded.

"'Three—a wealthy landowner who has built those riches through good honest endeavor of their own hands.

'Four—a person of good works of humanitarian kinds, or in the service of the Maidens.

'If there is a deadlocked vote, then said deadlock will be broken by the highest ranking noble from the realm from whence the original consort was chosen for the first born.

'If this is not possible, then the deadlock will be broken by the vote of the highest ranking noble present related to the first born.

'If the vote is disputed by the firstborn, then it will be referred to

and presided over by the ruling noble of the High Council of the First Maiden.

'At any time, the decision made can be reversed by the ruling noble of the High Council, and said solemnized pairing can be annulled if it so offends the High Council or places any Kingdom at a disadvantage by the choice that has been made.'

'Should such a commoner be chosen, they will have a title bestowed on them of Duke or Duchess. A suitable aligning bonding name is to be chosen to befit the circumstances. The union will be solemnized according to law and, when appropriately consummated, all children of that union will be eligible to ascend the throne.'"

Rosin tamped down the tiny flash of excitement even as she shook her head. "A commoner?"

Shamir smiled. "Yes, Princess, this widens your pool of choice enormously, but it will not be an easy path to travel. The criteria will be applied with stringent accuracy, as this would be the first instance of this type ever experienced in Maiden history, and the nobles bringing down this judgment will all have their own agendas and beliefs."

She couldn't bring herself to match his smile. Her thoughts span disconcertingly with this new knowledge. The full extent of this carefully thought out law. A law that ruled her, but one she had never known existed until this moment. "Stringently applied?"

Again, Shamir smiled. "Yes, only some of the nobles present here are aware of the full extent of the law as it is written. They will apply it to the letter, for fear of the High Queen. The others will apply it so because it is unknown to them, and they will not only fear the High Queen, but the very law itself. As it is written, it gives many of them an option to make a decision with such far-reaching effects for the first time in their lives. Dyanwen has lived by the strict, basic laws your parents enforced. The Sanjeva nobles know nothing of it, and the others, including Wilsea, know of it, but would never expect to take such an enormous responsibility themselves. Everything of such magnitude is referred to the High Queen."

"Shamir, if I choose to take this uncertain path. If I already have a commoner in mind, what would I have to do to bring such a case to the table? Mother Meg, you knew of this law, did you not?" She turned to her Moon Life Mother. "If Father Cad will approve this path, I want you to help me bring this case to the nobles?"

Meghan nodded, a satisfied smile curling her lips up in the corners. "Don't you fret about Cadmar? He will come around to our way of thinking."

"You know who I have chosen."

"Yes, my daughter, I do, and I approve your choice, but by the criteria set out, you may have a hard time gaining the nobles' approval."

"I know, Mother Meg, but Arlan is my choice. If they do not approve of this partnership, I will not make a union. I will abdicate and form a Bond of Le Chéile with Arlan, anyway. Enough is enough."

"My Daughter that is a huge step and brings its own risks. It is possible the High Queen will force you to return, and she will then find someone suitable. It would also be unwise to wait so long before rectifying the stewardship of your realm if it is to be salvaged. Devon will have it, and have Dyanwen and Wilsea cowering by then."

Rosin stirred restlessly on her bench. Her Moon Life Mother's warning made her uncomfortable. "I am aware of the death and destruction this will bring, but I will not be swayed from my choice. Now that I finally have a choice. Therefore, it will be up to them to make some sacrifice to protect their kingdoms, as I have had to do."

Meg smiled, a sly, smug gesture that teased the corners of her mouth as she nodded in approval. "That's my girl. You will make an invincible queen, Rosin."

"I must see, Arlan!"

"And if he refuses you?" Queen Meghan asked.

"Mother Meg, to be honest, it will shatter me."

Meghan stood and straightened her skirts. "Come then, let us get this over with. First, we will tell Cadmar the outcome and your decision. Thank you, Shamir, for your wisdom."

Shamir nodded.

Rosin limped forward and bowed low to the Moon Laurate. "Thank you, Shamir. Your knowledge is a truly valuable thing. When Keswin is mine, I intend to bring the new laws with me."

Shamir took her hand. "You will be a good queen, Rosin, and Arlan, a strong consort. Go with the blessings of the Maidens, child."

Bryne gasped and panted by the time they completed the hurried climb up the uneven stairs and entered the parlor. The King appeared surprised at their rapid return. His expression full of concern tinged with fear.

Rosin leaned close to her Moon Life Mother. "I think you should tell him."

Meghan nodded. "Cadmar, dear, we have a solution," she proclaimed grandly as she strode across the room.

King Cadmar frowned. "I have a feeling I'm not going to like this solution, my beloved. You both seem all too pleased with yourselves."

"Oh, don't be such a conservative, dearest, or you will be at risk of sounding like your late lamented brother."

"Well, tell me the worst of it, my queen."

"The laws state clearly that Rosin can from a Bond of Le Chéile with any worthwhile man not descended of the sixth maiden if there are no nobles willing. Shamir is making you a copy right now. Rosin has chosen Arlan as her consort."

"But we know nothing of this man, whether he is worthwhile or not. Surely there is another choice." A deep frown furrowed his forehead.

"Cadmar, the man in these circumstances, must be of her choice. In other words, a love match." Meghan danced on the spot with tiny steps.

"But too much is unknown. I cannot blithely approve this thing." Cadmar objected loudly, his face ashen.

"Of course not. It must be approved by the nobles here present."

"And if they do not give their approval?" Cadmar peered from one to the other.

Rosin lifted her chin so she could meet the king's gaze. "In that one moment, I will make the hardest decision I have ever had to make, and those who would suffer by it have my prayers, but believe me, I will not be thwarted. I will abdicate and leave Keswin to its fate, along with the other realms."

Cadmar frowned. "I do not like your tone, my child. You cannot abdicate. You cannot. I would suggest I meet with Arlan alone and put this proposal to him. I fear his refusal could send you spiraling into a deep melancholy."

"No, my Lord Protector, with respect, this is a task that I must do. I need to see the truth of his response reflected in his eyes. I have hidden nothing from him. My situation is a grim one so I will not blame him if he refuses me. I am Queen of Keswin and I must face the worst of it if I am to succeed. I can no longer afford to be a pampered and protected princess." She held his gaze and saw the flickering expressions cross his face. Disappointment, surprise, hurt, then grudging respect. "Much as I appreciate your offer."

Meghan clutched his arm. He glanced down at her, then back to Rosin.

Only then did she continue. "If my realm is to be restored, it must rise or fall on my decisions and my determination to see the hard ones through. This includes facing the fact that I might not be acceptable as a partner to the man I love. That I might not be considered worth the pain and trouble I come with. He may not want to take on the burden of royalty, and ruling, when a common warrior's lot would have immense freedoms by comparison. He may not want to live with the uncertainty that our bonding will be annulled by the High Queen, if she's not pleased. This, I shall face, and conquer, as I have the other hardships of the past moon-sweeps."

King Cadmar inclined his head, a sign of respect for an equal. "Your Majesty, my Moon Life Daughter, Queen of Keswin, on all levels, will I acquiesce to your request. Bryne, please carry my daughter, the Queen, out to the training arena."

The fact she had forged a new level to her relationship with the King of Tarlic delighted Rosin.

With a respectful bow, Bryne scooped her up in his brawny arms.

Cadmar turned to lead the way. "I believe your companion is training with my Master at Arms. Come, Bryne."

They rattled down the stone stairs, a kitchen boy running behind with her crutches over his shoulder. The clash of swords sliced through the air before they'd climbed halfway down the slow curve of steps. They stopped at the edge of the arena.

Arlan wore a full suit of armor, his face hidden by his helmet. His weapons glinted in the sunlight as he sparred with the Master of Arms.

Keegan had informed Rosin the two men had taken a liking to each other and trained regularly. Neither man managed to get the better of the other because they were so evenly matched.

A shiver flickered across her skin, her stomach flipped over and released butterflies as she watched the two men battle. Arlan, fit and back to full health, easily demonstrated his excellence as a swordsman.

Queen Meghan stood beside her, an arm around her shoulders, a wide smile on her face. In fact, since they'd been to see Shamir, the queen had not stopped smiling.

The king stood at her other side, his expression unreadable.

Rosin watched every move the two men made. Her heart skipped a beat, then raced, thumping behind her breast. With trembling hands, she clutched the stone wall that cordoned off the training arena and gazed at the man she loved. Suddenly, watching did not satisfy her. She wanted to touch him, hold him, breathe in his scent, and inspect every inch of him, wounds and all.

"You do not have to do this." Cadmar frowned down at her, his voice soft with concern.

Rosin shook her head. "Thank you. Please don't take my insistence personally, Father Cad, or as disrespect, but it is time for me to make my own decisions and to face my own demons now I am queen. I am not turning away from you, your love and support, or your wise counsel. Those things I value and never want to lose."

Cadmar smiled. "You will never lose my love, but now you also have my respect as an equal. It is hard for an old man like me to recognize that you are not only queen, but you have survived such hardships even I have not had to face. Survival of those horrors has forged strength in you not often seen in women so young. I see now your maturity and commitment to your duty and your throne, but that is not to say, as your Moon Life Father, I would not make it easier for you if I could."

"Thank you and yes, I know I'm torturing myself, but it's my decision. It's how it must be."

Cadmar sighed. "So be it, child."

She stood at the edge of the arena, suddenly shy, overcome with uncertainty, for she had not seen Arlan for more than eighteen moon-slides and she surveyed him with fresh eyes.

He had fashioned an elegant mask for his face. It hid his identity, but it also hid the disfigurement to his handsome features.

As the two men paused to catch their wind, Arlan saw her waiting. Immediately, he handed his sword to the waiting weapons boy and walked toward them. His wide, genuine smile remained on his mouth even as he bent his knee in respect to both her and Cadmar. The words he spoke were formal and appropriate.

"Princess, I am honored and pleased to see you are restored to full health. I have desperately wanted to see you, but your Moon Life Protector decreed it unseemly and open to misinterpretation."

"I know, Arlan. He only meant well for me. I am so glad to see you in good health, and training, no less, with my Protector's Master of Arms." She struggled to formulate the formal words. She desperately wanted to embrace him.

His smile widened the half of his mouth she could see.

She loved the way it quirked up at a crooked angle.

"He has been most generous with his time. His Majesty more than generous with his care of me as well." Arlan nodded respectfully in Cadmar's direction.

Cadmar smiled his acknowledgement, then turned to his Master of Arms. "Come, Kynan, we will walk. The Queen has some need of privacy."

Arlan's smile faded. "This sounds serious."

Rosin only nodded as she indicated he should stand.

The mask covering his disfigurement glowed and paled in the sunlight, making it impossible to read any expression from what remained showing of his face.

Rosin took a deep breath and clasped her hands tightly in front of her to prevent them from trembling. She contemplated her friend and protector. A multitude of memories flooded over her. How they had laughed together and hunted for food. How they had shared the warmth of whatever hidey-hole they could secure, and their care of each other's harms as they travelled through the rough terrain to Tarlic Castle.

Her heartbeat faster. She so wanted this man.

Since their arrival, Cadmar had clothed Arlan in a uniform of his own house guard, knee-high boots made of supple leather and provided new armor and weapons. She gave a small, satisfied sigh. The king had kept his promise.

It was extremely difficult, with the shame of rejection still stinging, to make herself vulnerable again, especially to this man, her friend, from whom she wanted more than friendship.

"Arlan, you know why I've come here. Why I've fought so hard to survive, and why I did what I did."

He nodded. "You're duty bound to save your throne, no matter what the cost."

Rosin nodded, then stared hard at the ground, trying to formulate her next words.

Arlan shuffled his feet. "Now you've come to tell me which lord has taken your hand in a Bond of Le Chéile . I knew it would come, but to be honest, Rosin, I think you already know I wish it wasn't so. I know I could never be considered. Unknown to all, and most likely a common warrior."

She looked up at him, trying valiantly to ignore the staccato beat that drummed crazily in her chest, making it so hard to breathe.

"Tell me, Rosin."

She shook her head, unable to speak through the clenching, choking emotion.

He stood motionless, watching her, searching her face for the answer. "If he be cruel, or old or bad tempered, I will..."

Again, Rosin shook her head. "No, Arlan. Nobody wanted me." The words creaked out, strangled by her humiliation and uncertainty.

"The patsy bastards. What is the matter with them? You're beautiful, courageous, brave, and smart. What? Couldn't they be seeing past the first resistance against their member that might prove them to be a better, bigger man because they had a maidenhead as their claim to fame?" The angry words burst out of him as if a dam of emotion had just exploded.

Rosin's face flamed at his crude reference to her lost virginity. She held up her hands, then shook her head. "Stop, Arlan."

He took a small step forward, then stopped. "My poor darling, that they should put you through such shame."

She so desperately wanted to reach out and stroke his hair, to touch the warmth of his skin, but she held herself in check. She must do what she had to in a manner befitting her station.

"I'm so glad they refused me, Arlan."

He studied every curve and shadow of her face before he delved deep into her gaze, searching for what he wanted to see. "But your throne will be lost."

Again, she shook her head. "I have been to see Shamir, Queen Meghan's Moon Laurate. He has great knowledge of the law. I have discovered it is far more complicated than I have been allowed to know. There is a clause that allows for circumstances like mine, where no noble is willing. It allows for me to form a Bond of Le Chéile with a commoner if he meets certain criteria." She looked directly at Arlan.

His expression transformed before her eyes. His scowling indignation melted into longing expectation.

"Arlan, I have come to ask you to be my consort. If you still have the desire for us to be together? Do you really want to make a Bond of Le Chéile with me, Rosin, a dispossessed queen for whose throne you will have to fight, and risk your life? I have little to offer you, not even my purity, and I may not even be able to have children and..."

He touched her lips with trembling fingers. "Shh, my love. I want nothing more than to be with you. These last moon-sweeps, my heart has broken afresh each day as negotiations for a consort were being conducted and the thought, I might never hold you again. You come this moon-slide with some miracle asking if I want you and yet you doubt my answer. This is more than I could ever have dreamed possible. My answer is yes, a thousand times over. All the rest does not matter."

She lowered her voice and leaned closer. "What I wish to do is to fall into your arms and hold you close, to kiss you, and love you, but I cannot," — she smiled up at him — "yet."

He smiled. "We will be together soon, my love."

"Then, as we are agreed, I will prepare. I'm not sure how this will work, but I would expect you will be summoned when required. Eight nobles remain, plus Dyanwen and King Cadmar. I have warned the King if the decision is not made cleanly and decisively, I will abdicate my throne and take my chances with the High Queen. They know the danger to their kingdoms in that, but I know this would also be risky to me because the High Queen would probably insist I return and bond with someone of royal blood. It is a chance I'm willing to take."

She waved her arm to summon the other two men, then she

beckoned Meghan from her discreet distance behind the wall. "It is agreed, My Lord Protector. Arlan will tender as my consort."

"Rosin, you still need the approval of the nobles." Cadmar cautioned, a deep frown furrowing his brow.

"I know, Father Cad, but if approval is not given, I will abdicate, regardless of the High Queen, and she can do nothing until after the thaw. I'm sure the nobles will understand the danger that will place their lands in."

"This is good. An excellent outcome should be forthcoming. I think this will be a beneficial union to all." Meghan looked up at her king and chortled.

"Meghan, please do not let the chariot out of the stable without a driver. It has not been approved yet." Cadmar remonstrated with her before he turned back to Rosin. "Child, would you be so harsh as to put others at risk?"

"Yes, Your Majesty, I would. I am tired of being manipulated and controlled by others. Either they make a decision I'm pleased with, or they will wait and suffer accordingly."

"Rosin, Your Majesty, will you not be a little more flexible?"

Rosin shook her head. "No. Being flexible will not get my kingdom in order and it will not be in my best interests. The evidence is shown by my current situation, decisions made by others for me that have not been at all flexible or good."

Cadmar nodded, but the frown remained. "Then we best prepare well, Rosin. Shamir is ready, and Kynan has agreed to be a support person for Arlan. He will give witness to his fighting ability and to his good nature."

Kynan bowed slightly to Rosin. "Your Majesty, I would be privileged to help your cause because I believe you could not find a better man than Arlan as your consort."

"Nor do I, Kynan."

Footmen hurried throughout the castle to summon the nobles, Rosin made her preparations with Shamir, Meghan, and Ashlynn by her side.

Ashlynn became absolutely beside herself at the news and proceeded to tear her wardrobe to pieces, literally, to find the perfect gown. "Dearest cousin, you are making a stand. You get to choose your own consort. Keegan will be so pleased. He has been arguing with Father for many moon-sweeps about his right to choose his own consort, or at least to have a say. Mother agrees with him, but Father is still a conservative at heart. Rosin, I'm so happy for you. To finally find happiness after what you have been through.

Rosin hugged her cousin. "Nothing is decided yet, Ashlynn." Even as she cautioned her cousin, she struggled to keep control of her own hope.

~ ~ ~

Arlan watched her leave with the King and Queen.

Kynan came to stand at his side and grabbed his upper arm. "Perhaps you should sit, Arlan. You are as white as the snow."

Arlan turned and stared blankly at Kynan.

Kynan led him to a bench and pushed him down.

Arlan collapsed. He shoved his trembling hands between his thighs. He glanced up as footsteps approached.

"What was that all about, Arlan? From the way you are looking I'm assuming she has found her consort."

Arlan stared up at Carrick and shook his head. "No-one...She's asked me."

"What?"

Arlan shook his head and tried to bring his roiling thoughts under control. "Apparently there is no-one willing nor suitable to be her consort so using the laws of the Maidens' she's asked me."

"Vipers curse, Arlan. Did you say yes?"

Arlan nodded. "It's not definite yet, but she's threatening to abdicate if they don't agree." His words barely squeezed out of his constricted throat.

Carrick whacked him on the shoulder. "By the Maidens' blessings, Arlan. I'm so pleased for you. You love her, don't you?"

He looked up. "Passionately, Carrick. The thought of her being bonded to some random male who may not be kind and respectful has been killing me."

"So, what happens now?"

"I will be summoned in due course to front the nobles. I'm trying not to get my hopes up."

Carrick dropped to the bench beside him. "Well, some news in addition. Apparently when all refused a consort, starting with Queen Brigit, the mother of her dead betrothed, all bar Sanjeva's Nexus Mostyn offered men, horses and equipment to get her started and they will join her to oust Devon in the thaw."

"How many?"

Carrick frowned as he calculated. "I'd say about three hundred including one hundred and fifty from Tarlic."

Arlan glanced at Carrick. "And the Commander?"

Carrick grinned. "Me. I suppose I'll have to get used to calling you, Your Majesty or something similar."

Arlan slapped him on the shoulder. "Not likely, Carrick. We're friends. Arlan it will stay. I'm surprised you agreed. I thought you were going to step down not head out into a battle that is near impossible to win."

Carrick frowned. "I wasn't interested until I heard it might be you leading us for the Queen. I hope I can still step down in a couple or so successions and buy a plot."

Arlan smiled. "If I become consort and we defeat Devon, I'll give you a moondust plot with the Queen's permission, of course."

"How you going to cope with being subject to a woman's rule even though she will be your bhean chéile."

Arlan chuckled. "I'd hope we would have a partnership, but I'll just have to pull my head in if she decrees something, at least in front of others."

~ ~ ~

In the smaller dining hall, Shamir sat at the head of the table with the Book of Laws open at the appropriate pages.

Rosin stirred restlessly in her chair. Finally unable to keep still, she hobbled up and down the room with loud, sharp clunks from her crutches. Dressed now in a deep green woolen gown, accessorized with a gold torc and bracelets borrowed from her cousin, she muttered her speech under her breath.

Shamir prompted her on where to make the points of law, and the king and queen added relevant bits of evidence to support them.

Her hands became clammy and her stomach twisted into a sizzling bundle of nerves. Her lungs clenched on each inhale in a desperate effort to stop her panicked breathing, becoming sobs of desperation. She breathed deeply and rehearsed until she heard them coming. Heavy footfalls in the hallway. Footfalls of impending doom, perhaps.

Rosin would not even contemplate losing this battle, but at the same time, she could not let unrealistic hope weaken her.

As they filed in and took their places around the table, she ceased her pacing to stand in regal aloneness by the fire, her hands folded demurely in front of her. She nodded acknowledgement as they passed. Each face held a mixture of emotion. Curiosity on all, while some held impatience, and in others, she read sympathy and interest.

Finally, Rosin stood alone at the head of the table beside the seated Shamir. "My lords and ladies, I thank you for taking the time to attend. On this moon-slide you will be making a historical ruling on a little used point of Maiden Law. I expect you to make a decision in harmony with your own conscience. I can arrange for a secret ballot, if so desired."

She had their undivided attention. It gave her great satisfaction to have taken them by surprise, but she sensed they were also wary.

She stood tall, watching each one closely. "I come before you this moon-slide as Queen of Keswin, dispossessed of my throne, orphaned by murder, then robbed of my innocence through rape by Lord Devon, Interloper, murderer, and obsessed madman."

They nodded in agreement, and some murmured in sympathy or anger.

"For those who do not acknowledge my authority as Queen of Keswin, please leave the room because you have no place here."

At her blunt announcement, the expressions of the two Sanjeva royal's hardened. Rexus Mostyn leaned in and whispered in the ear of his younger brother Cerdric.

Rosin strained to hear, but he spoke too softly. They made no attempt to leave.

"Who has had raids made on their realm by Devon since the massacre of my parents?" She looked around at them.

This time nearly every hand went up, except for the Sanjeva royals and King Cadmar.

She glanced around. "Who would be in a better defensive

position if Keswin had Maiden stewardship and freedom from Devon's hold?"

"What're you getting at, Your Majesty? Under your parents' rule, plenty of raids happened and not much help came." The big bear of a man from the small realm, Wilsea, to the east of Keswin, rose from his seat, his face a blustery red behind the thick ginger beard. "We have always struggled against Devon, and the Chattens. We've never had much support from your parents. I do not mean to malign the dead, but Fintain and Maeve's only goals consisted of bettering their own world. It's worse now because there is no defense between us and the Depcisians, or the Chattens. Add Devon attacking all the smaller communities and life is precarious for all. If you have brought us here to pose a solution, then I'm willing to listen. Otherwise, I am leaving now to defend my King's realm and the innocent people who are left."

"War Chieftain Bevan, I beg your indulgence, for I have only just begun to understand my parents' shortcomings and I am keen to rectify them. I am going to propose a solution, and if you will spare me some time, it will become clear." She made steady eye contact with the big man.

He stared back at her, unblinking, then glanced in King Cadmar's direction, before he sank down in his chair.

Rosin sighed with relief. She'd expected to be scuttled right there and then. "People, I ask you this. If I'm restored to the throne of Keswin, with a strong consort at my side, do you believe I could oust Devon from my realm, then with your support, bring a halt to his rampaging?"

After a short hesitation, they all nodded.

Queen Brigit stood. "If Keswin had a strong stewardship, together, we could bring an end to this reign of terror, but Rosin, the law demands you must have a consort."

"That is exactly where I'm leading, Your Majesty. My parents chose Eled, your second son, as my consort. I thought it a wise choice of an outstanding young man. Together, we would have made a strong stewardship, would we not?"

Queen Brigit blinked at her bluntness. "Yes, Rosin, you would have."

"So, my lords and ladies, I come before you on this momentous moon-slide to find a suitable alternative, an alternative you have not been able or willing to provide me. Without a consort, I cannot rule Keswin. Without a suitable noble tendering for my hand, I have no consort." She paused and let the impact of her words— carefully crafted as an accusation—fall between them.

Their embarrassment was tangible.

"I am determined to reclaim my throne, for the benefit of all here present, my realm, and my people. Therefore, I am determined to find a suitable consort."

They mumbled between themselves for a moment, then Queen Brigit stood again.

"Rosin, we have no one to offer for the role. We can do no more to help." She held her hands wide. "I don't know the answer to this problem unless we wait until the thaw for the High Queen."

Rosin nodded acknowledgement of the queen's words. "I understand your dilemma, so I sought advice from a wise man. A man deeply conversant in Maiden laws, a man trusted by my Moon Life Protectors, King Cadmar and Queen Meghan.

Shamir is a highly informed Moon Laurate. I have sought advice on how I can secure a consort when none is available and it appears I do have an alternative. This is written into Maiden law to ensure such a dilemma as mine is solvable. Shamir, please, will you read the appropriate law out for all to hear? For those of you who are already familiar with the law herein contained, I beg your patience and indulgence for the purpose of the clear understanding of the ruling you will make for me."

She stepped back from the table and turned toward the fire as Shamir began to read. His voice was warm and smooth in its deep timbre, deliberately soothing in tone as he spoke the ancient words.

Meghan gave an encouraging smile and a slight nod as Rosin struggled to stand still and serene while her heart beat furiously and her legs threatened to collapse.

Nobody moved. They listened in stunned silence, many having their rigid beliefs stripped from them in one fell swoop. Finally, Shamir fell silent.

After a short, deliberate pause, Rosin hobbled back to the table. She examined each face before her, trying to determine their reaction. "My lords and ladies, this moon-slide you have heard the full version of the Maidens' law on first born royalty securing consorts, particularly when there are none available."

"And this helps how, Your Majesty?" War Chieftain Bevan asked, a touch of impatience sharpening his tone. This extension of the law came as no real surprise to him. "There is no precedent for the use of this law. How do we know the High Queen will approve it being used for a decision of such magnitude and without consultation?"

"You are correct, Bevan, there is no precedent, but it is the written law as passed by the Maidens. These laws bind us all, including the High Queen. We all know she cannot be consulted before the end of the thaw or maybe even into the misting. Therefore, I seek your approval for a consort of my own choice, a commoner. He has sworn his fealty to me as Queen of Keswin and taken up the charge of seeing me restored to the crown..."

"A commoner!" Several voices scraped around the room.

Rosin held up her hands to silence them. "Yes, a commoner. As the law says, I can choose if he satisfies certain criteria. It is on this I ask your judgment. I do not want to delay my return to Keswin until after I seek a judgment from the High Queen or another noble is found, for by then, people, your kingdoms could be nothing, but piles of ashes ruled by Devon."

Bevan leapt from his chair, his face behind his beard as red as the hair on his head. "I sense a threat in your words, my lady, some blackmail perhaps."

"War Chief Bevan, I am merely stating how it is going to be. Either I receive an acceptable decision from you right now or I will abdicate, leaving Keswin with no stewardship until the High Queen can be consulted in the thaw. The consequences of that will be on your own consciences."

Queen Brigit stood, glanced around the room, then directly at Rosin. "How does this man meet the criteria set down in the law, Rosin?"

Her late fiancé's mother spoke softly, but firmly enough to subdue the dissent amongst the others.

"Your Majesty, the man I put forward is a warrior of great worth who fought gallantly against Devon and sustained horrendous injuries."

"I do not think this is enough, Rosin, you do not know who he has fought for before that moon-slide, if he has royal blood, if he owns land, or has done good works. You know so little of him, why are you convinced he is a good warrior?"

"Despite the defeat at Devon's hands, he tried to rescue me and then fought a good battle before succumbing. Since his arrival here at the castle he has shown all the manners of a gentleman." Rosin fought to keep the desperation she felt out of her tone.

Queen Brigit shook her head. "Even so, his suitability is questionable. I'm not convinced. Let us speak to this young man before making a decision."

Bryne had already left his post by the door to summon Arlan, so King Cadmar fetched refreshments to bide their time while they waited.

With a cursory tap on the door, Arlan entered moments later, fit, tanned, and every inch a senior officer of her Protector's army as he strode across the room.

Her heart leapt crazily, landed lopsided, then beat with a rapid uneven tattoo. Her throat constricted and tears welled in her eyes. Before this moment, she had never dared to hope he could be hers.

Arlan inclined his head to the King.

"Be seated, Arlan, we have some questions about your suitability."

Arlan slipped into the seat Bryne brought for him.

"So, Arlan, you have no memory of who you are?" Bevan asked.

Arlan met Bevan's skeptical expression. "No, my lord, I sustained a vicious blow to the head during a battle against Devon's troops."

"And no memories have returned?"

Arlan shook his head again.

Bevan continued his probing. "You have chosen to cover your face with a mask. One must ask if it is an attempt to conceal your identity which you claim not to know."

Arlan frowned. "I do not intentionally conceal anything, my lords and ladies." He reached up and took the mask off.

At the sight of his scars, a couple of the nobles gasped softly.

Arlan stared back at Bevan. "I chose to wear this mask so I do not frighten women and children with my deformity."

Bevan appeared slightly abashed at Arlan's bluntness. "So, you can substantiate nothing of your past or your character."

"Nothing, my lord, except that Rosin identified me as a member of the High Queen's Commissioned Warriors. I assume therefore

I am descended from the Maiden Arawen. And Master of Arms, Kynan says I have been trained by the Master Warrior Garven of Annaticcia."

Mostyn leaned in and muttered something to his brother.

War Chief Bevan glanced at his companion. He nodded.

"And royal blood?"

Arlan shook his head. "I do not know."

Queen Brigit now stood. "You have brought someone to speak on your behalf. Kynan, Master of Arms for King Cadmar, you are willing to recommend this man?"

"I am, Your Majesty."

Queen Brigit invited Kynan to speak with a wave of her hand.

"My experience with Arlan is that he is competent, educated, steady charismatic. Men will willingly follow him. In addition to my opinion, I can confirm Arlan has been trained by The Master Warrior Garven of Annaticcia. Very few warriors are trained by the Master Warrior of Annaticcia. They must be not only the best warriors and swordsmen, but also the best men; gentlemen at all times, educated and articulate. Master Garven only chooses men he believes capable of being inspiring leaders of men to be his students."

Despite Kynan's eloquent words, Rosin sensed the withdrawal of their interest and support. Even Father Cad appeared nonplussed at the lack of sympathy in the room.

Rosin decided to force the issue. "Enough of this dilly-dallying around. Is it not enough for you that this man of apparent good character and superior fighting skills declared his fealty to me? Is that not enough to answer the criteria? This commoner is my uninfluenced personal choice as consort. You who have refused to or been unable to offer a consort for me now have much to answer for. And you will answer."

Cadmar stood. "I would ask you for a compassionate vote and approval of her choice, which she has made under advice from me and Shamir. The Queen speaks wisely when she states that the longer Keswin is without solid rule, the more Devon will annihilate all the small realms. As he grows stronger, he will be harder and harder to eradicate and your people will grow weaker and more terrified."

"And what of the High Queen?" Bevan thumped his fist on the table.

"The High Queen can annul the bonding, or she can ratify it, as she sees fit. We will have made the decision within the guidance of the laws and for the right reasons, so she will be merciful. If we fail to make a wise decision, she may not be so merciful, especially if Keswin is destroyed and your realms are ravaged and starving. I suggest you weigh up the evidence then make your decision. I cast my vote in favor of Arlan, First Knight of Keswin, becoming the legal consort of Queen Rosin of Keswin."

Rosin smiled a tentative response to her Protector's vote then turned to the nobles waiting at the table. "Queen Brigit, gentlemen, do you wish for a secret ballot?"

Bevan shook his head. "Let's not be wasting time. A show of hands, people?"

The door creaked open. Una, Eled's younger sister, crept into the room and tiptoed up to Queen Brigit.

Rosin strained to hear what the younger woman whispered in her mother's ear.

Una kept her voice low, even as she glanced toward Rosin.

Brigit clasped her daughter's hand briefly. "Go, Una, this is not the place for you."

The younger woman left, her mouth drawn into a tight slash, her eyes downcast under the shock of white-blond hair that hung over her face.

When all, bar Queen Brigit, had voted, the score sat at an even four to four. Rosin's legs trembled and waves of nausea swept over her. The vote had come out closer than she'd hoped although she had expected nothing more from Bevan and Nexus Mostyn. Her success now depended on the approval of Dyanwen's queen. The thought of failure left her trembling.

"Your Majesty?" Rosin prompted the older queen.

The Queen of Dyanwen looked at her, her mouth moved slightly, but failing to get her words out, she took a generous sip of malt syrup and swallowed. "Your Majesty, Rosin, answer me one question if you please. Do you care for this man, Arlan?"

Rosin's stomach flipped and her head spun. She could barely speak with her dry constricted throat. "I... I... why do you ask, Your Majesty?"

"Please indulge the mother of your dead betrothed, Rosin."

"Your Majesty, are you insinuating something untoward?"

The Queen of Dyanwen shook her head. "No, Your Majesty, *I am not*. Please just answer my question."

Rosin glanced at Arlan. His face projected a blank mask, but she could see the emotions seething in the shadows of his eyes. She turned back to the table of nobles.

"Queen Brigit of Dyanwen, with respect, did you know your son had already given his heart to another?"

Brigit suddenly appeared tired, haggard. "Yes, Rosin, I did, and with his death I live with the guilt of not one death on my hands, but two, for his lady love took her own life the moon-wash she heard of his death. This is why I ask the question. Would you give your life for this man, Rosin?"

Tears sprang to her eyes. "Yes, Queen Brigit, I would."

Brigit turned then to Arlan. "And you, Arlan, First Knight of

Keswin, would you give your life for this woman?"

Arlan stood and walked across the small space that separated them. He took Rosin's hand in his then turned to Brigit. "Yes, Your Majesty, I would give my life for this woman."

Brigit smiled. "This is what I wanted to hear. One more thing before I cast my vote, your Majesty. You accepted my son's tender and with that came certain advantages to Dyanwen — trade routes and additional defensive capacity. With his death, these have become null and void. I need to know, under your proposed alliance with Arlan, a man of unknown background, where Keswin's loyalties will lie?"

Rosin stood tall and straight as she answered. "Your Majesty, Queen Brigit of Dyanwen, I stand before you and your peers and commit Keswin to meet the obligations that came with Eled's tender for my hand and its acceptance. Your son did not deserve to die the way he did. I feel responsible for your loss and to honor the tender agreement will go some way to easing the guilt I hold. It will also build a strong bond between Keswin and Dyanwen that can only benefit both realms and those around our borders. I have nothing with which to seal my commitment, and I hope my word in front of such witnesses as these will be enough for you to feel comfortable."

"I never questioned your word, Your Majesty, and I thank you for the generosity of spirit you have shown in honoring an obligation, which with my son's death has become null and void. I am satisfied."

The Queen of Dyanwen turned to the others. "Gentleman, I believe Queen Rosin will, if returned with a consort to Keswin, make a strong beneficial queen to her own people and to her neighbors. Therefore, I vote that Arlan, First Knight of Keswin, be approved according to Maidens' law. To be the legitimate consort to Rosin, Queen of Keswin, in the stead of my beloved son, Eled, who gave his life protecting her. My lords, those of you who have chosen to vote nay, I beseech you to recast your votes in favor of this match and help us form an allegiance so strong Devon will shrivel under the very thought of his opponents."

Rosin waited somewhat impatiently through a long silence as they consulted their own consciences. She had her answer, but she now teetered on a crevasse edge of uncertainty as the men before her considered the Queen's request.

Then one hand after another rose and Rosin watched in stunned silence and absolute wonder as, without a word being spoken, the group presented her with an absolute majority in approval for her chosen consort.

She stepped forward now. "I thank you all for upholding the law, despite its unfamiliarity. I promise you will not have cause to regret your decision. Keswin will be strong again, and in that, Keswin will be a powerful co-operative neighbor and a force for good, growth, and interdependent alliance in the battle against evil."

"With a majority approval and taking into account the urgency of the queen's need to return to Keswin, I suggest we proceed to make this a formal union right now," Cadmar declared.

Without further prompting, Arlan knelt and proposed his tender. Cadmar looked at Rosin and she nodded, to overcome with emotions to speak.

"Then it's settled," Cadmar said, rubbing his hands together. "A most agreeable arrangement."

Rosin and Arlan's gazes locked. She burst into laughter as he rose to his feet and pulled her up with him. He sought out Cadmar over her head. "So, what do we have to do to make this legal?"

"Will you officiate, Shamir?" Cadmar asked.

The Moon Laurate nodded all smiles with the outcome. "Then we shall start with the arrangements that need to be made. Come, children, we have work to do. My fellow nobles, I know most of you are eager to take your leave before this succession's early frost gets a hold and makes the land impassable until the thaw but I am sure Queen Rosin would be honored to have you witness her Bonding of Le Chéile.

All of those present nodded.

Cadmar hugged his Meghan. "Good. Bryne, summon the cook, the housekeeper, and the head gardener. Tomorrow moon-wash we celebrate."

"Arlan, if you agree, I want to bestow the title of Duke of Bekwen on you before you make your Bond of Le Chéile with the Queen tomorrow. It is fitting you have a title as consort to the queen. Now off you go." Cadmar flicked his fingers at them. "Meghan and I have work to do."

Without warning, Arlan scooped Rosin into his arms and hugged her tightly against his chest.

Giggles bubbled up. She felt warm and light as he carried her from the room, her damaged leg dangling awkwardly under her skirts as her feet bounced with his loping stride.

Neither of them felt the cold outside as Arlan wrapped her in his embrace. He trembled as she pressed against him.

"Arlan, my love, it is done."

He tightened his hold. "My love, I never thought to be yours, even though I was destined to love you until the time of my death. My heart is so full I think it will explode." He brought his head down and claimed her mouth, tenderly exploring her lips at first, but as the fire exploded between them. He deepened his kiss demanding a response from her.

She parted her lips and let him in.

He pressed her tighter to him.

She felt his need. Soon they would satisfy that need, hers as desperate as his.

After weeks of life and death struggle, suddenly, unexpectedly, she had her dream in her hands. She had been truly blessed with an awe-inspiring gift. Of course, there would be even greater struggles ahead. The High Queen might summarily annul her bonding, but for the moment, she wanted to savor her joy, the feel of Arlan's arms around her, wallow in the love they shared and the beating of their hearts in unison.

~ ~ ~

Trystan leaned against the low wall around the barracks. He hated being confined. His brother did not let him mix with royalty even though he was entitled to. Once he had fought it but now he could not be bothered with the misery that came with it. This time his frustration seethed hotter than usual. He knew Queen Brigit was in the castle and he would have dearly loved to reacquaint himself with her. He frowned. To still carry a torch for a woman after eighteen successions was pretty pathetic and he had only kissed her once. He watched the men below sitting around the fire pits drinking and gambling. Even Lukaz.

He heard Mostyn and Cerdric return from the conference to adjudicate on a consort for the Princess Rosin. Trystan sighed. He would have willingly tendered, but knew Mostyn would never approve.

He turned his gaze to the sky. The moons were rising. Each one ringed with a spangled band of ice as the frost settled in early. It was cold outside snow had fallen lightly just on sun fade.

"Trystan?"

He looked around as his half brother joined him.

"A moon beam for your thoughts."

Trystan grimaced. "They are not worth that much, Cerdric."

His half brother leaned on the wall beside him. "The little queen makes her Bonding of Le Chéile tomorrow to the common blood warrior they call Arlan. The one who brought her to Tarlic."

"I've heard talk he's a good man, but he is terribly scarred. He covers his face with a mask to hide his scars." He was in the dining room when we arrived. Some little viper was mouthing off about the Princess and her time alone with him. I smacked him and Commander Carrick confined him to the lock up. Arlan spoke then about what happened. He threatened anyone who spoke wrongly of the Princess with a meeting with the King or a duel with him. I saw him in the distance last moon-slide sparring with King Cadmar's Master at Arms. Kynan couldn't best him.

"Yeah, he is terribly scarred. He removed the mask at the voting this moon-slide. The little queen thinks she is going to take back her throne from Devon but Mostyn says she is young, foolish and delusional."

Trystan turned to look at his half brother. "With what legion?"

"Most of the nobles and royals have gifted her warriors."

"Devon has over a thousand they say."

"Trystan, she is on a fool's errand that's why no-one tendered for her hand besides the fact she was raped and miscarried the babe. Not solid gold material for any man."

Trystan frowned and sighed. "I would have tendered regardless of her reputation, but brother Mostyn would never have let me in case I contaminated Maiden royalty bloodlines."

"I suggested it and got cut down. Our brother is a viper's curse, Trystan, especially to you." Cerdric pushed up right. "So would you go with her?"

Trystan frowned. "On a fool's errand to my death. Yes, probably. Anything would be better than continuing my life as it is but there is no chance Mostyn's going to let me. He refused me permission to go to Gaud with Lukaz under the threat of all-out war against them."

Cerdric grimaced.

A heavy tread on the flag stones had them both turning and flinching.

"So, this is where you're hiding."

Trystan and Cerdic both inclined their heads.

"We were just discussing the little queen's futility in returning to Keswin and planning to defeat Devon. Trys and I think they are going to their deaths."

Mostyn sneered. "Too right she is. She has been gifted four hundred warriors of varying ability. Devon has over a thousand. That's why I was happy in the end to vote that common-blood warrior to be her consort. They aren't going to live long enough to breed."

"Trystan was just saying that and he's glad he's not going."

Mostyn glared at Trystan. "Got an opinion have you, little brother."

Trystan shrugged, not quite sure where Cerdric was going with his comments, but playing along with his lead. "Well, it is a futile effort and she's nothing more than a girl. They say she was raped and aborted her baby. I'm surprised even a common blood warrior would take her on but then he's scarred so badly he covers his face. Perhaps he's thinking he can give orders to royalty and his betters because he's bedding her. Regardless I wouldn't be taking orders from such."

Mostyn scowled. "Really, Trystan, just because you carry the title Dominus doesn't make you so high and mighty. The fact you are a base-born half breed would put you on a level with the little queen's consort, I would say or even below. Most common bloods are pure Maidens at least."

Trystan lurched one step forward his fists clenched then stopped. Rage tore through him. He dragged in a couple of deep breaths.

"I wouldn't if I were you, Trystan."

The three of them stood there motionless in the shadows.

Cerdric stepped forward. "Why don't you send him, Mostyn. It would get him out of your way. He would have to swear fealty to his little queen and therefore no longer able to lay claim to our realm and most likely he'll be dead before this succession is out. In the meantime he's going to have to bow down to a common blood warrior and take orders from a girl who thinks she's more than she is."

Mostyn looked from Trystan to Cerdric his expression tight and serious. His eyes squinted and his lip curled up.

Trystan glared at his brother. "For vipers sake, Mostyn, don't do this to me. I might be a pain in your side, but I don't deserve that surely?"

Mostyn suddenly smiled. "You know what, Cerdric, for once I think you have come up with a plausible idea."

"Mostyn, please don't do this."

Cerdric grimaced at Mostyn. "The little queen could make good use of him and his men."

"Such a waste of good men but I don't think that scabby lot, especially the half breeds, will take orders from any other and I don't want to mix them up with my finely tuned battalions." Mostyn turned to Trystan. "Little brother, Dominus Trystan of Sanjeva, you and your one hundred warriors are hereby assigned to Queen Rosin's legion. I offer without prejudice you and your men a Revocation of Allegiance"

"For viper's sake, Mostyn, don't do this. I'm your brother. You're sending me to my death." Trystan clenched his fists at his side trying to keep control of his elation and protest outwardly to his brother.

Mostyn waved his hand through the air. "It's done, Trystan."

"Noooo." Trystan howled and stamped his foot. "Reverse your decision, Your Majesty, please."

"Stop with the theatrics, Trystan, its unbecoming of a Dominus of Sanjeva or should I say a Commander in Keswin's army."

Cerdric smiled. "It will be alright, Trystan, and not for long once you confront Devon."

Trystan scowled at Cerdric not sure anymore if his younger brother was genuine of not.

Mostyn shivered and wrapped his cloak closer around him. "Vipers its cold out here. Come into the fire, Cerdric, we'll share a brandy to celebrate. Trystan, return to the barracks and make sure you report to King Cadmar first thing on the morning after I leave to advise of your addition to Queen Rosin's rag tag army. Farewell, brother."

Trystan inclined his head. "I didn't think you hated me this much, Mostyn."

"It's Your Majesty now, Trystan. You are no longer one of mine. And yes, I do hate you that much."

Trystan let his shoulders slump. "Farewell, Your Majesty, Dominus Cerdric." He turned on his heel and made his way along the path and down the steps to join his men and advise them of their fate.

Glee bubbled up inside as he loped down the steps two at a time. He hurried over and tapped Lukaz on the shoulder. "When you are free, Lukaz, we need to talk."

Trystan adjourned to his small Commander's room. His bags were already packed for his expected departure to Sanjeva the moon-slide after the bonding. He sat on his bed and hugged himself. He had no idea what the future held. Yes, he would probably die in battle with Devon as Mostyn had brought him to do anyway but until then he had freedom from the cruelty of Mostyn he had suffered for the last twenty or so successions.

Lukaz hurried through the door already gesturing.

Trystan smiled and grabbed his upper arms. "Lukaz, we've been assigned to Queen Rosin's legion. We are not going back to Sanjeva. We are free."

Lukaz lurched forward and hugged him. Gabbling madly.

"Slow down, Luakz, 'talk' to me."

Lukaz pulled back and signed.

Trystan nodded. "Yes, I'm happy. Cerdric did it. He told Mostyn I would hate to be assigned to a lost cause like Queen Rosin's."

Lukaz nodded a smile breaking across the darkness of his face showing his white teeth. His plaits bounced up and down.

"And yes I'll be taking orders from a common-blood warrior and a young woman. But Lukaz he seems a decent sort of man and from the way he spoke the other moon-wash he is not only in love with the Princess but has a great deal of respect for her. She must have a lot of guts to survive what she did and besides she can't be any worse than Mostyn.

Chapter 15

Rosin trembled, but not with the cold. On the dais, Arlan stood alone, dressed in black breeches, a long, royal blue woolen tunic, open at the throat, and a long, royal blue woolen cape, held on the shoulder by gold and silver brooch fashioned in the shape of the Bekwen crest. Around his neck hung an intricate gold torc, the male design that matched her own. Bonding gifts from her Moon Life Protectors, along with her bonding gown, made of the finest royal blue woolen cloth. For warmth, a fur-lined cape, trimmed with the white downy fluff of snow hare's pelt draped over her shoulders.

To her left, Father Cad waited for her to walk the small distance from the gate to the bottom of the stairs, and Shamir leaned heavily on a gnarled wooden cane, resplendent in a long green robe. Ashlynn had dressed in a pale blue woolen gown and acted as her assistant, helping her manage without her crutches. Mother Meg stood by Shamir, stunning in a russet wool gown that complemented her rich red hair and ivory complexion. Keegan stood beside his mother, his smile broad and genuine.

Even though Rosin knew his happiness was not all for her bonding, but mostly for his own possibilities after her victory with the Maidens' laws, she didn't care. After all that had happened to have people who loved her around as she became bonded, to the man she adored filled her heart with joy.

Snow powdered the ground and glistening icicles hung from

every rail of the lattice, making up the arbor turning the courtyard into a star-spangled dreamland.

Shamir glanced over at the assembled nobles. "My lords and ladies, this moon-slide Rosin, Queen of Keswin, will be bonded to Arlan, Duke of Bekwen. Any previous union is annulled. She will be bonded by the Laws of the Maidens and any children of this union will be entitled to ascend the throne of Keswin as legitimate heirs. Is there any who object?"

Except for a few quickly stifled snickers at the pointlessness of the question, there immediately followed a deep silence of consent. King Cadmar helped Rosin up the single step into the arbor. Arlan moved forward and took her hands. He smiled from behind his intricate bronze mask.

In response to the silence from the assembled lords, Shamir bowed to Cadmar, then turned to face Rosin and Arlan.

Rosin trembled. Not from the cold with her hands held in the warmth of Arlan's, but the memory of the last time she had stood thus. She scanned around. No one moved toward the arbor. She turned back to Shamir as he made the blessing for a long, happy, and fertile union.

She moved closer to Arlan.

He wrapped his arm around her shoulders, then took her hand in his. Together they held out exposed wrists, ready for the sealing of their union with the blending of their life-force.

Shamir withdrew his dagger. He asked for Cadmar's blessing, and all the nobles chimed in with enthusiasm.

Even though she expected and welcomed it, she still flinched at the stinging pain when the dagger broke her skin.

Before the blood had even beaded around the wound, Shamir bound her wrist against Arlan's, his blood blending with hers, staining the white bonding scarf red.

Arlan pulled her into his embrace and she went willingly to snuggle against the broadness of his muscular chest, feeling safe at last.

The only small doubts niggled were whether she could have children and how she would deal with the bonding bed. She trusted Arlan knowing he would never force or hurt her, but the memories of that horrible moon-wash remained fresh enough to haunt her at moments when she least expected.

They stepped up beside Shamir and Cadmar. "My lords and ladies, I now present Her Majesty, Queen Rosin of Keswin, and her chosen consort, Arlan, Duke of Bekwen."

The crowd of nobles shuffled a little until they had formed a corridor and Rosin and Arlan passed through arm in arm.

Inside the dining hall, the cooks and dining room servants had delicious, hot food ready—roasted meats and vegetables from the castle stores and hot toddies made with her Protector's fine imported berry wines. The fires roared at both ends of the hall, and Rosin quickly shed her cloak.

The fiddler and the flautist played light romantic melodies as a backing to the bard who sang of their love and of the brave deeds of all those present in both love and battles. The males far outnumbered the females, so when Meghan, Brigit, and Seana's dances were all accounted for, many of the younger nobles captured the hands of the serving girls and steered them onto the floor, swinging them around to the lilting music.

"Come, my darling, let us dance," Arlan said.

Rosin grinned and lifted the hem of her skirt just a little. "With this, my love?"

Without responding to her protest, Arlan placed his strong hands at her waist, then spun her around and around in time to the music. She gazed up into his eyes, crinkled at the corners because he smiled so broadly. The mask hid the horrible disfiguring scars.

Even though she understood why he wore the mask, she hoped when they were alone, he would remove it. She had seen the damage and wouldn't flinch like strangers did the first time they met him. Besides, she had bonded with him, loved him, scars and all. As they danced across the floor, Rosin realized Arlan had gradually moved toward the door and the waiting bonding suite.

They had barely fulfilled their required social obligations, but when some of the nobles made ribald comments, Arlan just laughed, then indicated Rosin's leg. "The queen has been on her feet all moon-slide. She is tired and needs to put her foot up."

Her face warmed. As they whirled out of the double oak doors, Arlan scooped her up into his arms and cradled her tightly against his chest as he carried her effortlessly across the courtyard, ignoring the robust cheers that echoed after them.

Arlan paused in the center of the path to capture her mouth with his, stealing a firm, caressing kiss. Rosin buried her face in his shirtfront to hide the heat burning in her cheeks, but as she breathed in the intoxicating scent of him, his chest shook with laughter.

She thumped his arm in a pretend show of anger. "Don't laugh."

But her show of shyness and mock anger only fired up his amusement even more, until he laughed so much, Rosin feared they would both tumble to the ground.

But moments later, Arlan easily shouldered open the heavy door of the bonding suite. He deposited her with exaggerated care in the middle of the bed and she sank into the deep maroon puffiness of the feather and down quilt.

He leaped and landed on his side next to her.

"Oh, Arlan."

"Ah, my love, at last we are alone and together. Rightfully."

He trailed his finger down her throat, past her cleavage, to the neckline of her gown. "And no maggots, no blood, and no cold."

Rosin's giggles faded. "But we do have a mask, my love." She reached up to untie the thongs that held it in place. "Please, take it off, Arlan. I want to see your face as it is."

He shook his head.

"Arlan, please? I don't want any barriers between us. Just you and me, as we are. Don't hide from me, Arlan. Besides, I would like to see how it has healed."

He smiled now. "Want to inspect your needlework, my love?"

"Yes, my dearest." She untied the thongs.

This time, Arlan made no attempt to stop her.

As the mask slipped from his face, Rosin studied his ravaged features. A wave of sadness washed over her at the extent of the damage and wished she'd done a better job of the repairs.

She reached up and ran her finger gently across his face, tracing the line of the scar from his forehead, past his eyes, across his nose to his mouth. Here she paused to slide her finger over his lips, the smooth warm skin tantalizing to touch.

He parted his lips.

Rosin slid the tip of her finger inside.

He met her tentative exploration with the tip of his tongue while at the same time pressing his lips together to imprison her finger.

Making no effort to remove the digit, she brought her thumb up and caressed the remainder of the scar across his jaw.

He opened his mouth, then nibbled, but she eased away from his ministrations to continue her gentle exploration. She caressed his throat, feeling the slightest of stubble rough under her fingers.

His Adam's apple bobbed up and down as he swallowed.

Sensuously, she slid her fingers down his chest to as far as his open shirt would allow.

Not satisfied with the simple touch, she leaned forward and kissed the scar where it travelled over his jaw and the corner of his mouth. The taste of him, like intoxicating wine swirling deep inside her, warmed every inch of her body, before it centered in her womanhood.

He moved his head just a fraction and his mouth covered hers, caressing, exploring lightly at first, then firmer. The hardness of his lips demanded a response as he brought his hand up, then cupped her head, his fingers tousling through her short curly locks.

She rested her head in his hand.

He released her mouth to shower light butterfly kisses over her cheeks, on the tip of her nose, then her eyes. He lowered her head onto the pillows, then drew back his gaze, focused on her with fervent intensity.

She knew what he sought. Some hesitation on her part, but she trusted Arlan and had determinedly pushed the haunting terrors into the backwaters of her mind.

This moon-wash, she wanted to give herself to Arlan without reservation, to share fully in their lovemaking. She would not let Devon's cruel assault come between them or turn her into a cringing ice maiden. No one would spoil her miracle.

With both hands, she cupped his face, drawing him close enough to feel the warmth of his breath on her skin. "My love, I want to be joined with you in every way. Make love to me, Arlan."

He placed a gentle kiss on her mouth before he sat up and, with one fluid movement, removed his shirt. Awe flooded her as she watched. The broad shoulders, the wide jagged scar that ran the full length of his chest, the deep muscular definition from chest to abdomen, and the sprinkling of light red-blond hairs that trailed down over his belly past his navel then disappeared under the waistband of his breeches.

His nipples were erect, begging to be touched.

She caressed the tips with her finger, then curled her finger around the nipple and traced a circle on the edge of the darker areola.

Arlan watched her touch him.

Self-consciousness flooded through her, but she didn't draw away. Instead, she flattened her hand on his skin, the nerve endings singing with the contact. With seductive slowness, she slid her hand over the hard ridges and slopes of his chest and abdomen.

He moaned softly. He smiled encouragement as she leaned forward to kiss his skin and leave an erotic trail of lip prints from the waistband of his breeches back to his nipples. She trailed her tongue around each nub in ever decreasing circles before suddenly taking one hardened tip into her mouth and sucking gently. Her action elicited another moan from her lover.

Emboldened by his response, she explored every inch of his torso with her hands and mouth.

His breathing quickened, became jagged, and he reached down and loosened the laces at the front of his breeches.

She followed his lead as he lay back and let her finish the task, tugging the edges apart, then pushing the inner flap aside to reveal a pair of white drawers.

Arlan lifted his hips and, with a wriggle, he kicked free of his breeches. His desire for her was acutely obvious through the thin material of his drawers.

She reached out tentatively and touched the hardness of his erection pushing against the material.

He gave a soft moan of desire and, with sure fingers, undid the laces on her bodice, revealing the shimmering under-garment that held her breasts. Her nipples were swollen and strained hard against the flimsy material, seeking release from their confinement.

With a small struggle, Rosin shrugged out of her bodice, then undid the ribbons holding her skirt at her waist. Her movements were made awkward by her splinted leg.

Seeing her struggle, Arlan simply put his hand under her bottom and plucked her skirt out of the way. Then, with eager fingers, Arlan lifted her camisole.

A wave of totally illogical shyness rushed over her. He had seen her before, had seen so much more than her breasts. But this was different. This time, she wanted to be desirable. She wanted him to want her.

He pushed her gently back onto the pillows. "Now, my lady, it's my turn to explore." Desire had darkened his eyes, his stiffened manhood throbbed between them.

Excitement sizzled through her, swamping the slightest edge of fear. Arlan would never hurt her. As raw passion flooded her body, it warmed her into a state of readiness for him, making moisture between her legs, and he hadn't even touched her yet.

He reached out and brushed her nipples with his palms. The erotic friction from the Calloused roughness marking his hands after years of swinging swords and slingshots made her skin tingle.

He cupped one breast after the other before he leaned down to nibble at her nipples, lick them, then finally suck on each.

The comfortable warmth inside her burst into liquid fire that roared through her veins.

Its heat exploded deep inside as he marked a fiery trail of kisses down her belly to the waist of her drawers. He paused just long enough to drag them from her body.

Now naked, only the light of the fire touched her pale skin with a golden glow.

He devoured her with an ardent gaze, his passion a glowing

flame that lit his face and hardened his body with a primeval response. But even then, he resisted his urges and gazed intently into her eyes.

"Arlan, I want you. I need you." She reached up to guide him to her so there would be no doubt she wanted him to love her.

He smiled, a knowing smile, as he bent his head and trailed kisses over her belly, then down to the mound that protected her now aching womanhood. He kissed the skin between the curly dark blond hairs before he carefully moved her broken limb aside.

Without a word, Rosin opened herself up to him.

He curled between her legs to drop minute kisses along her inner thighs, getting closer and closer to the heated flesh at the apex of her legs.

Rosin lay still, not sure what to expect as his fingers parted her outer lips. His caress was so gentle, so intimate, so erotic that her whole body sang in response. She could only see the top of his blond head between her thighs as his tongue lightly licked, tasting her. It bordered on being too intimate. The pleasure evoked, unbearably intense.

She trembled in response, clenching in eager anticipation as he sucked her tender folds, then dipped his tongue inside. The small, warm intrusion provoked spasms of delight. A cry burst forth when his tongue flicked over her nub of pleasure, then curled around the hard little protrusion. She arched her back, then lifted her body slightly to meet his ministrations as he took that nub of flesh between finger and thumb and gently slid his fingers up and down.

Wave after wave of exhilarating passion crashed over her. He caressed her entrance, just stroking and rubbing the sensitive flesh, using her own fluids to lubricate the action before his finger slipped inside. All the time, he kept caressing her most sensitive area as he moved his fingers in and out of her in a slow, sensuous motion.

The sensation polarized between her legs in an exquisite torment. She writhed to match and meet his movements. The friction built until a tingling fire pulsed and hummed through her body. She moved her hips against his hand as she reached for more, a desperate need to be filled, to be joined with him.

She could bear it no longer. "Arlan, stop, I can't..."

He chuckled, but didn't cease and a second later, the explosion hit her as a frantic, electrified sensation that crashed over and through her. Her inner flesh clenched, then spasmed as shudder after shudder vibrated her flesh and dissolved her bones.

"Arlan! Oh! Oh, Maidens' glory!" Her breath caught in her throat, her chest froze for a millisecond on each indrawn breath, and her throat burned as she gasped in mouthful after mouthful of air. The room swam, and nothing seemed real except the sensation of Arlan caressing her.

Sweat poured off her skin as she floated down. Small aftershocks rumbled through her body, weightless, uncoordinated, and boneless. She collapsed back onto the quilt, unable to move or think, soft moans still whispering past her lips.

Arlan chuckled softly as he trailed his lips up her body, then moved to lie beside her. He held her close as he showered her face and hair with kisses. "My little queen, my beautiful queen, you're glowing."

She smiled, then rested her head against his chest, purring at full volume just like a feline. Every cell in her body had relaxed into the mushy puddle of sated desire. She had never experienced anything like this before.

"Arlan, my love, in a while can we do that again?" Her question was barely a whisper because even her voice had collapsed in satiation.

"Oh, my lady, we haven't even begun yet." He nibbled her ear lobe, his hands already caressing her thighs and buttocks.

She leaned away from him, and he lowered his head to kiss her breasts. She cradled his head as she watched him suckle her nipples, pulling them gently so they stood out, pointed and erect. Then he kissed the tip of her nose before he rolled away from her just long enough to remove his underdrawers and when he stood before her in all his magnificence. Rosin stared at his nakedness, every inch of him, his member standing out long, thick, and hard with his desire for her.

He let her gaze linger on him for a while before he climbed back on the bed, then cuddled close. When his swollen appendage pressed against her stomach, she wasn't sure how it made her feel and couldn't quite banish the tiny edge to the pleasure his caresses had evoked. She pushed the memory of Devon's touch into oblivion, determined it would not interfere in her relationship with Arlan.

She drew in a deep breath and filled her lungs with his masculine scent, soon drunk on the heady mixture of Arlan. She planted teasing little kisses, alternated with nibbles on his warm skin. She tasted him, the faint taste of sweat, the sexually aroused male, and the lingering aroma of spicy soap. An aphrodisiac, all her own.

She had barely recovered from the pleasurable ache of her first orgasm when a new ache throbbed in time with her heartbeat. Her skin tingled and sizzled as Arlan left a fiery trail of kisses and caresses.

"My beautiful Rosin. I want you so much. I love you more than my own life."

"Love me, Arlan, love me."

"Are you sure, my love? I will not proceed unless you are sure you feel safe. When I touch you, there will only ever be pleasure."

"Love me, Arlan."

He captured her mouth as he pressed her back onto the bed. His hand slid over her belly, over her mound, then between her legs. This time, he continued to explore her mouth while his fingers delved into her and teased the tiny nub of pleasure with a gentle touch. He slipped another finger inside her and again moved it in a slow, seductive rhythm, instantly lighting up the embers of her first orgasm into raging flames of passion and lust.

She moaned against his lips and opened her mouth to invite him in. He tentatively dipped into her mouth, then withdrew before he deepened his kiss.

Rosin reveled in the taste of him, and the heightened sensations swirling around her body as they gradually centered in her nether regions. She lay back and parted her legs, firmly encouraging Arlan to move close.

He lifted himself and eased on top of her. His manhood pressed against her inner lips, but Arlan made no attempt to enter her. He waited.

She saw in his eyes. He wanted to take her, but he would not unless she asked him. She reached down between their bodies until she could curl her hand around his hard, throbbing shaft. With no hesitation, she guided him to her entrance, then lifted her head to whisper in his ear. "Take me, Arlan, I want you inside me."

She lay back and lifted her hips, feeling him ease just a little into her.

The sensation so incredibly intense as he slid slowly, but steadily into her. He paused for a moment before he moved in a steady rhythm, thrusting deep. Each time he entered her, Rosin lifted her hips to meet him, moaning as the sensations evoked spiraled out of control.

She cried out when wave after wave of pleasure crashed over her and instinctively, she matched his faster rhythm. Her whole body shook. Cry after cry escaped.

Arlan arched, his hips thrusting hard and deep. He groaned, covered her mouth with his, then stayed still, deep inside her.

A long sigh escaped as he relaxed and slowly lowered himself on top of her. He made no attempt to withdraw his member, instead holding her close as he rolled onto his side, taking her with him, his arms encircling her.

Still joined at the hips, Rosin sank into a sated boneless lethargy of ultimate pleasure. She luxuriated in the small after-pulses that thrummed through her body before they faded into contentment.

Arlan stroked her cheek, his thumb wiping the tiny rivulet of tears that had trickled unnoticed onto her cheeks. "Do not cry, my love."

She smiled. "Tears of happiness, Arlan."

He kissed her with a firm demanding exploration of her mouth and she responded with a daring exploration of her own. Breathless, they parted and breathed deeply, both of them smiling with lazy, sated smiles.

"Oh, my darling, you are so wonderful. I love you with all my heart and soul."

"And I love you, my beautiful, courageous, and regal Queen of Keswin, my lover, my friend, and my partner in life." He brushed his hand over her face, neck, and breasts. "No matter what we face in the future, my dearest Rosin, be it joy and happiness, or the cruelty of war and treachery, we will always have each other. Now snuggle down and sleep in the arms of your consort for the first time."

He kissed her lightly, held her close, then rested his head on the pillow beside hers. His warm breath fanned her cheek as she settled into the total softness of sexual, mental, and emotional satisfaction.

He slept before she did.

She lay there in the soft glow of the fire listening to her consort snoring softly, for the first time in her life totally content. Arlan's arms were the only place she wanted to be.

But even now, as she basked in the glow of their love, the desire, and the need to reclaim her throne throbbed strongly. All too soon, she would have to answer its demand.

Even Arlan's passionate lovemaking failed to still her mind. She lay in bed pressed against his warm, finely honed body and fretted about the future.

With an impatient flick of the quilt, she left the bed. The silvery moonbeams cast soft light across the room. She walked across the room to the window and stared out across the river flats. From this side of the castle, she could just see the river. From this distance, the two long boats belonging to the Wilsea contingent were mere darker shadows against the sandy banks. Snow fell, leaving a light dusting on the landscape.

"Come back to bed, my love. Nothing can be done before the Tidal Wash. We have the frost and the freeze to enjoy our bonding."

Rosin's first instinct was to snuggle down and close her eyes, but a sense of urgency prodded her.

"It's too long. Keswin can't wait that long. I can't wait that long."

TO BE CONTINUED...

ABOUT THE AUTHOR

Emily was a closet writer for several years before she got brave enough to share her work with anyone. She joined Eyre Writers Inc, a creative writing group in the seaside town of Port Lincoln and really began to improve. Her first book was a 100,000-word family saga novel but after a workshop on 'how to write a Mills & Boon', Emily embarked on a new direction – writing the Romance novel.

After being made redundant from the job she loved in 2011, Emily became a carer for her frail, vision-impaired mother and turned to fulfilling her dream of becoming a published author.

When Emily is not writing she enjoys spending time with family and friends, her three wonderful adult children, and her four adored grandchildren.

Emily also enjoys egg decorating and carving, reading of course, and painting and cooking when she's not writing.